WHITCHURCH-STOUFFVILLE PUBLIC LIBRARY

P9-CSH-059

WITHDRAWN

SEP 0 1 2020

CACTUS JACK

Other novels by Brad Smith

The Goliath Run
The Return of Kid Cooper
Hearts of Stone
Rough Justice
Shoot the Dog
Crow's Landing
Red Means Run
Big Man Coming Down the Road
Busted Flush
All Hat
One-Eyed Jacks
Rises a Moral Man

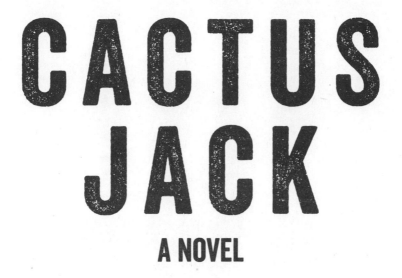

CACTUS JACK

A NOVEL

BRAD SMITH

Arcade Publishing · New York

WHITCHURCH-STOUFFVILLE PUBLIC LIBRARY

Copyright © 2020 by Brad Smith

All rights reserved. No part of this book may be reproduced in any manner without the express written consent of the publisher, except in the case of brief excerpts in critical reviews or articles. All inquiries should be addressed to Arcade Publishing, 307 West 36th Street, 11th Floor, New York, NY 10018.

Arcade Publishing books may be purchased in bulk at special discounts for sales promotion, corporate gifts, fund-raising, or educational purposes. Special editions can also be created to specifications. For details, contact the Special Sales Department, Arcade Publishing, 307 West 36th Street, 11th Floor, New York, NY 10018 or arcade@skyhorsepublishing.com.

Arcade Publishing® is a registered trademark of Skyhorse Publishing, Inc.®, a Delaware corporation.

Visit our website at www.arcadepub.com.

10 9 8 7 6 5 4 3 2 1

Library of Congress Cataloging-in-Publication Data is available on file.

Print 978-1-950691-45-6
Ebook ISBN: 978-1-950691-53-1

Printed in the United States of America

CACTUS JACK

One

THE BLIND OVER THE WINDOW HUNG by just a corner, allowing the midmorning light to stream into the room and across the bed where Billie lay, her right arm flung over her eyes to ward off the combination of the sun's rays and the fierce hangover she entertained. She was awake but fervently wished she wasn't. She needed to pee and she needed aspirin or something for her head, yet she couldn't bring herself to get up. She knew that both relieving her bladder and relieving the pain in her skull were good ideas, just as drinking tequila shooters for three hours the night before had been a bad one. Her entire head hurt, but after a moment she came to realize that her left eye was particularly sore. She gingerly touched her face, felt the contusion around the socket.

Beside her, Rory rolled onto his back and immediately began to snore, which was finally reason enough for Billie to get out of bed. She was wearing only jeans and a bra. She walked into the bathroom across the hall, her head pounding with every step. She washed down three ibuprofens with water directly from the faucet, holding her hair back with one hand as she drank.

She ran more cold water and splashed it across her face. She took a breath and looked into the mirror, staring at her swollen eye for a moment, turning her head one way and then the other as she tried to remember.

The tequila she recalled. The shots had been part of a juvenile drinking contest, something called the Name Game. Billie had played softball after work and in the bottom of the fifth inning she'd heard the rumble of the glasspacks and looked over to see Rory pull up onto the grass behind the bleachers in his Corvette. He wouldn't park in the lot with the rest of the cars and trucks; he was under the impression that the car was worthy of special attention and the rise behind the screen was just the place for showcasing. Typically, before cutting the ignition, he revved the engine loudly for ten or fifteen seconds, just in case there was somebody within a quarter mile who hadn't noticed his arrival. He shut it down and got out to lean against the hood (something no other living soul would be allowed to do), where he spent the next half hour smoking cigarettes as he watched the game.

Billie's team, the Broken Bombers, lost by a score of eleven to eight. They usually went to the Broken Rail—the bar that sponsored them—for wings and beer afterward. On the bench, Billie put her glove and cleats in her sports bag, keeping her head down, hoping to hear the rumble of the Vette's engine as it chugged away, but knowing that she wouldn't. Rory would want to come to the bar. He himself didn't play sports and in fact had no interest in baseball or anything other than cars and drywall, but he was jealous of Billie's time with the team and he also knew that the men's teams in the league hung out at the Rail. He was jealous of them too. He'd also been jealous of Billie's cat until it ran away. At least she told herself that it ran away.

She heard him calling to her as she made to leave and she walked over, trudging up the grassy slope. He was still leaning against the car.

"What's up?"

"Going to the Rail for beers," she told him. As if he didn't know. She went to the Broken Rail every Thursday night after softball.

"I was thinking we could get a pizza."

"I'm going to the Rail."

He shrugged. "That's cool by me."

She didn't bother to try to dissuade him. Such attempts in the past had only made him more possessive and suspicious. He didn't like her being on the team and had taken to asking her to do things on Thursday nights, hoping she'd choose him over softball. He rarely asked her to do anything the rest of the week, other than drink beer at his place and fuck. They'd been seeing each other for six months; she'd agreed to go out with him during the winter, when she'd been particularly bored with her lot in life. He was good-looking and physical and had come off at first as supremely confident, all things she liked in a guy. His insecurities had revealed themselves over time. Of course, that was the way it was in most relationships, but Billie had to wonder why it was always bad things that eventually came to the fore. Just once she'd like to date a guy and find out he'd been hiding the fact that he was really Francis of Assisi.

Rory, clearly not of Assisi, wanted to be around her whenever he could, even though he didn't want to do anything. He didn't have many friends of his own. Even the piston heads in Chillicothe avoided him once they realized he wanted only to talk about his own car. Theirs were of zero interest to him.

In the bar the team sat at a long table in the rear. They ordered beer by the pitcher and wings by the dozen. Rory sat beside Billie with his arm around her. She could actually feel herself cringe when he first did it and wondered how he didn't notice. His sole contribution to the conversation was to mention every ten minutes that Billie had struck out to end the game. The mentions got progressively less funny as the night moved forward.

Billie decided early on to have a couple of beers and a few wings and then leave. Then someone suggested the drinking game, and soon the shots arrived. After that, things grew real fuzzy real fast.

For the game, teams of four were made up; each team wrote down ten names on slips of paper and threw them in a hat. As each slip was drawn, an opposing team had to guess the name from clues given. The losers chugged tequila.

The competition—what Billie could remember of it—required a certain level of intelligence as well as general knowledge, and as such Rory hadn't done well, especially considering that none of the names in the hat happened to be Corvette or Stingray. Fueled by the Cuervo, Billie had begun to mock him, paying him back for his comments about her striking out, and he'd gotten pissed off, cracking back at her. The spat carried on when they got back to the house. The only reason she'd gone home with him was that she'd been too drunk to drive herself. When they got there, he started in on how she'd shown him up in front of her friends and how she had no respect for him. Finally Billie had told him to fuck off and said she would walk home. He'd caught up with her as she was going down the front steps.

Now she went back into the bedroom and picked up her team shirt from the floor. It smelled of beer. Rory was snoring, mouth wide open, a thin line of saliva running down his neck. She looked at him in disgust. Had she been that bored back in January?

She went out to the kitchen and put water on for instant coffee, then sat down, running her fingers over her cheekbone as she waited for the kettle to boil. After a bit she got up and looked in the fridge, but there was nothing there but leftover pizza and salami and cheese slices and beer. She wasn't hungry anyway. She made coffee and hoped that the painkillers would begin to work.

Carrying a mug, she walked out onto the back porch and sat down on the steps, the events of the night before weighing heavily on her. Rory's work truck, with A-1 DRYWALL printed on the door, was parked in the drive there, the box loaded with twenty or thirty pieces of sheetrock. The driveway sloped down toward the road out front. The yellow Corvette was parked at the bottom of the hill. As a rule, Rory put it in the garage every night, but she assumed he'd hadn't bothered when they got home from the Broken Rail. He'd been drinking as much as her and wouldn't have wanted to move the truck out of the way. Plus, they were still bickering and that would take preference over any shuffling of vehicles. Still, it was a rare occurrence, him leaving his precious baby out in the elements.

Billie sat there, looking at the car. She knew more about it than she did all the other vehicles she'd ever ridden in combined. It was a 1973 Anniversary model in canary yellow. The engine was 354 cubic inches and it put out 275 horsepower. Rory had spent nearly two thousand dollars on an after-market stereo system. For Billie's birthday in April, he'd bought her a thirty-dollar panties and bra set from Walmart. The underwear was also yellow. Just like the car.

Her head began to clear. Finishing her coffee, she shifted her gaze to the truck, reaching up to touch her cheekbone once again. After a while she got up and went into the house for her purse. It was on the floor by the couch. She looked around to see if there was anything else of hers in the house, anything she would ever need again.

The truck was a standard, floor shift. Billie put the transmission in neutral and released the parking brake and then got out. She stepped back as the truck began to roll forward, slowly picking up speed as it did. It was a heavy vehicle, a GMC three-quarter ton, made even heavier by the couple thousand pounds of sheetrock in the back. The Corvette was constructed mainly of fiberglass and plastic and was no match for the rumbling two-ton mass that smashed into it, crumpling the front fenders like tissue paper, crushing the hood and smashing the windshield like it was cellophane.

Billie assumed that the noise would be more than enough to wake Rory, so she cut across the lawn to the road and started walking quickly north, heading for home. She looked back a few times, expecting to see him in pursuit, but he never appeared. Apparently he slept through what, in his mind, when he finally awoke, would be nothing short of a holocaust.

Will got up to pee at around one o'clock and again at three. The only bathroom in the house was on the ground floor and he made his way down the stairs in the pitch dark, the loose treads complaining beneath his bare feet, the air inside the house still heavy with the humidity of the day. Both times after going, he drank from the bathroom faucet, the well water cold and chalky in his mouth, before going back to bed and uneasy sleep.

At twenty past four he was awake for good. He lay there in the big four-poster, the bed Marian had picked up at an auction outside of Junction City a couple of years earlier, wanting another hour or so of sleep he knew he wouldn't get. Lay there atop the sheets in the July heat, facing the wall rather than the window, not wanting to witness the coming dawn, knowing damn well that the morning sky would be yellow and cloudless, the air as dry as the Mojave. Just as it had been the day before and the day before that and all the days of the past seven weeks.

He got out of bed with the dawn, dressing in the half light, pulling on brown Carhartt pants and a faded blue shirt. In the kitchen he put coffee on and washed down his morning pills with a glass of orange juice while looking out the window to the outbuildings and paddocks down the hill. The farm occupied a corner between two roads and had two driveways, the main one off the county road that led to the house and a second two-track lane, running from the side road to the west, leading to the barns.

The two mares were standing in the shade of the big barn, head to flank, tails swishing the flies away. The gray colt was off on its own, in the corner of the front pasture nearest the road; it was looking west, as if in anticipation of something. Maybe the animal knew something that Will didn't. The grass in the pasture was nonexistent, nothing more than brown and brittle stubble poking through the red dirt.

When he finished the juice, he walked down the hill and ran water until the trough in the lee of the barn was half full, then tossed half a bale of hay over the fence, the sheaves kicking up dust as they landed. The colt, seeing the feed, came through the open gate to investigate while the two mares looked like they were deciding whether to leave the shade to come eat. The temperature, with the sun just now showing half on the horizon, was already in the upper eighties. Will watched the colt as it pushed the hay with its nose, not really eating so much as exploring. At two years and a few months, the animal was already sixteen hands, his barrel and chest heavily muscled. He was a dark steely gray and moved with a confidence borne of something Will had rarely come across in his seventy-three years, a quality innate to certain athletes and even in nonathletic types—salesmen and politicians, carpenters and mechanics, doers and watchers—whether they were good or bad or halfway in between. Whatever the quality, it was inherent. The colt had slid out of the birthing canal with the attitude.

The donkey began to bray from inside the barn then, no doubt sensing Will's presence. Will went and opened the door to the rear paddock, then let the jack and the nanny goat and the brown-and-white pony outside. The girl could tend to them when she got there. The donkey continued to complain as Will made his way back to the house for his own breakfast.

Marian had in the past few months pretty well cleared everything out of the fridge and cupboards that Will considered to be real breakfast food and replaced it with oatmeal and wheat germ and something called quinoa. After gazing unhappily into the pantry for a minute or so, he grabbed the keys to his truck and headed west to the Crossroads Café, five miles away at the intersection of the county road and Burton's Pike.

The place opened at six and was already half full when Will settled in at the counter. There were no surprises at the Crossroads, neither the food nor the conversation. Will could pick up the odor of frying bacon before he walked in, and as he sat on his stool sipping his coffee he could hear the popping of the grill, smell the grits and scrambled eggs even as he listened to varying opinions of the federal government, the goddamn Chinese, the lack of rain, and the possibility that Buck Barwell's wife did not leave him because she was screwing Larry Cantor, but rather because she was sleeping with Larry's daughter, the artist, newly returned from living a few years in London. Apparently the people seeing her coming and going from the Cantor place had jumped to the wrong conclusion. None of these news items would have been available to Will at home, hunched over a bowl of oatmeal sprinkled with quinoa and not enough brown sugar to satisfy a kangaroo mouse.

Bonnie, the owner, was working the fry pans and the grill, while Shannon, a university student and some distant kin to Bonnie, did the waitressing. By the time Will's breakfast arrived, the talk had moved past the sexual proclivities of Sally Barwell and landed on the topic of Mac McCoy's prostate. Mac, while studying the same menu he had read a couple of hundred times in the past year alone, decided to inform Shannon, impatiently awaiting his order, that his PSA number was an alarming seventy-three. Shannon, with a full diner to serve, had little time for discussing Mac's condition, even if she had any idea what the number might represent, which she did not.

"That number don't mean shit," Sudsy Jones announced from a corner table.

Mac ordered the country special, which he always ordered, before turning to Sudsy. "How's that?"

Will dipped the corner of his toast—whole wheat, one concession he'd make to Marian this morning—into the creamy yolk of an egg and ate while he listened.

"Forget about them numbers," Sudsy told him. "My daddy had a PSA of near two hundred and he told his doctor to stick his treatments up his ass. They was going to give him radiation and chemotherapy both. He didn't do nothing and he's still going strong. Eighty-eight years old."

Mac glanced at Shannon, who had moved off and was no longer even pretending to be interested. "But does everything . . . work?"

"What do you mean?" Sudsy asked.

At that, Mac clenched his fist and raised his forearm dramatically, the universal sign indicating an erection.

"He's eighty-eight!" Sudsy said. "What's he gonna do with a hard-on?"

Bonnie, scrambling more eggs, gave Will a look as he took a mouthful of grits, a look that said, *You see what I put up with every day?* But Will was pretty sure that Bonnie arrived every morning before the sun was up to pop biscuits in the oven and perc coffee and mix pancake batter because she wanted to do those things. She'd had plenty of offers on the place over the years and apparently never had the urge to bite. Her husband, Tim, was a scrap dealer with limited ambition. He was as likely to be found at home drinking beer in a lawn chair as he was out on the road, collecting junked farm equipment. Will suspected that Bonnie had little desire to join him in the yard. If the trade-off was listening to the occasional speculation about the virility of an octogenarian, then so be it.

Will felt a presence and looked to his right to see Stuart Martin slide onto the stool there. He removed his immaculate white straw Stetson and placed it on the counter. He gave Will a look, then nodded toward the corner table, where Mac and Sudsy were carrying on their medical discourse.

"Not exactly the deep end of the gene pool over there," Martin said.

No matter how accurate the statement might be, Will wasn't inclined to agree with Martin, who was a developer and a number of other things, most of which saw him kissing the asses of the so-called influential citizens of Marshall County. It was not surprising that he wouldn't have anything good to say about certain denizens of the Crossroads. He was a man who tailored his opinions to fit his surroundings and Will was damn certain that Martin would have little positive to say about him, if the circumstances and crowd were different. Will also knew that Martin was tight with Reese Ryker and that Will's name—if not his character—had been a popular subject with Ryker, ever since the gray colt had arrived on the scene.

Will finished his coffee and stood up. "I wouldn't be any kind of an expert on that."

"I would," Martin said. "How's your pasture holding up, Will?"

"What pasture?" Will put eight dollars on the counter and gave Bonnie a wink.

"I hear you," Martin said. "Damnedest drought I ever saw. I'm spending two hundred dollars a week on water just so my lawn doesn't die."

"I'm going to go before my heart breaks," Will said.

And go he did.

When he got back to the farm, a flatbed was parked by the barn and the driver was leaning against the fender of the truck, smoking a cigar that was down to its last inch and a half. The man was near Will's age, wearing a denim jacket and a greasy John Deere cap, pushed high on his forehead. Will glanced at his watch as he got out of the truck; it was seven forty. The seller had said the hay would be there around nine.

"You're early."

The driver shrugged. "I was on the road at three. Beat the heat."

"How's that working out?" Will asked.

"Not worth a shit but least this way I'm back home by noon or so."

Will walked over to look at the hay. It was a trefoil timothy mix and appeared to be pretty good quality. He yanked a handful from a bale and held it to his nose a moment. The driver pulled the lading bill from his jacket pocket.

"Hundred bales, right?"

Will nodded. "You can back around to the pole barn there."

The driver looked where Will pointed, to where the roof of the pole barn extended into the paddock. "Keep it out of the rain, is that the idea?"

"That's not even funny anymore," Will told him.

It took the two of them less than twenty minutes to unload and stack the hundred bales. The flatbed had at least ten times that on board; apparently Will's place had been the first stop. While the driver was restrapping the load, Will walked up to the house for the check he'd written earlier. When he returned, the driver was looking at the broodmares and the colt, standing in the shade.

"Never bought hay in July before."

"Need rain to grow pasture," the driver said. "That's a law."

Will handed him the check. After giving it the once-over, the man gave Will a receipt. "Masterson Thoroughbreds," he said. "You still in the game?"

"I am."

The driver took a moment to blatantly look over the farm—the unpainted barns, the house on the hill with its sagging porches—before turning again to the horses in the paddock. "What are you running?"

"That bay mare still races. Finished fifth last month at Chestnut. Laid up just now, though."

The driver looked at the bay, unimpressed. "Tough way to make a living, you ask me. Rich man's game, more than ever these days."

"I don't feel the urge to ask you," Will told him.

"I don't mean to offend, mind you."

"You couldn't offend me. I don't know you from Adam."

The driver smiled at that. He took a match from his pocket and tried to light the cigar stub. There wasn't enough left to smoke and he gave up, tossing the butt to the ground. He indicated the colt. "What do you got there—two-year-old?"

"That's right."

"Good-looking horse." The man's tone suggested that he was surprised to see such a horse at this particular location, as if he'd looked up to the house and seen Ava Gardner sitting on the porch. "You working him yet?"

"I am." Will took a moment, trying to decide if he even wanted to have this conversation with the man. "That chestnut by the trough is the dam. The sire is Saguaro."

The driver actually chuckled when he heard the name. "Did you say Saguaro?"

Will nodded. He wasn't sure why he felt compelled to tell this superior little prick who the sire was. Maybe he didn't like being looked down on by the guy who delivered his hay.

"That would be the same Saguaro who was sold to the Double R for twenty-some million dollars a few years ago?"

"How many thoroughbred stallions named Saguaro you know of?" Will asked.

The driver smiled again, clearly not believing a word. "Well— good for you, buddy. You might have yourself a real world-beater there. I'll keep an eye out for him, once you get him on a track somewhere. What do you call a horse like anyway—Man o' War?"

"I call him Cactus Jack," Will said. "You can pick up that cigar butt and take it with you."

Will turned on his heel and walked to the house, hearing the truck as the diesel engine fired to life and then accelerated up the drive toward the highway. Will didn't look back until he reached the porch, where he turned to see the flatbed moving north. The dust the truck had raised in the driveway hung over the farm like a brown cloud.

In the kitchen he got a glass of water from the sink and sat down at the scarred harvest table. Yesterday's mail was there, where he had tossed it after bringing it in from the box, not wanting to open certain letters. Like the one from the bank.

But now he did. The information inside was pretty much what he expected. Tossing the papers aside, he picked up the *Rancher's Journal*. Most of the news there was about the drought. Why did people feel obligated to report on the weather so much when it was all around? If it rained all day, the six o'clock news would have a five-minute segment telling people how it had rained all day, with some unfortunate reporter standing out in the deluge as if to prove it, while anybody with a window and the brains of a chigger already knew that it had rained all day.

He left the paper on the table and went to the sink for another glass of water. His doctor wanted him to drink at least eight glasses a day, to "keep things moving." He also wanted Will to walk an hour a day, or go to a gym for that length of time. He walked plenty around the farm, although he couldn't say how far in particular. As for going to a gym, even the doctor knew that wasn't about to happen.

Glancing out the window, he saw the little girl riding down the driveway on her bicycle. Her hair was tucked beneath a baseball cap and she wore pink jeans and a T-shirt with a picture of something—Will couldn't tell what—on the front. He watched as she leaned the bike against the barn wall and walked directly to the paddock. The colt came to her right away. She had a connection to the colt that Will did not. The horse dropped his head to push his nose through the fence rail, getting low enough for the girl to run her hand over it. Will could see her speaking to the animal and he wondered what she might be saying. After a few moments, she went into the barn. He drained the glass—two down and six to go—and went out the door.

The girl—Jodie was her name—was dispersing hay to the animals when he walked around to the back paddock. The goat, keeping its distance from the others, was standing in the shade of the building, chewing contentedly on a sheaf. The piston pump was *thump-thumping* in the corner, filling the claw-foot bathtub along the rail fence.

Will stood quietly by the corner of the barn. The girl, her tongue clenched between her teeth, didn't see him as she lifted a half bale of the new hay over the top rail to drop it into the corral. She watched as the donkey and pony came over and dug in. After a moment she went inside to shut off the pump. Returning with a brush in her hand, she saw him standing there.

"Good morning, Will."

"Hello, Sprout."

"I see we finally got our hay."

"We did." Will walked along the outside of the fence to look at the donkey. The animal, pulling at the hay, lifted its head and its ears went back. It had been leery of Will since arriving at the farm. Will could tell that the animal had been mistreated in its past, and probably by a man. The donkey was fine with the girl and even let her ride it without much fuss, although it preferred to move at a walk.

"Putting on weight finally," Will said.

"He sure likes his hay," Jodie said.

"You need to be careful with an animal," Will said. "A horse gets into the grain, for instance, and he'll eat himself sick. You ever see those chuckleheads at that all-you-can-eat buffet over to Junction City, stuffing their faces? Same thing with a horse, if you let him."

The little girl nodded slowly at the information, taking it in word for word, as she did everything she heard from Will.

"Figure out my share for the hay and I'll pay you," she said. "I got five dollars for helping my Aunt Micky clean a house in town on Monday and I have five more coming this weekend."

"I'll have my accountant look into the particulars," Will said.

"Are you having fun with me?"

"Nope," Will said. "We got no time for fun. We're running a farm here."

Jodie opened the gate and went into the paddock. "Go ahead and tease, but I have work to do. I need to brush that pony out. He looks like he took a dirt bath."

"All right," Will said. "I'm taking Jack over to Chestnut Field. I want to work him in the morning. I'd ask you to tag along but you need to brush out that pony."

Jodie stopped, trapped by her own good intentions. "Won't take me but ten minutes to take care of this pony."

"Oh—then you want to tag along?"

"Stop it."

"I guess I'll wait, then," Will said.

"You can sit in the shade and tease me while I work, mister."

"That's the best plan I've heard so far today," Will said.

He went over and sat, as she suggested. After a while, the goat left off the hay on the ground and walked over to the end of the paddock, where a narrow enclosure angled off to the barn. The spot, maybe fifteen feet by eight, was filled with junk—old fence posts, rolls of wire, paint cans and scrap iron, things Will had stowed there over the years when the paddock hadn't been in use. As he watched now, the goat, as goats will do, made an effort to climb atop the pile of posts.

"Get off there!" Will barked at the animal.

Jodie looked over as the goat turned and trotted away. She went back to work, brushing the pony's hide furiously, afraid that Will would change his mind about taking her with him.

"One of these days we need to clean that corner out," Will said. "Before one of these gets hurt. What is it about a goat that it's just got to climb?"

"Well," Jodie said slowly, "I guess we could do it today."

"No, we can't," Will said. "Today we're going to the track."

Two

FREDDIE'S FISH SHACK CATERED TO AN early dining clientele, most of whom were retirees. Billie's shift started at five and the place was already three-quarters full. She'd been on the move most of the day, fearful that Rory would show up at her place. By the time she walked home that morning, she deeply regretted destroying his car. Actually, she didn't regret the act itself; she'd come to hate the vehicle. But she was extremely nervous about what would happen next. She tried to calm down by telling herself that Rory would have the Corvette insured to the hilt. However, she also knew that a settlement would do nothing to temper his rage. He had an emotional connection to the vehicle that was odd, if not downright disturbing. Even if the insurance company managed to find the same forty-year-old model to replace it, he wouldn't be happy. And Billie doubted that the mess she'd left in the driveway could be repaired, not to Rory's satisfaction anyway.

At her house, she'd had a quick shower and put her work uniform in a bag and hoofed it the two miles to the Broken Rail, where she'd left her car the night before. The car was a fifteen-year-old Taurus that seemed to require constant repair—tires, alternator, brakes. If someone drove a truck into it, Billie would not shed a tear.

When she got to the parking lot at the Rail, she'd looked around as she approached her car, half expecting to see Rory lurking nearby. Surely he was awake by now and fully aware of what had happened. A sudden thought occurred to her: what if he didn't know *how* it had happened? Billie could say she'd left after he fell asleep and that sometime that morning—the neighbors or somebody who heard the crash would tell him when—the truck started to roll on its own. Of course, that would mean that Rory, when parking the truck, had neither set the brake nor put the transmission in gear. That was a stretch. The whole story was a stretch. Rory would know what happened. Rory knew Billie.

Leaving the parking lot, she'd stopped at the cosmetic counter at Target on the south side of town before driving down to the river, where she spent the rest of the day looking at the water and napping in her car.

Athena came on shift at six. Billie was waiting five tables and anticipating a grand total of maybe twenty dollars in tips. People who ate early were notoriously bad when it came to gratuities. She was picking up orders of the shrimp and chicken combo when Athena walked in the back door, buttoning her white shirt with the restaurant's name etched beneath the image of a smiling large-mouth bass. Her dreads were tied off at the back of her neck and she wore large gold hoops in her ears. She looked up as she met Billie, on her way with the plates balanced on her forearms.

"Got a full boat tonight—" Athena began and she stopped. "What the fuck is with your face?"

Billie kept walking. She delivered the entrees and then busied herself clearing dishes from other tables, taking her time, avoiding the conversation she was about to have with Athena for as long as she could.

When Billie returned to the kitchen, Athena was there waiting for her, arms crossed.

"I swear, I'm going to sue Maybelline," Billie said. "Go with the glow, my ass. Twenty-two dollars I won't see again."

"That sonofabitch," Athena said.

"How do you know I didn't take a line drive to the face last night?"

"You wouldn't have run off just now."

"I had shrimp combos getting cold."

"Something cold about this whole situation and it's not the shrimp," Athena said. "You call the cops?"

"No."

"Then I will."

"No."

"What do you mean no?" Athena said. "What is wrong with you?"

"I'm done with him," Billie said. "Isn't that good enough?"

"How the fuck is that good enough? Tell me how that is good enough."

Now Billie looked over to see Freddie, in the back by the fryers, watching them. Freddie was seventy-two years old and half-deaf but all his other senses were as sharp as the knives he honed daily. There was no little thing that escaped him, inside or outside of his restaurant. Billie was certain he was psychic on some level.

"Can we talk about this later?" she asked.

Athena saw where Billie was looking. "All right," she said unhappily. "You better come up with something good or I *am* calling the cops. You got that?"

Freddie's closed at ten. Rory showed up at nine thirty, coming in through the front door and into the foyer by the PLEASE WAIT TO BE SEATED sign. He stood there, arms crossed, projecting menace. Billie saw him first, mainly because she'd been watching for him. Then Athena noticed, because she'd been watching Billie. Her dark eyes flashed like a cat on the kill. Before she could move, though, Freddie had walked across the room to strike up a conversation with Rory. Freddie, who didn't know what was going on but knew something rank was afoot. He'd probably seen the bruise but chose not to say anything. That wasn't Freddie's style.

Rory, his nostrils flared and eyes glazed by what Billie assumed would have been a solid day of mournful boozing, outweighed the restaurant owner by probably sixty pounds. However, whatever reality Freddie was describing to him at this moment seemed to have an effect. Rory's eyes remained on Billie at the waitress station, but his ears belonged solely to Freddie. When he left moments later he gave Billie one last look, a look that told her that it wasn't over. She knew that, but at least she also knew now that whatever was going to happen, it wouldn't happen at Freddie's Fish Shack.

When the shift was done and the place closed, Freddie having gone home without talking to Billie about Rory or anything else, she and Athena lingered in the parking lot. Billie had some wine in the trunk of the Taurus for emergencies and Athena had a joint in her purse for the same reason.

"There was too much tequila," Billie said. She was sitting on the hood of her car. "That's what started it. And we were at the Rail and he's out of his element there. You know."

"He's out of his element most everywhere," Athena said.

"Yeah, whatever. So he was being mouthy, trying to impress people, and then I got mouthy back."

"So what? You're mouthy in general."

"Thanks." Billie poured more wine. They were using plastic glasses from the restaurant, the glasses they served juice in for kids. "So we ended up back at his place. That was my mistake; I should have just gone home. And—things got heated and, you know."

"No, I don't know," Athena said. "I don't know how this shit works."

"I woke up with a sore face," Billie said. "That's how it works."

"Except it's not supposed to work like that," Athena said. "And you know it. That fucking prick."

Billie released a long sigh and took a drink. The traffic on the thruway a hundred yards away was noisy, tractor-trailers running into the night, bound west to Chicago or east to Boston or New York.

"I'm trying to look at it as a good thing," she said. "I've spent all damn day thinking about it."

"Better think some more, if you decided it's a good thing."

"I'm looking at it as my way out. Now I'm done with the asshole forever," Billie said. "I know I should have been that first time but then he cried and swore it had never happened before and wouldn't again. Blah, blah . . . is there anything worse than a guy crying? It's fucking pitiful."

"Getting hit a second time by that guy is what's pitiful. You should have been out the door after the first."

"All right, all right," Billie said.

Athena took the joint from her purse and lit it, taking a deep pull before handing it over. Billie had a toke and began coughing.

"Watch it now," Athena said. "That's harsh shit." She took the joint back. "I never could figure what you saw in that prick anyway," she said, exhaling. "What—he make your socks roll up and down, that it?"

"Not likely." Billie had another toke, smoother this time. Old trickster.

"Then what? The man couldn't carry on a conversation unless it was about himself. Him and that fucking car. That it—you in love with the car, Billie?"

Billie told her what had happened that morning.

"Holy shit," Athena said. "No wonder he was giving you the stink eye earlier. You might just as well killed his mama as kill that car."

"See, that's what I've been thinking about," Billie said. "Why did I do that? What would possess me to destroy his car? All I can come up with is that somewhere in my hungover, pissed-off brain, I knew that if I did that, it was over. No more apologies, no more crying, no more nothing. Like this was some kind of instinctual defense mechanism that got triggered. This is my out."

"Except now you have to worry about the motherfucker wanting revenge."

"Oh yeah," Billie said, laughing. The weed was working. "Forgot about that."

"You cannot forget about that."

Billie glanced over. "What do you think Freddie said to him?"

"Oh, probably that if Rory started any shit in Freddie's, his fat white ass would end up in tomorrow's chowder. That's what I figure."

Billie had refilled her plastic cup.

"He's not going to forget about you, Billie," Athena said. "You saw how he was looking at you. You better lay low. Matter of fact, you better stay at my place tonight. I need to talk to you anyway."

"I don't need you yelling at me anymore," Billie said. "I told you I was done with him and that's not going to change tomorrow or next week or next year."

"I believe you," Athena said.

She took another toke and held the joint out, but Billie shook her head. Instead she reached into her purse for a cigarette. The pot nowadays was killer stuff and she couldn't handle more than a hit or two. She lit the smoke as Athena pinched the roach off and put it in her pocket.

"Turn down my kickass marijuana and smoke that shit," Athena said.

"Don't start."

"You said you were going to quit."

"And I am," Billie said. "I'm like Mark Twain. He said it was easy to quit smoking. He'd done it lots of times."

"Yeah, you and Mark Twain are two peas in a pod," Athena said, laughing. "I'm going to miss you."

"Maybe I will sleep on your couch, though," Billie said. "Give asshole a couple days to cool off." She paused. "What do you mean, 'miss me'?"

Athena reached for the bottle and filled the little cup before pouring more for Billie. "I'm getting out of here."

"Out of where—Freddie's?"

"No, out of Chillicothe. Out of Ohio."

"Where you going?"

"San Francisco."

Billie sipped her wine.

"So I wanted to tell you," Athena said. "Because I kind of feel guilty about leaving you alone here. I mean, who's going to look out for your skinny white ass?"

Billie shook her head. "At what point did you become my mother? I'm, like, a decade older than you."

"Yeah, but I'm way older than you . . . here." Athena tapped her temple with a fingertip. "That's what you need to realize."

Billie rolled her eyes. "So what's in San Francisco?"

"My aunt got me an internship with this designer there," Athena said.

"You want to be a designer?"

"You know that," Athena replied. "I told you that."

"You told me you wanted to be a singer, too. And a photographer and I don't know what else. So I'm taking all of this with a grain of salt."

"I figure to establish myself as a designer first. I got some serious talent in that department. About all you ever see me in is this fish shirt, but I got some moves when it comes to design. I'll show you some drawings."

Billie looked away toward the traffic on the thruway again. Athena watched her for a time, studying the bruise on her face. "I've always wondered who started that 'grain of salt' thing."

"What?"

"When you think about it, it makes no sense. Why not grain of sand, or grain of rice? Even then, it makes no sense."

"My grandmother used to say it all the time," Billie said.

"You never asked her what it means?"

"I know what it means."

"But where'd it come from? I doubt your granny invented it."

"Maybe she did."

"Nah, it's been around forever," Athena said. "People been saying it and nobody ever questioned it . . . until this very moment."

"You're right," Billie said. "That pot is badass."

Athena laughed. "Didn't I tell you?"

"So you're leaving," Billie said and took a drink. "What about Lesley?"

"Lesley and I are finished," Athena said.

"Good. I never thought she was right for you," Billie said. "Woman has no sense of humor, for one thing."

"She never knocked me around," Athena pointed out. "You know—like some people I could name."

"For fucksakes."

"But yeah, I'm leaving," Athena said after a long pause. "So what are you going to do?"

"About what?"

"Your life," Athena said. "You even listening to me?"

Billie shrugged. "I figure I'm doing it."

"Really?" Athena asked. "This is it? Getting high in a parking lot? Getting smacked around by Rory white trash? That's it?"

"That shit with Rory is done, as I've told you fourteen times in the past couple hours. And I never noticed you having any problems with getting high in a parking lot."

"You know what I mean," Athena said. "Didn't you tell me you went to college?"

"I did."

"For what?"

"Journalism and communications."

"And you graduated?"

"I did."

"And that led you to your current position at Freddie's Fish Shack?"

"That's right."

Athena finished her wine. The bottle was now empty. "What's so great about this place, that makes it better than home?"

"You just answered your own question." Billie hopped off the hood and walked over to toss the empty bottle in the recycle bin. Kentucky was where she was from. It was also where her mother had killed herself. "Anyplace is better than home."

Athena lived in a small apartment over a gallery downtown. The gallery sold mostly prints of cats and dogs and re-pops of movie posters. Billie went into the bathroom to brush her teeth, and when she came out Athena was sitting in a recliner with her laptop. There was a blanket and pillow on the couch. Billie stripped to her underwear and T-shirt and stretched out, adjusting the pillow beneath her head.

"You're a good friend, Athena."

"I know it."

Billie began to drift off. It had been a long day, following a brutal night. She was thinking about what Athena had asked. Actually, she was trying not to think about it. What was she going to do? She was thirty-two years old, working as a waitress, making eleven bucks an hour with minimal tips. She had a bruised cheekbone courtesy of someone who had been, up until twelve hours earlier, the man in her life. The highlight of her week was Thursday night softball.

She decided that not thinking about it was the better option, for tonight anyway. Such procrastination worked for Scarlett O'Hara. At least it had been working for her when the movie ended; hard to say what went down after that. Content in her solidarity with Miss Scarlett, Billie allowed herself to drift off.

"Pliny the Elder," she heard Athena say.

Billie opened her eyes. "What?"

Athena indicated the screen. "That grain of salt shit. Old Pliny started it."

Three

I T WAS LATE AFTERNOON WHEN THEY got back from Chestnut Field. They had spent the better part of the day there, depositing the colt in the stall Will had rented for the season and then arranging for Skeeter Musgrave to work the animal in the morning. Skeeter was a former jockey; Will had known him for thirty years or more and had used him as a rider for a number of those years until Skeeter couldn't make the weight anymore. He'd retired then, but within a year he was back at the track at dawn every day, working horses for any owner willing to pay him twenty bucks a toss. The money had nothing to do with it.

"What am I supposed to do?" he'd asked Will shortly after coming back. "Sit and watch TV every morning? Have you seen TV lately?"

There was a card running that afternoon, so Will and Jodie climbed into the bleachers and watched the first few races. As for wagering, they came up with a plan. Each race one of them would pick a horse and bet two dollars to win. They would alternate the picks from race to race. Will won the coin toss and chose the favorite in the first race and the horse finished second to last. Before the next race they went down to the walking ring to look at

25

the entries there, and Jodie settled on a tall chestnut gelding. The horse went off at eight to one and won going away. They collected nearly nineteen dollars.

Before the third race, Chuck Caldwell joined them in the stands. He was the track manager and he liked to cozy up to Will, mainly because Will had been around longer than just about any of the other owners and Caldwell liked to pretend he was part of the old boys' network, even though he wasn't. He was from back east—Connecticut or Vermont or one of those places—and he'd married a Lexington girl he met on vacation somewhere in Mexico. Her father knew the manager at Chestnut Field back then and had gotten Caldwell a job as an assistant. He was made manager when it was decided by the owners that he could handle the job without screwing it up. It had required some apple shining on Caldwell's part for that to happen, but he was fairly good at that. His wife made decent money in advertising, more than Caldwell, something she reminded him of quite frequently.

"I saw the colt in the row, figured you were kicking around here somewhere," he said as he sat down. He indicated the horses on the track, just now approaching the gate. "You making any money?"

"You're looking at your worst nightmare," Will said. "The kid and I are fixing to break this place today."

At that Caldwell laughed harder than was required. He had splotchy skin and thinning red hair and wore the same clothes every day—tan khaki pants and a black shirt with the Chestnut Field logo on the breast.

"You working the horse tomorrow, then?"

Will nodded.

"I might show up early to watch," Caldwell said.

Will knew that he wouldn't. He was constantly saying that he wanted to watch the colt run but Will got to the track at dawn and Caldwell three hours later. For their schedules to mesh Caldwell would have to be out of bed by five o'clock and Will didn't see that happening. But Caldwell seemed excited about the colt, if for no other reason than the fact that the animal's sire was Saguaro. Chestnut Field rarely was home to such lofty bloodlines.

"Any idea when you might run him yet?" Caldwell asked.

"Sooner than later," Will told him.

Caldwell hesitated. Will knew what was coming. "Any idea where?"

Will figured to run the colt right there at Chestnut. After all, that's where he'd been working the animal. The track usually ran a few juvenile races every year by midsummer. Will was waiting for things to feel right. He wasn't going to rush this horse. But he also wasn't going to tell Caldwell his strategy. He had a feeling that to tell Caldwell was to tell the whole world, and the colt was Will's business, not the world's.

"Still thinking on that," he replied.

Caldwell sat with them and watched the next race and then left, after receiving or pretending to receive a text on his phone.

"Do you like that man?" Jodie asked when he was gone.

"I guess I don't like him or dislike him," Will said after thinking about it.

"Me too, I guess," Jodie said.

For the next three races, they never got a sniff and decided to call it a day.

Will let Jodie cash the winning ticket and hold the money. When they got back to the truck, she handed it over to him.

"It's half yours," he reminded her.

"I owe you for feed," she said.

"We're going to keep that separate," Will told her. "Today's money is fun money. We split it straight down the middle. We'll worry about the feed another time."

They stopped for French fries and ice cream at a burger shack outside of the town of Chestnut. The bill came to within fifty cents of what they'd won.

"So we broke even," Will said. They were sitting outside, under an awning. The heat of the day melted the ice cream as quickly as they could eat it. "That's a good day in the thoroughbred game."

After eating they sat there for a while, watching the traffic pass. Will removed his sweat-stained Stetson and wiped his forehead with the sleeve of his shirt before putting the hat on again.

"You need a new hat," Jodie told him.

"Why do I need a new hat?"

"That one is dirty."

"Still does the job," Will said. "That pony was dirty and you didn't throw her away, did you?"

"No, but I cleaned her."

"I have a clean hat," Will said. "I save it for special occasions."

"What kind of occasion?"

"I can't think of one just now," Will admitted.

Jodie looked off toward the horizon, her eyes narrow. "What about when Cactus Jack wins his first race? Will you wear your clean hat that day?"

"I most certainly will."

When they got back to the farm, Will offered to give the girl a ride home.

"Throw your bike in the back."

"It's okay. I'll ride." And then she was on her bike and pedaling up the drive to the highway.

He had offered to drive her home in the past and she had always declined. She lived with her mother in a rented double-wide. The place was in poor repair and Will suspected that the girl was embarrassed by the fact. Well, Will himself wasn't exactly living in the Taj Mahal.

When she was gone, he ran water for the stock and then went up to the house and had a nap on the couch for an hour. It was still daylight when he woke up. He heated a cast-iron pan and cooked a flank steak alongside three eggs, sipping on a can of Budweiser while he did. He ate outside on the picnic table, on the deck overlooking the farm. Finishing the meal, he opened another beer and sat there as dusk approached. The sky to the west showed no remorse, clear and cloudless, marred only by the haze from the unrelenting heat. Down by the barn, the livestock were quiet. The mares stood not five feet from where Will had first seen them that morning. From the other side of the barn the donkey had brayed for a while over something and the goat had replied, as if telling the jack to be quiet.

It was nearly dark when Marian pulled up in her Honda SUV. She parked on the slope and got out, carrying a small cardboard box. Coming up on the deck, she walked behind Will and bent over to kiss him on the cheek, her free arm draped lightly around his neck.

"Hey, old man."

"How are you, Marian."

She moved around to sit across from him, placing the box on the table. She wore a navy skirt and a white blouse. Will looked at her legs as she crossed them. She had great legs for sixty-two years old. She had great legs for any age.

"Bourbon?" he asked.

"Maybe in a bit," she replied. "Too hot to drink, even."

He indicated the box. "What's this?"

"The bake sale at the church today," she replied. "Brought you some goodies that didn't sell."

"I get the dregs—is that it?"

"That's it." She turned to look toward the outbuildings and the assorted animals down below. "You get your hay?"

"Came this morning," Will said. "Some peckerwood delivered it."

She smiled. "Peckerwoods have to work, too."

"Price went up by nearly half," Will said. "And it's only going to get worse. They'll be trucking it from out of state next."

"We'll get rain."

Will drank from the can of Bud. "You keep telling me that but you don't say when. You worked all day at the church? Can't you talk to God about the weather, maybe put in a good word for me?"

"He has no interest in a sinner like you." Perspiring in the heat, Marian used her fingertips to push her hair back from her temples. "And yet He sees the sparrow fall. Isn't life strange?"

"Life around here is dry, I don't know about strange."

"I could do a rain dance for you."

"Worth a try."

She reached over to take the can of beer from him. She had a sip and gave it back. "You going to make it another year?"

Will was quiet for a time. "That two-year-old I dropped off at Chestnut Field today is half as good as I think he is, I'll be fine."

"Somebody was asking about that colt today."

"Well now," Will said. "That somebody wouldn't be Reese Ryker, would it?"

"It would. He came into the bake sale with his brand-new wife. Bought her some strawberry tarts before he made a point of striking up a conversation with me."

"Got hitched again, did he?"

Marian nodded. "And she's a looker, I can say that. You'd swear she stepped off the cover of *Vogue* magazine. Pleasant too, spoke with an accent of some kind."

"All his wives have looked like that. Must be his magnetic personality. What'd he have to say about the colt?"

"Asking about your plans for him."

"Worried I might be hitching him to a milk wagon, is he?"

"I don't believe that's his concern," Marian said. "He asked me when you planned to run him. I told him I didn't know. Which is what I would tell him even if I did know."

Will finished his beer and stood up. "You want one of these?"

"I'll just keep stealing from you," she said.

As he went inside, Marian stood and walked to the deck railing. In the gloaming she could see the mares lounging. Marian had ridden a little as a teenager in camp but in truth she knew nothing about horses, and less than that about thoroughbred racing. In the four years she'd been seeing Will, she hadn't learned much. As a rule, he didn't talk about the business end of things. She suspected that was because he was always either broke or close to it and didn't want her to think he was complaining about his impoverished state. However, she did know that there was a lot riding on the gray colt. She also knew of the unusual circumstances surrounding the animal's lineage, and why Reese Ryker was so concerned about it.

Hearing the screen door, she turned. Will walked over to hand her a cold can of beer. He'd brought two after all.

"Funny thing, I saw that snot Reese Ryker not two days ago," he said. "I was at the co-op and he was there, talking to the owner. Never said a word to me about the colt. Yet here he is, quizzing you."

"You know the man's ego," Marian said. She had a sip, wiping her mouth afterward. "He would never let on how you having that horse eats at him."

"Never occurred to him that you would tell me?"

"I said he's vain, not smart." Marian sat at the table again. "But he's bound to have that horse."

Will sat down, as well. "He's not going to get him, not as long as I'm above ground."

"Seems to me like a man who's never heard the word no."

"By my count, this is his fourth wife," Will said. "He must have heard it once or twice."

Marian laughed as she drank the beer. Will leaned forward and opened the corner of the box she'd brought with her.

"So what do we have here?"

"Low-fat muffins," Marian said.

"Christ. No wonder nobody would buy them."

"Far be it from you to try one before you start complaining about them," Marian said. "Have one for breakfast in the morning. Be a change from oatmeal every day, like the doctor prescribed. You did have oatmeal this morning?"

Will nodded as he took a drink.

"I wondered," she went on. "Because I saw a truck just like yours at the grits and grease down the road. Round about seven o'clock."

Will looked away a moment. It was nearly full dark now but the heat had barely relented. He glanced at Marian. "Spying on me now?"

"Hardly," she said. "I was headed to the church first thing. I guess I could start taking the long way around through Porterville, so I don't catch you cheating on your diet."

"For Chrissakes."

Marian took a long drink before returning the beer can to the circle of condensation it had made on the table, placing it precisely in the ring. "So how is the oatmeal down at the Crossroads? I bet it tastes just like bacon and eggs."

"It actually kind of reminded me of sausage and eggs." Will smiled. "Can we get back to where you promised me a rain dance?"

She watched him in the half light. "You know, if you were half as charming as you think, you'd be twice as charming as you are."

"That's a lot of fractions for an old shit-kicker like me," Will said. "You're saying, when it comes to women I'm no Reese Ryker?"

"You're no Reese Ryker." Marian smiled, letting him off the hook. "I wouldn't be within ten miles of this place if you were."

"Good to know."

"But you won't be getting a dance of any kind tonight. I have a meeting in town."

"Tomorrow night?"

"Sure, if you promise to stick to your diet," she said. "How's that suit you?"

"Right down to my boots," Will said.

Reese Ryker had indeed been born into it. His great-grandfather, Thomas Ryker, had arrived in Kentucky in the 1850s, coming out from Massachusetts with a new wife in a wagon and seven thousand dollars in a valise. He bought eight hundred acres of forest in Fayette County. Land in Kentucky was cheap then, and even cheaper yet when it was still nothing but trees. Ryker purchased eleven slaves at auction in Nashville and within three years had cleared the property, built a two-story house, and was raising crops, mainly rye and barley and corn. In 1859 he started the distillery that carried his name. When the war started two years later, he stood, as a man with eleven slaves would be inclined to do, with Leonidas Polk when he advocated secession. When that failed, Thomas remained on the fence for the duration, although family history insisted that he spent an evening in his own living room drinking bourbon with Nathan Bedford Forrest. Of course, if every southern gentleman who claimed to have pulled a cork with Forrest was telling the truth, it's doubtful that the general would have found time to do all the fighting that it was generally acknowledged he did. Not only that, but it's doubtful his liver would have lasted through Shiloh.

Thomas Ryker Jr. eventually took over the estate, which continued to prosper even when it became necessary to pay the workers. The distillery produced very good bourbon, considered high end, even in a state known for the liquor. The plant required corn and lots of it, and in 1912 Ryker Jr. was able to buy an additional five hundred acres, which upon his death in 1948 became the realm of his oldest son, Thomas III. At that time the Ryker name was associated mainly with the distillery, although the farm had continued to thrive.

Things took a downturn under Thomas III, who was a habitual gambler, a relentless drunk, and somewhat lazy to boot. Backed by what he mistakenly assumed to be an unlimited supply of capital, he married and divorced twice, spent weeks on end in Las Vegas, and left the running of the distillery and farm to underlings, some of whom were not particularly scrupulous about the accounts. When the cat's away and all that. By the time the second wife had left, with her own allotment of money, Thomas III was destitute to the point where he had to sell the distillery to a French consortium famed for its brandy. Thomas was also obliged to sell nearly all of the acreage accrued by his father and grandfather, retaining only ten acres surrounding the red brick mansion, built in 1899 on the original homestead.

By 1960 Thomas III was down to his last copper. He considered himself Kentucky royalty and could still play the part fairly well; he had a 1959 Cadillac convertible, unpaid for, and a fine wardrobe he'd bought back when he still had a few dollars in the bank. But his socks had holes in the toes and he owed nearly everybody within a hundred-mile radius—grocers, mechanics, the power company, and of course the bank. He was suffering from a deep depression and would from time to time find himself staring at the Navy Colt that had been owned, but never used, by his grandfather during the Civil War. However, it took skill to load the ancient cap and ball revolver, and courage to use it. It seemed he was lacking in everything.

He nearly begged off going to the Lexington Hospital Foundation Gala that spring, a fundraising dinner he had attended for years, usually with his wife of the time. But serendipity took a hand; had he stayed at home in his misery and self-pity, he would never have made the acquaintance of Shirley Reese, daughter of Frank Reese, founder and sole owner of Reese Department Stores, with over six hundred stores in forty-eight states. Not only would Thomas not have met Shirley Reese, he would not have asked her out to dinner the following night and several more times over the following weeks, and he would not have, obviously, married her that fall, in a small ceremony at the Ryker estate. Shirley was an only child, as luck would have it, and was considered somewhat plain in appearance and pathologically shy in public. These traits were of little concern to Thomas III. He found Shirley to be sweet and deferential and compliant. He also found her to be in line for an inheritance of around two billion dollars. If it wasn't a match made in heaven, it was close enough for Thomas III.

Thomas and Shirley had two children. Linda was born in 1962 and Reese the following year. Reese was of course named for his mother's family, in part to assuage the considerable concerns that Frank Reese entertained over the fact that his daughter had married an alcoholic spendthrift who might, when in his cups, be inclined to bet against the sun coming up tomorrow, if the odds were tempting enough.

Thus the fortunes of the Ryker name were once again reversed. Young Reese grew up on the old estate. His mother, who beneath her timid exterior was a woman with ambition and spirit, oversaw a complete restoration of the house and grounds. She had loved horses as a child, and with her father's passing in 1979, she and Thomas (she for the most part) decided to go into the thoroughbred business. More acreage was purchased, miles of white fencing erected; new barns were built, as were foaling sheds and a large training facility. The business was an iffy proposition, no matter how well backed financially, and Ryker Racing International had an uninspiring first two decades. Shirley enjoyed going to the track and watching her horses run; she was not obsessed with winning and could afford to lose. Thomas III couldn't care less. His coffers refilled, he went back to his vagabond ways. He died in 1999 and Shirley, mourning the man who she had loved as much as an absentee husband could be loved, had turned to Reese to run the stable. Linda had married a software engineer and moved to California. Reese had graduated from the University of Kentucky with a degree in business and dabbled in several start-ups, all financed by his mother and none particularly successful—a Jaguar dealership, a high-end restaurant called Reese's, a pipeline proposal that went nowhere but cost the family three million dollars in development fees.

So, at the age of forty, Reese took over the stable, renaming it Double R Racing. He suffered from his father's limited attention span, and so horse racing became the latest shiny thing to land on his radar. For whatever reason—possibly the fact that the actual work required to own a stable was not especially exerting—he took to the task. He took to traveling to all the venues where the biggest races were run—Louisville of course, New York, Baltimore, Dubai, California. He changed the way he dressed, he changed his speech, playing up the Kentucky accent he once had attempted to hide, and he changed his wife—three times. Yet for all his posing, he never felt accepted by the other big owners, the people who had been in the game for years and who, more significantly, had all won important races. Reese came to realize that he was a pretender. In fact, his second wife called him that as she was walking out the door. But he accepted the term (it was actually less painful than the terms of the divorce). He also knew that a pretender needed a crown. The crown Reese wanted was the Kentucky Derby.

Toward that end, he began to spend money, which the family still had in abundance, despite Reese's poor marital record. He hired one of the best trainers in the country, a taciturn type named Joe Drinkwater, and under his guidance he bought yearlings at the annual sales in Kentucky, Canada, and Florida—as many as fifty in a single year. Ryker horses began to win and the stable actually began to make money, finishing place or show in Triple Crown races seven times over a period of four years. But never first.

However, Reese was convinced that the day was coming. Ryker Racing was just one piece of the puzzle away from breaking through. Then, quite unexpectedly, that piece became available. Humphrey Brown, the billionaire Kentuckian and thoroughbred racing scion, with over a hundred Grade One victories to his credit, had announced that he would, upon turning eighty, be getting out of the business. Apparently he was determined to follow Warren Buffett's lead and give away as much of his money as he could in the time he had remaining. That meant that he would be selling off his entire stable, the jewel of which was a horse that was considered the top breeding stallion in the world—Saguaro. The seven-year-old had four years earlier finished second in the Derby, first in the Preakness, and second once again in the Belmont. The following year, the horse won the Breeders Cup Classic and was then retired to stud. Double R Racing put in a preemptive bid and was able to buy the stallion for twenty-eight million dollars. For a horse that commanded a quarter-million dollars for a single stud fee and one that would breed as many as a hundred or more mares a year, the price was not exorbitant, especially when it seemed to deliver, at long last, Reese's promotion from pretender to player.

They had acquired Saguaro three years earlier and that first spring had bred a dozen Ryker mares to the stallion. Of these, one showed such promise that even Joe Drinkwater had been seen smiling in the foal's vicinity. The colt, which they named Ghost Rider, was a mirror image of its sire. In Reese's fertile imagination, the animal was already the number one contender for the Triple Crown, even though the first of the three races, the Derby, was ten months away. But the two-year-old had already run five races—and won all five with blazing speed and unexpected stamina for an animal that young.

Five years earlier Reese's mother, feeling that Reese needed a real job, one with duties consisting of more than hanging around racetracks and acting a role, had purchased a television station—WTVK—in Louisville for him to run. It had been decided that Reese's title would be CEO. The studios and office space were on the outskirts of the city, near the airport. Reese had a spacious office on the top floor. At first he had gone there every morning, for a half day at least. The half days eventually turned into an hour or so, and then only once or twice a week. The station had been basically a turnkey operation when acquired, which meant that he had little to do there, although he liked to be involved with the hiring of the on-air talent. In fact, his third wife had been the anchor of the six o'clock news when he met her.

It was a forty-five-minute drive from the Ryker estate to the station. The day after buying the strawberry tarts from Marian at the church bazaar, Reese arrived there shortly past ten in the morning. He shared the top floor with Burt Collingwood, the station manager. There was a foyer, where the receptionist was, and two large offices, one on each side of the building. The interior walls were all of glass.

Burt was not in his office when Reese stepped off the elevator, but then he rarely was, spending most of his day in the studios below. The receptionist, also secretary to both Reese and Burt, was new. She was short and quite heavy, wearing a dress with a floral print. Reese stopped when he saw her.

"Good morning," she said, her voice a tentative singsong. If Reese had been more perceptive, he might have recognized the uncertainty in her tone, typical of someone very young starting a new job. Reese was not that perceptive.

"Where's Paulina?"

"Oh," the woman said. "She's not here anymore."

"I can see she's not here," Reese said. "If she was here, she'd be here. Right?"

The woman offered a weak smile, in case Reese happened to be joking. "I'm Michelle. You are Mr. Ryker, I know."

Reese had liked Paulina, although he'd never really gotten to know her. But she was of a type he liked. Tall and athletic. And she had a great ass. He frequently married such women.

"Do you have my messages?" he asked.

"I don't think there are any."

He went into his office without another word and sat at his desk for an hour, watching TV, flipping from ESPN to the news stations, mostly CNN because they had the best-looking correspondents. Reese wondered where Paulina had gone and why he hadn't been informed that she was leaving. He had hired her himself; she'd been working at a steakhouse downtown as a hostess and mentioned that she was looking for something else. After flirting with her for a month, Reese had created the job and offered it to her. Before that, both he and Burt had used the receptionist in the main foyer on the ground floor.

He watched the news a while longer. From time to time he harbored vague ambitions of running for office. He thought he might like to be a state senator, or even a US senator, but that would require a move to Washington. Either notion would have to wait.

Since the purchase of Saguaro and the emergence of Ghost Rider as a horse to be reckoned with, Reese had spent most of his mental energy fantasizing about what the colt would accomplish in a year, when the animal would race as a three-year-old.

Thinking about it now, he turned off the winsome women of CNN and left the office, thinking he would go to Churchill Downs, where Joe Drinkwater would be working the colt. The company currently had a dozen horses at the track.

"I'm gone for the day," he told the receptionist.

He took the elevator to the ground floor, where he found Burt Collingwood in the studio, going over some station logo artwork with a man in jeans and a faded hoodie.

"I was going to bring these up," Burt said when he saw Reese. "This is Jared Ross. These are the new logos we commissioned."

Reese ignored the artwork. "What happened to Paulina?" he asked.

"Are you kidding?" Burt asked.

"What do you mean?"

"We had to pay her off. What the hell, Reese."

"And then she quit?" Reese asked.

"You think she'd stay after that?"

"I never gave it any thought."

"Apparently not," Burt said.

"I liked Paulina," Reese said.

Burt let the matter slide. He held up the sheets with the various designs featuring the station's call letters. "What do you think of these?"

"They're fine," Reese said.

Burt looked at the kid Jared, cocking his left eyebrow just slightly, as if to say he was used to such apathy. "But which do you prefer?" he persisted.

"The red one," Reese said. "Who's the new girl?"

"Her name's Michelle," Burt said. "She has a degree from Northwestern."

"I don't think she's going to work out."

"Why not?" Burt asked.

Reese shrugged. "There's something off about her."

And he left.

Four

A THENA WORKED HER LAST SHIFT FRIDAY night, and she spent Saturday running around getting ready to leave. She was heading out for California Sunday morning, driving her white VW with 247,000 miles on the odometer. Before she left, she urged Billie to come with her.

"What am I going to do in San Francisco?"

"All else fails, same thing you're doing here," Athena had told her. "I hear they got restaurants out there."

It was Saturday night and they were sitting in Athena's kitchen drinking beer. Billie was still sleeping on the couch. She'd only been home briefly since destroying Rory's car, to pick up clean clothes and her mail. She hadn't seen Rory around but she was operating under the assumption that he was still plotting his revenge, though he hadn't come back to Freddie's.

"I don't know," Billie said now. "Where am I going to stay out there? You'll be at your aunt's."

"You are the most negative person I ever met," Athena said. "Where's that come from?"

"The fact that I live in the real world?"

"Fuck off with that."

Billie took a drink of beer. "How's life in California going to be any different than life here?"

"Let's see," Athena said. "Maybe in California you won't have a psycho ex-boyfriend stalking your ass?"

"We don't know that he's stalking me." Billie laughed. "We just assume he is."

"See how hard you laugh when the prick catches up to you," Athena said. "What about this journalism degree? You must have had something in mind when you got it. You wanted to work at a newspaper or what?"

Billie nodded. "Yeah, I thought I'd pick out a dying industry and aim for that."

"You could be on television, reporter or the chick reading the news, something like that," Athena said. "You got the looks for it, and you're fairly intelligent when you're not trying to prove otherwise."

"Who's going to boost my self-esteem when you're not around?" Billie asked.

"That's why you need to come with me," Athena said. "I wouldn't be surprised if my aunt knows somebody who knows somebody in television."

"Somewhere over the course of half a joint and two light beers, you have decided that I'm a bona fide TV anchor," Billie said. "By midnight I'll have won an Emmy."

"I won't be awake at midnight. I'm going to be on that thruway by six o'clock. If you intend to come with me, you better pack up your three pairs of jeans and five T-shirts, tell Freddie you're gone, and get in that fucking VW."

Billie went to the fridge for another beer. When she looked over, Athena shook her head in refusal. Billie popped the can and came back to the table.

"You go scout things out and then we'll talk," she said.

"Right."

"I'm serious," Billie said. "I do listen to you. And I know it's time for a change. But you have your own shit going on out there, and you need to focus on that. First we fix you and then we fix me later."

"I don't need fixing."

"But I do?"

"I'm like an umpire. I call 'em as I see 'em, baby. The bus leaves at six a.m."

Billie wasn't on it. She got up when she heard Athena moving about and helped carry her worldly belongings down to the parking lot. Athena handed over the keys to the apartment; the rent was paid until the end of the month, so Billie could stay on until then if she wanted.

"Don't forget to text," Billie said, and Athena was gone, chugging away onto Pine Street, heading toward the thruway, the backseat of the VW piled high with pillows and knapsacks and cooler bags full of snacks.

That night Billie, restless and bored, drove out to a bar called Shaker's on the highway south of Circleville. She was operating on the assumption that it was out of Rory's orbit. He had been born in Chillicothe, and, except for odd drywalling job out in the boonies somewhere, he rarely strayed very far out of town.

Shaker's was a typical shit-kicker bar, bad country music, lots of big-screen TVs, coin-operated pool tables in the back. The smell of stale beer permeated everything—the walls, the carpet, the patrons. A month of steam cleaning couldn't get rid of it.

Billie was surprised to see Goose Grayson working the bar. She knew him from Chillicothe; he used to play softball in the league and had slung beer at the old Templeton Hotel before it had burned down under not-so-mysterious circumstances, an insurance scam gone bad. Billie hadn't seen Goose since he'd quit playing ball a couple of years ago. She'd heard that his wife left him and that he'd taken the breakup badly. But badly enough to quit softball? That seemed a little extreme.

"What are you doing here?" he asked as he drew her a beer.

"Just out for a drive," Billie told him. He put the draft in front of her and waved away payment. She looked past him, to the other side of the L-shaped bar. A man, skinny as a snake, was sitting there watching Billie openly. He was sixty years old, maybe seventy, and wore a battered tan cowboy hat and snap-button white shirt with a frayed collar. When she stared him down, he didn't look away.

"I didn't know you were working here," she said, turning back to Goose.

"I moved up here last year. My girlfriend works at the GM dealership out on the highway."

A new girlfriend, Billie thought. Broken hearts mend.

"Still at Freddie's?" he asked.

"Still there," Billie said. "Crab cakes are my life."

"How's the team?"

"We're second-to-last place," Billie said. "But leading the league in hangovers."

A waitress came to the station with an order. As Goose moved off to serve her, Billie had a drink of draft and then turned on the barstool to have a look at the room. There was a lot of camo in evidence, on the men in particular, everything from pants to T-shirts to ball caps. Billie wondered if the socks and underwear were camo, too. She didn't want to find out. There were three girls at a table in the center of the room: college kids, no doubt, out slumming with the redneck crowd. They'd have stories to tell when they got back to school in the fall. They were drinking beer with shots and all appeared drunk. Two wore tight shorts and T-shirts, the third a short skirt. That one was showing a lot of cleavage too, and she had plenty to display. They likely weren't looking for romance in Shaker's, but they were sure putting the merchandise out there. Foolish kids.

When Billie turned back to the bar, the thin man was watching her again. Or still. His face was weather-beaten, his eyes wet behind heavy-framed glasses. Goose, idle once more, came over.

"Who's the bone rack in the cowboy hat?" Billie asked. "He's been eyeballing me since I sat down."

Goose had a look. "Never seen him before. You do realize that guys in bars look at pretty girls."

"Dude's old enough to be my grandpa," Billie said.

"That usually doesn't stop them," Goose said. "Hey, I heard about Rory's Vette."

Billie was still returning the skinny man's stare. "Yeah, that was a shame."

"Are you crazy?" Goose said. "He loves that car more than he loves his mother."

Now Billie turned to him. "So I keep hearing. But then, that's not hard to do. I've met his mother."

"Seriously," Goose said. "What were you thinking?"

"There wasn't a lot of thinking went into it," Billie assured him.

The waitress returned. Apparently the bourbon she'd ordered was to be straight up and Goose had poured it on the rocks. He gave her another shot and put the first one in front of Billie.

"My mistake is your free Jim Beam." He paused a moment. "You know, I was surprised when I heard the story. You never struck me as a jealous type, Billie. I always took you for the I-don't-give-a-shit type."

Billie took a slug of bourbon and chased it with the draft. "And what story would you be talking about, Goose?"

"What went down that night," Goose said. "You showed up at Rory's and found him in the sack with some woman. You lost it and went demolition derby on the man's Corvette."

Billie was quiet a moment. "And where did you hear this?"

"Buddy of mine over in Chillicothe."

"Where did he hear it?"

"He didn't say."

Billie reached for the bourbon. Of course Rory would come up with a story that made him look good. He couldn't very well tell the truth. "There's at least two sides to every story, Goose. Rory's either a ladies' man, doing two girls at a time, or a drunken asshole who likes to hit women. Take your pick."

"That how it was?"

"That's how it was."

"Then good for you, Billie."

Duty called again and Goose moved off to make margaritas for the college girls. Billie finished the bourbon and pushed the empty glass away before looking at the man in the hat again.

"Do I have spinach in my teeth?" she asked. "'Cause you've been staring at me since I walked in here."

"I know you," the man said. His voice was as cracked and worn as his complexion.

"I don't think so, Wyatt Earp. That line usually work for you, does it?"

"You're from Marshall, Kentucky."

At that Billie hesitated, reaching for the glass of beer as she attempted to place the man, trying to imagine what he might have looked like ten years earlier, or twenty.

"I used to live there," the man said. "You're Will Masterson's daughter. I knew your father."

"We're birds of a feather," Billie said. "I used to know him, too."

"I worked at all them little tracks around that neck of the woods," the man said. "Hot walker. I used to see your old man regular. I bought a Dodge pickup from him one time. A red Dodge, you remember that truck?"

Billie, finishing the draft, shook her head. "No."

"How's he doing these days?"

"Couldn't say."

Billie glanced to the rear of the bar and saw that one of the pool tables was now open. "Another beer here, Goose. And give me some change for pool, will you?"

"If you're talking to him," the man in the hat said, "tell him Jimmy Muirhead says hello."

Billie retrieved the beer and the coins from the bar, left Goose a five, and started for the table. "I don't expect I'll be talking to him."

She dropped the quarters in the slot and racked the balls and played a game of eight-ball against herself, shooting stripes until she missed, then spots. While racking for a second game, she glanced over to the bar. The man in the cowboy hat was no longer there, his empty glass all that was left. Billie looked around the place but the man was gone.

The truck had been a 1976 Dodge Ram, a red three-quarter ton her father had used to haul horses from track to track. Sometimes Billie would ride along, sitting in the passenger seat, punching up the AM stations on the radio. She had called the vehicle Big Red, the nickname of Secretariat, the greatest thoroughbred in history. She remembered the day he'd sold it, how sad she was to see it go. Funny she remembered the truck but not the man who bought it.

Playing again, she became aware of a guy leaning against the back wall, gripping a Miller longneck between his thumb and forefinger. He hadn't been standing there a few minutes ago but she'd seen him earlier with the camo-clad bunch in front of the TV, watching the Cleveland Indians. She'd noticed him because he was the one bucking the fashion, wearing jeans and a faded Joe Cocker T-shirt. He was a few years younger than Billie, she guessed, and not bad-looking. His hair was artfully messed up, held there with some product or another, but aside from that he was a good-looking man.

"You putting your quarters up?" she asked when she pocketed the eight ball.

"You might be too good for me," the man said.

"Spoken like a true hustler," Billie replied.

The man paid for the rack and they agreed on a dollar a game. "We have to play for something," Billie reasoned. "You got a name?"

"I'm Chris."

"Billie."

Chris wasn't much of a pool player. In fact, he made so many bad shots that Billie thought for a while that he *was* hustling her. It took her a while to realize he was merely inept.

"You from here?" Billie asked.

He shook his head. "Columbus. What about you?"

"Chillicothe," Billie said.

Chris dropped an easy shot in the side pocket but put too much on the cue ball, scratching in the corner. "Goddamn."

"They got pool tables in Columbus?" Billie asked.

He smiled at her. "Fuck you."

"Oh, my," she said, and then ran the table.

He paid her the dollar and while he racked for another game, she went to the bar and bought beers for them both.

"What are you doing here?" she asked when she came back and handed him the Miller.

"Working on a paving crew. We're doing the county road from here down to Henderson." He nodded toward the bunch at the front of the bar, still watching the ball game. "That's the gang."

Billie picked up the chalk from the side rail. "What do you do?"

"Rake and shovel mostly," he said. "Summer job, I'm a senior in college."

"What are you majoring in?"

"Sports psychology."

She broke the balls and made nothing. He walked around the table, inspecting what she'd left him.

"What does a sports psychologist do?"

Leaning over the table, he considered a bank of the four in the corner. "Convinces athletes that they don't suck, even if they do." He straightened, giving up on the bank shot. "What about you?"

"What about me?"

"What do you do?"

"Waitress."

"Really?" he asked, looking over. "Where?"

He seemed surprised to learn that Billie waited tables for a living and she didn't quite know what to make of that. Apparently even strangers thought she should be doing something else with her life.

"Seafood place in Chillicothe."

"Good food?"

"Not bad," Billie admitted. "The owner's the cook and he knows what he's doing."

Chris sank the two in the corner but hooked himself in the process. After he missed the next shot, Billie took over and he stepped back to watch. She was aware that he would position himself so that he could look at her ass while she played but she wasn't overly concerned about it. She was doing the same while he shot. She beat him again easily, and he paid her and racked for a third game. This time he bought the beers.

Billie made two stripes on the break and then two more before missing.

"Looks like I'm the one being hustled here," Chris said.

"Yeah, I'm up two bucks," Billie said. "This is big time."

"Maybe we should up the ante."

"What—you want to play for five?" Billie laughed. "Sounds like your schooling has gone to your head. Psychologist, heal thyself."

He managed to sink the seven in the side. It was hanging over the edge of the pocket; he could have blown on it and it would have dropped. "I was thinking maybe . . . I don't know . . . maybe we play for a back rub."

"Ah," Billie said. "There's hustlers and then there's hustlers. I think maybe we'll stick with the dollar."

He missed his next shot, then smiled at her. "I'm better at back rubs than I am at pool."

Billie laughed. "God, I would hope so."

She went back to work, dropping the fifteen in the side and the ten in the corner. She had just the nine and then the eight to go. Chalking her cue as she walked around the table, she looked over and saw Rory standing by the bar. Her heart jumped and she looked away immediately. Sonofabitch. How would he know where to find her?

Would Goose have made a phone call? No, he wouldn't do that. But maybe somebody else had. The place was nearly full and there could have been somebody there who knew who she was. Obviously the story of Rory's car was out there on the wire, and more than one version of it at that.

Not that it mattered how he got there. He was there and he was looking straight at her now. Billie wasn't sure why he hadn't approached yet. Maybe he was taking measure of the college kid, Chris, wondering if he was a threat if things got rough. Because things, Billie was certain, could get rough.

Which meant that she needed to get out of there. Her pulse rate still climbing, she lined up the nine, then turned and hammered the eight in the far corner.

"What the hell?" Chris asked. "You just lost the game."

"I guess I did," Billie said, tossing her cue on the table. "What do you say you and I go for a drive?"

Chris was clearly puzzled but he liked the idea. Billie nodded toward the back door and led the way. Outside in the parking lot, she remembered that her car was on the street out front.

"What are you driving?" she asked.

He indicated a pickup truck with MID-STATE PAVING on the door.

"Let's go," Billie said.

Five

WILL WAS DUTIFULLY COOKING HIS MORNING oatmeal when he heard Jodie calling for him from somewhere outside. He looked out the window and saw her running up the hill, wearing pink jeans and a yellow top. She burst through the door like a summer squall.

"Dory is hurt!" she exclaimed. "She cut herself on that scrap pile."

Will turned the gas off under the pot. "All right," he said calmly. "Let's have a look."

The nanny goat had a cut on her front leg, a couple of inches above the hoof. It was bleeding, but it wasn't deep enough that it needed stitches. Will hooked a lead to the animal and took her into the barn. Jodie held the goat's head still while Will washed the leg with witch hazel and smeared Barclay's Liniment over the cut before wrapping it with gauze and fastening it with tape. Instead of turning the nanny out again, they put her in her stall for the day.

"That'll keep her from further shenanigans," Will said. "After breakfast, you and I are going to clean up that pile of scrap."

They headed back to the house. The sun had been full up for an hour, promising another hot and cloudless day. The little girl walked beside Will, trying to match his long stride.

"What are shenanigans?" she asked.

"A good way for a goat to get into trouble," Will said.

"Can people get into shenanigans?"

"They certainly can."

"Did you ever?"

Will laughed and when he did he began to cough. He stopped walking for a moment until the fit passed. They climbed the steps to the back deck. Back in the kitchen, Will turned the gas on under the oatmeal.

"Did you have breakfast?" he asked.

"I'm not hungry."

"I didn't ask if you were hungry," Will said. "I asked if you had breakfast. Throw some bread in the toaster and we'll divide this oatmeal down the middle."

"Just like our winnings?"

"Just like our winnings," Will agreed.

She did as he suggested, standing by the toaster, waiting for it to pop as Will doled out the porridge. They put brown sugar and milk on the oatmeal and ate the toast slathered in strawberry preserves.

"I used to make breakfast for my daughter," Will said. "Sunday mornings we'd have pancakes. I used to make them in the shape of animals."

"No way."

His mouth full, Will nodded.

"What animals?" Jodie asked.

"Oh, different ones. She was always coming up with something new for me to try. I think she was trying to stump me. A giraffe one week, maybe an elephant the next. One time she wanted a pancake that looked like a duck-billed platypus."

"What is *that?*"

After they finished eating, Will went into the living room and brought back a volume from the encyclopedia set he'd bought secondhand thirty years earlier. He leafed through it to find a platypus to show the little girl.

"Is that a real animal?"

"It wouldn't be in the encyclopedia if it wasn't," Will told her.

"I never saw an animal like that before."

"Don't they teach you anything in school?"

She was reading the text beneath the picture. "I start fourth grade this fall. Maybe that's when they teach animals like this. Look what it says—they only have these in Australia and Tasmania." She hesitated on Tasmania, sounding it out.

"You sure about that?" Will asked. "I think I saw one under the porch last night."

"You did not."

"Could have been a possum."

Will had fed and watered the horses at daybreak. Now they decided to put the donkey and the pony in the barn with the goat, out of the way. He hooked the Case tractor to the hay wagon and backed it through the paddock gate and over to the scrap pile. He found work gloves for them both and they began to load the fence posts and wire and the rest of the debris onto the wagon. There were paint cans and scraps of two-by-four and plywood, left over from Will's various building projects over the years. As they worked, the girl talked and talked, which was not a problem. Will liked the sound of her voice.

"I can only stay until noon today," she said when they started. "I'm helping Aunt Micky again this afternoon."

"We'll be finished by noon. What are you and Aunt Micky doing?"

"She cleans houses."

"Does your mom work with her?"

"She used to."

Will, trying to pull a tangle of wire from under the pile, gave up and went into the machine shop for a pair of pliers. When he returned he began to cut the wire into shorter lengths that he could pull free.

"Is your mom working now?"

"No." The girl paused a moment, looking not at Will but at the scrap pile. She sighed. "She's got a new boyfriend."

"And what does he do?"

"Not a whole lot that I can see, Will. They were still in bed when I left this morning."

"What's his name?"

"Troy Everson."

Will rolled a heavy cable reel out of the way, pushing it over by the wagon. The day was growing hot and he stopped to wipe his brow. He had known Troy Everson's father, Ronnie. He was a shiftless little bastard who couldn't be trusted with an Indian head nickel. Somebody shot him in Willisburg ten or twelve years earlier, over a debt or a woman or maybe both. He had survived the stomach wound but Will hadn't heard of him since. Presumably he'd moved on, away from the man who had found reason to fire a bullet into his belly.

All Will knew about the son was what he'd read in the weekly paper and heard in the local bars and diners. He was apparently in the business of recycling auto parts, stealing cars and trucks and cutting them up and selling them piecemeal. Whatever his skills as a mechanic, his expertise as a thief was lacking as he kept getting arrested, although running a chop shop was considered petty crime in the county and he usually spent just a few months in jail before being kicked loose to go back to his thieving ways. Will also recalled a story that he'd been mixed up in dealing drugs, too— selling crack or meth or whatever it was that kids were using to fry their brains these days.

And now, it seemed, he was mixed up with Jodie's mother. Will wasn't happy with the news. It was none of his business but that didn't mean he was thrilled to hear it. The girl, pulling fence posts from the pile, had fallen silent. For somebody who could chatter like a magpie she didn't have much to say about her family life as a rule. The fact that she spent most of her free time at Will's spoke volumes anyway.

"Where's Tasmania?" she asked after a time.

"Down there by Australia somewhere," Will told her. "We can look it up later if you want."

"That would be cool."

"It would be cool," Will mimicked. "You know, you can have those encyclopedias if you want them. My daughter used them all the time when she was your age."

"Didn't she have a computer?" Jodie asked.

"No. Most people didn't have computers then. She didn't need a computer. She had those encyclopedias. Plus she was smart, like you."

"Do you think I'm smart?"

"I think you're as sharp as a tack."

Jodie frowned. "Does that mean smart?"

"It does."

"Sharp as a tack," she repeated to herself, so softly Will could barely hear it. "Does your daughter have a computer now?"

Will knelt down to snip more of the tangled wire. He stood, winding the wire into a ball before tossing it onto the wagon. "I don't know. I expect she probably does. Even I got a computer, although I'm not exactly a going concern on it."

"Where is she anyway?"

"Ohio somewhere, far as I know."

The girl was nine years old but she was perceptive enough to know when to leave a thing alone. Maybe her own experience informed her of this. Whatever the reason, she didn't press Will on the matter.

By eleven o'clock they had the pile of scrap reduced to nothing but a few odds and ends on the ground and the large cable reel by the wagon. Jodie was raking the dirt and telling Will about a birthday party she'd been at the previous weekend.

"And then Bailey said that Dylan asked her first. But Chandra said that wasn't true."

"What's Dylan saying?" Will asked.

"Dylan's not saying anything. You know what boys are like. They don't say nothing if they can get away with it."

"I've heard that."

Jodie tossed a coffee can on the wagon. "And I'm not even telling you what Jeremy did."

"Who's Jeremy?"

"Jeremy is Bailey's brother. He's older than her but he acts younger. He can be a real brat, especially if he's with Teddy because Teddy likes to stir the pot, or at least that's what Bailey's mother says."

"All these characters, I'm going to need a scorecard pretty soon," Will said. He put his shoulder against the cable reel and began to lift.

"Melissa says that Bailey is just lying," Jodie said as she continued to rake, gathering the last of the wood splinters and wire into a pile.

Now Will lifted the reel, got his legs under it, and heaved it onto the wagon. As he did, he released a sudden moan. Jodie looked over just as he fell backward to the ground. His right hand was pressed to his chest and he was gasping as if he couldn't catch his breath. His eyes were wide open, looking at the bright cloudless sky that had tormented him these past weeks.

"Will!" the little girl shouted and ran to him.

Billie stood by the living room window, looking to the street out front. The rain that had chased them from the quarry the night before hadn't amounted to much. There were no puddles in the driveway and the pavement was already dry. The pickup with the paving company logo was parked alongside the house in plain sight. It was the first time Billie had slept at home since remodeling Rory's Corvette. She assumed by now he would know she had overnight company. If he was driving to Circleville to look for her, he was surely checking out her house on a regular basis. But she wasn't concerned. Like most bullies, Rory was a dyed-in-the-wool coward. He wouldn't come calling, knowing there was a man on the premises.

He hadn't followed when they had left. Billie saw his truck in the parking lot, the front end still damaged, the headlight held in place with wire. She had expected him to come crashing out the back door of the bar, but he hadn't, possibly for the same reason he wouldn't come to the house—Billie's guest. Maybe he merely wanted her to know of his presence, that he hadn't forgotten about her. If so, it was a psychological ploy that she would have guessed was beyond him, but then who knew what went on in that mind of his?

They had driven off in the truck, heading south. Leaving the bar's parking lot, Billie had been obliged to give a condensed version of the Rory saga, calling him a jealous ex-boyfriend who was having trouble moving on. She didn't feel compelled to mention the physical abuse, or the beloved Corvette that now resembled an accordion. On the way out of town they picked up a six-pack of beer at a mini-mart.

"Where to?" he asked.

"Drive," she said.

"We could go to the motel where I'm staying but I share a room with one of the guys," he said. "They'll be rolling in soon."

"Do I look like the type of girl who would go to a motel room with a guy I just met, even if I did kick his ass on the pool table?"

"I guess not," he said with a smile. "But I'd be a fool if I didn't try."

Halfway to Chillicothe there was an abandoned quarry a couple of miles from the highway where the locals sometime went to swim. Billie showed him the side road and they turned off. It was an overcast night but very warm, and there were a half dozen cars parked along the lip of the quarry. A few people were swimming; the rest were kicking back, drinking beer and wine and playing music.

They parked away from the others and sat on the tailgate of the truck. Billie began to relax. Seeing Rory not twenty feet away had unnerved her. She was going to have to deal with him at some point, but it wouldn't be tonight. Once again she prided herself on her ability to procrastinate; as a rule it had served her pretty well to this point. But it seemed it wouldn't work with Rory, not forever. As for the here and now, though, she had a warm night, a cold beer, and a good-looking kid to flirt harmlessly with.

"So this is where you're from?" he asked.

Drinking, she shook her head.

"Then how'd you end up here?" he asked. "Let me guess, it had something to do with a guy."

"Nope. It had something to do with a girl."

"Ooh . . . really?"

"Relax," Billie said. "What is with you guys anyways? A girl I went to college with was from Chillicothe. A few years back I came and stayed with her a while. Started working at Freddie's. She got married and moved to Chicago and I just stayed on. So far, anyway."

"Where you from?"

"Kentucky."

"So where did you go to college?"

"Kentucky at Lexington."

He drained his beer, then reached for another. "And why didn't you graduate?"

"I did graduate," Billie said. She turned to look at him. "Are you always this presumptuous? First you're surprised that I'm *just* a waitress and now you're assuming I didn't finish school. You want me to conjugate a couple verbs for you to prove it?"

He smiled. "I guess I deserved that."

"What's your story?" she asked. "You got your summer job, and you're hanging out in the bars, sniffing around the girls like a dog in heat. I bet you have a girlfriend back in Columbus. A looker with a flat belly and a button nose who thinks you are the bee's knees."

"Now who's being presumptuous?" he asked. "Nope, no girl-friend. I had one, going back to high school, but we split up last winter."

He got down from the tailgate to move in front of her and stood there, smiling, for a moment. Billie's knees were apart and he moved between them, his legs against her thighs now. "So here I am, drinking beer with a looker with a great body and a button nose. And I'm thinking there's no reason why I shouldn't kiss her."

"I don't have a button nose," Billie said and then she kissed him.

She walked from the living room to the kitchen and began to make coffee. Getting out of bed, she'd pulled on shorts and a T-shirt and gone into the bathroom to wash her face and tie her hair back. As she waited for the coffee maker, her cell phone rang in the front room and she went to find it. It was in her purse, where she'd tossed it on the floor beside the couch when they'd come in last night. She recalled making out there before they'd gone into the bedroom. She remembered thinking that she wasn't going to have sex with him, right up until she did.

It was Athena on the phone, calling from somewhere in Kansas. Checking in, as she had promised.

"Why are you talking so low?" she asked after she gave Billie the update on her drive.

"I got a college boy in the bedroom," Billie said. She'd walked back into the kitchen.

"No shit?" Athena laughed. "Glad to know you're moving on. So—how was it?"

"None of your business."

"Why not? Is this something serious—this college boy?"

"I met the guy in a poolroom twelve hours ago," Billie said. "There's nothing serious about it."

"Then tell me about it," Athena said. "What did you guys do?"

"Really?"

"I need details."

"We had a lovely evening. Couple of beers, nice conversation."

"That's not what I meant."

"I know it's not what you meant," Billie said. "My coffee's ready, gotta go. Call me tomorrow."

She heard Athena laughing and calling her a bitch as she hung up. She poured a cup of coffee and sat down at the kitchen table. Hopefully, the guy sleeping in her bed would give her a ride back to Circleville, where she'd left her car. He was going to be late for work. She had mentioned that to him the night before but he hadn't seemed overly concerned about it. At the time, they were busy pulling each other's clothes off, so she could understand why. She knew all about shifting priorities when it came to sex.

Now she heard him in the bedroom, shuffling around. He went into the bathroom and a minute later she heard the toilet flush. He came down the hallway and into the kitchen after that, wearing just his jeans, pulling his T-shirt over his head.

"Hey," he said.

"Good morning."

He stood there in the doorway, looking around, at one point dropping his head to glance out the kitchen window to the truck outside. He grimaced slightly, as if realizing that not only was he missing work, but he was in possession of a company vehicle in the process.

"There's coffee," Billie said, indicating the pot.

He poured a cup and added milk.

"All I have is brown sugar," Billie said.

"This is good," he said and came to sit across from her. He tried the coffee, then set it aside to cool. He looked at her a moment, as if slightly amused by something. "It's Chris."

"I know your name," Billie told him.

"I figured maybe you thought it was 'college boy.'"

Billie took a moment. "Well, that's what you get for eavesdropping on phone calls."

He smiled at that and took another sip of coffee before looking at his watch.

"You have time to drop me at my car?" Billie asked.

"Sure."

Billie raised her cup. "We can drink these on the way if you want."

"Trying to get rid of me?"

"No," she said. "I just assumed you needed to get to work."

"You assumed right." He took another sip. "I had fun last night."

"So did I," she said. "Shooting pool and drinking beer and having sex—you really can't go wrong. And you're not even good at one of those things."

"Please tell me you're talking about pool."

Now she smiled and drank her coffee. She could see now how young he was, not so much in appearance, but in every other way. She wondered if the ex-girlfriend back in Columbus had been his only experience with a woman. It seemed highly unlikely.

"We could do it again," he said.

"You'll have to work on your game."

"Yeah, I wasn't referring to the pool."

"I knew that," she said and then she didn't say anything else of an encouraging nature. She didn't need a kid ten years younger than her falling in love with her, or even falling in infatuation with her, though it might be fun for a month or so. But she already had a stalker out there on the loose. She didn't want to trifle with the kid's emotions. Of course, she had to consider that maybe that was just what he was doing with her. Maybe he was just a horny kid who liked the idea of fucking an older woman for a few weeks. The very thought that she was suddenly the older woman hit her right between the eyes.

"We need to go get my car."

Her phone rang then. Crossing to the counter, she picked it up and looked at the display, a Kentucky number she didn't recognize. She considered not answering but she did, hearing a voice that was just vaguely familiar.

"Yeah, this is Billie," she said.

As she listened, she crossed the room to sit down at the table again. She picked up her cup and then set it aside. Running her fingers across her forehead, she exhaled heavily, staring at the tabletop.

"When?" she asked.

Six

THE ONLY BLACK DRESS THAT BILLIE owned was a cocktail number, quite short and cut low. She bought it for a friend's wedding and had worn it three times since, twice more to weddings
and once to a New Year's Eve party at the local golf course in
Chillicothe. It had been an unpleasant evening. The guy she was
with got drunk and started a fight with the man who had married
his ex-wife, even though it had been he who left the marriage, not
the other way around. Apparently he hadn't minded leaving his
wife as long as she never dated anyone else for the rest of her life.
Disgusted by the whole sordid mess, Billie had ended up taking a
cab home.

The dress was not suitable for a funeral. Driving to Marshall
Thursday morning, she stopped at a mall on Lexington's south
side and bought a dress off the sale rack, a black shift that came
to her knees and had a high scoop neck. She bought shoes, too.
Given her time constraints, she wore the clothes as she left the
store, stuffing her jeans and shirt in a bag. The counter woman
who took her money regarded her like a woman on the lam from
something. Billie could imagine her calling Homeland Security
after she left.

She'd worked the night before and left Chillicothe that morning, heading straight to the funeral. It was raining when she got up and it never let up as she drove west. At times it was a deluge, coming down in sheets. Twice, she was swamped on all sides by tractor trailers throwing rooster tails of water against the windshield of her Taurus. She'd had to pull over until the torrent subsided.

Leaving the mall, her car turned over slowly three or four times and then stopped. She had cables in the trunk but it took her fifteen minutes before she could convince anybody to give her a boost. Most people looked at her as if she were trying to sell them something. Finally a man with a long gray ponytail agreed, pulling his van up close. Once the Taurus was running, the man launched into a story of how he'd driven across the country in 1967, looking for America. Billie had finally begged off when she realized that the story might just take as long as the trip itself.

Her father was at the Browning Funeral Home in Marshall. It was the only funeral parlor in town and Billie had been there a number of times growing up. Because of the weather and the stop at the mall, she arrived fifteen minutes before the service was to begin. She was met inside the front door by a nervous-looking bald man in a navy-blue suit. Whether he was anxious about Billie's late arrival or just in general, she couldn't know. He greeted her solemnly and led her at once to the back of the home, where she was allowed to look at her father one last time before the casket was closed.

The old man was dressed in a suit, a brown single-breasted that Billie recognized. White shirt and black string tie, his preference on the rare occasion he got dressed up. He looked older because Billie hadn't seen him in ten years, and he looked bad, because he was dead.

She stood by the casket for a couple of minutes while the bald man hovered nearby, his concentrated efforts not to be obtrusive making him even more so. Finally Billie reached forward and laid the palm of her hand on her father's chest.

There was a seat reserved for her in the front row of the chapel. As the man led Billie in, she noticed that the room was nearly full, although she didn't really recognize anybody in the blur of faces. Already sitting in the row was a woman of about sixty or so, and Billie assumed the woman was her father's girlfriend. Did people in their sixties and seventies use terms like girlfriend? Maybe Billie would have to learn things like that. Wasn't it just a few days ago she had thought of herself as an older woman?

"Billie, this is Marian Dunlop, your father's close friend," the man said. "Billie Masterson."

Her father's close friend (apparently *that* was the accepted term, for today anyway) stood up to shake Billie's hand.

"Hello Billie," she said. "I wish we were meeting under different circumstances."

Billie didn't manage to say anything and afterward wondered why not. But what would have been appropriate? *Delighted to meet you?*

As there was no other family present, it was just the two of them in the front pew. Billie had an aunt who lived in a nursing home in California, and there was an uncle, too—a perpetually broke dreamer that her father had never had much use for, living somewhere down south. Florida maybe. Neither was there, nor had Billie expected them to be. She was sure there were people in the chapel behind her who had been surprised to see her walk in.

The woman beside her looked over and gave her a smile that was sad but somewhat reassuring. Billie reacted by looking away. She wasn't in the mood to be reassured about anything, particularly not by the woman who had been sleeping with her father these past years.

The man who had called her at home Monday morning was a lawyer named David Mountain Clay. He had been Will Masterson's attorney and friend for three or maybe four decades and Billie remembered him quite well, even if she hadn't recognized his voice on the phone. He stood several inches over six feet, and the last she'd seen him he had weighed in the neighborhood of three hundred pounds. When she was a little girl, Billie had been under the impression that one of his names was Mountain because he resembled one. On the phone three days earlier, he'd mentioned that her father's girlfriend would be speaking at the service and asked if Billie wished to say something, as well. She'd declined. What would she say about the man she'd spoken to a half dozen times in the past ten years that wouldn't sound like hypocrisy?

A Baptist preacher led the service, offering the standard sermon, talking about a house with many rooms, one of which was apparently being prepared at that moment for Will Masterson's imminent arrival. There was a hymn—"Just a Closer Walk with Thee"—sung by those present or at least those willing to join in, and a couple of prayers. The preacher had nothing of a personal nature to say about the deceased, which made sense because Billie suspected that the two men had never met. It was possible that her father had become devout in recent years, but she doubted it. After finishing the second prayer, the man introduced the woman sitting a few feet away from Billie.

Billie watched closely as the woman walked up to stand in front of the gathering. She was quite lovely, with sharp features and a strong chin. She looked fit in a black cotton dress that stopped above her knees. She had very good legs. Billie could see how her father would be attracted to a woman like that, although she wasn't sure what the woman might see in a crusty old horseman set in his ancient ways and possessed of a stubborn streak as wide as the Mississippi.

While Billie was wondering about the attraction, the woman at the pulpit proceeded to spend the next ten minutes explaining it, and in doing so she mentioned that the man in question was indeed a throwback and that he also had a stubbornness to him that would have made a mule blush, in her words. She talked as well about his kindness and his heart, which she said had a hard shell and a center of marshmallow.

Sitting there listening, Billie began to resent the attractive woman with the strong voice and even stronger memories. She'd known for some time that her father had a girlfriend, but in her mind's eye that woman had been a mousy little thing, subservient to Will Masterson, stopping by unannounced to clean his house while all the while hoping for a marriage proposal. That was not the woman speaking to the crowd of mourners this minute, telling of how she and Will, after too much wine one night, had fallen asleep in a hot tub and had awakened to find that the power had gone out, dropping the water temperature to a teeth-chattering level. The laughter in the room did nothing to quell Billie's feelings of resentment.

When the woman was finished and had returned to the pew, the preacher told the gathering the details of the interment, inviting any who were interested to attend. He then led the congregation in the Lord's Prayer. The woman named Marian Dunlop recited it strongly and so Billie did not.

Will had a burial plot behind the Baptist church in the village of Westbrook, fifteen miles west of Marshall. His parents were in the graveyard there, as were his grandparents and various aunts and uncles and a few cousins. Billie's mother was not there. She'd left behind a will and in it she'd instructed that her ashes be scattered in a small lake where she had vacationed with her family as a child. A final "fuck you" to her husband, Billie had always assumed. The rain had continued throughout the service and seemed to pick up as the pallbearers carried the casket across the grass to the gravesite, where a tent had been erected. The mourners followed, at least those of them hearty enough to brave the storm, and they all crowded together beneath the tent as the preacher said the final words.

Looking around, Billie recognized a number of the mourners, including the monumental David Mountain Clay, who caught her eye and nodded. He'd grown old, his face fleshy, his eyebrows as craggy as those of a musk ox. There were a few kids in attendance, which surprised Billie. They must have been dragged there by their parents or grandparents. Billie also noticed Reese Ryker among the mourners, standing directly across from her, beside a beautiful dark-haired woman about Billie's age. Why would Ryker be there? Billie knew him mainly by sight. When she was a little girl, she and her friends would ride their bikes past the Ryker estate and stare at it in wonder—the fencing and the barns and the paddocks, the gardens around the main house. It was a place out of a story book. When Billie got older, she came to know that it was Reese's mother who was the force in the family, and that Reese was, as Will Masterson described him, a fart in a mitten. Yet here he was today, watching the man who had opined that being laid to rest.

The bald man from the funeral home had given Billie a red rose, which he told her she might place on the casket if she so desired. Not knowing what else to do with the flower, she obliged him and then Marian Dunlop did the same. The preacher invited all those assembled to the community center in Westbrook, for "a time of fellowship." At that point, everyone turned and headed through the rain to their cars, parked in the church lot and along the road out front. Many people had brought along umbrellas and they shared them with those who hadn't. Billie walked alone across the wet grass, angling to her car, parked on the roadside. The bald man had wanted her to ride in the funeral home limousine to the grave-yard but she had begged off, saying that she didn't want to have to return to Marshall afterward. In truth, she did not want to share the car with her father's articulate girlfriend.

She didn't want to go into Westbrook for any fellowship either but she knew she should make an appearance. Glancing over to the church parking lot as she walked, she saw Reese Ryker talking to the woman Marian there, holding an umbrella over the two of them, while the dark-haired fashion model stood off to the side in the drizzle. So that's why Ryker was there, Billie thought. He was obviously friends with the woman who had—according to her, anyway—captured Will Masterson's heart. Billie couldn't see her father moving in Ryker's circle, or getting anywhere close to it, but then she'd been gone a while. Maybe the old man became upwardly mobile in his older years.

But she doubted it.

There was what appeared to be a new Porsche Carrera parked behind her car, and she didn't have to speculate on who the owner would be. There were a lot of pickup trucks in the parking lot along with a few SUVs and smaller American cars. But only one brand-new Porsche. When she looked back toward the church, the car's owner was still talking to Marian Dunlop, laughing about something one of them had said. Apparently to some people the day was a joyous occasion.

The basement of the community center was low-ceilinged and quite small, and the crowd there, with the offer of free food and coffee, was standing room only. Billie poured a cup for herself and stood off to the side near the exit door, which she planned to use as soon as was politely feasible. A few people came over to speak to her—mostly men and women of her father's vintage. They asked how she was, where she lived, what she was doing now. None seemed overly impressed with her position at Freddie's Fish Shack.

She saw David Mountain Clay when she arrived—he was hard to miss—standing near the dessert table talking to Marian, who seemed to know everybody in the place, including the church-women in the kitchen who had provided the meal and were even now making up more sandwiches and refreshing the coffee urns. Once the well-wishers had wandered off from Billie, Clay made his way over, the coffee cup in his huge hand looking like a child's plaything, something from the Betty Crocker Kitchen set Billie had once owned. He extended his free hand.

"How are you, Mr. Clay?" Billie asked.

"Finer than frog's hair," the lawyer said. "I didn't know if you'd remember me."

"You thought I might not remember the giant who sat at our kitchen table drinking whiskey and playing cribbage with my father until all hours of the morning, the two of you pounding the table and cursing like sailors?"

Clay smiled. "Four bits a game, those were important contests."

His teeth had yellowed over the years and his jowls hung like a bulldog's. In his halcyon days as a litigator he had worn a fringed buckskin jacket to court and kept his hair long, well past his collar. The jacket was not in evidence today but the hair was still shaggy, turned nearly snow white. He looked all right though, Billie thought, like a lion that had managed to survive the vagaries and pitfalls of a cutthroat career and life in general mostly intact.

"How did you find my number?" she asked.

"Your father had your number," Clay said. "Along with his sister's and brother's. Your aunt couldn't make the trip from the west and I couldn't find your uncle. The number was no longer in service."

"That sounds like Uncle Randy," Billie said. "His whole life has been a bunch of numbers no longer in service."

Clay drank off his coffee and looked for a place to set the cup. "And how is your life in Ohio?"

"Peaches and cream," Billie said.

"Did you ever marry?" Clay finally put the cup on a chair rail along the wall, where it balanced precariously.

"Not that I recall," Billie replied. "What about yourself?"

"Still blissfully wedded to the former Florence Raymond Townes," Clay said. "God bless 'er."

Billie had no idea if the old lawyer was being sarcastic or not. She had never been able to tell, even as a little girl, when he would regale her with improbable stories of his ancestors, most of whom he claimed to have been bosom buddies with, people like Daniel Boone, Andrew Jackson, and Abraham Lincoln himself.

"Where is Mrs. Clay today?" Billie asked, looking around. She didn't recall if she had ever met Clay's wife. The lawyer and her father had been drinking buddies when Billie was young, but he and his wife hadn't socialized with Billie's parents. Her mother wasn't much for Kentucky society, especially toward the end.

"In Chicago with her sister," Clay replied. "Shopping and theater and all that. Their annual pilgrimage."

A woman came out of the kitchen just then to retrieve Clay's coffee cup from the chair rail, presumably before it fell. He watched her, smiling and ducking his head like an errant child. Will Masterson's "close friend" Marian was busy laying out more food across the room. Billie gestured toward her.

"What's the story there?" she asked.

Clay turned to look. "Your father had his gallbladder removed, I don't know, four or five years ago. Marian was the attending nurse at the time. They hit it off, you might say."

"Isn't that romantic?" Billie said. "She still a nurse?"

"Retired now," Clay said. "She's quite active in the community, and with the church."

"Gosh, she and my father were soul mates," Billie said.

"Sarcasm is a poorly constructed cloak," Clay said, turning back to her.

"Was I being sarcastic?"

"You know it and I know it," Clay told her. "So what are your plans now?"

"Heading back home," Billie said. "Thinking I might sneak a couple of those brownies into my purse on my way out the door."

"Home being?"

"Home being home," Billie said. "Where I live. I seem to remember you being a lot smarter than this, Mr. Clay."

"And I remember your sass," the lawyer replied. "No, I thought maybe you were referring to the farm, which was your home for many years. I thought you might stick around a couple of days."

"I have no reason to stick around."

"Well, you are wrong about that," Clay told her.

"Why's that?"

"Because there are matters that require settling." Clay paused, enjoying the moment. "I seem to recall you being a lot smarter than this, Billie."

She laughed. "We're quite a pair, aren't we? Apparently we don't have enough brains between us to light a match. We ought to run for office."

"I have been asked, believe me," Clay said. "I assume you wouldn't possess a house key to your father's place."

"I don't remember there ever being one," Billie replied. "He never locked the place."

"He did in recent years," Clay said. "The changing landscape of our world, Billie. People who do drugs tend to steal things to pay for those drugs. If they were to apply those efforts and that ingenuity to hard work, I daresay we would be living in Valhalla."

"Valhalla," Billie said. "You haven't lost your flair for hyperbole, Mr. Clay. Didn't your great-great-grandfather once wrestle Davy Crockett?"

"Did I say that?" Clay asked. "Well then, I suppose it must have happened." He dug into his pants pocket and produced a key. "For the house. You might as well stay there while you're here."

Billie did not immediately reach for the key. "I'm not sure the old man would want me to."

"Well, you're wrong about that, too," Clay said.

Seven

SHE WAS SURPRISED AT HOW LITTLE the place had changed. Driving out to the farm along the county road south of the village of Westbrook, she hadn't known what to expect. Given her father's relationship with the woman who'd spoken at the funeral, she was prepared to find the house completely renovated—granite counters in the kitchen, en suite bathroom, couches and chairs from IKEA. Maybe an Impressionist print or two on the walls. In truth, though, she would have been surprised to see any of that. The old man wouldn't have the money for those things or the desire for them if he did. He wasn't much for change.

She was right in that. Inside the house she found the same old GE fridge, the same stained plywood cupboards, and the same living room furniture. The place did look somewhat cleaner than when she'd been there last, at which time the old man had been living the bachelor life. But the house even smelled precisely as she remembered it, a combination of man and farm and horses, of sweat and leather and fried bacon and boiled coffee and dried manure and Barclay's Liniment. The smells of Billie's youth.

There were a few touches that might have been attributed to the girlfriend—a fancy coffee maker in the kitchen, a blender (what

would her father do with a blender?), and some items of clothing in the bedroom that Billie couldn't see him wearing. There
were things in the bathroom—soaps and lotions and an electric
toothbrush—that weren't Will Masterson's, either. The only other
addition was the deck built onto the rear of the house, overlooking
the outbuildings down the slope. On it was a large wooden table
surrounded by a half dozen chairs made of wicker, and one of solid
wood. Billie knew which chair was the old man's.

She brought her clothes in from the car and changed back into
the jeans and cotton shirt she'd left Ohio wearing. She folded the
new black dress and put it in her bag, wondering when she might
have occasion to wear it again.

She found a half-full bottle of Woodford Reserve in a kitchen
cupboard and carried it and a glass outside to sit in one of the
wicker chairs. The rain had stopped. The downpour had flooded
the farm and now the rainwater rushed across it from east to west,
overflowing the swale that dissected the property, gushing through
the culvert under the rear driveway before hurrying to the pond at
the bottom of the west pasture.

Pouring a couple of ounces into the glass, she looked absently
toward the outbuildings and as she did three thoroughbreds came
out of the pole barn—two bays and a dark gray—stepping tentatively into the muddy paddock. The gray was just a colt, Billie
could see, and he spotted her immediately, lifting his head high in
the air, as if he could pick up her scent. The other two horses were
probably broodmares. They moved around the corral with their
noses down, searching for graze. Billie wondered if they'd been fed
today. She had to assume that somebody would be taking care of
that. Maybe the girlfriend and if not her, then certainly David
Mountain Clay.

She lit a cigarette and drank the bourbon and tried, as she had
the past few days, not to feel guilty about the fact that she'd gone
eight years without seeing her father. And about the fact that now
she would never see him. It hadn't been a conscious decision on

her part. Never had she said to herself, or to anyone else, that she would never see him again. She had been bitter after her mother's suicide, and even more bitter about the fact that her father wouldn't discuss it with her. It was as if he wanted to pretend that he had nothing to do with it, and how could he pretend that if he was to have an actual conversation with Billie about it?

Still, she had always assumed that she would see him again. She hadn't thought about it because she had chosen not to, like with a lot of other things. Which was why it seemed she was constantly having conversations with people—like coworkers or pool-shooting university students—about what she planned to do with her life. She didn't know the answer because she chose not to think about that, either. She wasn't a planner, she was a doer, she told herself—although she couldn't offer up any evidence that she'd done much of anything of late.

Besides that, it took two to tango. If the old man had at any time in the past years called and said he wanted to see her, she would have obliged him. Did he think she would just show up out of the blue? He probably did. Then again, maybe he didn't think of her at all anymore. After all, he had his eloquent girlfriend to keep him company, to cook his meals and rub his sore back and whatever other services she provided, probably expertly. Billie didn't want to think about that, either.

She had a long swallow of whiskey and wondered why she was being so hard on the woman. Would she have preferred the old man spend his last years with some shrieking harpy who demanded that he buy her clothes and take her to dinner every night? Then again, maybe that's exactly who this Marian Dunlop was. Maybe today was all an elaborate act and she had everybody fooled, rural Kentucky's answer to Meryl Streep.

Movement from the back driveway caught her eye and she looked around to see a little girl on a bicycle heading for the barn. Dodging the puddles in the lane, she never looked toward the house until she stopped to lean the bike against the machine shed. When she saw Billie, she turned away so quickly that Billie thought she was up to no good. She was wearing a blue baseball cap and she removed it, revealing a mass of dark curls that Billie recognized. She'd been one of the kids huddled under the tent at the graveyard. She didn't look toward the house again but went directly into the barn. Moments later, the side door opened and the girl proceeded to lead a succession of animals into the far corral, beyond where the three horses stood in the mud. There was a donkey, a brown-and-white paint pony, and finally a nanny goat. The girl, who had been wearing sneakers when she arrived, now wore black rubber boots. Billie, transfixed by the scene, waited to see what might emerge next. She wondered if the old man had invested in a traveling circus. Maybe there were elephants and jugglers and a trapeze artist living in the barn.

Instead of more livestock, though, the girl next dragged a bale of hay outside, where she removed the strings and distributed a couple of flakes each to the animals before going back for another bale, which she spread out for the horses in the near paddock. She did not once look up again to the deck where Billie sat watching. It seemed she was making a conscious effort not to do so.

Which suited Billie just fine. She didn't need any interaction with the kid, whoever she happened to be. It was obvious that somebody—probably David Clay—had hired her to tend to the stock until things were sold off. Billie wouldn't interfere with whatever arrangements had been made. Interfering might lead to someone suggesting that Billie do it, and she had no interest in that. She did wonder why they hired somebody so young. The kid looked about ten years old. Was help that hard to find in this part of the country?

When she had scattered the hay for the horses, the girl turned and went back into the barn again. Billie knew from experience that cleaning stalls would be next on the list. It was a good job for a ten-year-old kid: it would build character, which would allow her, when she was thirty-two, to sit on the deck and sip bourbon.

Billie heard a vehicle then, coming up the front driveway on the far side of the house, stopping there, the engine shutting down. The car door opened and closed and then Billie heard the creaking of the screen door out front. Moments later, the woman who would be Streep walked out of the house and onto the deck. She was still wearing the black dress but she had changed her shoes, ditching the pumps for a pair of flats.

"Hello," she said. Her tone was neither friendly nor unfriendly.

Glass in hand, Billie half turned in her chair and nodded. Marian Dunlop hesitated, as if she might walk over to Billie and perhaps even offer her hand again. She seemed to think better of it and moved to the edge of the deck, where she leaned her elbows on the railing and looked for a long while at the rain-soaked farm. Billie watched her in silence, wondering why she had shown up so soon after the funeral. Maybe the place was now hers and she was there to run Billie off. But David Clay wouldn't have insisted that Billie stay here if that were the case.

Unless, of course, he and the woman were in cahoots.

For Christ's sakes, Billie thought, *get a grip on yourself. Since when did you ever worry about things you couldn't control and—more to the point—couldn't care less about?* She smiled and drained her glass, then reached for the bottle. The bourbon might be all she would get from the old man, and if that were the case, she was absolutely fine with it. Woodford made a good whiskey.

The woman shifted her gaze to the west pasture now, where the pond continued to rise, and she spoke without turning. "He'd have given his eyeteeth for a quarter inch of rain these past weeks. And here it's done nothing but, since the day he died."

Billie didn't say anything. She poured from the bottle and then capped it. As she drank, Marian turned to look at her. Her eyes were hazel and at this moment seemed to suggest they were amused by something.

"Are you going to offer me a drink?"

Billie indicated the bottle. "Help yourself."

"No thanks."

Now Billie smiled. "You're not in the temperance league, are you?"

"Not quite."

"Then what's the problem?"

"Not in the mood, I guess," Marian said.

"Well, I hope it's not something I said."

"I think we can safely assume that it's nothing you said," Marian replied. "Because you really haven't said a fucking thing so far. If I didn't know better, I'd say you were mired in a good old-fashioned pout."

"But you don't know better," Billie said.

"How's that?"

"You don't know better. You don't know anything about me."

"That's not true," Marian said. "I know all kinds of things about you. He never mentioned that you were a pouter, though."

"I'm not fucking pouting."

Marian finally smiled. "Did you ever know a pouter who didn't say that?"

Billie was getting hammered and she knew it. She had another sip of whiskey and turned her attention to the activity down the hill, where the animals were eating the forage, moving it with their noses through the mud. She made an effort to maintain a neutral expression, to offset the recent accusations of pouting. She had no idea how she looked. For an absurd moment she considered whistling a tune to display her nonchalance. She was saved from such foolishness by the little girl, who emerged from the barn at that moment, pushing a wheelbarrow full of manure, leaning into it, her little muscles straining with the effort against the new mud. Billie grabbed at the lifeline.

"Who's the kid?"

Marian turned. "Her name's Jodie. She lives the next road over."

"Kinda young for a hired hand, isn't she?"

Marian watched as the girl maneuvered the load through the muck to a manure pile outside the paddock. When she tipped it up, the wheelbarrow went sideways and the girl went with it, falling to one knee before getting up and righting it.

"Your father first made her acquaintance at an auction over by Victortown. I don't know all the details except that the donkey there was lame and on the block. Sold for seven dollars and the girl was the buyer. Will arrived home with both child and donkey. The nanny showed up next. It belonged to one of her school friends and was headed for the smoker. The pony was being mistreated by some idiots who operated a riding stable in Greenville. You could count the animal's ribs when it got here."

"The old man was never one for taking in strays," Billie said.

"You talking about the animals or the kid?"

"Both."

"I think her home life is pretty shitty," Marian said. "Her father was in jail and when he got out, he took a powder. Apparently her mother's had her problems, alcohol and drugs, doesn't work much to speak of."

"What's the mother's name?" Billie asked, wondering if she knew her.

"Shelly Rickman."

Billie knew the family. "Who's her father?"

"I never heard a name but I know he's gone," Marian said. "The mother's with Troy Everson now."

Billie knew that name, too. "I would have assumed that Troy Everson would be in jail by now."

"He just got out."

The kid pushed the wheelbarrow back into the barn. Watching, Billie realized she'd just had what could pass as a conversation with her father's girlfriend. Not a conversation that was really *about* anything, just a needy kid that Billie would in all likelihood never see again. She had a sip and relaxed a little, no longer on defense.

"So the old man adopted her," she said. "And I noticed a woman's clothes in the master bedroom. Some pajamas even. Seems as if he had lots of female company of late."

"Not as much as he would have liked."

Billie started to respond but then stopped. She wouldn't take the bait. It was too late for all that now anyway. She knew it and she assumed that the woman at the railing, watching her, knew it, too.

"I expect you stopped in for a reason," Billie said. "And you don't want a drink so I'm thinking it must be business. So now what?"

Marian came over then to sit at the table. "Now nothing, Billie," she said calmly. "I was in love with your father and I think he was in love with me. My heart is broken." Her voice cracked and Billie thought for a moment she would break down. But she wouldn't, not here and not in front of Billie. "My heart is broken. I came here because I knew you were here and I thought it might help if I could talk to the other woman he loved. Obviously I was wrong about that, and that's okay. I've been wrong a good many times in my life. But you are just as wrong if you think I want anything. The only thing I wanted was buried today in that church graveyard."

As she spoke, Billie sat looking at the tabletop, the glass of bourbon propped on her knee. When Marian stopped talking, she looked at her.

"All right."

Marian nodded. "As far as my clothes and whatever else I have here, I'll have them out of here tomorrow."

"You don't have to do that," Billie said. "Christ, the place might be yours. You were obviously a bigger part of his life than I was."

"I don't want it," Marian said. "I have my own house in town. When he was alive, this was my favorite place in the world to be. We sat at this table a thousand times, Billie. But we won't again. If he's not here, then neither am I." She paused, still watching. "I hope we're clear on that. Do you have any questions?"

Billie drained her glass and placed it on the table. At the moment she couldn't think of a single one.

Marian turned to go but then stopped. "Listen, I know things were not great between your father and you."

"I doubt you know the whole story," Billie said. "I doubt he told you about my mother."

"I'm sure he was sorry about what happened," Marian said.

"Did he tell you that?"

"No. I told you, we didn't talk about it. I knew about your mother . . . what she did. But we never talked about it. I didn't feel it was up to me to bring it up."

"Then you don't know that he was sorry."

Instead of going to the TV station, Reese drove out to Chestnut Field the next morning, where he had coffee with Caldwell. He'd called the manager the day before, while driving home from Will Masterson's funeral. They'd met a few times, both at Chestnut and Lexington Downs, and Reese had always got the sense that Caldwell was looking to move up, away from the B track, and the B track characters who came with it.

The two men sat on the patio by the stretch. The field was dark that day, and a number of trainers were working horses on the rain-soaked track. Reese paid them little mind. What did he care about claimers and five-year-old maidens? He was aware, however, that Caldwell was curious and maybe even excited about Reese asking to meet. It had never happened before.

"How's your year been so far?" Reese asked when they had their coffee.

"So-so," Caldwell replied. "Up a bit from last year."

"The place looks really good," Reese said. He indicated the infield, which had been replanted that spring with roses and geraniums.

"My idea and my design, too," Caldwell said. "It took some convincing. Just between you and me, ownership here is somewhat lacking in imagination."

"Well, it looks like Churchill Downs," Reese said, lying. "The reason I'm here—are your sheds all full?"

"Nearly," Caldwell replied. "We might have a couple of stalls along the back."

Reese nodded. "That probably won't work, then."

"What do you mean?"

Reese hesitated, as if wanting to release his story slowly. "I was thinking of maybe renting a row of barns here. I have so many fucking horses I can't run them all at Keeneland or Louisville. Maybe I'll have to wait until next year." He paused for effect. "Or look elsewhere."

"Hold on," Caldwell said. "Let me think here. I could probably shuffle some sheds around. I've got horses here that are just taking up space. I might be able to clear up an entire row if I had a few days."

"You have horses here that aren't running?"

Caldwell nodded. "Some are hurt, some are just here for the workouts."

"Didn't Will Masterson run out of here?"

"He did," Caldwell said. "I guess you heard that he died."

"That was a shame," Reese said. "I never knew the man well. Did he have any horses here when it happened?"

"That two-year-old was here," Caldwell said. "Well, you know that story—the colt's by your stallion."

"The colt's still here?"

"No. Will ran him the day before he died, though. He didn't like to leave that horse here, seemed like he was awful possessive of it. And it's only, what, twenty or thirty miles or so to the home farm."

"Wonder what they'll do with the horse now?"

Caldwell shrugged. "No idea. I expect you'll see it for sale."

"I suppose. Who did Masterson have working him anyway?"

"An old jock named Skeeter Musgrave."

"Where could I find him?"

Caldwell indicated the horses on the track. "He was just out there ten minutes ago, breezing a horse for McDaniels. You want to talk to him?"

"I do," Reese said. "And see what you can do about finding me some stalls. I like the way you operate, Chuck."

"I will," Caldwell promised. "I absolutely will." Reese got to his feet.

"I was reading about Ghost Rider in the journal this morning," Caldwell said then. "You've got a juggernaut on your hands there. You're taking him to the Breeders, I assume?"

"I certainly am."

"Then I expect you're gearing up for all the extra publicity that's going to come with that situation. And then next spring in Louisville. Knock wood."

"RR Racing can handle it."

"I'm sure," Caldwell said. "But I just thought I'd mention that I'm quite experienced in that field." He chuckled. "Sort of find myself underused around here. Not playing to my strengths."

"What field?"

"Public relations," Caldwell said. "I have a degree from Dartmouth and I did some work for the New England Patriots for a while." Caldwell wasn't going to mention that he was an unpaid intern for the team.

Reese considered this, or seemed to. "Let me think about that. I might just need a man. Now let's find this Skeeter character."

Eight

THE NEXT MORNING, BILLIE MADE USE of the fancy coffee maker and carried a cup with her as she took a walk around the farm. The rain had done its job and the day dawned as fresh as Eden. The water running beneath the lane had subsided overnight and the pond was nearly full. The pasture already showed a tinge of green where it had been brown the day before. The air smelled of rebirth and promise. It was as if the drought had never occurred. How twenty-four hours could change things so completely bordered on miraculous.

Before setting out, she found a pair of rubber boots her size—Marian's, she assumed—to wear on her walk. The low areas were muddy yet, with pools of dirty rainwater gathered here and there. She did a circuit around the thirty-acre property, strolling through the small bush lot at the rear of the farm, where overhead the leaves of the maples and white oaks and hickories were still dripping. She flushed a cottontail from some brush and spotted a skinny coyote before it trotted off, crossing the side road to run into heavier bush to the south. A sense of déjà vu hung from Billie like the raindrops from the trees.

Her coffee was gone by the time she reached the barns on her return. The horses and other animals were outside in their respective paddocks. Billie looked to see they had water—the rain had taken care of that—but didn't bother to feed them. She assumed the kid named Jodie was coming again. If Billie fed the horses and left, the girl might show up and feed them again. Or worse, assume her job was unnecessary and not come back.

The broodmares stood off by themselves beneath the pole barn, but the colt came over to Billie as soon as she came near. He was a good-looking horse. If he was a two-year-old, as she suspected, he was big for his age, fully developed across the chest and haunches. He was curious, reaching his nose across the top rail to sniff her. After a moment she gave in to his flirtations and ran her hand over the animal's forehead. Then she turned and headed back to the house. She didn't need to get involved with the colt or anything on the place—not the feeding or watering or cleaning of stalls. She'd shoveled enough horse shit to last her.

The phone was ringing when she walked into the kitchen. She let it ring and then heard her father's voice, talking on an old school answering machine. Billie didn't know that anybody still used such a thing. There was a beep and she heard the melodious whiskey voice of David Mountain Clay.

"Billie, it's lawyer Clay here. Pick up if you're there."

She went to the phone and said hello.

"How's your schedule this morning?" Clay asked.

"Is that a joke?"

"Have you eaten yet?"

"No. I've just made my rounds of the estate, making sure the cotton's as high as an elephant's eye and all that."

"I'll buy you breakfast. Meet me at Mom's Diner in Marshall in half an hour."

"It's not really called Mom's," Billie said, but the old lawyer had already hung up.

The place was in fact called Mom's Homestyle Diner. It was in the middle of the business section—such as it was—of Marshall. Billie parked on the street across from the restaurant and got out to have a look at what had once been the heart of the town. The buildings were the same but most of the retail shops she'd known were gone, no doubt victims of the big box stores she'd driven past on the way into town. Mowat's Hardware was now a convenience store, and the shop where Billie had purchased her dress for the prom had a blinking sign out front that read Big Stan's Tax Services. Billie was not in the least sentimental about the demise of the dress shop, as the prom hadn't gone well, in spite of her dazzling emerald gown with the rhinestones on the bodice and what was to be her first and last date with Craig Sensabaugh. Instead of spending a memorable night at the ball, she'd gotten pie-eyed on cherry whiskey and then into a fistfight with Valerie Simpson, whom she found behind the gym, inspecting Craig's tonsils with her tongue.

Lawyer Clay was waiting for her inside Mom's, sitting in a corner booth with a cup of coffee in hand and a folder before him. He hadn't ordered yet, he told her, and waited until she looked over the breakfast menu.

"Mom's world-famous flapjacks," she read.

"And you accused me of hyperbole," Clay said.

The young waitress, who was multipierced and colorfully inked and probably not Mom, hovered nearby. Billie settled on French toast, even though the dish, according to the menu, had not yet gained world renown. Clay asked for the mushroom and cheese omelet.

"How did you sleep in the old homestead?" he asked when the waitress was gone.

"Like a woman who had Woodford Reserve for dinner and the same for dessert."

"You must be hungry this morning, then."

Billie indicated the folder. "What's that?"

"That is your father's will."

The waitress brought coffee for Billie and utensils for them both. Billie splashed milk in her cup and had a sip. It was very good coffee. Maybe there was more to Mom's than Billie suspected. She wondered at her propensity for cynicism.

"Shouldn't the girlfriend be here for this?" she asked.

"The girlfriend has a name."

"Marian," Billie said. "Shouldn't Marian be here for this?"

"She doesn't need to be. Outside of two small codicils, you inherit everything." Clay set his coffee cup aside and opened the folder. "That's the good news."

"And what's the bad?"

"Well," Clay said slowly, "you've inherited a considerable amount of debt."

Billie laughed. "That's the one thing my family's known for. Why wouldn't the old man want to pass it on?" She paused, thinking. "How can you inherit debt anyway?"

"Technically, *you* can't," Clay told her. "The farm has debt, and you have inherited the farm."

Billie considered this. "Am I allowed to turn down an inheritance?"

"You mean, like somebody asking you to dance?" Clay asked, clearly amused.

"Like somebody asking me to dance and then charging me a thousand dollars for the pleasure."

"No."

"All right," Billie said, preparing herself. "How much debt?"

"Who knows?" Clay said. "It's not something your father would ever confide in with me. He wasn't a complainer. But I know there's a mortgage on the farm with the bank, and likely a second mortgage there, as well. And then a considerable back tax bill, as well as a number of smaller debts. Oh—and a demand note with some grape grower over in Monticello."

"A what?"

"Like a private mortgage," Clay said. "Your father would have needed only to keep up on the interest. Not a big concern at this time."

"Have you got a ballpark number on the total debt?" Billie asked.

Clay shrugged. "I do not. Maybe a hundred thousand, maybe one fifty."

"And how much is the place worth?"

"Possibly two hundred," Clay said. "The outbuildings are not in great shape and the house is . . . well, modest, I might say. You could add in a few thousand for the broodmares. As for the gray colt named Cactus Jack, I couldn't say. I can tell you that your father was very optimistic about that particular horse."

"My father was always optimistic about one horse or another," Billie said. She indicated the paperwork on the table between them. "That would be the same man who died in hock up to his ears."

"It didn't weigh on him, I can tell you that," Clay assured her. He paused a moment, glancing from the paperwork to Billie. "I daresay if you sold the place, somebody with new money would snatch it up, bulldoze everything, and build an ugly mansion there, with wrought-iron fencing and stone lions guarding the gate."

Billie shrugged her indifference to that scenario. She recalled that whenever David Clay talked about people with new money, he was usually referring to anybody who had arrived in Kentucky after the Truman administration. The food came then. Clay's omelet was enormous, as befitted the man about to devour it. Billie's French toast looked good to the eye and was served with fresh strawberries and real maple syrup, not the fructose mucilage found in most diners.

They began to eat while Billie processed what she had heard. If Clay's assessment proved to be accurate, and she had no doubt it would, then she stood to break even when all was said and done. Which meant that she would get nothing, exactly what she had expected and, for that matter, desired. Unfortunately, she would have to invest some time and effort in order to end up with that nothing, something she had not expected. There would be lawyers (the giant sitting across from her being one) and realtors and tax people and various debtors to settle with. It seemed a lot of work just to finish at zero. But she would have to do it. What choice did she have?

The waitress refilled their cups as they ate. Billie's meal was, she had to admit, excellent, maybe even deserving of flapjack status when the time came to redo the menu. They were both finished eating before she spoke again.

"What about the codicils?"

Clay wiped his mouth and reached for the paperwork. "Nothing of consequence. Your father left a few personal items for Marian Dunlop. And a thousand dollars for Jodie Rickman, the young lady with the orphan animals."

"She can use the money to trailer them out of there," Billie said.

The waitress brought the bill and Clay claimed it, looking it over like a mining assayer appraising a suspicious gold nugget before placing it and twenty-five dollars on the table. He pulled an ancient watch from his pocket and checked the time. Billie resisted an urge to ask him of the piece's provenance; surely it had once belonged to some historical figure—William Tecumseh Sherman or at the very least Stephen Douglas.

"I assume then that you intend to sell the farm?" His voice and manner were suddenly distant.

"What the hell else am I going to do with it?"

"I think your father always hoped that you would eventually come home. That you would want to run the place."

"That sounds like a great idea," Billie said. "It being such a moneymaker and all."

Clay gathered the paperwork. "Well, it's only my two cents' worth, but I think that's what he hoped for."

"Maybe he should have told me then. He could have picked up the phone."

"And you could have picked up the phone. It seems to me that you were the one who shut down communications."

"If you know that, then you know the reason why," Billie told him.

Clay shook his large head and kept shaking it while he seemed to struggle with something. "All right, I've had enough of this. It's time somebody straightened you out. There's something you need to know. And it might very well hurt you."

Billie stared at the old lawyer. "Then I don't need to know it."

"You do," Clay said. "And I'm not going to apologize for telling you. Your mother didn't kill herself because of anything that went on between her and your father. And you goddamn well know it, Billie. Tell me what you remember of your mother. Think back to when you were growing up."

"What do you mean? She was my mother."

"Tell me what you remember of her. Day to day."

Billie didn't want to reply. Not only did she not want to address the matter, but now she was resentful of the old lawyer's challenging tone. "My mother was sick a lot. That wasn't her fault."

"And what was the nature of her illness?"

"A lot of things. She had back problems, stomach problems. A lot of things. There were days she couldn't get out of bed."

"Billie," Clay said. "She couldn't get out of bed because she suffered from depression. You knew it and your father knew it and nobody talked about it because your mother refused to acknowledge it. She saw it as a sign of weakness. So your father took on everything. Protecting her. Protecting you too, Billie. You were at the university before your mother finally got treatment. Maybe she waited until then, keeping things from you."

Billie stared into her coffee cup. This was the conversation she didn't want, the one she'd been avoiding most of her life. "I knew about the depression. How could I not? I'm not stupid, you know."

"Did you know she took shock treatments?"

The information gave Billie pause. "No."

"While you were away at school," Clay said. "The drugs weren't working, not long term anyway. The doctors kept tweaking them, as they do. I have a feeling she was looking at the electroshock as a last resort. I only heard all this afterward, you understand."

Billie drank off her coffee and then looked to the waitress, needing a refill. She was fuming. "And you've decided to tell me now this so you can justify my father having a stupid fling. Is that the way it is? You think it was okay for him to do that to a woman who was barely hanging on?"

"Your father had a fling, as you would call it, because your mother was sleeping with another man. A man who ultimately spurned her. Your father couldn't bear it. It was ripping him apart, Billie. And he couldn't talk to you about it because he was still protecting you. And your mother too, even then. Maybe that was his great error in all this. Fathers protect their daughters, whether they be three or thirty. He never got around to treating you like an adult. Maybe he was waiting for you to act like one."

"Fuck you, Clay. You sanctimonious asshole." Billie looked away from him now, glaring out the window, at the people on Main Street walking past. She fought an urge to get up and run away. She waited for a response that didn't come. After a time, the big man's silence hung over her like a shroud.

"What man?" she asked.

"A professor at the college. He was a tweedy little shit whom she idolized for some reason. He used your mother for a few months and then married one of his students."

Billie fell silent again and then she turned on Clay. "My mother never killed herself over a failed love affair."

"No, she did not," Clay agreed. "It was nothing more than a symptom."

Billie found that she was pissed off now that he had dared to agree with her. "Why the fuck are you telling me this? You sonofabitch. You heartless sonofabitch."

"Will Masterson was my lifelong friend and you've been punishing him for years for a crime he didn't commit. I've decided I won't let you live out your life under that false impression. Like I said, I don't apologize for it. I spoke my piece."

"You spoke your piece," Billie echoed. "I guess you're happy now."

"Not in the least. I wish your father had called you. I wish you had called him." Clay got to his feet. It seemed an effort for him to lift so much bulk into a standing position. "I can tell you this. Nobody knows how much time they have to do the things they intend to do. I'll see you, Billie."

Billie stood, as well. "I'll need a lawyer to handle the sale."

"There's plenty of them around," Clay said and left.

Driving back to the farm, Billie kept thinking about what she had just learned. She felt betrayed by David Clay. But how would she have felt if he hadn't told her and she somehow found out he'd been keeping the truth from her? Just as betrayed. She had no doubt it was true. She remembered her mother taking the classes and bringing home books on obscure Italian poets. Billie had never laid eyes on the professor. What had Clay called him—a tweedy little shit? How could her mother fall in love with a man like that? But Billie knew she wasn't happy with her life on the farm. She tried to be, but trying to be happy when there was no happiness present was a futile task. Maybe the tweedy little shit provided her with something to hang onto. For a while anyway.

Billie had only found out about the waitress her father was seeing after her mother took the pills. She had then jumped to conclusions that had apparently not been quite accurate. And Clay was right: Billie ended up punishing her father for something he hadn't done. Why didn't he tell her the truth? Billie knew the answer to that, too; if she didn't, lawyer Clay had laid it out pretty clearly over breakfast. Will Masterson was merely protecting her, as he'd done since the day she was born.

David Mountain Clay had also been protecting her. Today he decided to stop. And the reason he decided to stop was—at least in part—because she told him she was going to sell the farm. Well, what was she supposed to do? She was taking what appeared to be the only practical way out of the situation, and he'd acted as if she had spat on her father's grave. He and the old man had been good friends for a lot of years; maybe that was the problem. But wasn't he required, as the probate attorney, to set aside his opinions, especially those of a personal nature? Billie didn't need him to tell her what she *should* do.

At the house, she poured another cup of coffee and sat in the kitchen for a time, thinking about what she had learned that morning. As disturbingly enlightening as it was, she decided she couldn't let it prejudice her thinking about what she needed to do now. In terms of the farm, whatever action was practical before Clay's revelations was still practical. She reminded herself that although there was no real upside to the situation, there wasn't a downside, either. All she needed to do was to go forward, deal with the paperwork, and get the estate settled. Hopefully she wouldn't lose any money in the process, because she didn't have any to lose. Sitting there, it occurred to her that there was no reason why she couldn't head back to Chillicothe and conduct things from there. All she needed was a lawyer—probably not David Clay, given his attitude when leaving the diner—and a realtor. Easy peasy, as Athena would say.

She sat there, absently drumming her fingers on the old harvest table. The pine top was scarred by several generations of abuse by plates and saucers and pots and pans, by rings left by liquor glasses and beer bottles, by random scratches and cigarette burns, by gouges made by impatient children (Billie among them) with knives and forks. Billie thought she recognized the rings from her mother's martinis. They had grown in volume and frequency toward the later years. There was family history ingrained on that tabletop, one whose code could never be broken. The table, like Will Masterson, was a survivor.

She glanced over to the answering machine on the counter. After a moment, she took her phone from her purse and punched in the number. She listened to her father's voice on the tape, then hung up before the beep. She did it again and then a third time before setting the phone aside. Wiping her eyes, she stood up and looked out the window in time to see the little girl heading into the barn. A few minutes later, as she'd done the day before, she emerged into the corral on the other side, dragging a bale of hay.

Billie watched for a while. When the girl finished with the feeding, she hooked a lead on the pony and led it into the barn. Billie went out the back door and started down the hill, lighting a cigarette as she walked. It was late morning and the day was fifteen degrees cooler than the one before. The storm had seen to that, chasing the humidity across the Mississippi to the plains.

The girl had the pony tied to an upright wooden beam and she was feeding it pieces of apple when Billie walked unnoticed through the open door.

"You're a greedy guy, Mister Buster," the kid was saying.

"You named your pony Mister Buster?" Billie asked.

The girl looked at Billie for a half second and then away. "He was already called that when I got him. I didn't want to change his name and confuse him."

"I could never tolerate a confused pony," Billie said.

The little girl had no reaction to that but instead picked up a brush and began to groom the pony's withers, which were streaked with mud. No doubt the animal had been rolling over in the wet paddock. Billie took a drag on the cigarette.

"You're not supposed to be smoking in here, you know."

"You're not supposed to be giving me orders," Billie said. "It turns out this is my barn now."

"I guess that makes it okay for you to be foolish."

"What did you say?" Billie asked.

The girl turned away from her and went back to her grooming. Billie stared at her a moment before looking down at the cigarette in her hand. The kid was right, of course. Billie had walked into the barn without even thinking about it. Her father would have kicked her ass. He'd smoked most of his life but Billie had never once seen him, even when he was in his cups, light up in his barn or anybody else's. Billie knew better, but what bothered her was the fact that she'd forgotten. What was wrong with her? She walked over and flicked the butt into a mud puddle outside the door.

"You happy now?" she asked, returning.

The kid kept up her brushing and made no reply.

"I'm told you're Jodie," Billie said.

The kid nodded, still focused on the job at hand. The pony, however, sidestepped around to give Billie a look. He was restless and not particularly enamored of the brushing. Most ponies Billie had known were cantankerous and often downright mean.

"I'm Billie."

"I know who you are."

"Then I guess that means you know what's going on. You know you're going to have to start thinking about what you want to do with your little petting zoo here. I'll be selling the farm."

The girl didn't reply at first. Billie began to wonder if she was dimwitted (although she was smarter than Billie when it came to the issue of smoking in the barn). Marian Dunlop was right about one thing—she was a pretty little girl. Today she had her thick dark hair tied back at the nape of her neck, tucked beneath a baseball cap with the Cardinals logo on the front. The bill of the cap was frayed. Whether it was a nod to the current style or just a really old cap, Billie couldn't know. In spite of her dark complexion, the girl's eyes were blue. That would be the Rickman in there. The family was all blonde and blue-eyed—and shiftless for the most part. From what she had seen of the kid so far, it seemed to Billie that she hadn't inherited that.

"Maybe whoever buys it will let them stay," the girl said softly. "I pay for their keep."

"That'll be for the new owners to decide," Billie said. "I wouldn't get my hopes up if I were you. A wise man told me over breakfast that anybody buying the place would be after the property only. Which means they'd be bulldozing the buildings."

The girl stopped her brushing. "How can you let them do that?"

"They come up with the money, they can do whatever they want."

"This is your family farm."

"Well, it's also the real world, kid. The place is up to here in debt. A mortgage, back taxes, power bills. Got those horses to feed. All of that costs money and there isn't any."

"Will always managed."

"Will was the one who created all the debt," Billie told her. "You do get that?"

The girl went back to brushing the pony but her heart was no longer in it. Apparently a short conversation with Billie was all that was needed to sour her mood. First lawyer Clay and now a little girl. Billie was having quite a day, spreading optimism and goodwill wherever she went. After a few more strokes with the brush, the kid untied the animal and led it to the door and released it outside into the paddock. She stood there for a time, with her back to Billie. *She's going to start bawling*, Billie thought. When the little girl turned, though, her eyes were dry.

"I have a thousand dollars," she said. "Or I will have. Mr. Clay told me that Will left it to me. You can have that to help pay the bills."

"Jesus Christ," Billie said. "I'm not going to take your money. You should blow that on video games and CDs."

The girl frowned. "Nobody buys CDs."

"You know what I mean," Billie told her. "That's found money. Blow it. What's wrong with you?"

"There's nothing wrong with me," the girl said. "Those animals are my responsibility. I have to take care of them."

"How old are you?"

"I'll be ten in October."

"Then act like it," Billie said. "You shouldn't be worried about looking after things, especially things like ponies and goats and whatever."

"You had a pony when you were my age. His name was Little Joe."

Billie regarded the girl a moment. "Sounds as if you and my father were besties. What else did he tell you?"

"Nobody says besties," the girl said. "He told me you wanted a pancake that looked like a platypus."

It took Billie a moment to realize what the kid was talking about. She remembered the old man making pancakes in the shape of animals, but she didn't specifically recall a platypus. If Will had told the girl about it, though, it was true. The old man obviously had a better memory than Billie, about some things anyway.

"So my father made you pancakes, did he?"

"No," Jodie said. "He made me oatmeal. Marian told him he needed to eat oatmeal for breakfast."

Billie had heard enough about her father and the two women in his life. She had come down here to tell the girl that she and her animals were going to have to vacate the premises, and all this talk about her father wasn't helping matters. She didn't need to hear about the conversations between the two of them, about duck-billed platypuses and a pony named Little Joe, after the character in *Bonanza*, a show that had been off the air for ten years before Billie was born but one that she and Will had watched in reruns almost every Saturday morning.

"Well, I have things to do," she told the girl, wishing now that she did. "I just wanted to give you the lay of the land. It doesn't have to happen today. Like you said, maybe whoever buys the place will let you and the herd stick around. But you'd better be prepared for otherwise."

She walked out before she could hear any more protest. As she passed the paddock, the gray colt trotted over to her but she ignored him, heading up the hill to the house and not looking back. She'd had enough interaction for the day, whether it be with kids or horses or oversize lawyers. She'd been home for a day and a half and already it was too much.

Nine

THERE WAS BEER IN THE FRIDGE, a local brand that she hadn't heard of, and after a lunch of crackers and cheese she opened a bottle and carried it out onto the deck. This time she sat in her father's chair as she drank the lager and tried to think about what she needed to do in order to extricate herself from the farm. She found that her thoughts kept returning to her mother.

Of course Billie had known that her mother had emotional issues. She'd had her ups and downs over the years, but who didn't? Billie was of the opinion that people were fucked up in general, even the ones who seemed to have it together. There had been a time when Billie had wondered if her mother's problems stemmed from her marrying the wrong man. But that wasn't even true. She hadn't married the wrong man; she'd married the wrong circumstance. Billie doubted she was ever really happy on the farm. She'd met Will Masterson at a wedding in St. Louis, where she'd grown up. The bride was a childhood friend and the groom a cousin of Will's. Apparently a whirlwind romance had followed, the horse farmer and the debutante, and the two got married before Billie's mother even realized how her life would change.

When Billie was little, she and her friend Glenda from town had for a time become enamored of the classic movies channel. The two of them came to compare Billie's parents to mismatched characters in film, convinced that Will was Gary Cooper and her mother Jean Arthur. The martinis helped with the comparison. Of course it was nonsense: even Gary Cooper and Jean Arthur weren't Gary Cooper and Jean Arthur.

The good times in Billie's memory bank far outweighed the bad. Her mother sewed and played the piano and showed Billie how to do both. Not particularly well, but it didn't matter. She had days when she would wake up literally singing "Oh What A Beautiful Morning." And others when she wouldn't get up at all. Billie later recognized her behavior as manic depressive, or bipolar, or whatever the current term was. But she obviously had never appreciated the depth of her mother's problems. Billie assumed that everybody suffered to some degree. There were days even yet when she didn't want to get up.

But now David Clay had taken it upon himself to tell Billie more than she wanted to know. Maybe he'd done so, as he suggested, to vindicate his old friend Will Masterson, or maybe he'd done it to convince Billie to keep the farm. Probably both. Whatever the reason, Billie didn't feel particularly appreciative of the effort. And if Clay thought his little revelation session was going to change her mind about selling, he was dead wrong.

Now she needed to put things in motion and she was unsure of how to do that. Lawyer Clay would be able to guide her, but she didn't feel like asking him, not after what had happened. She would let things settle for a couple of days. Maybe then she'd be less angry with him, and at the same time maybe he'd come to realize that selling was the prudent move, something he should have known all along. It could be that his sentimental side regarding his old friend was clouding his pragmatism. She would never have expected that, not from David Mountain Clay. Not only had he always considered himself to be the smartest man in the county, there was a very good chance it was true.

Of course, she hadn't expected any of this. Certainly not her father dying, even though he was seventy-three years old and had spent at least sixty of those years eating bacon for breakfast every day. The oatmeal had arrived on the scene too late. Still, it was unexpected, as was everything and everybody Billie had encountered since. Like Marian, who, as it turned out, was probably not a shrew, although Billie was still unsure exactly what to make of her. And the little girl, so cute she should be in commercials, who had somehow taken up the spot in Will Masterson's heart once solely reserved for Billie.

She finished the beer and went inside for another. When she came back out, she saw one more thing she couldn't have expected—the silver Porsche Carrera winding its way among the puddles in the back drive. Billie opened the beer and sat down, watching the car. Why would Reese Ryker come up the back drive instead of the main one leading to the house? Of course, that was the secondary question. Why was he there at all?

He parked beside the machine shed and got out. He was apparently alone today; there was no stunning brunette lounging in the passenger seat. He spotted Billie up above immediately and waved and she raised her hand tentatively in reply. He started toward the house but stopped when he got past the barn and saw the thoroughbreds in the paddock. He walked at once to the gate. Billie watched, thinking the colt would go to him as it had her. But the animal stayed its ground. Reese stood there for longer than she would have expected, staring at the horse while not giving the broodmares a second glance.

Finally he turned and came toward the house. He was wearing a blazer and a white shirt with blue jeans. When he got near, Billie could see the jeans were neatly pressed, with a crease in them. What had her father called the man—a fart in a mitten?

"Hello, Billie," he called as he stepped onto the deck, smiling and attempting a hale and hearty tone that somehow didn't fit him. "You look comfortable."

"Got my feet up and my mind in neutral," Billie said, her words betraying her mood. But she wasn't going to tell Reese Ryker her thoughts. She wondered if she was required to offer him a beer. She decided against. She couldn't be providing beer to every person who dropped in unexpectedly. And uninvited to boot. "What brings you out this way?"

Reese gestured pointlessly toward the south. "Oh, I had some business and driving home I realized I was close by. Thought I'd stop and say hello. We never had a chance to speak at the funeral. My wife and I had a previous engagement and couldn't make it to the community center."

"You missed out on some kickass brownies."

The statement seemed to give Reese pause. He was looking his age, Billie thought, which would be somewhere north of fifty, maybe fifty-five. There were pouches beneath his eyes and his hair was colored an odd shade of maroon. She could see evidence of expertly installed hair plugs in the front. He had a deep tan that was either unhealthy or artificially applied. His teeth, when he had smiled at Billie, were brilliantly and unnaturally white.

"I just wanted to express my condolences," he said then. "I knew your father a good many years."

Billie mumbled thanks as she wondered at the accuracy of what she'd just heard. Had Will Masterson gotten chummy with Reese Ryker? It seemed unlikely, but if he had, it probably had something to do with Marian Dunlop. Maybe she—like Ryker—was what passed for a Kentucky blueblood herself. Whatever the case, it really didn't matter to Billie, and in truth it was none of her business who her father had chosen to hang out with in his later years—whether it be feisty matrons or curly-haired waifs or spray-tanned billionaires.

Reese had turned and was now looking the place over, taking in the fields and the bush lot and the pasture to the west. He did not glance toward the barns and the horses there. Billie watched him, wondering what she might add to the conversation.

She decided on, "You got your new car all muddy."

He turned to look at the vehicle. He seemed puzzled by the remark. It occurred to Billie that he had never washed a car in his life and so he didn't have any reaction to getting one dirty. No doubt somebody in his employ would wash it and the next time he got behind the wheel it would be spanking new again. Billie wondered what he would say if she ran a truck full of drywall into the front end of it.

He looked back to her. "Will you be taking the place over?"

Billie took a drink. "And do what with it?"

"I couldn't say," Reese said. "But it's your family farm."

"You think I could make a living off thirty acres?"

"I would not think that, no," Reese said after a moment. He shrugged and smiled his pointless smile. "I often wondered how your father made a go of it. But I knew nothing of his financial situation. A gentleman does not ask that of another gentleman."

Not even a sure-enough good buddy? Billie wondered.

"The truth is, though, I have always liked this particular piece of property," Reese continued. "I've been looking at small farms in the area lately. I'm not sure how much you follow the thorough-bred game these days—"

"Not at all," Billie interjected.

"Well, you might not be aware that Double R Racing is a very big player on the world stage. Very big and getting bigger. I'm involved in every aspect of running the stable, top to bottom. I need a place to train some foals, get the young colts away from the older stallions."

Well now, Billie thought, smiling to herself. She knew that things would eventually begin to make sense, and now—roughly twenty-four hours after her father had gone into the ground—they had.

Reese Ryker had a few hundred acres of his own—Billie couldn't say if it was four hundred or six hundred or a thousand—with a mansion out of a Hollywood movie and flower gardens and miles of paddocks and she had no idea what else. So why would he be looking at Will Masterson's thirty-acre spread, with a house and outbuildings that were probably teardowns? The story about a training facility for young colts seemed like a leaky vessel. Billie had a drink of beer and looked at the barn roof, where her father had, over the years, nailed odds and ends of ribbed steel to keep out the rain.

"You sound like a man looking to buy some real estate, Reese."

"I'm always interested in land, Billie," he replied. "It's in my blood. My father had a saying—always buy land, they don't make it anymore."

That saying was older than spit. Billie wondered if Reese actually believed that his father had come up with it. The stories she'd heard growing up about Reese's old man were about a guy who dedicated his every waking hour to pissing away the family fortune. Billie doubted there had been much land acquisition in the mix. Of course, that didn't mean that Reese's father hadn't passed the old adage on to the son. Talk was cheap. Cheaper than farmland.

Reese made a point of looking at his watch, a clunky mass of gold on his wrist that looked as if it weighed eight pounds. "I need to run. I actually stopped to extend an invitation. I would have called but I didn't have the number. My wife and I wanted to ask you to dinner tonight, at the restaurant at Lexington Downs. They have a fantastic new chef there, a woman they poached from some bistro in Paris. Paris, France . . . not Kentucky. I have a horse running in a stakes race tonight—a two-year-old filly that looks quite promising. I was thinking we could have a bite and watch her win. Might be a nice evening out for you after . . . everything."

Billie started to say no but then heard herself accepting. *Why not*, she reasoned. She could sit on this deck, bored to tears, or she could go out for the evening, to a tony racetrack restaurant for a meal cooked by some hotshot chef from Paris. France, that is.

She was curious about Reese Ryker, his alleged friendship with her father, and his obvious interest in the farm. It was evident that dinner at Lexington Downs was about more than just dinner. She might as well find out. If she was going to sell the property—and she was—then she'd prefer to sell it to a man with deep pockets. What was it to her that the man himself was no deeper than the mud puddles he'd driven through to arrive here today?

They arranged to meet at the track at seven o'clock. Billie had nothing dressy—other than the black dress she'd bought the day before—so she wore jeans and a white blouse, along with a pair of black cowboy boots she found in her father's bedroom. They were women's boots, with red stitching and soft tooled leather. They were beautiful, and Billie was pretty damn sure she knew who owned them.

Reese and his wife were already there when she arrived, sitting at a table by the floor-to-ceiling front windows that overlooked the track. Billie hadn't been there in years—the place had undergone an extensive renovation. The restaurant was large, maybe a hundred feet long, with a retro-looking bar running along the back wall, done in oak paneling and brass railings. The bartenders, both men and women, wore crisp white shirts with red suspenders. The thick carpet underfoot was the color of Kentucky bluegrass. Classical music played softly in the background.

Reese stood as Billie approached. "There you are. This is my wife, Sofia. Billie Masterson."

Billie shook hands with both. The woman was more beautiful up close than she'd appeared from a distance. Her eyes were dark, nearly black, and her skin a natural tan. She said hello, solemnly expressing her condolences. She had a slight accent—Spanish or possibly Portuguese. She wore a short blue skirt and a red top of some silky material. There was a diamond on her ring finger the size of a hickory nut.

The two of them were drinking red wine and Billie joined them. Reese had already ordered appetizers—smoked salmon and shrimp puffs and sushi—but told Billie to add anything she wanted. She deferred.

"The chef's special tonight is quail," he said as he poured wine for her. "But everything on the menu is good. The steaks are amazing, first class."

They held their glasses toward one another and drank. The wine was good, better than the boxed stuff Billie had been buying back home at the Piggly Wiggly.

"How are you called Billie?" Sofia asked. "Are you named for the famous outlaw, Billy the Kid?" The word *kid* emerged from her ruby lips as *keed*.

"I was named for a more obscure outlaw—my father," Billie said.

Sofia smiled. "What nature of outlaw? A politician perhaps?"

"Billie's making a little joke," Reese said. "Her father was not an outlaw. His name was William."

Sofia nodded. "Ah, yes. I see."

Reese announced that they should bet a little during dinner, so while they waited for the appetizers, they looked over the program. The restaurant offered tableside wagering. The first race was a sprint with nine entries and everyone at the table came up empty. The winner was an older gelding that paid thirty-eight dollars to win.

"Oh, that is the horse I should have bet," Sofia exclaimed.

"Hindsight," Reese told her.

"The bane of every horseplayer who ever drew breath," Billie said.

"So you know about this business?" Sofia asked.

"Just that part."

The food arrived. The server who brought it was not the one who had taken their order, and there had been a mixup somewhere along the line. She brought antipasto instead of sushi. Reese explained the error to the woman, in a voice usually reserved for errant children, his tone bordering on sarcasm.

They began to eat. Billie tried the shrimp and had a sip of wine, watching Sofia over the rim of her glass. She could not have been much older than thirty, somewhat earthy and sensuous, not what

Billie would have expected. She went after the food with enthusiasm.

"How did you guys meet?" Billie asked.

Reese waved at the scene beyond the windows, where the track ponies were leading the horses for the next race out from the tunnel below. "This game. Sofia's father is the best thoroughbred trainer in Europe. We did business together, and Sofia and I met through him."

"He would not say he is the best in all of Europe," Sofia pointed out. "He works at a small track near Pamplona." She smiled. "We are peasant stock."

"False modesty," Reese said. "Who needs it?"

Billie put a sliver of salmon on a cracker and popped it into her mouth. "So you work with horses, too?" she asked Sofia.

"I know nothing about horses." Sofia gestured to the track. "This is the distance I like to be from them, so I can see how beautiful they are, how fast they run, but I don't have to know how they sometimes will kick and bite a person."

Billie smiled at her and was about to ask what—if anything—she did for a living when Reese interrupted.

"What are you doing now, Billie? You're in Ohio, right?"

Billie nodded. "Chillicothe. I'm a waitress at Freddie's Fish Shack. You ought to try our deep-fried cod bits."

Reese smiled thinly. When he reached for an appetizer, Billie noticed how soft and pink his hands were, the nails perfectly manicured. She doubted his involvement in every aspect of his stable—top to bottom, he'd claimed—included cleaning out stalls or throwing hay bales, or doing anything that might risk a man getting a hangnail. But she couldn't hold that against him. It was one of the privileges of ownership.

They ordered their entrées. A few minutes later, the second race was off. The lead horses came down the stretch four abreast and remained bunched as they crossed the finish line, too close to call.

"It was six!" Sofia shouted. "I am certain it was six number horse."

She was right. In a photo finish, the number six was the winner, paying five dollars and eighty cents on a two-dollar bet. Still, Sofia was ecstatic.

"I win!"

"The woman has a knack," Reese said. He looked at her a moment, as if indulging her, before turning to Billie. "What did you bet?"

"The two horse," Billie told him. "It should be crossing the finish line any time now."

By the time the third race ran, their food was there. Sofia had the winning ticket again, another favorite. Her delight in this never faltered. Billie picked another pretender that finished far up the track. Reese, cutting into a slab of prime rib the size of a hubcap, nodded toward her.

"What are your plans long term?" he asked. "I assume you're not looking at being a waitress forever. Don't you have a journalism degree?"

"How would you know that?" Billie asked.

His mouth full, Reese shrugged. "I heard it somewhere. Not true?"

"It's true."

"But you've never used your diploma?"

"Once," Billie said. "I rolled it up and swatted a fly with it."

Sofia looked up from her quail and laughed out loud. Reese appeared annoyed as he went back to his beef. Chewing slowly, he looked out over the track. The crew was setting up the temporary fencing for the next race, a mile and an eighth on the turf.

"You must have had a notion of using it at some time," he suggested after a bit. "Were you thinking of reporting?"

"I'm not sure," Billie said as she reached for her wine. They were on their second bottle now. "I may have watched *His Girl Friday* too many times when I was a kid. I was a big Rosalind Russell fan."

"Did you ever think about TV?" Reese asked. "Maybe in the field—news anchor, something like that?"

"I might have," Billie admitted, thinking of Athena. "I finished school over ten years ago. I can't recall what I was thinking. I really can't recall what I was thinking ten days ago."

"You probably wouldn't know this, but I own a TV station," Reese said. "WTVK in Louisville. It's regarded as one of the top small-market stations in the country. We're always looking for talented people. And you certainly are attractive enough to be on air."

Billie glanced at Sofia, who was watching her, her eyes bright. Billie wondered about the people who were deemed *not* attractive enough to be on television. Or at least on Reese Ryker's station. Were they ever invited for seared quail with asparagus tips? Probably not, unless they had farmland to sell, as well.

"I have no experience," Billie said. "I wouldn't know which end of the microphone to hold."

"They could put a little sign on it," Sofia said. "This side up. No?"

Billie smiled as Reese gave his wife the look of indulgence once again. He let the matter slide; apparently he'd said all he wanted to for the time being. He was one for planting seeds, Billie thought.

The stakes race was the seventh on the card. Reese guaranteed that his filly—a sleek bay named Kiss Me Kate—would win without breaking a sweat. He was wrong on both counts—the two-year-old was perspiring quite heavily as she crossed the line behind six other runners. Reese sat stone-faced, looking down at the horses as they filed back toward the tunnel.

"I knew he was the wrong jockey." He was seething quietly, his upper lip curled. "Maybe next time they'll listen to me." He took a moment to settle himself before glancing over at the two women. "As long as the horse is healthy, what do I care? I think it's time for some brandy."

They had a round of cognac, a vintage from France that Billie had never heard of but endorsed by Reese as "the best," and then, after deciding they would bet the last race, they ordered another. When it arrived, Reese finally got down to it.

"What *are* your plans for the farm, Billie? Are you thinking of selling?"

"I am," Billie said. "Isn't that why you invited me here tonight?"

"Absolutely," Reese said. "We thought we would ply you with food and liquor and offer you ten cents on the dollar."

Sofia turned her smile on Billie. "How are we doing?"

Billie raised her glass. "I can't recall when I've encountered better plying. Although we need to talk about that ten-cent figure."

"Oh, they are off!" Sofia exclaimed, meaning the race.

It was a mile on the dirt. A squat chestnut gelding left the field in its dust and paid twelve dollars to win. Sofia again had the ticket. As she went to cash in, she was beaming like a child showing off her prize calf at the county fair. Billie, for her part, never picked a single winner the whole night. Looking at Reese Ryker, considering the man and his intentions, she wondered if that was a bad omen or a good one. Or nothing at all.

"I'm obviously interested in the property," he said. "It's the size I want and it's close enough to the home farm to be practical in terms of moving horses back and forth."

"Would you bulldoze the buildings?" Billie asked.

Reese had a drink of the cognac. "I probably would." He paused, making a show of reconsideration. He was a lousy poker player. "Actually, I would hang onto the house. I have a groom renting a place in town. Got a wife and a couple of little kids; he could stay there."

"Well, I need to talk to a realtor, I guess," Billie said. "I have no idea what the place is worth."

"I would call more than one, if I were you," Reese told her. "Have the place assessed and then I'll make you a proposition; perhaps you and I can make a deal outside of real estate. Save you the broker's fees. That money might as well be in your pocket as theirs."

Billie had already considered the possibility and would have suggested it if Ryker hadn't.

"Tell you what," Reese said then. "I'll even take the stock off your hands. Turn those old broodmares out to pasture and let them graze. We can figure out a price for them, too."

Billie nodded as Sofia returned with a fistful of dollar bills and a smile as big as the moon.

"I guess you'll be picking up the check," Reese suggested.

"The horse wins me nine dollars," Sofia said. "Do you think that will cover it?"

"Not even the sushi," Reese said, looking impatiently across the room, where their server was chatting with the bartender. "Looks as if Beyoncé there is on a break. Imagine that."

He went off to settle the bill. Sofia drank off the last of the cognac and pushed the snifter away before turning to Billie.

"You two have discussed your business?"

Billie, still focused on Reese's attitude toward the waitress, turned. "To a point."

"Do not let him lowball you," Sofia said, smiling. "Is that the correct word—lowball? He has plenty of money. He might as well give some of it to you. But not all, of course." She laughed.

"I appreciate that," Billie said. "Although I'm sure he wouldn't." She found herself liking the woman, whereas she had been thoroughly prepared not to. "What do you do when you're not taking advantage of the pari-mutuel system?"

"I am a singer," Sofia said. She seemed surprised that Billie didn't know this. "I make . . . pop music . . . you call it here. I am recording next month some new songs. In Los Angeles."

Since arriving back in Kentucky, it seemed that things were being revealed to Billie in slow motion, as if she were walking underwater. Her father's relationship with Marian Dunlop, for instance. David Mountain Clay's review of the finances of the farm, and his petulant take on Billie's intent to sell. Reese Ryker's invitation to dinner with his gorgeous young wife. At least now

Billie could see that situation for what it was. A fifty-ish billionaire with hair plugs and a fake tan, and an aspiring singer twenty years or so his junior. Nothing new under the sun here. As deliberate in their arrival as these revelations had been, none had been particularly surprising when they got there. Billie wondered if she would ever be truly surprised by anything again.

They walked out together. Reese's Porsche was in a preferred lot somewhere, while Billie's car was in general parking, with the rest of the great unwashed vehicles of the ordinary punters. When Billie thanked the couple for dinner, she received a handshake from Reese and a rib-cracking hug from Sofia. For someone who looked like a runway model, she was incredibly strong. Peasant stock indeed.

On the drive home, Billie stopped at a corner store and picked up a real estate flyer. Back at the farm, she sat at the kitchen table and went through the paper, circling the names of the two realtors with the most listings. She would call them in the morning.

There was one beer left in the fridge. She cracked it and went outside to the deck. She stood by the railing, drinking and listening to the sounds of the night—the wind in the pines emitting a low whistle, the soft guttural noises from the horses below. She could smell the manure and the hay and the pungent mud of the now-filled pond. From the road she heard a hot rod downshifting as it approached the stop sign, glasspack mufflers rumbling like distant thunder. The driver turned onto the highway and then pounded the vehicle through the gears as he headed for town, for cold beers and female companionship, Billie presumed.

The sounds and smells of her youth, she thought as she drained the bottle and headed for bed. Lost to the years.

Ten

THE REALTORS WERE QUICK TO RESPOND. By noon they had both been there and gone, after doing quick evaluations of the property. And they were clear that it was the property—not the buildings—they assessed. Neither bothered to even enter the barn or machine shed, nor did they ask to see the upstairs of the house. The first agent was named Habib—a Pakistani with a British lilt—and the second a woman named Lorelei, who looked like a country and western singer from fifty years ago: big hair and an accent straight out of *Hee Haw*. She drove a pink Cadillac. Billie spaced the two appointments an hour apart but Lorelei was early; her Caddy and the departing Habib in his Audi met in the driveway.

Whatever their differences in background and accents, the two were in lockstep on everything else, including price. Habib said he would put the place on the market for two hundred and ten thousand, while Lorelei came in at two fifteen. Either scenario would leave Billie with about two hundred grand after fees—that is, if the asking price were met. Roughly enough to break even and exactly what David Clay had predicted.

As Lorelei was driving off, Billie saw Jodie pedaling up to the barn on her bicycle. When the little girl looked up to the house,

Billie turned and went inside. She poured a cup of coffee and sat down at the kitchen table. She wondered how soon was too soon to call Reese Ryker. She didn't want to appear overly eager. Then again, she didn't want the opportunity to pass her by. He was hot for the property for whatever reason, but maybe a week from now that wouldn't be true. After all, he was a fart in a mitten and such a man might be capricious. Billie wanted to get on with things. Maybe she could get Ryker to pay the assessed price of two fifteen. That would get her square with what was owed and leave her with a few dollars for her troubles.

Either way, she wanted it done. She wasn't use to dealing with— well, pretty much anything. Her life was simple and purposefully so, if she didn't count the abusive ex-boyfriend and the fact that everybody she encountered was of the opinion she was stuck in a rut of some kind. But Billie could argue that ruts themselves were simple things. Uncomplicated things.

She was thinking of making something for lunch, and realizing there wasn't much available for the making, when she heard a tapping on the back door. She turned to see Jodie standing there, outside the screen.

"I need your help."

The piston pump in the barn, bought used by Will Masterson two or three decades earlier, lost its prime occasionally and wouldn't draw. When that happened, a steel plug on top of the pump needed to be removed and the pump filled with water. The girl knew that; she'd watched Will do it a dozen times. However, she wasn't strong enough to remove the plug. When she and Billie walked into the barn, the pipe wrench from the machine shed was already there, on the shelf beside the pump, alongside a bucket half-filled with water from the diminished trough outside.

"You have to take out that plug," Jodie said.

"I know what I have to do," Billie said.

Will Masterson would never tighten a bolt or a nut if he could overtighten it. It was all Billie could do to get the plug out. Twice the wrench slipped and she fell backward. She felt the little girl's eyes on her, judging her, wondering if she was up to the task. Finally the plug turned. When it was out, Jodie indicated the bucket.

"You have to fill it to the top."

"I've done this before," Billie said again.

"I wasn't sure," Jodie said. "Looked to me like you were never going to get that plug out."

"It's out, isn't it?"

Billie filled the pump and put the plug back finger tight, in case more priming was required. Jodie flipped the switch; the pump ran noisily for a bit and then they heard the water gushing into the trough outside. Jodie walked to the door and watched before turning to Billie.

"Thank you."

"It's all right," Billie said.

"Maybe you could leave the plug a little loose and I can do it next time. That way I won't have to bother you."

"You didn't bother me." Billie could have added that there weren't going to be too many next times, but she didn't. Still, she torqued the plug to her own specs, not Will Masterson's. When she was done, the girl was looking out the open door.

"The way that front pasture's greenin' up, we might be able to turn the horses out before long."

Billie looked past the kid to the field, where the grass was beginning to grow after the drought. She was somewhat unnerved by how the little girl used Will Masterson's words. The pasture greening up.

When Jodie went outside again to check the level of the water trough, Billie looked around the pump room and noticed a car battery on a shelf by the door, alongside her father's old battery charger. Probably a spare the old man had picked up somewhere. It was Billie's now, and she might have use for it. When Jodie returned, she caught a flapping loose sole of her running shoes on the doorsill and stumbled. She righted herself without falling, then walked over to switch the pump off.

"You need new shoes," Billie told her.

The little girl looked at her feet. "I guess."

"So buy yourself a pair. You get that money from David Clay yet?"

"Not yet," Jodie said. "I have to save that money for my animals anyway." She paused. "At least until I know what's going to happen."

I can tell you what's going to happen, Billie thought. But she didn't say it. She already had, and the girl hadn't listened.

"Do you mind if I stay here for a while and work on the cart?" Jodie asked then. "I need to sand it some more before I can paint it."

Billie looked at the pony cart on the sawhorses. Most of the paint was worn off or chipped away and she could see where the kid had been sanding the rest. The sulky had once been bright red. Billie knew because she had painted it herself. Will had made the harness, or rather he had cut down a harness that had once been used on a Clydesdale owned by his father.

"Does your mother know where you are?"

"Yes."

"And it's okay if you spend the whole day here?" Billie asked. "Don't you have stuff to do?"

"What kind of stuff?"

"Kid stuff."

"She doesn't—" the girl began and then stopped. "It's okay. I only live over on the next road. She knows I'm here."

She had started to say that her mother didn't care but had stopped herself. Now she was looking at the cart, as if it were the only thing in the world for her. Billie shook her head. She hoped that Reese Ryker wouldn't take too long with his offer.

"You can stick around," she said. "If you're going to be painting in here, open the doors. I don't need you keeling over from the fumes. Or better yet—drag the thing outside."

"I don't have any paint yet. I have to buy it when I get my money."

"You're going to buy paint for that old cart but not shoes for yourself," Billie said.

The girl shrugged. Billie left her there.

Back at the house she turned her mind away from the exasperating kid in the barn and thought again about lunch, which made her wonder if the little girl had eaten, or brought something with her. It wasn't Billie's concern, she decided. The cupboards offered up cans of soup and sardines (her father ate sardine sandwiches on a regular basis, which lingered on his breath for hours—how had he ever landed a girlfriend?) and stale crackers. The fridge wasn't any more promising, although she considered a grilled cheese sandwich before realizing there was cheese but no bread. *No beer either*, she reminded herself.

Grabbing her keys from the table, she went out the front door and got into her car. The engine turned over slowly but fired. Driving off, she took care not to look down the hill to the barn where the little girl was sanding away on a pony cart that would in all likelihood never be harnessed to her orphan pony.

On the main street in town she drove past Mom's Homestyle Diner. She could see through the plate glass that the place was turning a brisk luncheon trade but she wasn't interested in going in. David Clay might be there, plowing through a plate of chicken wings or spaghetti while offering sage advice and tall tales in equal measures to the locals. Billie was not in the mood for his sagacity today.

The Bellwood Hotel, which sat in the northeast corner of the town square, had a restaurant on the ground floor, she recalled. She parked in the municipal lot behind the main drag and walked through the square, past the statues of soldiers from the various wars of the past couple of centuries, men depicted variously in buckskins and butternut, wearing puttees and coonskin caps, carrying flintlock rifles and assault weapons. All of them looked upward, advancing on some unseen enemy, their faces etched with valor, courtesy of some anonymous stonemason.

The restaurant in the old hotel had two rooms—a pub out front and a dining room to the rear. The place smelled pleasantly of linseed oil and draft beer. Billie was about to take a stool at the bar when she recognized the bartender as Mike McCall, whom she'd gone to high school with. They had been acquaintances more than friends; she remembered him as a silent type, not into sports or cars or juvenile delinquency, which was why they hadn't been close, she realized. She had no opinion about him one way or another but she didn't feel like getting trapped in a conversation with someone who might be interested in catching up, especially when they had nothing to catch up about. She turned and made her way to a corner booth. After a time, Mike spotted her; she waved and asked across the room how he was doing. He asked the same and that was it. If only everything were that easy.

A waitress appeared and Billie ordered a beer and a burger with fries. Sitting there, waiting for her food, she was bored and noticed a discarded newspaper on a table near the front windows. She went over to retrieve it and as she did, she glanced into the dining room. Marian Dunlop was at a table there, with three other women, all nicely dressed, all with silver hair. She sat sideways to Billie, in conversation, and didn't see her. Billie grabbed the paper and retreated to her booth, out of sight.

The paper was the *Marshall Gazette*, which came out every Wednesday. There were more pictures than articles inside, and most of the images were of various sports teams from the local high school, although there were a few of the bowling leagues—both men's and women's—and from the service clubs around town. One page was devoted to the criminal activity in the county for the past week. There had been two car accidents, one charge of under the influence, several break-ins, and a domestic assault. Billie thought she might see the name Everson among those charged but she did not.

The waitress brought the burger, which was passable, and the fries, which were cold. She ate the burger while reading the classifieds. There was a livestock section with a couple of dozen animals for sale—horses and goats and rabbits and alpacas. It occurred to her that she could run an ad and sell Jodie's animals that way. Find a good home for them and give the kid a few bucks to boot. Maybe she could buy some shoes that weren't falling apart. Why wouldn't her mother do that? Presumably her money was being spent on other pursuits, Troy Everson among them.

Setting the paper aside, she glanced toward the front door and saw Marian standing at the till there, settling her bill. As she waited for her change, she turned and looked directly at Billie. She stared for a few seconds before turning away. *That's good*, Billie thought. *Pay your bill and off you go.*

But she knew of course that wouldn't happen. Of all the gin joints in all the towns in the world.

"You could have asked," Marian said as she approached.

Billie looked up at her from the booth. The older woman wore a green summer dress and flats. Her sunglasses were pushed up into her thick hair and she had a brown leather purse of distressed leather looped over her shoulder.

"I'll bite," Billie said. "Ask what?"

"If you could wear my Tony Lamas."

Billie hesitated. When she'd returned from the track last night, she'd taken the boots off inside the front door and left them there. Which meant that Marian had been at the house that morning and seen them. How else would she know that Billie had worn them? But when was she there? Billie had driven straight from the farm to the restaurant and when she arrived Marian was already there, in the dining room with her silver-haired posse. She had to have been in the house while Billie was down at the barn with the kid, priming the pump. So she was there, did a little snooping around, and then left without talking to Billie. Wasn't that interesting? The woman had an agenda after all, although Billie had no idea what it was. Not yet, anyway.

"I must have missed you this morning," Billie said.

"Missed me where?"

"At the house."

"I wasn't at the house."

Now Billie was getting aggravated. "Then what's this about the boots?"

"You could have asked before you borrowed them," Marian said. "I would have said yes. They're just boots, for Chrissakes."

"What—you got somebody following me?"

Marian laughed. "You've been gone too long, Billie. Around here, people talk. If you have dinner in the dining room at Lexington Downs with Reese Ryker and his latest wife, chowing down on quail and sipping red wine and cognac, and if you're wearing kickass Tony Lamas while you're doing it, people are going to notice. And some of those people are going to run and tell me about it, hoping that I might give a damn when I don't."

"Ah, but here you are," Billie said.

"Hey, women and their boots, right?"

Billie showed her palms. "Won't happen again."

Marian turned as if to go, but then stopped, as if something were holding her there against her will. "Has he made an offer yet?"

"Ryker?"

"Yeah, Ryker."

"No, but he's going to."

"You going to take it?"

"He's offering me more than market value," Billie said. "I guess I would be a fool not to." She paused briefly. "You're suddenly acting as if you have a dog in this fight, after telling me the other night you didn't. All I'm trying to do is pay off the old man's debts. You do understand that, right?"

"I'll bet he's offered to buy the livestock, too."

Billie had a drink of beer, wiping her mouth afterward. "What if he has? He can have the goddamn horses. More money for me. Like I said, I'm not making any off the farm."

"Take the money and run, then," Marian said. "Take it and ske-daddle back to Ohio. That way you won't hear people laughing at you."

Billie had had enough of the cryptic nature of the conversation and of the woman's attitude in general. She didn't care for people who let on that they knew more than everybody else in the room. For one thing, they usually knew less.

"What the fuck is your problem?" she asked.

With that, Marian laughed again. That didn't help the situation, not from Billie's standpoint anyway. If there was one thing worse than being talked down to, it was being laughed at.

"You really believe that Reese Ryker is wining and dining you because he's desperate to buy Will Masterson's thirty acres? You haven't stopped to ask yourself why?"

Billie shrugged. "I don't care why. I look at him and I see some rich asshole with too much money and not a lot of brains. The world's full of people like that. We have one in the White House right now."

"Listen," Marian said. "You can do whatever you want. But you really need to know one thing—Ryker doesn't have the slightest interest in the farm. All he cares about is that gray colt."

Billie had the mug of beer halfway to her mouth. She hesitated, thinking back to the young horse in the paddock. Of how Ryker had stopped to appraise the animal when he'd come to call yester-day, never giving the broodmares a glance.

"What's so special about the colt?"

"Well now, you've been here three days and you're finally asking a question," Marian said. "Maybe there's hope for you yet, Billie Masterson."

With that, she unslung the purse from her shoulder and sat down in the chair opposite. Since spotting her earlier, Billie had been fervently hoping the woman wouldn't come over and join her. Now she wasn't so sure.

"I've been here three days and I haven't told you to go fuck yourself . . . yet. Answer the question."

Marian turned in her chair, looking toward the bar. "If I'm going to get cursed at, I want a beer." She signaled to the waitress. "Bring us a couple of drafts."

Billie saw that her glass was nearly empty and drained it before looking at the older woman across from her. "Well?"

"You know of a horse named Saguaro?" Marian asked.

"Yeah, I've heard of Saguaro."

"That's the sire."

Billie sat silently for a moment, wondering—once again—if there was something she was missing. She seemed out of step with everyone she met or talked to. Dealing with these people was like playing Scrabble blindfolded.

"The old man drove a twenty-year-old pickup," she said. "He couldn't afford Saguaro's stud fee if he sold his soul to the devil. So what are you talking about?"

"Your father considered himself an expert on two things," Marian said. "What were they?"

Billie shrugged. "I have no idea. Whiskey and women."

"I'm not going to comment on that," Marian said. She paused as the waitress delivered the drafts. She had a drink before looking at Billie again. "He knew horses and he knew cards, particularly cribbage."

"I guess," Billie said.

"Now you know who Humphrey Brown is, right? The multi-billionaire?"

Billie nodded. "Except I heard he gave it all away."

"Apparently he did, or most of it, anyway," Marian said. "But before that, going back three years, he owned Saguaro. He made a lot of money off the horse, not that he needed any more money. And he liked to play cribbage with your father in the lounge

of the old Paducah racetrack. One night they got into a mara-
thon match—cards and bourbon, I'm sure you know the routine.
Sometime around three or four in the morning, they decided on
one last game. Now how can your father compete financially with
Humphrey Brown? He can't, obviously. So they set the stakes for
this one game—Will's old pickup truck against one service call
from Saguaro. And Will won the game. About a month later he
trailered that chestnut mare over to Brown's stable in Louisville
and had her bred. All legal and registered. The stud fee was one
dollar. A week after that, Brown sold Saguaro to Double R Racing,
owned by your new best friend Reese Ryker. Of course, Brown had
known all along he was going to sell the horse. What did he care if
Will got a foal out of the deal?"

Billie reached for the fresh draft. "So Reese wants Cactus Jack
because he owns the sire."

"That's right," Marian said. "But he more than wants it—he's
obsessed with the colt. He apparently went ballistic when it
leaked out what had happened between your father and Brown.
He couldn't believe that Brown bred the top stallion in the world
to one of Will Masterson's B track broodmares. He actually offered
your father a hundred grand for the mare while she was in foal."

Billie shook her head. "And the old man turned him down. Of
course he turned him down. Why would a man ass-over-teakettle
in debt want a hundred thousand dollars when he could stick with
a pig in a poke?"

"And who are we talking about here?" Marian asked. "Not only
did he turn Ryker down, he named the colt Cactus Jack. One cactus begets another."

Billie thought about it a moment. "So—that whole song and
dance last night was about the colt, not the farm. Why wouldn't
he just make me an offer on the horse? I couldn't care less about
the animal."

"He's probably worried he'd find out that you're your father's
daughter," Marian suggested.

"Nice try," Billie said. "But that sentimental shit doesn't pay the mortgage." She turned the draft glass in her hands. "Besides, how does Ryker even know the horse can run? That's a crapshoot even when both the sire and dam are top of the line. And three years on—doesn't he have lots of colts already from Saguaro?"

Marian scoffed. "Come on, he's not going to run him. He's going to geld him. He doesn't give two hoots about the colt. All he cares about is the bloodline. That's all those people ever care about. You think he wanted Will to run that colt and maybe win some races and then stand the horse at stud? Advertising him all over the world as being by Saguaro? Not a chance. And now it sounds as if he's worried you might try the same thing. One thing he's got going for him is your ignorance of the situation."

"Until now," Billie said as she took a drink. "But doesn't everybody in the business know about the colt? It must be common knowledge."

Marian shrugged. "Everybody looked at it as a joke. Eccentric old Humphrey Brown playing a prank on the thoroughbred world. Plus, he didn't much care for Reese Ryker and I think he liked getting the last laugh on him—*after* he sold him Saguaro for twenty-seven million dollars."

Billie remembered something from the night before and smiled.

"What?" Marian asked.

"Apparently Ryker owns some TV station?"

"Yeah, in Louisville."

"Well, he came this close to offering me a job there last night," Billie said. "Told me I was purty enough to be on air. Pulling out all the stops, I guess."

"You're pretty enough," Marian said, "and you're white enough, too."

"Really?" Billie asked. "That's the way it is?"

Marian, drinking, didn't respond, but then she didn't need to. Billie considered Ryker's attitude toward their server at the restaurant the night before. His attitude toward everything, it seemed.

"I could sell the colt to somebody else."

"You could," Marian said. "I told your father that. He said it wouldn't fetch a big price because of the dam. He said that nobody knows how good a two-year-old is going to be anyway, no matter what the blood."

"I just said that."

"I heard you. Your father wouldn't sell him anyway. He wanted to run him. He thought the horse was something special."

Billie remembered what David Clay had said, about the colt and her father's expectations. "That would be the latest in a long line of horses he felt that way about," Billie said. "Like I said, he drove a twenty-year-old pickup."

Marian shrugged. "He liked that truck."

"He could have learned to like a brand-new one, if he wasn't broke his whole life."

Marian took a drink. "Well, I felt an obligation to explain the situation. You do what you want to do, Billie. And you're welcome to wear the boots whenever you want."

Billie smiled. "They're nice boots."

Marian pushed the half-full glass aside and stood up, reaching for her purse. "I have to go to the city."

"I have no choice but to sell," Billie said quickly, stopping her. "I don't like Ryker misrepresenting himself, and to tell the truth I don't like him, either. But I have to sell to the top bidder. That's just business. And if a gray colt that I first laid eyes on three days ago has to lose his testicles in the process, that's the way it has to be."

"Then that's the way it will be," Marian said. "The beers are on me."

Billie watched as she paid on her way out. When she was gone Billie sat there alone and finished her beer, then reached for the one left behind by Marian.

In the parking lot her car wouldn't start again, the battery barely turning the engine over. A man and a woman in a van were just leaving and they jumped the Taurus for her. On the way out of town she stopped at the Quikmart, leaving the car running, and picked up bread and cheese and eggs and more beer. There was a deli counter off to the side, with sandwiches made to go. She got a chicken salad on whole wheat. Approaching the farm, she drove around to the side road and into the back lane leading to the barns.

Jodie had managed to put the wheels on the pony cart and drag it outside into the sun. She was sanding away at the buggy shafts as Billie rolled to a stop, dust in her hair and on her face. Billie got out, carrying the groceries and beer.

"You need a dust mask," she told the girl.

Jodie looked at her but made no reply. Billie reached into the bag for the sandwich and tossed it on the seat of the cart.

"I bought an extra sandwich and now I'm not hungry," she said. "You might as well have it or it'll go to waste."

Jodie stared at the package as if it might be booby-trapped. Billie put the groceries on the hood of her car and went into the pump room. She connected the charger to the battery on the shelf and plugged it in. The gauge showed it as half-charged. Leaving the charger connected, she retrieved the groceries and walked up the hill to the house. When she got to the back door, she turned to see the little girl sitting on the dusty cart, eating the sandwich.

Eleven

MIDAFTERNOON, BILLIE PULLED ON OLD JEANS and a T-shirt and went down to check on the battery, which now showed a full charge. She went into the machine shed for some wrenches and when she came out the gray colt trotted over to her, putting his head over the paddock fence. She stopped to have a better look at him, reaching out to run her hand along the horse's forehead.

"I've been hearing stories about you," she said.

She went to work removing the dead battery from her car. The clamps were corroded and she had trouble loosening them. The wrench wouldn't hold and twice she skinned her knuckles when it slipped.

The pony cart still sat on the sawhorses in the drive. It looked as if the sanding were finished, or as finished as it would get. Jodie was in the back paddock. Billie had seen her from the pump room; she'd put a halter on the brown-and-white pony and had the animal on a lead, working it, talking softly as she did. Billie could hear Will Masterson in the words.

It took a combination of penetrating oil and vise grips and swearing to remove the old battery from the Taurus, but after a half hour she had success. The new (used) battery went in much easier.

After tightening the connections, she smeared the posts and connectors with axle grease to prevent further corrosion, again hearing her father's voice in her head.

As she worked, she toyed with the idea of calling Reese Ryker. *Might as well get on with it*, she thought. She had no desire to wait a few days and even less to wait a few weeks. As she was closing the hood on the car, she heard a noise and looked up to see the Porsche pulling in the front driveway by the house, rendering her concerns moot. Let him be the eager one; now she could play the reluctant seller.

Wiping her hands on a rag she'd found in the shed, she started for the house. Reese met her by the back deck, wearing designer aviator sunglasses, black dress pants, and a short-sleeved polo shirt with the Double R Racing logo on a breast pocket from which a sheet of paper was protruding conspicuously. Approaching, Billie was aware of her dirty jeans and grease-smeared T-shirt. She was annoyed that she would care how she looked but she did.

"I was in the neighborhood—" he began.

"What about a beer?" she said, thinking that she didn't need to hear once again how he just happened to be in the neighborhood. *Try telling the truth for once*, she thought.

He hesitated. Maybe he didn't drink beer. Maybe it was overpriced French cognac or nothing at all.

"I'll have a beer," he said. "What do you have?"

"Bud," Billie said and went into the house to retrieve two bottles. When she returned, Reese was sitting down. He had removed the shades and put them on the table. She handed him a beer, then sat opposite him and took a long pull on the bottle. Watching him, with his too-white teeth and his bronzed complexion and his expensive clothes, she began to feel a little contentious, knowing now what she hadn't before. But she couldn't let that influence her. She reminded herself that all she cared about was settling things up and heading home. As she had told Marian, it was business. She wasn't in the mood for small talk, and fortunately, neither was

Ryker. He took the smallest of sips from the bottle before pulling the paper from his shirt pocket.

"I was at my lawyer's office this morning on another matter and while I was there I had him draw up an offer sheet for your farm. I might as well tell you that I did talk to a realtor who I happen to trust, and he gave me a ballpark figure on what he might assess the place at. Sight unseen, granted, but he knows the area and he knows the business. Given what he suggested, I think you'll find this a fair number."

Billie glanced at the sheet, skipping over the legalese to the number at the bottom. The offer was three hundred thousand. Reese's trusted realtor buddy was a little on the high side, unless Reese had upped the number himself, looking for a strike on his first cast. If he thought that three hundred grand was bait enough for Billie to take, he was absolutely right.

"Did you get a chance to talk to anyone yet about an appraisal?" he asked.

Billie, still looking at the number, nodded.

"That offer is rock solid," Reese added. "Am I in the ballpark?"

Billie leaned forward to put the paper on the table. "You're in the ballpark."

She told herself she wasn't lying. After all, who knew the definition of *ballpark*? It seemed to her that a word used as a metaphor couldn't have a precise definition. So she was sort of telling the truth, not that she had any particular aversion to lying. Everybody did it, under certain circumstances. If your friend gets a haircut that makes her look like a mangy sheepdog, you don't tell her that. And in this case the man making the offer was the liar, or at least the one misrepresenting himself. If he would not tell the truth, then Billie would, in her way. She indicated the paper.

"That's for lock, stock, and barrel?"

"That's it." Reese gestured behind her. "Like I said, I might rent the house out to one of my employees." He turned in his chair to look down the hill. "The buildings—I don't know. I'll want to build a new stable."

"And the horses?"

"Probably let them go at auction," Reese said.

"You wouldn't want to run that two-year-old?" Billie asked. "I noticed you looking him over the other day."

Reese laughed. "Do you know how many two-year-olds I'll be running this year? No offense to your father, Billie, but that horse might be a five-thousand-dollar claimer at best."

Billie took a drink of beer. "But the sire isn't a five-thousand-dollar claimer."

She had succeeded in rattling him. To try to hide it, he reached for the beer he didn't want and had another sip, nodding his head slightly in agreement. He could hardly disagree. And did he actually think that Billie wouldn't know that the colt's sire was Saguaro? But then she hadn't known, not until a few hours ago.

"No, it's not," he said after a moment. "The thing is—you need the blood from both sides of the equation when breeding. And the dam in this case—well, again, I don't want to offend your father."

"The dam ain't up to snuff," Billie suggested.

"That's the hard truth of it," Reese said. "Bloodlines are bloodlines, doesn't matter if you're talking about horses or dogs or people even. There's an old saying—you can't make a racehorse out of a pig."

"But you can make a very fast pig," Billie said. "That's from Steinbeck. Or did you think that your father came up with that one, too?"

Reese stiffened in the chair. "I don't know where it came from. I'm just telling you that it takes two to tango. I already own the best two-year-old in the country, in my opinion, a colt named Ghost Rider. I'm running him in the Mercedes Mile next month and then he's going straight to the Breeders Juvenile. Which he will win. He's by Saguaro and a mare named Lady Jane, who has Northern Dancer in her line. *That's* the type of breeding that creates champions."

Billie felt somewhat satisfied that she had raised his ire, even if it had required insulting his father to do it. She looked down the hill. Jodie was now brushing the pony out, while the donkey and goat stood by, watching the proceedings as if they thought they would be next.

"And you'd bulldoze the barns?"

Reese nodded. "They look like they're about ready for the wrecking ball."

"Any chance you could do something for the kid and her little menagerie there?"

Reese regarded the scene below for a moment. "What would you suggest?"

"I don't know," Billie said. "I thought you might have a couple of open stalls somewhere, with all your holdings."

"For donkeys and goats? I think it unlikely." He looked again. "Is that your daughter, Billie?"

Billie shook her head. "Some stray my father took a shine to. Lives the next road over. Typical story, broken family." She took a swig of beer and kept talking, against her better judgment. Why not let it go and stick to the business at hand? "You know how it is. She's got this little family of animals to love because she's never known any at home."

"And the cycle will repeat itself," Reese said. "That's the way it is with these people. I don't know what the solution is. In the end, they certainly don't contribute anything positive to society."

Maybe all they needed was a father smart enough to marry an heiress with a couple billion dollars in the bank, Billie thought, watching the smug face across from her.

"I guess it comes down to the blood, like you said," she suggested, baiting him. "Maybe what we need in this country is a sterilization plan." She paused, watching him. "Start gelding some people. What do you think?"

Reese laughed. "I've heard worse ideas. Looking at that girl there, I'd say her breeding was definitely in question."

"What are you suggesting?"

"That you don't have to be a dog to be a mongrel," Reese said smiling.

Billie felt her blood rise as she glanced down the hill to the girl.

"This one here is a stubborn little thing," she said, trying to control the fury in her voice. "Got a bit of a mouth on her, too."

"Comes with the territory," Reese said. "You can only imagine what she hears at home."

Billie nodded as she took a drink. The beer tasted like ashes. "You know who she reminds me of?"

"I can't imagine."

"Me," Billie said. She reached for the paper with the rock-solid three-hundred-thousand-dollar offer and folded it in half before handing it to Reese Ryker. "I've changed my mind. I think I'll stick around a while."

Billie called David Clay to make sure he was available and then changed out of her dirty clothes. Before walking down the hill to her car, she had a thought and went into the cellar of the house. The old man had always kept random cans of paint—half or quarter full—down there among the cobwebs, out of the weather if the temperature dropped below freezing. The cans were lined on a shelf upside down, his method for sealing the lids. She was counting on Will Masterson's packrat mentality, but she really didn't expect to find what she was looking for. She did, though. There were brushes there too, thoroughly cleaned, their bristles wrapped tightly in cellophane.

Beside the barn the pony cart was still balanced across the sawhorses and Jodie was back at her sanding. Billie set the half gallon of paint on the ground and placed the brush on top.

"You keep sanding and there'll be nothing left of that cart but dust. It's time to start painting."

Jodie looked at the dried paint along the lip of the can. "It's red, like before."

"Of course it is," Billie said. "Will Masterson was of the opinion that red was the only color suitable for barns, tractors, wagons, and bicycles. Pony carts, too. Make sure you clean that brush when you're finished. I saw a can of turpentine in the shed."

It was past five o'clock when she drove into Marshall. David Clay said he would be in the bar of the Bellwood Hotel and that's where she found him, sitting at a table opposite the booth where Billie had eaten lunch earlier that day, where she'd had the enlightening conversation with her father's girlfriend. Had that really only been a few hours ago?

"Tell me about the old man's plans for that colt," she said when she was sitting across from him and waiting for a beer.

Clay was drinking bourbon and water. He'd ordered another when Billie had asked for beer. "Why would you want to know that?"

"Why do you think?" Billie asked.

Clay rattled the ice in his glass. "I figured the animal to be in Reese Ryker's barn any day now. I hear that the two of you are doing business together."

Billie shook her head. "For a guy who has spent his whole life stretching the truth like a rubber band, I'm surprised you would pay attention to idle gossip."

Clay was not offended in the least. In fact, he smiled and waited until the waitress arrived with the drinks. "Your father was going to race the colt," he said when she was gone. "What on Earth did you think he would do with it?"

"I'm asking about specifics," Billie said. "Where was he working it? And when was he going to run it?"

"He's got a stall over at Chestnut Field," Clay said. "As for when, I have no notion. Soon, I would think. You know the thorough-bred game, Billie—midsummer you start to see the juveniles run."

"What little I knew I forgot," Billie said.

Clay poured the dregs of his first drink—if it actually was his first—into the new arrival. "What happened between you and Mr. Ryker? Don't tell me he couldn't meet your price."

"We had philosophical differences," Billie said.

"I can just imagine." Clay drank from the glass. "And now you've come to me, seeking counsel. I hope you don't think I can tell you how to make a go of things out there on the homestead, in light of the mountain of debt you've inherited."

"Are you fucking kidding me?" Billie demanded. "You're the one who got all pouty when I told you I was going to sell the place."

Clay laughed, his big stomach heaving. "It's my nature to be devil's advocate. I do it mainly for my own recreation. I'm too old and fat for sex and I hate golf. What else is there?"

Billie drank her beer and said nothing. She'd let the old lawyer enjoy himself for a while. In due time though he would keep talking, because that was also his nature.

"All right," he conceded. "I would say that you are correct—the gray colt is the key if you intend to get out of hock. So you have two choices—race the animal and hope he's got a modicum of the speed his sire had, or put him on the market today, before he runs even one time, and see what kind of a price he'll fetch based on his lineage."

"On the subject of the colt," Billie said, "is there any particular reason that you didn't want to tell me that the fucking horse was by Saguaro in the first place?"

"Language," Clay lectured. "That's twice now. Keep in mind this is a public house."

"Fuck you."

"There's the hat trick." The lawyer laughed again. He was having a very nice time, it seemed. "Would you have everything handed to you on a platter, Billie? If so, you should have made the deal with Ryker."

"Not an option," Billie said. "What do you think the colt's worth?"

"I haven't a clue," Clay said as he took another drink. "I suspect not a whole lot, untested as it is. People are going to look at the dam. You'd have to find someone willing to take a gamble on the horse being something special. Otherwise, I don't know, you might get twenty or thirty thousand for him."

"That's not going to get me out of the red."

"No, it's not," Clay said. "So sell the colt to Ryker."

"No."

"Okay." Clay drank half the whiskey in his glass and looked at Billie's beer, which was nearly full. "Who's paying for the drinks, by the way?"

"You are."

"I'll have another anyway."

"I thought you might," Billie said. "Okay—let's say I can't sell him for a price. What do I need to do to get the horse ready to run?"

"You need a trainer first," Clay said. "I guess you could start at Chestnut Field. Your father considered that his home track. The manager there is a man called Caldwell. He's a carpetbagger, a bit of a lickspittle, but he knew your father and might be able to point you in the right direction. How do you intend to pay a trainer, though? Do you have money?"

"Not so you'd notice."

"Your father left you a little bit," Clay said. "I don't know if it's enough because I don't know what a trainer makes. If you found one genuinely excited about the colt, perhaps you could work out some sort of a contingency agreement."

"Do people still use the term *carpetbagger*?"

"I do."

"Because you're ancient?"

"Because I'm colorful."

Billie took a swallow of the cold draft, thinking about her situation. Growing up, she'd spent a lot of time with her father around the various racetracks in the state, but she couldn't say she knew much about the game. Back then, it was more about being with him. She had picked up a little, through osmosis, but she never felt as if she needed to study the business because he knew everything there was to know. Not that said knowledge ever led to any kind of financial success.

"This all sounds pretty iffy to me," she said.

"What does?"

"Betting everything on a horse that's never run before."

"That's because it is," Clay said. "Matter of fact, some might say it's downright foolish."

Billie looked at him for a moment. "Anybody ever tell you that you are an infuriating man?"

"A number of people. Mrs. Clay mostly." Smiling, he took another drink. "Look at it this way, Billie. You can take a chance with the horse, and if it doesn't pan out, you still have the farm, which you can sell for enough money to get you clear on the debt. Which, I might remind you, was your intent all along. So why not take the chance? You could look at it as a challenge, maybe one that you've been wanting on a subconscious level. Maybe even needing, at this point in your life."

"Little bit of bourbon and you get all psychoanalytical," Billie said.

"How do you know I've only had a little bit?"

Billie glanced around the room, which was filling up, people getting off work, she guessed. Many wore jackets and ties. She wouldn't have guessed that Marshall had much of a white-collar labor force.

"Are you suggesting that the old man set this up on purpose?" she asked.

"Not at all," Clay said. "He didn't intend on dying last week. He was going to run that colt himself. No, this is more a matter of serendipity. An extremely underrated facet of life—serendipity. Don't you agree?"

"I've never given it much thought," Billie said.

"I have," Clay said. "As a matter of fact, when I was a young man, I dabbled in the thoroughbred game myself. I bought a colt at the Keeneland auction one year, a beautiful chestnut sired by the great Secretariat. I named that animal Serendipity."

"Could he run?"

"Not a lick," Clay said as he drained his glass. "Not a lick."

Twelve

CHUCK CALDWELL SAT BACK IN HIS chair with his feet on the desk and studied the woman standing across from him. He had been expecting her, after getting a heads-up from Reese Ryker the day before. Ryker had called to discuss the stalls he wanted at Chestnut Field and then casually mentioned that Caldwell might be getting a visit from Will Masterson's daughter. Reese hadn't said that the woman was a looker—tall and blonde, dressed in jeans and a tank top beneath a faded green work shirt. It occurred to Caldwell that Reese had called just to bring up the woman's name. As far as the stalls went, he seemed to be hedging his bets on the subject. Caldwell got the sense he was being tested.

"Your father did have a stall here," Caldwell told the woman. "After he passed—we assumed it wouldn't be needed."

"Was it paid for?" Billie asked.

"I'd have to check the paperwork," Caldwell said. "Some owners pay monthly, in which case it would lapse in a few days."

"Could you do that?"

"When I get a chance, yes."

Billie stalled, apparently hoping he would check while she waited. He had no intention of doing that. Why check when he already knew the answer?

"I'm in the market for a trainer," she went on. "Could you recommend one?"

"For that horse?" Caldwell said. "I don't think so."

"And why not?"

Caldwell leaned forward to grab a pack of gum from his desk. "I understand there were some questions about the animal. Ethical questions."

"What are you talking about?"

Caldwell put a piece of gum in his mouth. "With regards to timing. Your father said that he bred his mare to Saguaro a few days before Humphrey Brown sold the stallion to Reese Ryker. Reese Ryker wonders if that's true. He wonders if he made the deal for the stallion and then Brown had the horse breed your father's mare after the fact. Which would mean that Reese Ryker should have been paid the stud fee."

"That would mean that both my father and Humphrey Brown are guilty of fraud and of doing something pretty unethical," Billie said. "Two guys who were in the thoroughbred business their whole lives."

"There's a theory that it was all a joke, concocted by the two of them to thumb their nose at the game." Caldwell crumpled the gum wrapper and lobbed it into a waste basket in the corner, a direct hit. There were other wrappers on the floor surrounding the basket.

"Except that neither one of them would do that," Billie said. "Funny—I've spent some time with Reese Ryker recently and he never mentioned this fraud theory to me. You think it would have come up. Maybe he was too busy trying to buy the colt from me under false pretenses. Maybe he came up with this new story after I told him to take a flying fuck at the moon yesterday."

"I doubt you spoke like that to a man like Reese Ryker," Caldwell said. "Do you have any idea how much he's worth?"

"You saying I can tell a poor man to go fuck himself but not a rich one?"

Caldwell shook his head. He wasn't going to trade barbs with the woman. "The story is out there. If I was a trainer, I'd be wary of getting involved."

"But you're not a trainer," Billie said. "What are you again?"

"I manage this facility and have been doing so for fifteen years," Caldwell said. "Part of my job is to keep everything that happens here above reproach."

"Wouldn't finding my father's rental agreement fall under that category?" Billie asked.

Caldwell smiled and said nothing, chewing the gum.

"One other thing," Billie said. "I need to talk to a workout rider named Skeeter Musgrave."

"Musgrave," Caldwell said slowly. "I don't know that name."

"For somebody's who's been running this place for all those years, you don't seem to know much," Billie said. "I'll be back for that agreement."

The first person Billie ran into when she went to the backstretch knew who Skeeter Musgrave was and where to find him. The man was sitting in a lawn chair in front of one of the sheds. He was all alone, sunning himself, his eyes closed beneath a battered fedora.

"I've been working the colt," he said when Billie asked. His voice was as rough as quarry rock. He looked Billie over, but not in the lascivious manner that Chuck Caldwell had. Skeeter Musgrave was simply sizing her up, as if he might be able to judge her potential with a critical first look. Billie's father had a habit of doing the same thing. He was wrong as often as he was right but that never stopped him from doing it.

"I saw you at the funeral," he said. He pushed the hat back onto his forehead, revealing a widow's peak of steel gray. His nose and cheeks were shot with tiny red lines.

Billie hadn't noticed him at the time, but then there had been fifty or sixty people there and at the graveyard afterward. At five foot two or three, Musgrave would have easily gotten lost in the shuffle.

"I thought you might come around," he said. "Are you looking to sell the colt?"

"I'm not sure what I'm going to do with him," Billie admitted.

"If I was a little bit younger and a lot richer, I'd make an offer on him."

"Why?" Billie asked. "Is he that good?"

"I have no idea," Musgrave said. "He can sure as hell run but that don't mean diddly until you get him on a track with eight or ten other horses. *That's* when you find out where the bear shit in the buckwheat."

Billie hesitated, then decided she could live without clarification about defecating bears.

"Have you seen the workouts?" Musgrave asked.

"No."

Musgrave got to his feet and started for a black pickup truck parked along the shed row lane, the fenders encrusted in mud, the wheel wells rusted out. He walked with the peculiar gait of most jocks and ex-jocks, slightly bowlegged, with rolling hips and a pronounced limp. He reached through the open window of the truck to retrieve a notebook.

"Your father has these numbers somewhere but I always keep a record of my own," he said, returning. "Don't ask me why." He leafed through the pages until he found what he wanted. "Cactus Jack—here we are. Three furlongs in thirty-three two. Four furlongs, forty-five two and forty-four eight."

"And that's good?" Billie asked.

"That's good," Musgrave said. "I mean, it ain't stop the goddamn presses good, but the horse has got some speed. Can't tell how it might finish, not until you get to the dance. But there's something more than speed to consider."

"And what's that?"

"That horse knows who he is," Musgrave said. "You see that every now and again, with horses and with, I don't know, ballplayers and the like. It seems as if the game slows down for them while it's speeding up for everybody else. You get that colt out there on the dirt and the animal is just plain relaxed. Not a lot of thoroughbreds have that; a thoroughbred's wound up by nature and by breeding. They say Saguaro had it when he raced. I expect that's where this colt got it."

"I just talked to a guy named Caldwell who says he doesn't think my father had a stall rented here for the season."

Musgrave shook his head. "That boy up there in the office knows about as much about the business as I do about the Russian ballet. Ask to see the agreement."

"I did," Billie said. "He said he'd have a look for it after he finished chewing his gum. Or something like that." She paused. "So you would recommend I run the horse?"

"I would."

"I need a trainer," Billie said. "And I don't have much money to pay one. Can you suggest anybody?"

"That'll work for free?" Skeeter squinted as he considered the question. "There's a couple here I like," he said after a moment. "I don't know that they're looking to work on the cuff. But I can give you their names."

"I'd appreciate it."

The old man jotted down a couple of names in the notebook, then paused for a bit before adding another. Tearing the page from the book, he handed it over. "You talk to Reese Ryker about the horse?"

Billie was looking at the names. "I have talked to Reese Ryker about a number of things. Why do you ask that?"

"He was here," Skeeter said. "Yesterday. He was asking about the colt and then he told me that he had a claim on the animal. Said that Saguaro belonged to him when he bred your father's mare."

"Do you believe that?"

"Not on your nelly."

"You said he was asking about the colt?"

"He was."

"What was he asking?"

"Same thing you're asking," Skeeter said. "About the workouts, the times, all that. I didn't tell him nothing."

"Why not?"

"I didn't like the way he was asking."

When Billie got back to the farm it was nearly noon. The pony cart was sitting in the sun by the barn, gleaming with a fresh coat of paint that was, Billie discovered when she touched it, still wet. She looked around for the little girl but she wasn't there.

But Marian was. Her SUV was parked by the house, the back hatch open. When Billie walked inside, she was coming down the stairs carrying an armload of stuff. There was a large cardboard box on the dining room table. Inside Billie could see books and toiletries, a few items of clothing, a pair of pink slippers. The Tony Lama boots with the red trim were on a chair.

Billie merely nodded when Marian said hello. She wasn't happy that the woman had walked in with nobody there. And it bothered her that it bothered her. It wasn't a matter of trust, so what was it? Maybe just the fact that Marian was more at home in the house than she was, that she'd had more of Will Masterson these past years than Billie. But whose fault was that?

"I had no idea how much stuff I had here," Marian said. "I let myself in. I didn't think you'd mind."

Billie shrugged.

"I'll leave my key," Marian said, sensing the attitude. "I thought I'd better do this now. I wasn't sure how far along you were with Reese Ryker."

"How far along?" Billie asked.

"Toward selling the place."

Billie went into the kitchen and got a beer from the fridge. Opening it, she walked back into the living room. "I'm not selling the place. I wouldn't sell those ratty slippers to Reese Ryker."

Marian looked at the slippers, which were practically new. "You're not selling to Ryker, or you're not selling at all?"

"I don't know," Billie said. "But not to Ryker."

She drank from the bottle and went over to the window. Looking down the hill, she saw the gray colt standing by the hayrick with the two broodmares. Jodie must have fed them. The pony cart sat gleaming in the afternoon sun. Billie thought back through the years to when she had painted it. She'd gotten more red on her than on the cart, it had seemed. It was oil-based paint and her mother had scrubbed her for a half hour to remove it. Billie wondered if Jodie had gone home in the same state. Would her mother help her clean up? Probably not.

Billie turned to see Marian putting more stuff in the box. "I was just over at Chestnut Field, talking to a little old guy who tells me that I should race the colt. He says the horse is fast and that he knows himself, or something like that. And there was something else about a bear shitting somewhere."

"I always liked old Skeeter."

"You know him?" Billie said. "Of course you know him. You and the old man were attached at the hip, apparently. You can probably tell me where the registration papers are for the colt, and the damn lease agreement for the stall at Chestnut."

"That stuff is in a box under his bed," Marian said. "Where else would Will Masterson keep his valuables? I have to say, you seem a little on the crusty side today, Billie. Even for you."

Billie took another drink but said nothing. Marian watched her a moment and then shrugged. She walked over to retrieve a framed print of Elvis Presley from a sideboard along the wall. There was a twenty-dollar bill tucked along the edge of the glass.

"I'd like to have this if you don't mind," she said. "Will bought it for me when we went to Graceland. When I wasn't looking he signed Elvis's name on the twenty and tried to tell me it was genuine."

"Take it," Billie said.

"I just want the print," Marian said, sliding the bill out from under the glass and handing it to Billie. "The money is yours."

"Graceland," Billie said. "Did he just want to be your teddy bear?"

"All right," Marian said. "I won't tell you any more stories about Will and me."

"Did you slow dance to Nat King Cole?" Billie asked. "He and my mother slow danced to Nat King Cole."

"We danced to Tony Bennett."

"I don't care," Billie said.

"Then you shouldn't have asked."

Billie stuffed the twenty into one of the Tony Lama boots and left. She walked outside to the deck and stood there for a while, drinking the beer. Down the hill the colt was now trotting back and forth along the paddock fence, watching her, as if he knew he'd been a topic of conversation of late. As if he too wanted to get on with things. After a while Marian came out to put the house key on the table.

"So tell me," Billie said, still watching the horse. "How come you and the old man hit it off? What did you have?"

"I didn't have anything," Marian said. "The answer is simple. When I first met your father he was pushing seventy. If he'd been twenty-five years younger, we'd have never lasted. You know he was a wild one. Where do you think you got it from?"

"You saying I'm just like him?"

"Seems to be the consensus."

"Sounds to me like you've been talking to lawyer Clay," Billie said. "You probably know that he told me the truth about my mother."

"Yes, and I wish he hadn't."

"Why?"

"Because if your father had wanted you to know, he'd have told you."

"Maybe he should have," Billie said.

Marian looked at her but said nothing.

"Well, I know now," Billie said.

"Are you any better for the knowledge?" Marian asked.

"I can't answer that," Billie told her. "I guess I'm no worse."

Thirteen

IT WAS BILLIE'S BAD LUCK THAT the quarter horse racing circuit had moved out of Kentucky ten days earlier and was now in Missouri. She passed a few days weighing her options, or rather watching them diminish, then on Sunday she got into her car and drove west.

She'd had an unproductive week. Chuck Caldwell had told her that she had no right to the stall Will had rented at Chestnut Field, even after Billie had shown him the contract she'd found, as Marian had said she would, in a shoebox under her father's bed, along with the registration for Cactus Jack, a few photos of Billie as a child riding her pony, her parents' marriage license, and an Army Colt revolver that looked as if it might have gone up San Juan Hill. Caldwell had said that the contract didn't mean anything, as the agreement was made with Will Masterson, not Billie.

Billie also got the sense that Caldwell had been talking to any number of people about Reese Ryker's claim regarding the colt. She had contacted eight trainers over the course of the week and every one of them said they didn't believe his theory, just before saying that they didn't want to get involved with a horse that might become part of a legal battle. Before leaving that morning,

Billie had called David Mountain Clay and given him an update, thinking he might dispense some sage legal advice. The man was uncharacteristically quiet and not in the least bit helpful. Maybe he was pissed off that Billie had called on a Sunday.

Luke Walker wasn't on the list Skeeter had given her. He'd been Billie's idea, one that she would file under the category of last resort. She caught up to the quarter horses in Poplar Bluff. The track there was a few miles out of town, near the east bank of the river and beneath the bluff itself. By the time Billie arrived and paid her admission, the card was half over. She didn't spot Luke until the last race, which he won aboard a muley-looking bay gelding that was listed as eleven years old in the program. Under Luke, the horse looked like it had wings.

Billie went down to the backstretch after the race and immediately ran into Steve McGee, who was loading the very same gelding into a double trailer. At first he didn't recognize Billie.

"Goddamn," he said when he did. "What the hell are you doing here?" He looked past her, as if he might see something there that would explain her sudden appearance.

"Looking for Luke," she said.

"Luke?" He seemed surprised by that too and why wouldn't he be? Billie was fairly surprised herself. "Well, you just missed him. He jumped off this gelding and into a Camaro with some girl that's been hanging around here all night."

That part did not surprise Billie. "Any idea where they went?"

"It's Luke," Steve said. "You know where they went. He's been drinking at a place called the River Flats, on the way into town. You can't miss it." He eyed Billie narrowly. "Why do you want to talk to Luke?"

"I'm not sure that I *want* to," Billie said. "But I feel like I need to."

The River Flats was a honky-tonk bar with a corrugated steel roof and a gravel parking lot. The place was relatively busy for a Sunday night—cowboys and cowgirls, bikers and carpenters, teenagers and geezers trying to look like teenagers, their hair spiked, noses pierced. There was a band playing, and what they lacked in talent they made up for in volume. The lead singer was a tall redhead, a walking tattoo with a screeching falsetto.

Billie found a place at the bar and ordered a Bud. She'd spotted Luke Walker when she entered, sitting at a corner table with a half dozen people, among them a young woman of twenty-five or so—a voluptuous girl whose cropped T-shirt did nothing to hide that fact. She was, Billie suspected, the driver of the Camaro Steve had mentioned. Luke, holding forth, had eyes only for the girl and hadn't noticed Billie's arrival. As she drank her beer the band announced that it would take a break, mercifully, and the room grew somewhat quieter, at least quiet enough for Billie to hear Luke's familiar voice in full storytelling mode.

"I still say that sonofabitch Nevada Ned loosened my girth when I wasn't looking," he was saying. "Anyway, halfway down the track my saddle starts to slide and I'm hanging on to this nag like a flea on a jackrabbit. By the time I crossed the finish line I'm sitting on that horse's rump, holding onto the reins like a man driving a goddamn stagecoach." He paused to look at the pretty girl. "At this point I feel compelled to tell you that I did win the race."

"Nobody loosened your girth." This from a bearded man in a black cowboy hat, sitting at the table. "You were nipping at the Jim Beam all day and forgot to tighten it."

"I ain't going to admit to any such thing as that," Luke said.

He laughed, looking around the room as he did, and it was then that he spotted Billie. A moment later he was standing beside her. He was not much older than she, but he could have passed for ten years older. He was skinny as ever, with a face that had been exposed to too much sun and too many midnights. He smelled of horse and sweat and of Luke. When he smiled, she saw he was missing a tooth.

"Now where in the hell did you come from?" he asked.

"How are you, Luke?"

"If I was any better, there'd be two of me."

"There has to be a law against that," Billie said.

"Now Billie," he said. "Hey—I heard about your old man. I would have come to the funeral but I was racing up in Montana. Sorry to hear it, though."

Billie nodded. "Can I buy you a beer?"

"You can buy me a whiskey. If you still love me, you'll make it a double."

"A single it is then," Billie said, lifting a hand to get the bartender's attention. When she indicated Luke, the man nodded. Of course he knew what to bring. Half the bartenders in half the states of the union would know.

"You look good, girl," Luke said.

"You look like a boot that somebody left out in the weather all summer long."

"Christ," Luke said, falling silent for a moment. "I thought you were in New York City."

"I was, for about ten minutes once." The drink arrived and Billie paid for it. "Ohio recently. But right now I'm back home."

"Actually right this minute you're in Missouri. Why is that?"

"I inherited a two-year-old thoroughbred that might have some potential. I'm looking for a trainer."

"Well, don't be looking my way," Luke said. "I lost my thoroughbred license a few years ago and I don't care to ever get it back. You have to be rich to run thoroughbreds these days."

"Just what I needed to hear," Billie said. "Seeing as I'm church-mouse poor. What do you have to do to get your license reinstated?"

"Suspension's over, so just pay the fee. But I told you—that ain't happening. I'm strictly a quarter horse man these days." Luke took a drink, eyeing her. "You didn't drive here from Kentucky to ask me to train a horse for you?"

"I did."

"Kentucky is full of trainers."

"None of them want to work this horse," Billie said. "None that are any good anyway. Reese Ryker has put the word out that I'm poison and Cactus Jack is damaged goods."

"What's a Cactus Jack?"

"The colt that I drove two hundred miles to talk to you about."

The bartender brought another whiskey and another Bud for Billie. She paid.

"*Cactus* Jack," Luke repeated. "Not that colt by Saguaro, that little deal your old man and Humphrey Brown dreamed up. He's two already?"

"That's the colt."

Luke thought about it a moment. "Can he run?"

"He hasn't raced yet but his workouts are good."

"When you going to race him?"

"When I get a trainer," Billie said. "Are you having problems with your hearing?"

"My hearing has always been fine," Luke said. "It's my judgment that gets me in trouble."

"Or lack thereof."

He ignored her, something he was always good at, when it served him. But she could see his brain working now, that same brain she had many times suspected was incapable of functioning very well. When it came to horseflesh, though, he was capable of operating on a different level.

"You say the workouts are good? How good?"

Billie told him.

Luke nodded and had a drink, grimacing as if he were fighting an internal battle with himself. "All right, we go to Tennessee in the morning. Running there through the weekend. I figure to be back in Kentucky, I don't know, next Monday or Tuesday after that. I might stop and have a look. Just a look though. It could be I can recommend somebody for the job."

"Okay," Billie said.

"You want to come join us?" Luke said.

Billie shook her head. "I'm going to drive home. Besides, it looks like you got your hands full with that poor girl who can't afford a T-shirt big enough to cover her boobs."

"Watch it—that's my new girlfriend."

"Really? What's her name?"

"Her name is Loretta."

"Loretta who?"

Luke hesitated. "We really haven't gotten around to last names yet. She's only been my girlfriend for a few hours."

"You'll be a teenager when you're ninety, Luke."

"A man can only hope," Luke said as he headed back to the table.

Billie got back to the farm at three-thirty in the morning. She went to bed and fell asleep immediately, something she hadn't been doing of late. Then again, she'd been up for nearly twenty hours and behind the wheel for half of that time. When she woke the sun was full up and streaming in the window. Since arriving back at the house she'd been sleeping in the room that had once been hers. The same double bed was there, although it had been piled high with her father's books and work clothes and other items. Apparently the room had taken on the role of a large junk drawer. She could have slept in the master bedroom but it didn't feel right, especially knowing that the old man had been sharing the bed with his girlfriend these past few years. *Girlfriend* seemed an odd term to use for a woman of Marian's age but Billie couldn't come up with another. *Partner* seemed to suggest a business arrangement, or people who were herding cattle. *Significant other* sounded clinical—and had too many syllables anyway. *Lover* she didn't want to think about.

She heard voices when she woke and got up to look out the window. David Mountain Clay was standing in the lower driveway by the barns, talking to the girl, Jodie. The lawyer was in his shirtsleeves and he had his pants hitched up nearly to his armpits. He was of course doing most of the talking, words that Billie couldn't make out. But she had to assume that he was asking of her whereabouts.

She got up and pulled on the clothes she'd worn for her trip to Missouri, then went into the bathroom to pee and wash her face. Going out the back door, she saw by the kitchen clock that it was ten fifteen. As she started down the hill, David Clay glanced at her, then said something to the girl before getting into his Lincoln and driving off without another look Billie's way.

"What the hell was that?" Billie asked.

Jodie turned to her. She wore rubber boots that were caked with manure. Apparently she'd been cleaning stalls. "What was what?"

"He left," Billie said. "Wasn't he looking for me?"

"I don't think so," Jodie said. "He was looking for me."

Billie watched as the Lincoln made its way along the county road, heading back to Marshall. "Why?"

Jodie reached into the pocket of her shorts and produced a check. "He gave me this."

She held the check out, but Billie already knew what it was. Nice to know that David Clay was looking after the little girl while he barely gave Billie the time of day when she'd called on Sunday.

"I can pay you for my share of the hay now," Jodie said.

"Don't worry about it," Billie said absently.

"I have to pay my share. Will would never say how much I owed so you have to decide."

"I said don't worry about it. Put the money in the bank. And buy yourself some sneakers. Those you're wearing weren't worth ten cents and now you've got red paint all over them."

Jodie fell silent then. It seemed as if something were bothering her, and it occurred to Billie that it wasn't her shoes.

"What?"

"Can you cash the check for me? I don't have a bank account."

Billie wondered if other nine-year-olds had bank accounts. Did she at that age? She couldn't remember but she guessed that she probably did. She would get money for birthdays and other occasions and deposit it. "Get your mother to cash it."

"You can't do it?"

The situation was suddenly clear. Billie put David Clay's rude departure out of her mind, at least for the time being. The little girl didn't want to hand a thousand dollars over to her mother, who didn't work for a living and was apparently spending her days in the company of a petty thief named Troy Everson. Billie didn't blame her. She wasn't thrilled that it fell to her to come up with a solution, but evidently it had.

She glanced toward the front pasture. A few days earlier she had turned the two broodmares and the gray colt out into the field, where the grass was lush and green after the rains. The three were now grazing along the edge of the pond. On her drive home last night, Billie had decided that she needed to get the lease situation at Chestnut Field settled before Luke Walker arrived to look at the colt. In fact, she hoped to have Skeeter Musgrave start exercising the horse again. Before that could happen, she was going to have to deal with Caldwell's contractual bullshit about the stall at Chestnut. She could always trailer the colt back and forth to the track every day, but she'd rather not do that. The horse needed to be in one place. Her father wouldn't trailer the animal every day, so neither would Billie.

"I'm going to Chestnut Field after lunch," she said. "First we'll go to town and you can open an account."

Jodie took a breath, obviously daunted by the task. "Is it hard to do?"

"Not when you have a check for a thousand dollars. They'll probably give you a toaster."

"A toaster?"

"Never mind."

Kentucky First National had been Billie's bank when she was a kid and she decided it would do as well as any other for Jodie. It was downtown, in a four-story granite building with a cornerstone that read 1892. It turned out that Jodie needed the signature of either a parent or a guardian. Billie offered to cosign but was rebuffed.

"My mom will sign," Jodie said.

Billie wasn't happy with that scenario—she suspected that the thousand dollars might not last long around the little girl's mother—but there was nothing she could do about it.

Billie intended to drop the girl off at the farm when they had finished her business and told her so as they walked to the parking lot.

"Why can't I go to Chestnut Field?"

"Because it's not a place for kids," Billie told her.

"Will used to take me."

"Good for Will."

"He told me he used to take you."

They were driving out of town in Will Masterson's truck. The salvaged battery in Billie's car had lasted until her return from Missouri, and when it went dead she gave up and moved on to the old man's truck. It was a five speed on the floor. It had been years since Billie had driven a stick but after a few lurching stalls, she found it was like riding a bike. An old bike with fading paint and an engine that smoked when first started up.

Billie glanced over at the kid, who was buckled in the passenger seat and staring straight ahead.

"I said, Will used to take *you*," the girl repeated.

They were at a stop sign by the highway. Left was Chestnut Field and right was back to the farm. Billie hesitated before turning left.

"You're a pain in the ass," she said.

At Chestnut they parked in the lot reserved for owners and trainers and riders. *Might as well stake my claim*, she decided. She was already on the shit list there, through no fault of her own. There was a card at the track that night, but for now the club-house was nearly empty. Walking through the doors, she spotted Caldwell standing near the wickets, talking to a security officer in a blue windbreaker and baseball cap, a walkie-talkie clipped to his belt. As Billie approached, Caldwell finished his conversation and dismissed the man. Billie didn't wait for him to speak.

"I'll be trailering a horse here in the morning," she said. "And I'll be using the stall my father paid for. If you intend to stop me, you'd better have the cops on hand. And maybe your lawyers too, for that matter."

"Oh, relax," Caldwell said. "Nobody's calling the cops."

"Good," Billie said, backing up a bit. "I'm just saying I don't expect any trouble from you. You got that?"

"I got it," Caldwell said. "I got it when you sent your muscle this morning. Why are you even telling me this?"

What muscle? Billie thought.

"You'd better watch your step," Caldwell said. "That's all I have to say. I have powerful friends, too."

He walked off without saying any more. Billie glanced at Jodie, who'd been standing behind her.

"What the hell was that?" she asked.

The girl shrugged her small shoulders. Billie decided to go out to the shed row, to be sure the stall was empty. Caldwell had backed down a little too quickly for her liking and she suspected he was up to something, but the stall was vacant and clean.

"So are we going to bring Cactus Jack here tomorrow?" Jodie asked.

"*We* aren't doing anything of the kind."

Walking out, they came upon Skeeter Musgrave. He was sitting on a bench in a shaded area between the clubhouse and the track, wearing a denim jacket and work pants.

"Hey," Billie said, approaching. "What are you doing?"

Skeeter shifted his weight, leaning to one side. "Just stopped to rest this damn hip. Feels like we got some weather coming."

"I was going to try to find a phone number for you," Billie said. "You want to breeze a horse for me in the morning?"

Skeeter thought it over before nodding. "Sure."

Walking closer, Billie saw the neck of a flask protruding from the jacket pocket. The man was sober, though.

"Hey, Jodie bug," he said then.

"Hey, Mr. Skeeter," she replied.

Billie glanced from the old man to the girl. "Okay, I'm going to trailer the colt here first thing. Where do I bring him?"

"Jodie can show you."

"I'll be alone."

"I want to come," Jodie said. "I know what to do."

Billie ignored her and kept looking at Skeeter. He pointed to the track, by the three-quarter turn. "There's a gate over there where I can meet you. What time?"

"You tell me."

"Six?"

Christ, Billie thought. "Six it is."

"I thought I'd be seeing you," Skeeter said.

"Why's that?"

"I saw what happened this morning. I was hanging around the barns and after a bit I come to the clubhouse to get a coffee and a fried egg sandwich. That's when I saw the giant."

Jodie's eyes widened.

"You saw a giant," Billie said.

"Yup," Skeeter said. "A giant with long white hair, and he had that peckerwood Caldwell backed into a corner by the front office and man, if he wasn't making that boy eat a bucket of shit." Skeeter glanced at the girl. "I mean a bucket of poop."

"What were they talking about?" Billie asked.

"They were talking about you."

Billie considered that. "Specifically?"

"Specifically about the stall your father rented for the season. The giant was explaining to the peckerwood how it was."

"And what was the peckerwood saying?"

"He was agreeing most wholeheartedly with the giant." Skeeter smiled. "Wouldn't you?"

"I would," Billie said, picturing the scene in her mind. "I'll see you in the morning."

Jodie didn't say anything until they were almost to the farm. Billie was quiet too, thinking the day had gone better than most she'd had of late. Finally the girl looked over at her.

"Was the man really a giant?"

"No."

"What was he?"

"He was a lawyer," Billie said.

They raced on Saturday at a track east of Nashville, near the town of Lebanon. Luke rode his bay gelding and won big. Steve's mare pulled up the first time out and he had to scratch her. It looked like a tendon problem but he wasn't sure. If it was bad, he'd be in the market for another horse to run.

That evening they ended up at a bar in Nashville. There was a pretty good band, playing old school country, and dancing, with lots of pretty women doing the dancing. They'd left the horses at a friend's farm a half hour out of the city and rented rooms at a motel on the north side of the city. It was late when they got back.

Luke's room faced east and on Sunday morning the bright sun sliced through the open blinds, crossing his face like parallel lasers. Waking, he opened his eyes and closed them at once. He could smell the woman's perfume on the pillowcase and the sheets. He tried to will himself back to sleep, wishing he had some Oxy or even a couple aspirins. He'd had a scrip for Oxy, for his knee, but it had expired. The doctor was a suspicious type who didn't want to write another.

After a while he rolled over onto his back and reached for the woman but came up empty. He sat up and looked around the room. Her purse and jacket were gone and so was she. He put his head back on the pillow and closed his eyes, relieved that she had left. He wasn't up for any shenanigans this morning and he didn't feel like talking to a stranger at that hour, either.

He managed to fall back asleep. When he awoke for the second time the sun had cleared the window and the room was in half darkness. He got up and had a leak, then stepped into the shower. When he came out of the bathroom a few minutes later he noticed his wallet, lying on top of his clothes where he had tossed them the night before. He opened it up; the money was gone.

He met Steve for breakfast at the motel coffee shop.

"How much was there?" Steve asked.

"The four hundred I won," Luke said. "Minus whatever I spent last night in that honky-tonk."

"When are you gonna fucking learn?" Steve asked.

"Learn what—not to trust people?"

"Not to let your pecker do your thinking for you," Steve said. "How you going to find this woman? Do you even remember her well enough to tell the cops what she looks like?"

"I'm not calling the cops," Luke said. "Maybe she needed the money for something."

"You are unbelievable."

"Hey—twenty-four hours ago, I didn't have that money. I still don't. Easy come, easy go."

"The Luke motto."

Luke had some scalding coffee. He'd bummed some aspirin from Steve and his head was beginning to clear. He hoped that he spent a lot of money at the bar last night. That would mean he'd only lost a little bit to the woman.

"I'm heading to Kentucky today," he said. "Can you get the horses? I'll catch up with you in Indiana."

"Yup. What if you hire on with Billie?"

"I ain't training no thoroughbred," Luke said. He glanced out the window to where his Ford pickup sat in the parking lot. He was low on gas. "You got a hundred you can lend me?"

Steve gave him the "when are you gonna learn" look again. The waitress came over, carrying a pot of coffee. "You all need a refill?"

Luke pushed his cup forward. As she poured, he kept his eyes on her face.

"You're a very beautiful woman," he said. "Shouldn't you be modeling someplace?"

The woman smiled just slightly before glancing at Steve, her eyebrows rising. Luke sipped the hot coffee and watched her walking away.

"You are pathetic," Steve told him.

"'Cause I like women?" Luke asked. "What's pathetic about that? Now what about that hundred, bud?"

Fourteen

THAT NIGHT BILLIE WAS SITTING ON the back deck, listening to the crickets and smoking cigarettes. She had decided she would quit the latter, and every time she thought about it, she lit one up. She was bored with thinking of all the things she was required to think about. Bored with worrying that she didn't know what the hell she was doing. She didn't know enough about the racing game to fool herself into believing she could make money from it. Her father knew the business inside out, upside down, and all around, yet he had operated on the thin edge of bankruptcy his entire life. And if Billie thought that pretty colt trotting back and forth along the fence in the front pasture would be the great leveling agent in all of this, she needed to think again. There had been dozens of colts and fillies over the years, all pretty, all destined for greatness, and every damn one coming up short.

A little past eight she got into Will's truck and drove into Marshall. She found a bar she'd never seen before in a strip mall west of town, a place called Sneaky Pete's. She sat in the truck for a few minutes, wondering why anyone would call their bar sneaky. Was that supposed to represent something positive to people? Billie wouldn't buy a car from someone who called himself sneaky. She wouldn't go to a sneaky doctor, or a sneaky accountant. She might hire a sneaky private investigator, but that seemed the exception to the rule.

She went inside anyway. There was music playing and a large dance floor. She stayed until past midnight and almost went home with a guy she danced with a half dozen times. He said he sold software and was in Kentucky a couple days every month. Such noncommittal opportunities usually appealed to Billie; she probably would have taken this one if she didn't have to be up at dawn to trailer-load the colt. Not only that, but she stopped drinking around eleven o'clock, switching to tonic water. Before heading home, she necked with the guy in the parking lot for a while before politely turning down his request for a blow job. He had seemed like a nice guy up until the last, and maybe he was. Billie had been hearing that these days blow jobs were like handshakes to teenagers, but she wasn't subscribing to that adjustment of social mores. Maybe because she wasn't a teenager.

Five still came early. She made coffee in the half light, her head groggy from the beer and the hour. She would eat later. Carrying her cup down the hill, she watched as the colt came loping toward her, obviously more awake than she was. The broodmares, maybe aware they weren't going anywhere, were grazing along the far edge of the field. Billie had hooked the horse trailer to her father's truck the day before. The rig sat parked by the machine shed, under the brightening sky.

Jodie was leaning against the fender of the truck, her thin arms crossed, eyes defiant. She wore faded jeans and a jacket. She must have gotten up at half past four to get there.

"You're here early to tend to your little flock," Billie said and walked past her to the rear of the trailer.

"I'm going to Chestnut Field."

"Not with me, you're not." Billie swung open the doors and dropped the ramp.

"He knows me better than you."

"Who does?"

"Cactus Jack."

"Well, he's going to be disappointed," Billie said. "'Cause today it's just me and him."

When Billie walked to the pasture gate the horse trotted over to her, as was his nature. She led him out of the pasture and across the lane to the trailer. There he stopped dead, looking into the trailer's dark interior. Billie stepped onto the ramp and pulled, but the horse would not move.

"Come on!" she urged.

"He won't go in," Jodie said.

"He has before, obviously. I doubt the old man walked him twenty-five miles to Chestnut."

She pulled again. The colt outweighed her by roughly eight hundred pounds; she was not going to move him. Jodie turned and went into the barn and came out moments later with a grain pail containing a couple of handfuls of oats. She stepped past Billie and showed the colt the pail before moving deeper into the trailer. The horse followed her, bumping Billie aside in his haste. The girl clipped the trailer leads on either side of the halter while the animal buried his nose in the pail. Walking out, she gave Billie a look.

Billie said nothing as she pulled up the ramp and closed the trailer doors. She was moving around to the driver's door of the truck when she heard the girl's small voice.

"You're not taking any tack?"

Billie stopped. "Wouldn't Skeeter have it?"

"No."

Billie went into the tack room at the front of the barn. There were a half dozen saddles there and as many bridles. After a moment the girl came in behind her and pointed to a saddle before lifting a bridle from a peg on the wall. Billie carried the tack outside and put it in the box of the pickup, then moved to the door again.

"You need hay. And a water bucket."

Billie exhaled and turned back to the barn again. She didn't look at Jodie as she threw four bales of hay into the truck and climbed into the cab. As she drove off, she glanced in her rear view and saw the girl standing there in the lane, watching.

When she got to the end of the lane, Billie stopped. There was no traffic at that hour. Half of the red sun was showing on the horizon, casting the fields and forests to the east in an ethereal pink light. She sat there idling for a full minute and then got out.

"Well, come on," she called.

On the drive to Chestnut Jodie was happy, as a kid might be who had gotten her way. She told Billie in great detail about a movie she had watched with her aunt the night before, something about a whale and a mouse. After the movie review, she began a story about her next-door neighbor, who sometimes hoed his garden in his underwear.

"Do you have a vegetable garden where you live?" she asked when she finished.

"No," Billie said.

Jodie sighed, looking out the windshield to the morning sky. "It's a beautiful day, isn't it?"

Billie nodded.

"Red sky though," Jodie said. "Will said red sky in the morning meant we could get rain."

Billie had heard that too, from the same source. "Listen, kid, I really don't have a lot to say in the morning."

The girl was quiet for a few seconds. "You don't have a lot to say in the afternoon, either."

Skeeter was waiting at the gate, as promised, sitting in his truck. When he saw them, he waved them forward and then led the way to the shed row. They put the colt in the stall and fed him hay. There was a tap along the wall outside the stall. Jodie filled the bucket without being told to and hauled it inside. Billie stacked the rest of the hay alongside the shed and pulled a tarp over it.

"When do you want to take him out?" Billie asked, watching the horse. He had ignored the hay and was pacing about in the stall.

"In a bit," Skeeter said. "Let him settle down first, get used to where he's at. He hasn't been here for a couple weeks." He watched the horse for a moment, then indicated the clubhouse in the distance. "You guys eat anything? Coffee shop will be open. Let's get a cup of joe and a sticky bun."

The sun was full up by the time they had their food. They walked outside to sit on the benches along the track to eat, not far from the finish line. Billie noticed that Skeeter sat with his right leg straight out, favoring the hip.

There were a dozen or more horses out on the dirt, running under the gaze of owners and trainers who each held cups of coffee in one hand and stopwatches in the other. The track was largely silent apart from the rhythmic thudding of the horses' hooves. It was a sound Billie had always liked. There was a musical cadence to it, something primal and soothing. She could remember mornings like this with her father, when he was one of the men with a coffee and a stopwatch, and Billie would be beside him, huddled against the cold dawn, watching her breath on the air and listening to the sound of the hooves. The men would get to talking and sometimes they'd forget that Billie was there. They might be telling a story about what they'd gotten up to the night before, with a girlfriend or a woman they'd met in a bar. Before things got too raunchy, Will Masterson would cut them off.

"Little pitchers have big ears," he'd say.

Billie glanced over to where Jodie was sitting quietly, nibbling at a jelly donut as she watched the action on the track. She'd insisted on paying for her own breakfast. She was serious in that insistence, as she was in most things. Too serious for a little girl, Billie thought, although she was hardly an expert on the subject. Maybe she had been serious too at that age.

She turned to Skeeter. "Did my father talk to you about when he figured to run the colt?"

"He was aiming for a sprint here at Chestnut, first week of August," Skeeter said. "But we're set back now, horse hasn't been worked in near two weeks. Might be too soon, running him then."

"How will we know?"

"I say breeze him short a couple days, then see how he is. Move him up in distance from there. You'll know if he can handle six furlongs."

Billie nodded, watching a young woman go loping by on a large bay colt, the woman standing in the irons, laughing at something.

"You do realize you can't run a horse without a trainer," Skeeter said. "And you don't have one. Or do you?"

Billie took a sip. The coffee was weak but hot. "Not at the moment. I think Mr. Caldwell put the word out that I'm persona non grata. Every time I talk to a trainer, he runs away like I've got leprosy."

"What is persona non grata?" Jodie asked.

"It's Latin for leprosy."

"What are you going to do?" Skeeter asked.

Billie had another sip of coffee before setting it on the bench beside her. "I talked to a guy named Luke Walker. He used to train thoroughbreds but these days he's into quarter horses. He said he'd have a look at the colt."

"He might come on as trainer?" Skeeter asked.

"He was kind of vague about that," Billie said. "Vagueness is one of his strong suits. He said he might know somebody, that kind of thing."

"I remember that boy," Skeeter said. "He started right here at Chestnut, you know. He knew his way around a horse. He was an up-and-comer—I recall him running horses all over the state—Churchill, Keeneland, Paducah. Always wondered what happened to him."

"Too much partying, that's what happened," Billie said.

"He did have that reputation." Skeeter chuckled. "I also recall that his brain kept getting caught in his zipper."

Billie glanced at the little girl beside her and then back to Skeeter. "Little pitchers have big ears."

Reese Ryker stood in Caldwell's office, by the window overlooking the track, and watched as Skeeter Musgrave loped the gray colt back toward the gate, where Billie Masterson and the girl Reese had seen at the farm were standing. Billie had a stopwatch in her hand and when Skeeter pulled the horse up, she showed the face to the rider.

"So now she has a stall," Reese said. "Isn't that wonderful?"

Caldwell was sitting at his desk across the room. He'd been reading *People* magazine when Ryker arrived.

"Wasn't much I could do about it, Reese," he said. "Short of out-and-out breaking the goddamn law, which would have landed me in court. The agreement was signed, paid in full for the season."

"Why is Daniel Clay sticking his fat nose into it?"

"I hear he was pals with Masterson. Looking out for the daughter, I guess."

"He ought to look out for himself," Reese said. "I happen to own a TV station. Maybe I'll have my investigative team look into Mr. Clay's record." He turned. "You ever know a lawyer didn't have a few skeletons in his closet?"

"What's done is done," Caldwell said. He wished Reese would get off the subject of David Clay. "So she can work the horse. How's she going to run him without a trainer?"

"How do you know she's hasn't found one?"

Caldwell got to his feet and walked over to the window. "Lookit down there, Reese. I see that old piss tank Musgrave, the smart-mouth bitch, and a child. I don't see a trainer."

Reese had to concede the point. "But we have to assume she's still looking."

"Looking and finding are two different animals," Caldwell said. "The word is out there that you might have a legal claim to the colt. These small trainers don't want to run afoul of you. The way I see it, she'll get discouraged at some point and put the colt on the block. Then he's yours."

"I'm not sure she'll sell to me. I seemed to have rubbed her the wrong way."

"How so?"

"I don't know," Reese said. "You know how women are. They don't have to have a reason to do an about-face. It can't always be their periods, can it?"

"You wouldn't have to buy him under your own name, though, would you?" Caldwell asked.

Reese considered it. "What are you thinking?"

"Wouldn't be hard to find an intermediary. I could help you out with that."

Reese turned back to the window. Skeeter had climbed down from the horse and they were leading the animal to the shed rows. They looked like a happy little family in a Rockwell print, if Rockwell were to paint a picture of a drunk, a foul-mouthed waitress, and a white trash orphan.

"Might be something to consider."

"I wouldn't have any trouble coming up with somebody discreet," Caldwell said.

I bet you wouldn't, Reese thought.

"What's going on with that PR position job at the Double R?" Caldwell asked. "Are you still looking at hiring somebody?"

"Still discussing it in-house."

"It makes a lot of sense," Caldwell persisted. "The Double R is a going concern. And with that colt Ghost Rider . . . well, let's just say you've got a superstar in the making there. You'll need somebody to handle publicity."

Reese looked at Caldwell and nodded slightly. "You're on the short list. You need to keep me in the loop with that colt. You hear?"

"Yes, sir."

"And let me know if David Clay shows up here again."

"He won't," Caldwell said. "I put the run on him yesterday."

Like hell you did, Reese thought and left.

Fifteen

LUKE STOOD TRACKSIDE, HIS FOREARMS OVER the rail, stopwatch in his right hand. Billie was a few feet away and Jodie was sitting on the rail. They all watched as Cactus Jack galloped past, with Skeeter aboard. Luke clicked the watch and had a look.

He had shown up at the farm the night before, having just arrived from Tennessee, driving a red Ford F250 that had seen some hard miles. The windshield was cracked, the front fender dented, and one headlight held in place by duct tape. The tires were caked in mud, as if Luke, leaving Tennessee, had pointed the truck north and not bothered with the modern improvements known as roads. The mufflers were rusted through; Billie had heard the engine barking from a half mile away, and so she was standing on the back deck when the truck pulled in the lower laneway and rolled to a stop by the barn. Luke got out and started up the hill, walking stiff-legged, like a man who had driven for several hours without stopping to stretch his legs. Or a man who had fallen off any number of horses, dirt bikes, and barstools in his time and was now paying for the countless fractures, sprains, and torn muscles he'd suffered.

"I wouldn't say no to a cold beer," he said as he approached.

"You're a constant surprise," Billie told him and went inside for two bottles. They sat in the dying light, drinking. With an effort, Luke kicked off his worn Frye boots and set them aside. His gaze settled on the broodmares at pasture.

"So where is this wonder horse?"

"We've been working him at Chestnut Field," Billie said. "Your old stomping grounds."

"We? You got a mouse in your pocket?"

"Got an old boy named Skeeter Musgrave working him."

"I know Skeeter." Luke took a drink. "You stretched him out yet?"

Billie hesitated. "Skeeter?"

"The colt."

"Oh," Billie said. "Looks like tomorrow."

"So you intend to race him?"

"Depends."

"On what?"

"On whether or not I have a trainer."

Now, at the track, Billie watched as the colt under Skeeter passed by and then she turned toward Luke. "What'd he do?"

"Three furlongs, thirty-two seven."

"He can do better than that," Jodie said. "He was lugging at the turn."

"How'd you like to go sit in the truck?" Billie said.

"I wouldn't."

She'd been at the house again at dawn and this time Billie hadn't argued. There didn't seem to be any point in it. But Billie had to wonder yet again how a nine-year-old could be up and out the door at first light. Where was the mother, and what the hell was she doing? Shouldn't she be making the kid breakfast and nagging her to brush her teeth, that type of thing? It was what Billie's mother had done, at least on the days she'd managed to get out of bed before noon. Later on, there were many when she did not.

They all watched as Skeeter loped the horse toward them, pulling the animal up short of the rail. The colt wasn't breathing hard.

"He was lugging at the turn," Skeeter said.

Jodie shot Billie a look but she wouldn't meet it. She saw that Skeeter was limping even more than usual as he walked the horse out before leading him back to the stall. At Luke's suggestion, Billie and Jodie rubbed the animal down while he and Skeeter went for a stroll along the track. Billie kept an eye on the two of them. Skeeter was doing the talking and Luke the listening, which was rare. When they returned, Skeeter said he had to be getting home. Billie watched as he climbed into his truck, grabbing the steering wheel with one hand and the door post with the other and lifting himself in.

Luke had been there when they arrived earlier, a half hour past dawn. Leaving the farm the night before, he'd told Billie he was staying at a buddy's place outside of Junction City. He'd shown up this morning wearing the same jeans and T-shirt as the day before, along with a beat-up straw Resistol, pulled down to hide his eyes. Billie wondered if he had slept in his truck. She could have offered him the couch in the farmhouse but she didn't want to give him any ideas, given their history.

Now he suggested they get something to eat and the three of them walked over to the clubhouse. They sat outside in the morning sun with their fried egg sandwiches and coffee. Jodie had juice. Out on the track there were other trainers working other horses.

"So tell me the plan here," Luke said.

"There is no plan," Billie told him. "That's the beauty of it. I have no idea what I'm doing."

"That's the beauty of it?" Luke asked.

"I'm joking," she told him. "I remember when you used to have a sense of humor."

Luke started to tell her to fuck off but caught himself, glancing at the little girl. He took a bite of his sandwich and washed it down with the weak coffee. When he turned his head, Billie saw that he had a mouse beneath his left eye that wasn't there the night before. Apparently he'd had a night. Back when she knew him, and dated him briefly, he was always getting into fights, usually over a girl. He was famous for saying that he was a lover and not a fighter. He lost a lot of fights and won his share of girls, so maybe he was right.

"The plan is, I either race the colt or sell the colt," Billie said. "My father thought the horse was special. I have to take that with a grain of salt, as Pliny the Elder would say."

Luke turned to her. "Who?"

Billie shook her head and continued. "Thing is, I'm not exactly in love with the idea of racing him if he's going to finish up the track and cost me money in the process. If selling is the smart move, then that's what I'll do."

"You can't sell him," Jodie said.

"Remember what I told you about the truck?" Billie said to her.

"So why am I here?" Luke asked.

"There's a theory out there that you know horses," Billie said.

"And you want me to be the one tells you what to do?" Luke asked. "Why would I take that on? I don't know if the horse is any good. Only God knows that and even God bets across the board sometimes. You got offers on him?"

"Not exactly."

"What the hell does that mean?"

"It means I don't have an actual offer I would consider," Billie replied. "But Reese Ryker would buy the colt today if he could."

"That dipshit—why does he want him?" Luke asked.

"Because he owns the sire and apparently he's afraid that I'm going to dilute the line by breeding the colt to every broodmare in Kentucky. He's convinced that the dam is of inferior blood. He's all about the blood, that boy."

"So he'll geld the horse," Luke said. "That's why you don't want to sell to him."

"One reason."

"What's the other?"

Billie glanced at Jodie. "I don't like his cologne."

Luke laughed. His laugh had acquired a whiskey crackle to it, a sound Billie recognized from a number of her father's friends who had liked to bend an elbow.

"There's something else you should know," Billie said. "Ryker's been telling people that Humphrey Brown bred Saguaro to my father's mare *after* he sold the horse to Ryker. So he figures he's got a claim on the animal."

"You got the colt's registration?"

"I do."

"Then Ryker's just flapping his gums."

"Speaking of papers," Billie said. "What about your license?"

"I'm still thinking about that. Whether or not I need this in my life."

"What does Skeeter think?" Billie asked. "Or did you two go for a walk earlier to talk about fall fashions?"

"Skeeter likes the colt. Skeeter likes him a lot." Luke sat quietly for a time. "That's something else you have to consider. You can't keep asking that old man to work that colt. He can't hardly get in and out of his truck, his hips are so bad."

"I saw that," Billie said. "I smelled whiskey on him this morning, too."

"Well, he ain't drinking at six a.m. for pleasure," Luke said. "That's painkiller, that's what that is. He don't want to say no to you because of your old man. But you need to find somebody else to work the horse."

Jodie got to her feet. "I have to use the bathroom."

Billie looked around. There were washrooms just inside the clubhouse doors. Jodie walked away, depositing her cup and napkin in the waste basket beside the benches.

"What's the deal here?" Luke asked. "Is she yours?"

"No, she's not mine," Billie said. She told Luke about her father and the kid, the shortened version.

"Donkeys and goats," Luke said. "I'll be damned."

"I'm certain you eventually will," Billie said. "Are you going to train the horse in the meantime?"

Luke fell silent again. Billie didn't like it when he was quiet. It suggested he was using the part of his brain that operated on logic, and the logical decision might not be the one she wanted to hear. But then again, maybe it was. Maybe she should sell the damn horse, sell the farm, and head out. That was the original plan. When had she decided it was no longer in her best interests? When she found out that Reese Ryker was an entitled racist asshole? What did that have to do with Billie's best interests? Nothing she did would change what he was.

"I'd like to stretch him out," Luke said. "See what he's like at six furlongs. Let's do that and then we'll talk some more. But you have to decide whether you want this, Billie. I was real happy racing my gelding on the flat tracks and then you came along."

Billie was watching the clubhouse doors where the girl had gone. Through the glass she could see the washroom door as well, and she had seen Jodie go inside but she didn't know if she was alone in there or not. How long did it take to go pee?

"You listening to me?" Luke asked.

"Yes," she said.

"You want to run the goddamn horse or not?"

Billie kept her eyes on the clubhouse and then Jodie emerged, walking toward them wearing the same serious look, wiping her hands on her jeans. Maybe the washroom was out of paper towels.

"Yes," Billie replied.

Sixteen

Caldwell called Reese Ryker from his office as he was watching the horses out on the track that morning. Or rather, as he was watching one horse. He told Reese what he was seeing.

"Come to my office," Reese said.

Caldwell had been waiting for an invitation to the sprawling stables of Double R Racing for a while now, thinking it would be the next step toward getting hired there. "I can be at the farm in half an hour. How do I find your office?"

"I'm not at the stables, I'm at my TV station."

So Caldwell was obliged to drive to Louisville, an hour's trip. He arrived in the middle of rush-hour traffic and got stalled on 64 for thirty minutes. In the mezzanine of WTVK, it took him a while to get past reception; apparently Reese hadn't told anybody he was coming. When he was finally ushered into the glass-walled office on the top floor of the building, he found Reese sitting behind a large desk, talking to a man in a leather bomber jacket and jeans. The man was tall and thin as a sapling, with dirty blond hair that reached the collar of the coat. He was on his feet, leaning with his back against a plate glass window overlooking the city, doing something on his cell phone.

"Mr. Caldwell, Mr. O'Hara," Reese said in a bored voice. Then to the man by the windows, "Show him the picture."

The man named O'Hara turned the phone around to show Caldwell the screen. There was a photo of Luke Walker there, apparently taken a few years earlier. The picture was from *The Racing Journal.*

"That him?" Reese asked.

"Yeah," Caldwell said. "I told you it was him. He used to train horses at Chestnut Field."

"Well, Luke Walker doesn't have a trainer's license," Reese said.

Caldwell shrugged and moved to sit in a leather chair across from Reese. "I'm just telling you he was there this morning when they worked the colt. He was talking to the exercise rider afterward for a good bit. So I put two and two together and called you. Isn't that what you wanted me to do?"

Reese nodded toward the man by the windows. "Mr. O'Hara has been busy on Google. Walker was suspended four years ago. For doping horses, according to the internet. What do you know about that?"

"It happened over at Sutherland, so I only know secondhand," Caldwell said. "He was accused of doping but it was never actually proven. He claimed there was a false drug test. So it was kind of left up in the air. There were people who believed it both ways."

"You're saying he wasn't convicted," Reese said.

"Well, *convicted* would be the wrong term."

"Don't tell me how to talk," Reese snapped.

Caldwell backed up. "All I meant is that it's not a court of law. If it was, though, I guess you'd have to say he wasn't found guilty."

"Then why the fuck was he suspended?" O'Hara asked. The man had a high-pitched voice, almost feminine, and he was clearly pissed that his information was being called into question.

"He got suspended for taking a swing at the guy who accused him," Caldwell said. "Another trainer, claimed he lost a big race because Walker was doping." He looked at Reese. "The suspension was only for six months, though. How do you know he didn't get reinstated?"

"Because we just checked," Reese said. "You think this is amateur hour? He doesn't have a license here or anywhere else in the country. So why's he hanging around your track and looking at my colt?"

"Your colt?" Caldwell said.

"Yes, my fucking colt. One way or the other."

"I don't know," Caldwell said emphatically.

"Is that woman going to run the horse?" Reese asked.

"She hasn't entered him in a race," Caldwell said. "That's all I can tell you."

"Why haven't you asked her? Sounds as if she's been working the horse every day. Why haven't you asked the exercise rider?"

"She doesn't have a trainer," Caldwell said. "So she *can't* run the horse."

"But she now has a trainer looking at the horse," Reese said. "If I'm this Walker, and I'm looking to get back into the thoroughbred game, and some ditz calls me up and says she's got this colt that just happens to be out of the best fucking stud in the country, then what am I going to say? 'No thanks, I'll wait until something better comes along?' I don't think so."

Caldwell didn't think he was required to answer, so he didn't. Reese glanced over at the thin man for a moment before turning back to Caldwell.

"All right," he said. "You can head back. I've put a call in. If Mr. Walker applies for reinstatement, I'll know about it. You might want to strike up a conversation with the Masterson woman. Pretend you're on her side. Maybe she'll tell you her plans."

"I believe that boat has sailed," Caldwell said.

"Try," Reese said and gestured with the back of his hand toward the door. Dismissal.

Caldwell stood up. "Uh, I updated my résumé. I was wondering—do you have an email address over at Double R where I could send it? Or I could drop off a hard copy."

"Yeah, drop it off," Reese said absently, punching something up on his cell phone.

"Okay then," Caldwell said, thinking about the hour's drive he'd just made to have a five-minute conversation he could have had over the phone. Plus it had cost him fifteen dollars to park. He was feeling a little left out, but then he usually felt that way after dealing with Reese Ryker.

"Let's see what the deal is with this guy Walker," Reese said to O'Hara when Caldwell was gone. He was still looking at his phone. "You know, seems like he was a pretty good trainer at one time. Shit, he ran in the money 42 percent of the time in 2011 at Keeneland." He looked at O'Hara. "Why would he quit?"

"Because he was cheating and got caught."

"If every trainer who ever doped quit the business—well, we'd be running low on trainers," Reese said.

"If he's looking for a way back in, maybe he wants to come work for you," O'Hara said.

Reese thought about that. The idea had appeal.

"You could always ask," O'Hara said. "You said this woman doesn't have any money, right? If the horse doesn't run in the money, how's she going to pay him?"

"Oh, she's broke," Reese said. "I have a feeling it's in the blood. You're right—if he's willing to work for a one-horse operation like she's got going, you'd think he'd jump at a job at my stable." He paused. "But maybe there's more to the boy's story than meets the eye. Maybe he's a drug addict or something like that. Let's find out. I'm going to tell them downstairs that you're working on a story for me and to give you full cooperation. You can use that new assistant producer's contacts. What's her name—the one with the big tits and the short hair—Melissa maybe?"

"I'll find her."

"We need to get this done before they race the fucking horse," Reese said. "I'm afraid the thing will win and that'll change everything."

O'Hara started for the door and stopped. "He can't win if he can't run."

"I've thought about that, too," Reese said. "Keep that one in your pocket for now. Let's find out what Luke Walker's game is first."

Driving home from the track with Jodie in the passenger seat, Billie wondered if the kid intended on hanging around the farm all day. Surely she had more in her life than shoveling goat shit. She had been at the farm every morning since Billie had come home (if home was where she was). It didn't take a whole lot of analyzing to figure out why she was there—she obviously preferred the farm over her own place. But Billie wasn't looking for a best friend and certainly not one who couldn't see over the dashboard of the truck. Today the problem was resolved when they pulled into the lane.

"I have to get going," the girl said. "I'm helping my aunt this afternoon."

"Helping her what?"

"Clean a house in Crabapple Orchard."

Billie was still trying to get a handle on the girl's situation. She'd mentioned helping the aunt before. So what was that about? Was the aunt using the kid as free labor or was she looking out for her, giving her something to do away from a home life that Billie was assuming was fucked up, given the principles and the fact that the girl had said that the mother and boyfriend weren't much for getting up before noon?

"What's your aunt's name?"

"Micky."

"Your mom's sister?"

The girl nodded. "Sort of. They have the same mother but different fathers."

"And she cleans houses for a living?"

"Yup. And she works at a restaurant, too. It's called Sarah's Place."

"In Marshall?"

"It's in Lexington."

Billie was assembling a portrait of the half-aunt in her head and it was, surprisingly, not a bad picture. She had two jobs and paid at least some attention to the kid. It sounded as if she had the mother beat by a country mile. "You want a ride home?" she asked.

"It's okay."

"I can drive you."

"I'll ride my bike."

Before going into the house Billie saw that the flag was up on the mailbox, so she walked out to get her father's mail. Instead of adding it to the pile on the dining room table, today she sat down and started opening letters. Aside from a couple of junk mail offers from investment firms that obviously had no idea what Will Masterson's financial situation was, she was looking mainly at bills. Overdue at that and most marked urgent. She opened the envelopes one by one and made separate piles on the table. Gas company, telephone, power, the county tax department, feed store, American Express. And several notices from the Kentucky First National branch in Marshall. When everything was open, she sat back and studied the sheer volume of paperwork while wondering about the best way of dealing with it. Billie had never really been in debt, not even going through college. She'd received some scholarship money and paid for the rest as she went, through whatever she earned working and money she got from her father. Looking at the paperwork in front of her now, she had to wonder how he'd ever managed that. Never once had he mentioned that he was short on cash. Not this short, anyway.

She went into the kitchen and made a pot of coffee. Returning with a cup, she sat down with the stack of paperwork and began to cull the herd. Most of the bills had been sent more than once, some several times, the amounts due increasing exponentially each time. She crumpled up each of the earlier versions and tossed them aside, leaving only the most current of each. The pile was now slightly less daunting, even if the amount owing was not. She thought she should total up what was due but then decided against it, knowing the number would merely serve to depress her.

Instead, she called David Mountain Clay's office. The secretary wanted to know what the call was concerning before putting the great man on the line. Billie was reluctant to discuss her finances with a stranger and so the two went back and forth for a bit; apparently lawyer Clay had managed to hire a secretary who was nearly as aggravating as himself. Billie told herself that it would not be in her best interests to tell the woman to go fuck herself.

"It's about money," she said finally.

The secretary requested that Billie be more specific.

"He owes me money," Billie said.

The next sound she heard was the honeyed accent of lawyer Clay. "I do *not* owe you money."

"I know you don't," Billie said. "But it got you on the line."

"What's the problem now, Billie?"

"The problem is I'm sitting here going over my father's sad finances. I have maybe a thousand dollars in a bank account back in Ohio. I can use that to pay what the old man owed Marshall Feeds and have enough left over for a draft beer—maybe. However, that leaves me a little short when it comes to these other creditors, such as—well, pretty much everybody in central Kentucky, by the looks of it."

"So you decided to get me on the phone under false pretenses."

"Tell your receptionist to work on her people skills."

"Miss Willard has been diligent in protecting me for thirty-one years."

"A delicate little thing like you needs protection," Billie said. "Enough of that. Did you tell me that my father had some money in the bank?"

"I did."

"And am I allowed to use his money to pay off his bills?"

"It's not his money," Clay said. "It's yours."

"If it's mine, then why don't I have access to it?"

"You do. If you give me your banking details, I can have the money transferred to your account today. Or if you prefer, you can come here and I will give you a check for the full amount."

Billie exhaled. "Is there a reason you haven't told me this? Is this standard procedure for a lawyer, or is this something you've come up with on your own to annoy people? By the way, I seem to recall you driving out to the farm to pay that little girl a thousand dollars that my father left *her*."

"She's nine years old," Clay said. "Do you wish that I treat you as such?"

"Sure, if it means giving me money."

"You have a copy of the will, Billie," Clay said. "If you take time to read the document in its entirety, you will find no evidence anywhere of your father requesting that I babysit you."

"I'm betting I won't be the first person today to tell you to fuck off."

"You would," Clay said. "My clients are in general much more courteous than you."

"Well, I suspect I'm getting special treatment so I figured I might as well return the favor. Okay, how much money are we talking?"

"I believe it's in the neighborhood of twenty-five hundred dollars."

Christ, Billie thought. "He's thirty grand behind on his taxes alone, David. Did you know that?"

"I didn't know the number. I suppose I knew the ballpark, had I given it any thought."

"So what do you suggest I do with the twenty-five hundred? Buy lottery tickets?"

"The lottery is a tax on the stupid, Billie."

"Yeah, I wasn't serious."

"If I were you, I would give a little to the county," Clay said. "Say, five hundred dollars, just so they know you're thinking of them. And do the same with some of the other bills, particularly the local creditors. You'd be surprised how much goodwill you can buy for a few dollars. And keep the lights on at the same time."

"I guess," Billie said.

"Throw the American Express bill in the trash. Credit card companies are an abomination, the interest rates they charge. Let them try to sue a dead man for nonpayment."

Billie smiled. "See—you can be likable if you try."

"The bank poses a bigger problem," Clay said. "I'm going to assume they're looking for money, too."

"Yup," Billie said. "And apparently have been for a while now."

"I thought as much." Billie heard a creaking sound, like a chair being moved. She could picture the old lawyer in his lair, lounging behind a wooden desk, surrounded by antiquities and awards and God only knows what else. "They're probably in a position where they could foreclose soon."

"Like how soon?"

"Again, I don't know the details. I suggest you talk to them."

Billie gave it some thought. "I'll stop at your office and pick up the check this afternoon and then go to the bank. I might as well open an account while I'm there. That's what we nine-year-olds try to do when we get a nice inheritance check."

"Miss Willard will have it ready."

"I can't wait to meet her," Billie said. "One other thing. I hear some Falstaffian character was out at Chestnut Field, throwing his weight around, no pun intended. I would thank the crusty old bastard but I wouldn't want to embarrass him."

"Goodbye, Billie."

Seventeen

THE ALARM WENT OFF AT SIX and Billie reached for it blindly in the half light. The clock was ancient, like most things in the house, save the coffee maker and blender. It required winding and lost on average four minutes a day. Billie pulled on jeans and one of her father's work shirts. She'd been borrowing his oversize shirts for a while now. She either had to go shopping or make a trip back to Ohio to pick up her own clothes. While she was there, she should probably give up the rental on her apartment, as well. Athena sounded happy to be in California, said she wasn't planning on coming back. Neither was Billie, but that didn't mean she couldn't decide any day now that she didn't want anything to do with the situation here. She might decide on a whim to sell and then—like Huck—light out for the territories.

She washed her face and went downstairs to make coffee. The sun was up and she kept watch down the hill for Jodie to arrive. It was only after she'd poured a cup that she remembered the girl was helping her aunt again today. That was fine; Billie wouldn't have to worry about the kid for a change.

They were going to work the colt at seven o'clock and it was a few minutes to the hour when Billie arrived at the barns at

Chestnut. There were plenty of people and horses wandering back and forth from the track, but nobody was at her stall. Cactus Jack was standing with his head over the half door, watching her. She filled the plastic water bucket and carried it inside. The horse drank and then lifted his head abruptly and pushed his nose against her, dripping water down the front of her shirt.

"Don't be kissing up to me because the kid's not here," she said.

When she stepped outside, she saw a young guy approaching. He was jockey-sized and black, with close-cropped hair and a serious look about him. She looked away and he called out to her.

"Ms. Masterson."

"Yeah?" she said, turning. She was aware that the front of her shirt was wet and she wiped at it ineffectively.

When he got close, he extended his hand. "I'm Tyrone Howe."

Billie shook the hand as she considered the name. "Tyrone Howe used to ride for my father twenty years ago. You're not him."

"That was my old man."

Now Billie gave the youth a closer look. "I used to give you jujubes back in the day. You wouldn't eat the yellow ones."

Tyrone Howe smiled. "I don't remember that. I do remember you."

"You've grown up," Billie said. "I mean, not a lot."

Tyrone gestured to the colt behind Billie. "I'd like the ride on that gray, if you're planning to race him."

"So you're a jock," Billie said. "How's your father?"

"He passed a year ago. And I heard about your father. I'm sorry."

Billie nodded but didn't say anything, not wanting to encourage a club for newly orphaned racetrack kids. "Where have you been riding?"

"Here a bit," Tyrone said. "A few mounts over at Sutherland. I haven't won but twice so far, so I'm not exactly setting the world on fire. Not yet."

"But you intend to?"

"What would you think if I said I no to that?"

Billie laughed. She could hear the rumble of exhaust from the direction of the gate, meaning Luke had arrived. She thought it was strange that Skeeter was not there yet. Skeeter who was always at the track at first light. It took her a moment to realize why he wasn't.

"You were talking to Skeeter," she said.

Tyrone nodded.

"You here to work the colt this morning?"

"That's up to you, Ms. Masterson."

"Stop calling me that. It's Billie." She turned as Luke rolled to a stop and got out of the Ford, looking ragged and half-asleep. Billie wondered if he ever woke up looking any different from that.

"This is Tyrone Howe *Junior*," she said to him. "He's a jockey and he wants to work my horse today."

Drowsy appearances aside, Luke was quicker to put two and two together than Billie. "I guess you were talking to Skeeter."

"Yes, sir."

"How old are you?"

"Twenty-one."

"Still got your bug?"

"I do."

Luke turned and looked at the horses out on the track and didn't say anything else. Tyrone, uncomfortable under the silence, walked over and made a show of admiring the horse in the stall. Billie watched Luke, who seemed to be taking his own sweet time considering the young man. She grew impatient; they weren't buying a house here, just hiring an exercise rider for the day. What was he waiting for?

"What do you think?" she finally asked.

Luke was still watching the horses on the track. "Well, I said I wanted to stretch that colt out this morning." He turned to Billie. "And Skeeter ain't here, I'm too heavy—and you're a girl."

"You are such a fucking asshole."

Luke smiled. "I just wanted to make sure you were listening. Let's put Mr. Howe on the horse. See if there's any mutual admiration happening there."

With Tyrone in the irons, they ran the colt flat out for six furlongs. When the young jockey loped the horse back to the rail where Billie and Luke stood, his eyes were like a kid's at his own surprise birthday party.

"Wow," he said as he slid down from the horse. He stood there a moment, looking at Billie.

"What did he do?" Billie asked.

"One eleven flat," Luke said.

"And how's that?" Billie asked.

"If it ain't wow, it's damn close to it," Luke said. He slipped through the rail fence and took the reins from Tyrone. "I'll walk him out."

Tyrone stood uncomfortably as Luke led the horse for maybe twenty yards before turning. "You around tomorrow?"

Tyrone nodded. "I'll be here at six."

"Put your feet up then," Luke said. "I'll be here at seven."

With the horse walked out and rubbed down, Luke told Billie to come with him to his truck. She got in the passenger side, pushing aside a pile of clothes and fast food wrappers and empty beer cans. Luke took a copy of *The Racing Journal* from the dash and opened it to a page he'd marked.

"*This* is where we're going to try him," he said. "A sprint right here at Chestnut, for juvenile non-winners. Purse is twenty-two thousand five hundred."

Billie looked at the date. "That's just a week from Saturday."

"That's right."

"Is he ready?" Billie asked. "Are you ready? You need to get reinstated."

"Done."

"What?"

"I went down yesterday and got my license back."

Billie thought about that. "Seems like you all of a sudden want to move on this."

Luke nodded. "I got to thinking after I left here yesterday—either we're going to do this or we're not. I got no desire to play fiddle-fuck around with the horse for three months just to have the animal spit the bit his first time out. Let's run him and see if he's got some mojo."

"And after today you figure he has?"

"He's got speed," Luke said. He looked out the truck window to where the colt was standing in the stall, his head over the half door, watching them. "You used to play softball, Billie. You ever—"

"Still do."

"What?"

"First base for the Broken Bombers."

Luke gave her an annoyed look. "Yeah, whatever. What I was saying—you ever see a guy warming up in the bullpen, throwing a hundred miles an hour, and then he comes in the game and can't get nobody out? Well, sometimes a horse is like that. What you see in the workouts doesn't make it to an actual race, where he's got seven or eight other horses crowding him, not to mention the crowd noise, the lights, the starting gate, all that song and dance."

Billie had a look at the form. "Let's be optimistic here," she said. "Let's say he runs a good race, maybe finishes in the money. When could we run him again?"

"Now who's the one wants to move fast?" Luke asked.

She sighed and put the form on the dash. "I went to the bank yesterday. The old man wasn't what you would call diligent about making his mortgage payments. They're getting impatient. The loans manager is somebody I went to high school with—Kellyanne Cruickshank. We weren't exactly tight back then. I might have even been mean to her and I think she just might be harboring ill feelings. She said they've been waiting for me to put the farm up for sale. Who is she to assume that I don't have the money to pay off the loan? Do I look like I don't have a pot to piss in?"

Luke gave her the once-over, the dirty jeans and faded work shirt, stained now with slobber from Cactus Jack.

"Oh, fuck off," she said.

Luke laughed. "You're saying you need some money short term. By the way, I'm deferring my fee until we race the horse. But don't you get to thinking I'm not in this for the dough-ray-me. I'm not exactly flush myself these days."

"When were you ever?"

"Which one of us is crying poor here?" he reminded her. "All right now, say the horse runs a good race and comes out sound. We could run him again in—oh, three weeks. But let's not get ahead of ourselves. First thing you need to do is enter the horse in that race on the sixth. It looks as if they have a couple spots open." He searched through the debris on the seat and produced a paper. "I made a copy of my license for you. That shithead Caldwell might want to see it. I'm a little worried about that boy. Is he going to give you friction on this?"

"No."

"You seem pretty sure about that."

"He's afraid of my giant."

Luke looked at her. "Are you stoned?"

Now Billie laughed. "We don't have to worry about Caldwell."

Luke shrugged. "Another thing—has this horse been in a starting gate yet?"

"A couple times, according to Skeeter."

"We need to work on that too, starting tomorrow. And I didn't notice you paying Tyrone anything for the ride today."

"Oh, shit," Billie said. "I need to pay him."

"Sounds to me like you got a lot of people out there need paying," Luke said.

"No shit," Billie replied.

Caldwell was polite to the Masterson woman, even though she didn't know what the hell she was doing. The horse she was entering, for instance, was still in her father's name and so was the stable called Masterson Thoroughbreds. He told her that she needed to get both things changed over. But he entered the two-year-old Cactus Jack in the sprint she requested anyway, contingent on the changes. He resisted a strong urge to tell her to get the fuck out of his office and come back when she didn't have her head up her ass, but he knew that telling her that would only result in another visit from David Mountain Clay and that this time the old lawyer would be thoroughly pissed off, as opposed to his last visit, when he was merely simmering, a state that just the same put the fear of God—or whomever it was that Clay represented—into Chuck Caldwell.

So he did what he had to do and then showed Billie Masterson the door. Getting shed of her didn't improve his mood any, as now he had to call Reese Ryker to tell him what had just happened. Reese Ryker was not going to like it.

Caldwell sat there for a time, his cell phone on the desk a couple feet away, dreading the conversation. He wouldn't tell Ryker about the advice he'd given the woman about taking ownership. What Ryker didn't know wouldn't hurt him. Well, it might, but when it did at least it wouldn't have Caldwell's fingerprints on it.

Caldwell thought back to the conversation he'd had with Ryker a few days earlier. As he was leaving, he'd asked about submitting his résumé to the Double R and Reese had told him he could drop it off. He hadn't been enthusiastic about it but he had said it. Today would be as good a day as any, Caldwell decided. If he was going to get his ass reamed, he could at least get something out of the trip. He opened his laptop and brought up the résumé and printed it out.

It was just before noon as he approached Lexington. The home farm for Double R Racing was southeast of town about ten miles. Caldwell had been by the place many times but never inside the gates. Getting close, he decided he needed a drink before breaking the bad news to Ryker. He kept going, to the outskirts of the city, where he pulled into the parking lot of a strip club called Honey Bunnies. Unlike the Ryker stables, Caldwell had been there many times.

He sat at the bar and ordered a steak sandwich, then drank vodka with tonic and watched the girls as he waited for his food. There was a stage at each end of the bar, and—as the sign outside boasted—continuous entertainment. When Caldwell walked in, a black girl was just beginning her routine. She wore a faux leopard-skin bikini and then she didn't wear it. At the far end, a young woman with long red hair was suspended on a stripper pole, her legs wrapped around the pole above her, her hair reaching the floor. Caldwell enjoyed his vodka as his gaze went from one dancer to the other, like a man watching a tennis match.

When the redhead finished, another girl—introduced as "the mesmerizing Jasmine"—came out immediately. She had close-cropped dark hair and looked a little like a young Audrey Hepburn. A very young Audrey Hepburn. She wore a short white dress and cowboy boots. Caldwell was certain there was an age requirement for strippers in the state but he didn't know what it was. He assumed it would be at least the same as the drinking age. The girl on the stage looked no older than sixteen. Of course, looks could be deceiving, as she was also staring at Caldwell right now in the most alluring way. She *looked* as if she were infatuated with him when all she really wanted was for him to come closer and slide some folding money in her G-string. *Good luck with that*, Caldwell thought.

He had two more vodkas along with his lunch. He was about to settle up when the young Audrey Hepburn known as Jasmine slid onto the barstool next to him. She was now wearing a short black skirt and a yellow V-neck that showed her cleavage. She asked that Caldwell buy her a drink, so he did. They flirted for a bit and then she suggested a transaction that had a lot of appeal, one he probably would have taken her up on if he weren't on a mission. Out of curiosity he asked for her rate and she told him two hundred for an hour. He scoffed at the number and she got a little pissy. Sensing there was no deal to be made, she took her free drink and moved on. When Caldwell left the bar, she was sitting with two guys in business suits at a corner table.

He was feeling the liquor as he drove toward the Ryker estate. He was also feeling a bit nervous about showing up unannounced. He had no idea if Reese would even be there. He could be in Louisville, pretending to run his TV station. A half mile from the stables, where the white fencing began, Caldwell pulled over and punched the number into his phone. The man answered on the fourth ring, calling Caldwell by name.

"Yeah, there's been a development," Caldwell said.

"What happened?"

"I'm just down the road from the stables," Caldwell said. "Thought I'd drop off my résumé. Are you there?"

There was a pause. "Pull up to the house."

Caldwell had his invite to the big house. Approaching, he saw the Porsche parked in the circular drive alongside a Jaguar roadster and a black Land Rover. Caldwell pulled his Cherokee up behind the Jag, wishing now he'd stopped to run the car through the car wash on the way. As he was getting out, Ryker's wife, Sofia, came out of the house. Caldwell had seen her at Keeneland once but only from a distance. Today she was wearing tight black jeans and a white T-shirt with a lunging panther across the front and stiletto heels that had to be five inches high. Caldwell had no idea how women didn't fall over wearing those things.

"May I help you?" she asked in a strong accent.

"Chuck Caldwell," he said. "I run Chestnut Field."

"Yes?"

"Reese asked me to stop by."

"He is in the house," she said as she walked to the Jag. "Bye bye."

As Caldwell climbed the wide steps the front door opened and Reese stepped out. His hair was mussed and his eyes heavy. He looked as if he'd just gotten up from a nap. Maybe Caldwell had woken him with the phone call. He indicated some white wicker chairs on the porch to his left and moved to sit in one.

"She entered the horse," Caldwell said as he sat down.

Reese took a deep breath but didn't say anything. Then his eyes seemed to notice the Jaguar, just now pulling out of the long drive and turning onto the highway out front.

"Where the fuck is she going?"

Caldwell hesitated. "She didn't say."

Reese shook his head. "When are they running him?"

"A week Saturday, a sprint at Chestnut."

"So I guess she has a trainer," Reese said. "You wouldn't let her enter a horse without a trainer, would you?"

"No, I wouldn't. Luke Walker got his license back. I saw the paperwork."

"Luke Walker," Reese said. "What a joke. Mr. O'Hara did some digging on him. He's a habitual fuckup, it would appear. He's a boozer and a gambler and whoremaster. Earns a dollar and spends two."

"I've heard the stories," Caldwell said. "He showed up driving a truck I wouldn't give you five cents for. But they gave him a license, so I have to let him race if he wants to."

"At least until he fucks up again," Reese said. "We've been keeping tabs on him. He stays on a farm outside Junction City and spends his evenings drinking in a bar down the road." Reese glanced over. "And every morning he pays you a visit at Chestnut."

"He's not coming there to visit me," Caldwell assured him. "I've never even had a conversation with the man."

"Perhaps you should. You could ask him why he's working for Billie Masterson."

"Maybe he's fucking her. Good-looking woman."

Reese shook his head. "Even if he is, why would he want to hire on with a one-horse stable? Unless he sees something in that colt."

"He can train other horses, too," Caldwell said. "He's a free agent."

"Do you see him training other horses?" Reese asked.

"No, but he was just reinstated. I doubt he's exclusive to the Masterson woman. Like you said, she's only got the one horse and who knows if the animal can even run?"

"He may have options he hasn't considered," Reese said. "Think about it. If you were Luke Walker, with a five-cent truck and the ass out of your jeans and no prospects other than a colt that has never been raced—what would you do if I asked you to come and work for me? I have more two-year-olds on this farm alone than I can count. Wouldn't that have appeal?"

Caldwell nodded but remained silent. He was thinking about how Reese Ryker had described Luke Walker. Boozer, gambler, whoremaster. How hard could it be to trip up a guy like that? And how grateful would Reese be if he could do it?

"But then you'd be stuck with him," Caldwell said.

"Temporarily," Reese said. "The price you pay. But Billie Masterson would not be racing that horse next Saturday."

"That would be one way to handle it."

Reese turned. "Well, at the moment I don't have another. Do I?"

Eighteen

They had ten days to get the colt ready to run. Billie kept asking Luke if that was enough time and he kept ignoring her. He and Tyrone would breeze or gallop the horse on alternate days. With Skeeter up, Will Masterson had already had the colt switching leads and he took to it well. There was a training starting gate in the infield and Luke had the colt in there every day, with Tyrone in the irons, practicing the break.

Most of the time Billie hung around the track, watching and feeling useless. Most days Jodie came with her. Cactus Jack seemed to love the kid, probably because she'd been around the colt more than the rest of them and had a habit of spoiling him. She'd been quiet of late, uncharacteristically, and Billie wondered if things at home were more fucked up than usual. The kid was still at the farm every morning at first light.

Billie had made nominal payments to the feed store and the power company. She went back to the bank and met again with her old high school acquaintance, Kellyanne. Since their first meeting, Billie had been trying to remember the nature of their relationship back at good old Marshall High. Kellyanne Cruickshank had been snobbish and petty and Billie recalled that her father was an accountant for a John Deere dealership, which meant that he was a white-collar type, which also meant that Kellyanne considered herself to be on a slightly higher social plane than the other kids. She and Billie didn't hang out. Kellyanne was in the math club, while Billie smoked joints and drank lemon gin in the parking lot on Fridays before the football games. To make matters worse, from Kellyanne's perspective anyway, joint-smoking and gin-drinking Billie got better grades than math-club Kellyanne, and a scholarship to boot.

There had also been an incident at a school dance. Billie's memory was fuzzy on the details but it seemed to her that she might have left with a boy who Kellyanne had set her sights on. It also seemed that Kellyanne was taking a long time to get over high school.

Not that Billie would have recognized her. Her hair was now straight and blonde and cut short and spiky. She wore suits to work, with very tight skirts and high heels. She was brisk and authoritative and seemed to want to impress upon Billie that she had achieved much in life while Billie was still slouching around in jeans and work shirts, out of work and mired in inherited debt. She had a point in all that, Billie had to admit.

"If it was up to me, we would demand payment on the mortgages today," Kellyanne told her point-blank. They were sitting in her glass-walled office at Kentucky First National.

"Then I guess I'm glad it's not up to you," Billie said lightly, hoping to inject a little humor into what Kellyanne had obviously decided was a humorless situation.

"Mr. Brock is pretty soft on some things," Kellyanne added.

Billie didn't know who Mr. Brock was but didn't ask. Presumably he was somebody who held Kellyanne in check up to a point.

"So you've been here all this time," Billie ventured. "Are you married with kids and all that?"

"This isn't a social."

"No, I see it's not," Billie said.

"The clock is ticking."

Billie told that to Luke when she got to the track later. It was noon Monday and she and Luke were sitting on the tailgate of his truck along the shed row, drinking take-out coffee. Tyrone had just left; he had two mounts later that day in Keeneland. Billie had remembered to pay him. He was working the colt for twenty dollars a day, on the agreement he would get the ride come Saturday. Billie was getting a bargain, both with the jockey and Luke himself, and she knew it.

"How are we going to know if he's ready to run?" Billie asked.

"He's ready to run today," Luke said. "Running is the easy part. Hell, a toddler can run. It's all the rest we got to keep working on. I had a horse once, the starting gate opened and that animal just stood there. The rest of the field was in the back stretch before that horse finally wandered out of the gate. Never ran again. Never ran then, come to think of it."

"You said the colt was breaking well," Billie said.

"He is. I'm just giving you an example of how things can go sour."

"It can be depressing, talking to you."

"You want sunshine and lollipops?" Luke said.

Billie wouldn't mind a little sunshine and a few lollipops but she didn't say so. "What about Tyrone?"

"What about him?"

"Is he the right jockey?"

Luke looked at the horse in the stall. Jodie was feeding the animal bits of carrots and he was leaning his neck out over the door, reaching for more.

"Tyrone will be okay," Luke said. "Keep in mind he's got his bug and that helps us. He's a little green but he gets along with the colt well. Sometimes a jockey just needs to keep out of the horse's way, let him do his thing. But I figure he knows that. Shit, he was probably on a horse before he learned to walk. It's in his blood."

"There's that word again," Billie said. "You sound like Reese Ryker."

"Well, there's a reason that Saguaro gets a quarter million dollars to mount a mare. And that's the same reason I'm sitting here. That colt there feeding his face on carrots is a good-looking animal, but if he wasn't by Saguaro I'd be up in Indiana right now, racing my bay on the flat track. So you can't come down too hard on Ryker, not for that anyway."

"I wasn't talking about horses so much."

"What do you mean?"

"Let's just say that Ryker has some political views I don't agree with."

Luke shrugged. "Well, I can't comment on that. All I know is horses."

"And honky-tonks and poker games and pretty girls."

Luke laughed as he tossed the dregs from his cup onto the grass. "I'm a goddamn Renaissance man and I didn't even know it."

Billie and Jodie left shortly after that. As they were driving through the gate, the girl looked over at Billie.

"What's a bug?"

Billie turned onto the highway. "Something that crawls in your ear at night. Lays eggs inside your head and makes you crazy."

"Be serious."

"An apprentice jockey gets a five-pound weight allowance. They call it a bug."

"How come they call it that?"

"They just do."

"That's not an answer."

"It's the only one I got, kid."

On the drive back to the farm, Billie decided she wouldn't go to the track the next day. She was worrying over the colt like she would over a child being sent off to school for the first time. She needed to trust Luke and Tyrone and stay away for a day or two. If she wasn't going to the track she might as well drive back to

Chillicothe. She needed to give up her apartment and empty her meager bank account. She could probably do the banking over the phone, but she wanted her clothes and her laptop and a few other things.

She drove the truck into the lower lane and parked by the barn. Shutting the ignition off, she glanced over at the silent little girl. She was still wearing the worn sneakers. In fact, Billie hadn't noticed a single purchase she might have made with her windfall—not a shirt or a bell for her bicycle or even a goddamn ribbon for her hair.

"I'm going to Ohio today and I won't be back until tomorrow. Can you look after things here?"

Jodie glanced around. "What things?"

"Feed the stock. Muck the stalls. Make sure everything has water."

"The mares are out to pasture and they have water in the pond. And I always take care of my animals. You don't need to tell me."

"Just look after things, okay?" Billie said. "And I thought you were going to buy new sneakers. Did you open a bank account?"

Jodie said nothing.

Let it go, Billie thought. *Why do you want to get involved with something that's none of your business!*

"What did you do with the money?" she asked. "Blow it at McDonalds?"

"No."

"Then what?"

The girl exhaled. "My mom needed help with the rent."

Shit, Billie thought. *This is what happens when you ask questions you don't want the fucking answers to.* Not that it would stop her, not now. "How much did you give her?"

The girl looked away.

"All of it?"

"She needed help with the rent," Jodie said again. "The house where I *live,* okay?" She opened the door and got out.

Billie got out, too. Jodie was already on her bike, eager to be gone.

"Just look after things," Billie said. "I'll be home tomorrow. I'm going to pay you."

"No. I owe for hay."

"When my father was alive, who was the boss here?" Billie asked.

Jodie wouldn't look at her. "He was."

"And who's the boss now?"

Watching the little girl, with her eyes fixed on the road out front and her jaw tight, Billie remembered that her father used to say that there was nothing in the world more stubborn than a child. Not that a person became less stubborn as they grew up (Billie was evidence of that), but they learned how to manage it better, how to disguise it as something else, whether it was feigned indifference or even ignorance of certain facts. But nine-year-olds didn't hide behind disguises. They were too pure for that.

"You are," Jodie said at last.

"Okay," Billie said. "I'll see you when I get back."

Luke had been staying at Nick Hartwick's farm on Knob Hill Road, west of Junction City. By luck, when Luke had pulled into his drive, Nick was just a couple days away from heading out on a six-month contract as a pipefitter in Alberta. He had arranged for a neighbor to look after his place while he was gone. He had ten acres of pasture and was grazing two paint quarter horses and a half dozen yearling steers. The horses actually belonged to Nick's ex-girlfriend Becky, who had left a few months earlier, returning to her sad-sack husband who had promised her that he was a changed man. One reason Nick was going to Alberta was that he didn't want to be there when she found out that the ex-husband was the same mean prick he'd always been. Then she'd be back on Nick's porch, her suitcases and guitar in hand, and it would start all over again.

So the timing was right when Luke arrived. He offered to tend to things on the farm in exchange for lodging. He also hit Nick up for five hundred dollars, seed money, as Luke had put it. Nick didn't mind; he'd been willing to pay the neighbor kid fifty a week to feed the stock, so in the long run he would be saving money, even if Luke didn't pay him back. And Nick knew that Luke would eventually repay him, although it might take a few years. Not only that, but with Luke on the premises full-time it would discourage thieves or druggie nesters looking for a warm place to crash.

The house was a frame building, story and a half, and Luke took the front upstairs bedroom as his own. He passed his mornings at the track, training Cactus Jack. Afternoons he tended to the ex-girlfriend's horses and the Hereford steers. If needed, he fixed fence and cut grass. In the evenings he usually headed to the Junction Tap House, on the highway a few miles away. The food there was edible and he could usually hustle up a pool game. Thursday was euchre night and Luke considered himself an expert at the game.

He drove there around six o'clock on the Tuesday before the race and settled in at the bar. He asked for a large draft and a corned beef sandwich. The place was mostly empty but slowly filled as Luke ate the sandwich and talked football with the bartender until he found out the man was a Patriots fan.

By nine o'clock he was playing shuffleboard with a guy who looked like a golfer on TV—polo shirt, khaki pants. He'd come in an hour earlier with a young woman wearing tight jeans and a sleeveless black T-shirt. She had short hair under a Cubs cap. She was good-looking. The guy couldn't hit a rock if his life hung in the balance and Luke beat him easily three games in a row, two dollars a game. Then the girl challenged him. She was better than the guy but not by much. She was very friendly though, which more than made up for her lack of skill. Luke was surprised when the guy announced that he was leaving, saying something about work in the morning.

"What are you going to do?" he asked the woman.

She looked at Luke. "Another game?"

"Sure."

She turned to the guy. "I'm going to hang here for a bit."

The guy had no problem with that, it seemed, and off he went. The woman went to the bathroom and while she was gone Luke went to the bar and bought beers for them both.

"He your boyfriend?" he asked when she came back.

"Fred?" she asked. "No, we're just buddies. We went to high school together." She smiled at Luke. She had a nice smile. "Fred's not my type."

"You look like you could still be in high school," Luke said.

"Give me a break, man," she said. "I get that all the time. Shit, I'm twenty-five years old."

"What do you do?"

"I'm a teacher. And it's summertime so I get to stay out as late as I want."

"What's your name?"

"Rachel."

"I'm Luke."

Rachel picked up the fresh draft and had a drink. "I want to tell you something, Luke. Before I leave here tonight, I'm going to kick your ass at this game."

"A woman needs a goal in life," Luke said.

They played the first end, with Luke making three points. He wasn't taking it easy on her, not yet, but he might just do that if it looked as if it might work to his advantage.

"You say Fred's not your type," he said. "What is your type?"

She threw the first rock and it skidded to a stop inside the single line. She smiled without looking at him. "I kinda like cowboys."

When Luke woke at dawn the woman was gone. The first thing he did was reach for his jeans on the floor to make sure his wallet hadn't been cleaned out. His money was safe. Thinking that maybe she was still on the property, he looked out the window to the yard below and saw that her car was gone. She'd followed

Luke home in a red Mustang convertible that looked brand-new. Apparently schoolteachers made good money.

He had a slight hangover but it wasn't debilitating. He had stuck to draft beer even when Rachel had tried to talk him into doing shots. He knew he had to be at Chestnut early. He wondered if he was maturing at long last; in the past, whenever a pretty girl suggested shots, Luke was all over the idea.

Still, he felt wrung out and it wasn't hard to know why. It had been quite a night. The room was in disarray, the sheets twisted together, both pillows on the floor. Luke had no idea that schoolteachers were so adventuresome. This schoolteacher anyway. She was into everything he suggested and had a few ideas of her own. At some point she took out her phone and asked Luke to take pictures of her in different poses. Luke hadn't been too interested in the idea; he didn't quite understand the obsession kids had with taking photos of everything they did. He didn't get Snapchat and Instagram or any of the rest of it. He had a flip phone he'd bought in South Dakota ten years ago. He didn't know how to text and didn't want to learn. Tweeting was, quite literally, for the fucking birds.

But of course he had obliged the woman. She was beautiful and naked and horny. So he had taken a few pics and then they fucked. Then she took some pics and they fucked again. Boy, did they fuck.

He was surprised that the woman was gone. She seemed like the type who might want to stay for breakfast and have a serious conversation. Luke would have no time for the first notion and not a lot of interest in the second. He had no idea when she left. He wondered if she woke up feeling sheepish about her actions the night before. Maybe it was something she'd never done before and she was guilty about it. Luke hoped not; guilt was a useless emotion as far as he was concerned. He wondered if he would see her again.

He had a quick shower and got into his truck and headed for Chestnut. He hadn't gotten any more than about three hours' sleep, he guessed, and he was weary, his head fuzzy. They were stretching the colt out to a mile today. Tyrone was there, waiting, as he always was. He was working horses for other trainers too—Luke suspected he was short on money—but he said that Cactus Jack was his first priority. Billie was not anywhere to be seen and so neither was the little girl.

The colt's numbers at eight furlongs were as impressive as they were at the shorter distances. After they galloped him, they worked him breaking from the training gate for a time. Returning to the stall, Luke rubbed the colt down and fed him before heading back to the farm. When he got there, he found a black Pontiac Sunfire by the barn. Luke parked alongside and got out to walk around the building. A woman with curly brown hair to her shoulders was in the pasture field with the two paint quarter horses. She was feeding them something from her hand—sugar cubes or the like, Luke guessed. He had never seen the woman before but he knew who she was. He leaned on the fence and watched her. When she finally turned, she feigned surprise at seeing him there. Unless she was stone deaf, she'd have heard his exhaust when he pulled in.

"Hey there," she said, walking toward him. She had some curves to her and was pretty sexy, wearing a tank top and jeans. Brown suede cowboy boots. She had an abundance of freckles on her arms and shoulders and everywhere else, Luke guessed. "Nick around?"

"Nope."

"I'm Becky."

"I figured that."

"Where's he off to?"

"Alberta."

That gave the woman pause. "Canada?"

"That's the only Alberta I know of," Luke said. "Something I can help you with?"

"Who are you again?"

"Name's Luke. I'm looking after the place for a bit. He said you might come around, depending on your circumstances."

"What the hell does that mean?"

"You know. How's things working out with the hubby?"

The woman Becky was immediately offended. "Why is Nick telling you my business? I don't know you from a load of hay."

"He asked me to look after his ex-girlfriend's horses," Luke said. "It was only natural for me to ask him why the hell he was taking care of them, you being gone and all. I wasn't aware that the information was top secret."

Becky looked away. "When's he coming back?"

"Not sure," Luke said. "I do know he has a woman up there in the tar sands. I believe she's a wealthy oil tycoon."

"What?" Becky demanded. "He's shacked up with somebody already?"

"Nah," Luke said. "I made that up, just to see what you'd say."

"You think you're a funny man."

"I'm kinda hungover so I'm not really thinking that much at all."

"That's obvious," Becky said. "If you're looking after the place, you should know that I've advertised my paints in *Ranchers Monthly*. So there might very well be people coming by to look at them. I'll try to be here when that happens but if I'm not I'd appreciate it if you could show any prospective buyers the horses. And if you could do it without being an asshole, that would be a bonus."

"Nick never told me what a sweet talker you are."

"You started it."

"I guess maybe I did," Luke said. "All right then, I'll do my best to accommodate you, Becky. And if Nick calls I'll tell him that you came around, just like he said you might, looking all mopey and full of regret and such."

"Did you already forget the part about not being an asshole?"

"Shit," Luke said. "I need to write that down somewhere."

Becky left then, getting into her beat-up Pontiac and throwing stones as she accelerated down the driveway. Luke watched her for a moment and then turned to have a look at the two quarter horses in the field. In the house he scrambled three eggs and washed them down with a beer before heading to the couch for a nap. He told himself he was getting too old for this shit. He drifted off thinking about the schoolteacher.

Nineteen

WHEN SHE GOT TO CHILLICOTHE, BILLIE went to her place first. Driving into town, she began to worry about running into Rory. But it was a workday and he would be on a job somewhere, she reasoned. It would be a fluke for him to stumble across her, unless he was watching her place, and she doubted he would be doing that after a month or so. He was probably under the impression that she had left town for good. Hell, maybe he'd even had the Vette repaired by now and everything was cool once again in the narrow sphere of Rory's world.

There was a volume of mail inside the door of her place, 90 percent of it flyers and junk mail. She went through it quickly, deciding that none of it required her attention before tossing everything into the recycle bin out back.

She intended to take whatever clothes she could jam into her one suitcase and leave the rest to Goodwill. There wasn't much else in the apartment she wanted. The furniture wasn't worth hauling to Kentucky and there was no place to put it there anyway, unless she wanted to store it in the barn, where the mice would get at it. Wandering back and forth through the house, she was marginally disappointed to realize there really was nothing there with any sentimental value, unless she counted the picture of her with the Broken Bombers on top of the TV. What did it say about her that she had lived over three decades without becoming attached to anything? She told herself that it was merely evidence that she was a practical person. Yes, that was it.

She needed to talk to her landlord, who lived next door, to tell him that she'd be giving up the apartment. Her rent was a few days past due and he would be making an issue of that. She'd been late in the past but never more than a week or two. Now she was about to tell him that she was moving out without notice. He would whine about it and Billie would listen to him for a bit and then leave.

She made coffee and sat in the living room, thinking about what she was about to do. Giving up the house meant she was committing herself to the situation in Kentucky. A practical person (which she had just recently decided she was) might argue that there was a very good chance she'd be selling the farm in the near future. Or losing it to the bank. And then where would practical Billie be? Her mother used to criticize her father for putting all his eggs in one basket. Not only was Billie about to do that, she was about to use the same damn basket.

Aiding and abetting her were a trainer coming back from suspension, a man whom Billie had always known to be the walking definition of the word *reckless*; a jockey who offered enthusiasm but not much in the way of experience; and a cantankerous old lawyer whose sentimental side when it came to Will Masterson might be trumping the pragmatism for which he claimed to be known. To that mix Billie could throw in her father's girlfriend, who had lately seemed to wash her hands of the whole lot, although Billie's attitude toward her might have encouraged said washing.

None of it seemed particularly encouraging to practical Billie and most of it registered as downright foolish. She finished her coffee, rinsed her cup in the sink, and went next door to pay the coming month's rent. After that, she'd have to reassess.

Leaving town the following day, she stopped by Freddie's Fish Shack, pulling into the parking lot behind the building just as Freddie himself came out the back door, carrying a plastic garbage bag and heading for the dumpster in the alley. He glanced at the truck without recognition as it pulled in and looked away, tossed the bag into the dumpster, and started back for the restaurant. Billie rolled down the window and called to him.

"Billie," he said as she got out. "When did you get back?"

"I don't know that I am back," Billie said. "How are things?"

"Same old," Freddie said. "One day the same as the next."

"Living the examined life," Billie suggested.

"Not sure that peeling potatoes and deveining shrimp fits the description." Freddie looked her over for a moment, as if her appearance might inform him of how she was now. "You hear from Athena?"

"She texts me," Billie said. "Still trying to lure me to California."

Freddie took his cigarettes from his pocket and put one in his mouth before offering the pack to Billie.

"I'm off them," she said.

Freddie lit up and blew smoke into the air. "California—that where you headin'?"

"Not just now," Billie said. "I was here overnight and heading back to Kentucky. I had to pick up some things."

"What's going on in Kentucky?"

"I'm on the farm. My father left me a dog's breakfast—horses and debts and other assorted entanglements. The odd donkey and nanny goat. I'm still sorting out what to do with it all. I have a two-year-old thoroughbred I'm thinking of racing."

"You never told me your father was in the racing business," Freddie said.

"I guess it never came up."

"My old man played the ponies." Freddie hauled on the cigarette again and smiled. "He had a saying. You know how to make a small fortune on the horses?"

"Start with a big fortune," Billie said.

Freddie laughed. "That's it."

Billie reached over and took the cigarette from the old man and had a drag. "You're a bad influence," she said, handing it back. "So—you seen Rory boy around?"

"He doesn't come here," Freddie said. "Say what you want about Rory, he can take a hint. I see him though, time to time." He hesitated. "Ordinarily I wouldn't say anything because I'm not real interested in all the soap opera shit that goes down in this town. But I'm thinking you might be happy to hear that Rory has a new girlfriend. Or somebody he's been seeing anyway. So that might be good news for you."

Billie nodded. "Bad news for her, but good news for me."

"I don't know anything about the woman. Let's hope she isn't the type to go to customizing the man's car for him. Although I might categorize that as reap what you sow, asshole."

Billie smiled again. "I love you, Freddie."

The object of her affection flipped the cigarette into a corner. "I guess you won't be coming back here to work ever again, will you?"

"You never know."

"Oh, I know," Freddie said. "There were times when I considered firing you, just to get you motivated in another direction. Untapped potential, that's what everybody said about you."

"And I never get tired of hearing it."

Freddie smiled. "I'm glad you stopped by. Where'd you get the truck, anyway?"

"I inherited it," she said. "I was hoping for a yacht."

"What would you do with a yacht?"

"Sail away," Billie said. "I would sail away."

Billie arrived back at the farm late in the afternoon. She parked the truck by the machine shed, noticing Jodie's bike there, leaning against the paddock fence. Billie got out and walked through the barn. The pony and donkey stood in the far paddock, their tails chasing flies in the afternoon sun. The goat was lying on its belly in the dirt, front hooves tucked beneath it, chewing a mouthful of hay. The little girl was nowhere to be seen.

Billie spotted her when she started for the house. She was standing on the back deck, turned sideways to Billie, and she looked to be arranging something on the table there. Curious, Billie went over for a look.

On the table were brand new jockey's silks, in gold and green. The letters MT were embroidered prominently across the back of the shirt. The girl had been busy smoothing the clothes out for Billie to see and now she turned, proud of her efforts and obviously anxious for Billie's reaction.

Billie wasn't quite sure what her reaction was. "Where did these come from?"

"Marian brought them."

"Why the hell would she do that?"

The girl's enthusiasm began to slide. "For the race Saturday." She seemed puzzled that Billie didn't get it. "It's Cactus Jack's first race."

"How would Marian know that he's running?"

"I don't know but she did," Jodie said. "She said she ordered these silks for Will a couple months ago. It was going to be a surprise." She hesitated. "Don't you like them?"

Billie moved closer and ran her fingers over the stitching. They were quality silks. "They're okay, I guess. Nobody asked her to do this."

"I guess she wanted to do it."

Billie went into the house and got a beer from the fridge. When she came back, she stopped outside the door. "You want anything?"

"I have to go," Jodie said. "I waited for you to see the silks."

Billie exhaled and sat down. "They're nice. And to tell you the truth I never even thought about what Tyrone would be wearing on Saturday."

"There are silks in the tack room, in the wooden chest," Jodie said. "The same color as these but they're kinda—" She stopped.

"Kinda what?"

"Kinda not nice like these."

"Yeah," Billie said and took a drink. "So when was Marian here?"

"After lunch. I was trying to hook the harness to the pony cart and she drove in the front lane and came down and asked where you were. I told her you were in Ohio and she asked if you were coming back. I think she was joking."

"She's a riot."

"Do you know how to do the harness for the pony cart? Will was going to show me."

Billie did know how to do the harness, or at least there was a time when she had known. What she knew now and what she didn't know was getting fuzzier by the day.

"We can take a stab at it," she said.

"You can teach me, instead of paying me to look after things."

"I can do both."

Jodie was quiet for a moment. "How come you don't like it when people do things for you?"

Billie had the beer can halfway to her mouth. She looked briefly at the silks, arranged carefully on the table by the little girl. "What makes you ask a question like that?"

"I just wondered. That's all."

"Didn't anybody ever tell you that curiosity killed the cat?"

Jodie stood up and started down the steps, heading for her bicycle down the hill. She took about twenty steps before turning back.

"I can figure out the harness by myself."

Well shit, Billie thought as the girl got on her bike and rode away.

Twenty

L UKE'S FIRST IMPULSE WAS TO SAY no to Reese Ryker, but after talking to the man for a couple minutes on the phone he decided it might be fun to meet up. He could play along for a while, hear what Ryker was offering, and then have the pleasure of telling him to go piss up a rope. The idea had a lot of appeal and besides, Luke was bored. He'd been sitting on the porch of the farmhouse near Junction City, drinking beer and counting his toes, when Ryker had called. Luke told him he could be at the stable in an hour, which gave him time to drink another beer.

Seeing Ryker's operation up close was not something that factored into things. Luke had seen fancy stables before, and lush pastures and mile after mile of pristine white fencing. He'd grown up in Kentucky after all, and even though he hadn't been raised on an estate, he'd seen enough of them that they held no interest for him at this point. There had probably been a time when he had been impressed by such trappings and a later time when he had resented them, but since losing his license a few years back he'd grown to believe that money didn't mean shit when it came right down to cases. Or maybe he just told himself that because he was chronically broke.

There were some nice vehicles in the circular drive in front of the Ryker mansion. Luke parked his truck beside a white Jag and got out. The sun was high and the interior of the Ford was hot as he drove, the air conditioning having gone south a few years earlier. Standing in the concrete drive, Luke removed his Resistol and wiped his brow with his forearm. He was about to climb the flight of stairs to the front door when he heard his name. He turned to see Reese Ryker standing in the doorway of the main stable. He was dressed in white, shirt and pants and ball cap with RR across the front. Only a man who had never gotten his hands dirty would wear white in a horse barn. Luke knew the man by sight but had never spoken to him before the phone call earlier. He looked different from what Luke remembered, older and younger at the same time.

Luke shook the soft hand offered to him. He saw Reese's eyes flick over the dirty truck in the driveway. There was something satisfied in the look, as if it confirmed something to him. The man was as transparent as glass.

"How'd you like to look at some horses?" Reese said.

"Why not?" Luke said. He was already enjoying himself.

First stop was the main barn, where the stallion Saguaro was installed. Luke had never seen the horse up close and he was impressed, but then how could he not be? The animal had presence and attitude and was a superstar in the racing world. He seemed to know that he was something special; Luke had seen that in horses before. They said that Cigar had it, Secretariat had it. Saguaro definitely had it. Although Luke never mentioned it to Reese Ryker, he could see a lot of the colt Cactus Jack in the sire. His eyes were slightly wider than most thoroughbreds and the gray of the horse's coat was highlighted with tiny white flecks.

"You ever see a better-looking horse?" Reese asked.

Luke admitted that he had not.

He got the grand tour then, through stables that were cleaner that a lot of motel rooms Luke had slept in, along tree-lined lanes bordered by pastures where broodmares grazed alongside their foals, by a training track where runners were being worked. Amid the riders and grooms was a man in a fedora and Double R windbreaker, leaning on the rail of the track. Reese pointed to him.

"Come on, I want to introduce you to Joe Drinkwater."

Joe Drinkwater heard their approach over the sounds from the track and turned. It took him a moment before he spoke. "Hello, Luke."

"How are you, Joe?"

Reese hung back a moment. He seemed almost miffed that the two men knew each other. Apparently he'd been looking forward to (further) impressing Luke with the fact that he had Joe Drinkwater training his horses.

"Where have you been anyway?" Joe asked.

"Racing quarters," Luke said.

"That flat tracking is for kids," Joe said. "You getting rich?"

Luke laughed. "Not hardly."

"Oh, he's doing all right," Reese said. "You should see the truck he's driving."

Joe turned on Reese, his eyes hooded, and he made no reply. Luke didn't know Joe Drinkwater well, but he knew the look. He'd seen it with enough trainers and vets and hot walkers and grooms. They had to work with certain owners but they weren't required to like them.

"Did you breeze Ghost Rider this morning?" Reese asked.

Joe nodded.

"And?"

"Twenty-seven seven."

Reese looked to Luke for his reaction. He was like a kid who had turned a cartwheel and was now expecting praise for it. Except it had been the horse that turned the cartwheel, under the guidance of Joe Drinkwater. All Reese Ryker did was write the checks. Luke didn't feel obliged to compliment the man for that.

"Come on," Reese said. "I want to show you that colt."

They walked back to the house and got into a Jeep to drive to the far end of the farm, where the young horses were. Reese parked beneath a large shagbark hickory tree and they walked across an expanse of lawn to a pasture field enclosed by more of the white fencing. Inside were a dozen or so two-year-olds. Luke went to the fence and looked them over. It was an impressive display of horse-flesh—bays and chestnuts and grays, all muscled and sleek and all of them from blood. At the end of the field was a smaller paddock, separate, and inside a large gray colt was trotting back and forth.

"Come on," Reese said.

Even Luke, who had for the past few years purposely ignored whatever was happening in the thoroughbred world, had heard about Ghost Rider. The colt was considered the best two-year-old prospect in the country, which was why the animal had his own pasture. Two-year-old colts were like teenage boys; they liked to fight to show which had the bigger cojones. Ryker wasn't going to risk an injury to his prize prospect over a schoolyard scrap.

"What do you think?" he asked.

Luke nodded his appreciation. The colt they were admiring didn't come over to them; he continued to trot back and forth, watching the other horses. Luke thought about Cactus Jack. That colt was a sociable animal. That could have been in the blood too, from the dam's side.

"Saguaro is the sire," Reese said.

"I believe I read that somewheres," Luke said.

Reese stood watching the colt, half smirking. "I guess we have something in common then."

"I don't own a colt by Saguaro," Luke said.

"But you're training one," Reese said. "And *one* would be the key word in that sentence. What are you going to do when you find out that horse of Masterson's runs like his mother and not his father?"

"I ain't going to sit down and cry, I'll tell you that," Luke said. "I've been around the block once or twice."

"You need to come and work for me, Luke," Reese said. He indicated the horses in the field. "There's a lot of talent there. Joe Drinkwater can't train them all and I don't know how many years he's going to keep working anyway. I've been looking into you, Luke. It's time you started using your God-given talent. I'd start you at two thousand a week and then you'd have your percentages on top of that. You could be a rich man."

"Maybe I'm already rich."

Reese laughed. "You'll pardon me for doubting that."

Luke looked at the muscled colt a little longer. "I'm going to have to say no. I've made a commitment to the owner."

"An owner that won't even be in the business a year from now."

Luke shrugged. "I still have to say no."

He was expecting a bigger reaction from Reese Ryker. Instead he got no argument at all. On the drive back to the house, Reese talked of other things—the warm weather and the fall elections. He told Luke that he had been approached to run for office but declined. For now, he said.

They parked the Jeep in front of the house. Luke thanked Reese for the tour and walked to his truck, still thinking that Ryker's recruitment effort had been on the weak side. He had expected a full court press. Not only that, but Reese Ryker—who was used to getting his way—was taking Luke's rejection in stride, as if the offer had been for a cup of coffee rather than a job.

"I almost forgot," Reese said as Luke opened the truck door. "There's something in the house I wanted to show you. Come on in."

Luke smiled as he followed Ryker up the steps. So the boy had an ace up his sleeve after all. What would he offer now? A house in the country with servants and a limo service? Sixteen vestal virgins? Reese led the way through a large living room with vaulted ceilings and pictures of African wildlife on the walls into a den of sorts, with a bay window, dark paneled walls, and a desk the size of a pool table. There was someone there, as if waiting for them, a tall skinny guy with lank blond hair, sitting in a leather chair, one leg over the other.

"My associate Mr. O'Hara," Reese said.

The associate never stood or offered his hand. Luke nodded to him, wondering where this was leading. The whole situation had taken a turn and Luke couldn't figure the direction. But he had a gut feeling they were through talking about a job offer.

"I mentioned earlier that I have been looking into you," Reese said, taking a seat behind the desk. "Mr. O'Hara was doing the actual looking. He tells me you don't have much of a social media presence, Luke."

"I got zero social media presence," Luke said. "You didn't have to pay somebody to tell you that."

"That's not quite accurate." Reese reached into a drawer and brought out a manila envelope. "I have these on a thumb drive but Mr. O'Hara suspects you don't own a computer." He pulled a dozen or so glossy photos from the envelope and slid them across the desk. "I believe you know this person?"

Luke glanced at the pictures. A glance was all that was required. They had been taken in his bedroom a few nights earlier.

"Yeah, she's a schoolteacher, name of Rachel. What of it?"

"You're close," Reese said. "Actually, she's a school*girl*. Her name is Brenna Simpson and she's seventeen years old. She goes to private school in Louisville. And—well, you know kids today—everything they do, they feel a need to post pictures of it. She sent these to a friend of hers, bragging about—what did she call it—a dirty night out in Junction City. These kids are so smart and yet they don't seem to realize there is no such thing as a private photo these days, unless you take it with a Polaroid and hide it under your mattress."

Luke could feel his heart in his chest. "She told me she was twenty-five."

The associate O'Hara made a chortling sound. When Luke glanced over, he was looking out the window, a slight smile on his face.

Reese shrugged. "She could tell you she was the quarterback for the Green Bay Packers but that wouldn't make it true."

Reese reached forward to spread the photos out on the desk. "I have to say that she looks very young to me. And acrobatic too, I might add. I just wanted to show you—oh, here we are—we have a couple of nice shots of you too, Luke. You and your seventeen-year-old girlfriend."

Luke wouldn't look at the pictures again. He was thinking of reaching across the desk and taking Ryker by the throat. Presumably that was why the silent associate was there, to prevent such a thing.

"This gets better, Luke," Reese went on. "As I'm sure you know, the age of consent in Kentucky is eighteen. Which of course means that you are guilty of statutory rape. The irony here is—this girl's father is a district attorney in Louisville's second division court. And he's known for having prosecuted a number of statutory rape cases. He seems to be on a bit of a crusade about it."

"She said she was twenty-five," Luke said again. "What about the bar? They were serving her."

"Maybe her father will go after the bar for serving his daughter alcohol under age," Reese said. "But I'm thinking he'll want to go after the rapist instead. I'm thinking he'll want to put you away for a number of years. A good number."

In a daze Luke turned and sat down heavily in a chair across from Ryker. He stared blankly for a moment at the photos spread across the desk. "How?"

Reese nodded toward the blond man. "I asked Mr. O'Hara to keep tabs on you. I'm pretty sure he's had tougher assignments. You drive to the same racetrack every morning and you drink at the same bar every night. You left there Tuesday around eleven o'clock with the girl following you in her car. Her license number led to her name and then a little cyber-sleuthing led to . . . these." He indicated the pictures.

Luke glanced again at the skinny man in the chair by the wall. "That can't be legal."

Reese laughed. "I'm pretty sure it's not. Do you want to call the cops, Luke?"

O'Hara was still smiling, proud of his work. Luke kept a baseball bat behind the seat of his truck. For a moment he entertained the thought of getting it and laying waste to the room and to the two smirking assholes in it. But he knew that wouldn't change anything. He needed to find out what would.

"What can I do here?" he asked. "How many people have these pictures?"

"Good question," Reese replied. "Mr. O'Hara notified the girl and she told her friend. They of course removed them from the internet. Do others have them? Maybe so, maybe not. If so, they wouldn't know the implications and they wouldn't know who you are anyway." He smiled. "Luke, you look a little peaked. Would you like a drink?"

"No. Tell me what you want."

Reese shrugged, looking over at O'Hara for a moment. "Well, obviously the job offer is no longer on the table. I was hoping you'd take me up on that and then none of this unpleasantness would be necessary."

"Tell me what you want."

"Come on, Luke. You know what I want."

Twenty-One

I T WAS SHORTLY BEFORE NOON SATURDAY when Billie came out
of the house and walked down the hill to the barn. Jodie was
there and had been all morning. A few days earlier she and Billie
had sorted out the old harness and hooked the pony to the freshly
painted cart. The pony was having none of it. The animal was
cantankerous by nature and had obviously never been hitched to
anything before. Again Billie had been reminded of the ponies
she had known growing up; few had been particularly agreeable.
After a couple of hours trying to convince this one to pull the cart
up and down the lane, they had given up and put a saddle on the
animal. The pony had history with a saddle and allowed Jodie to
ride her around the yard for a bit. The cart would go back into
the machine shed. Maybe in thirty years another little girl would
decide it needed a coat of paint.

This morning Jodie had led the donkey outside and was brushing him as Billie approached. Billie suspected that the girl was
concerned that the jack was feeling left out of things, with the
pony getting all the attention of late. Billie doubted that a donkey's mind went in that direction. Next they would have to worry

221

about the goat's abandonment issues. When Jodie saw Billie now, she straightened from her work and stared.

"What?" Billie asked.

"You're wearing a dress."

"I know I'm wearing a dress," Billie said. "I'm a girl. Girls wear dresses."

"I didn't think you did."

Billie, all nerves this morning, affected a haughty southern accent, filched from her hero Scarlett. "Well, I'm going to the racetrack today, young lady. I have a two-year-old colt that shows promise. I thought I would gussy myself up to a certain degree."

"You're funny."

"Thank you, child." Billie turned toward the truck, which she had taken time to wash the day before. "Well, I'm off."

"Wait a minute, I'm not ready."

"Where do you think you're going?"

"To Chestnut Field."

"Is your goat racing today?"

"I'm going with you to see Jack race," Jodie said. "I've known him longer than you."

"What's that got to do with anything?"

"He'll want me there."

"How do you know what he wants? Is he a talking horse?"

"I'm going," the girl said.

"Do you think I'm going to let you accompany me to the race-track, wearing those dirty old sneakers? On an important day like this? Not on your life."

Billie turned and headed for the truck. Jodie stared after her.

"Why can't I go?"

Billie opened the passenger to retrieve the shoebox on the seat there. She returned and handed it to the little girl.

"Put these on and let's get moving."

Jodie opened the box to see the pink Adidas inside. She smiled.

"These are so cool!"

The girl thanked Billie three times as she put the donkey in the paddock and they started out. A mile south on the highway was the intersection of the side road that led to Jodie's house. Billie had a look down the road, realizing that she hadn't never actually seen the place.

"Did you tell your mother what you're doing today?" Billie asked.

"She doesn't care."

"I'm sure she does."

The kid didn't respond. Billie could see the wheels turning though as she searched for a way to change the subject.

"Does your mom know about your animals?"

"Of course."

"What does she think about them?"

"She thinks they're a waste of money."

Billie kept her eyes on the road and told herself to shut up, not to comment on a woman who didn't work and who took her ten-year-old daughter's inheritance to pay the rent and then told the kid that her animals were a waste of money. Billie couldn't see an upside to commenting on that. Besides, today was a good day for the girl. And maybe for Billie, too.

"We need carrots," Jodie said. "I want to give him carrots after he wins. Can we stop at the market? I know the man there and he gives me the old ones."

"Do you think Cactus Jack is going to win?" Billie asked.

"I know he's going to win."

Billie wished she were as certain. Other than the aftermath of the incident with Rory's Corvette it had been a long time since she had been nervous about anything. She hadn't slept well the night before and when she had nodded off, she had strange dreams, none of which had anything to do with what would happen today. She dreamed she was back in school but couldn't speak when she tried to answer a question. And she dreamed that she and Athena were in Spain, her subconscious summoning up a country she'd never visited. When she woke up, she felt drained.

Today would inform her of something, even though she wasn't sure what that something might be. But she was sure that by the time evening rolled around, she would have a clearer picture of what she was doing and whether she should be doing it. There was more to it than just that—at some point she'd come to realize that she was looking at today as possibly a vindication. For herself and for her father. She had stayed away too long and now she couldn't help but feel that this was the last thing the two of them would ever do together.

She and Jodie went to see the colt when they got to the track. Tyrone was hanging around the shed row. He had two other rides that day but he was staying close to Cactus Jack. He looked more nervous than Billie felt.

"You see Luke yet?" Billie asked.

"Not yet," Tyrone said. "Figured he'd be here this morning but I haven't seen hide nor hair."

Billie thought it strange but she didn't tell Tyrone that. There were still two hours until race time. "When are you riding first?"

"Next race," Tyrone said. "I better get over there."

Billie looked at the kid. "Let's go to the grandstand and watch. Maybe we'll put a couple of dollars on Tyrone's horse."

It was two dollars Billie wouldn't see again. The horse stumbled out of the gate and fell behind at once, finishing sixth in a seven-horse field. Billie watched but her mind wasn't on the race. Her mind was up in the clubhouse lounge, where she had spotted Reese Ryker and his wife a few minutes earlier, sitting at a table by the outside railing. Across from them was Chuck Caldwell. Billie didn't have to wonder why Ryker was there.

She and Jodie watched the next race before going back to the barns, and as they walked along the lane they spotted Luke's truck coming through the gate. He pulled up and parked but didn't get out. He sat there behind the wheel, staring straight ahead. It seemed he hadn't noticed Billie and the girl walking directly toward him. When he did, he opened the door and stepped down.

He looked like shit. Even to Billie, who had long ago accepted that Luke always appeared a little worse for wear, he looked like shit. She had no doubt that he'd tied one on the night before and although she wasn't happy with the timing, she told herself that it wouldn't matter. The work with the colt had been done and it was the horse that would be running the race, not the trainer.

"Don't do that," Luke barked as he approached.

Billie turned to see Jodie feeding the colt a piece of carrot. The little girl stepped back as if she'd seen a snake.

"It's half a carrot," Billie said.

"And I'm the trainer," Luke told her. "I don't want the horse fed before a race."

"Rough night?" Billie asked.

"My nights are none of your concern."

Billie looked at him evenly for a moment, trying to figure what was going on with him. Who knew—maybe he was as nervous as the rest of them and his anxiety was causing him to act like a prick. Whatever the cause, Billie had no intention of enduring it.

"I'll see you in the saddling barn," she told him.

She and Jodie went back to the grandstand. They bought popcorn and sodas and stood outside by the walking ring, watching the entries for the next race as they filed out onto the track. Billie didn't have any appetite but the girl did. She was totally at ease; it seemed as if her young heart couldn't conceive of the day being anything but a success. Billie was envious.

Luke himself led Cactus Jack to the saddling barn before the sixth race. Billie told Jodie to stay close to the rail and followed. Tyrone came out of the jockeys' room, wearing the new silks and an expression like a teenage bride. When the colt was saddled, a walker led him along the path to the walking ring, lined by bettors wanting a look at where their money was going. Billie stood in the middle of the ring, beneath ancient sugar maples, and watched the rest of the entries circle around her.

Reese Ryker and Sofia were along the rail, as she had known they would be. Spotting Billie, Sofia shouted her name and waved like they were old friends. Billie wondered if she knew that her husband was there hoping that Billie's colt would break a leg. She wondered if Sofia cared what her husband wanted. Probably not.

When Billie turned she saw Luke and Tyrone now standing at the number four post, where Tyrone would mount up. They were talking in earnest, words she couldn't hear.

"Change of plans," Luke was telling Tyrone. His voice was low and he kept his eyes on Billie across the way as he spoke. "I want you to take him to the front. Right out of the gate."

Tyrone stared at Luke. "You're not serious?"

"Goddamn right I'm serious."

"That's not what we talked about," Tyrone said. "This horse needs to come off the pace."

"Well, I changed my mind," Luke said. "I think he can wire it. Bring him out flying."

Tyrone waited a moment. He looked toward Billie, as if for assistance, but she was out of earshot. "Luke, this horse has got all kinds of late speed. All due respect—"

"All due respect *what?*" Luke snapped. "You're a fucking bug boy with three wins. I was training thoroughbreds when you were still pissing your pants. Now you bust him hard out of that gate."

Billie came closer as the call came for riders up. Luke hoisted Tyrone into the saddle and walked alongside the colt toward the exit.

"Flying," was the last he said.

They watched the race from the railing near the finish line. Luke was quiet even yet, still sullen. Over the years she'd known him, Billie had seen him at his lowest—hungover, beat up, dejected—but she'd never seen him as he was today. When she tried to make eye contact, he wouldn't oblige.

Before the horses went into the starting gate, Billie turned to look for Ryker again. What did he hope to accomplish by being there? Or was it that he couldn't keep away? She saw him up top again, at the same table. And then she spotted Marian, in the stands below, sitting alone. Billie stared at her but she didn't return the look. It seemed she was focused on the horses, just now entering the starting gate.

"Will he be okay coming out of the gate?" Billie asked Luke.

"He's got no problems with the gate," Luke said.

Billie didn't know why she'd asked that. She knew that the colt had been breaking well in training. Maybe she'd been hoping for a civil reply from Luke, a change in his tone. She didn't get it.

And then they were off. Cactus Jack came out of the gate like his tail was afire, moving at once to the rail, flying flat out. The colt had a five-length lead on the pack at the first turn and was increasing it with every stride. Tyrone didn't let up, keeping him tight to the rail as they barreled out of the second turn and into the backstretch.

"He's winning!" Jodie shouted. She had climbed onto the wooden railing.

Billie glanced at Luke. He was staring straight ahead but she could have sworn he wasn't watching the race. His eyes seemed fixed on some point far away, as if imagining a better place in a better time.

In the back stretch it was Cactus Jack by fifteen lengths, but Billie already had a bad feeling in her stomach. And then the field began to close. By the three-quarter pole the colt had run himself out. The rest of the field went past him one by one. By the time the gray colt came down the stretch, the race was over. Billie could see that Tyrone was holding him up. There was no point in pushing him now. Dead last was dead last.

Beside her Jodie was in tears. Billie glanced up and saw Ryker laughing. Maybe somebody had told a joke but she doubted it. She looked for Marian but she was already gone.

Luke dutifully walked out onto the track as Tyrone brought the horse back to the finish line. Billie followed.

"I'm sorry, Billie," the jockey said. He looked close to tears himself.

Billie shook her head. "Don't worry about it."

"I'm sorry," he repeated.

"No," she said and she didn't say anything else.

They turned the horse over to a hot walker and then they went back to the barns. Luke hadn't spoken a word since the race ended, not to Billie, not even to Tyrone. Jodie was still sniffling as they reached the stall. She was the one who *knew* the horse would win.

"What happened?" Billie asked as they waited for the colt to return.

"Horse got beat by the field," Luke said. "That's what happened."

"But why?"

Luke smiled like a man with a bad toothache. He wouldn't look at Billie or the little girl. He had not met Billie's eyes since the race had ended. Of course, he hadn't looked at her before the race, either.

"You just never know with a two-year-old," he said. "I've been trying to tell you that all along."

"It's just one race, though," Billie said. "It doesn't tell us much, does it?"

"Maybe not." Luke was now staring at his truck, as if leaving were the only thing on his mind. "But it's going to cost you money to go forward. I can't keep working for nothing. And there's entry fees, vet fees. Gets to the point where you're throwing good money after bad."

"I don't have it to throw," Billie admitted.

The hot walker was leading the colt along the lane toward them.

"You might get a price on him if you were to sell now," Luke said. "Somebody willing to look past what happened today. He's still got the blood."

Billie watched him as his eyes flicked from the colt and out to the track and then to the grandstand. Anywhere but Billie, it seemed.

"Hell, you never wanted to be a horse farmer anyway, Billie. You run him last a couple more times and he won't be worth an Indian nickel."

"You saying you're done?" Billie asked him.

"That's what I'm saying. Been a waste of my time. Should have stuck to the quarter horses in the first place." He went to take the lead from the hot walker.

"Leave it," Billie told him. "We'll take care of him."

Luke shrugged and started for his truck. "No point in me sticking around then."

"Luke," Billie said sharply.

He stopped but didn't turn. "Yeah?"

But she'd only called to him because she wanted him to look at her. And that was something he wasn't going to do.

"Nothing," she said to his back.

She watched as he got into the truck and pulled a U-turn and idled off along the lane. As he neared the gate, she saw his brake lights flash as the truck stopped. It sat there for maybe a minute; it seemed as if Luke were talking to somebody, but at that distance Billie couldn't see who. Finally he drove away and she took the lead from the walker. She and Jodie were rubbing the colt down when Reese Ryker showed up, as Billie knew he would.

"Tough day," he said. "I have to say, I thought maybe you had something for a while there, Billie. And then . . . well, then all those other horses ran right past yours."

"What do you want?" Billie asked.

"Just thought I'd stop and ask what your plans are moving forward."

"The sweat hasn't dried on my horse yet," Billie said.

"My offer still stands."

"So does my answer," Billie said. "Why are you so eager to buy a slow horse anyway?"

"Maybe I'm sentimental," Reese said. "I own the sire. I might just as well own the foal. Keep it in the family."

Billie moved around the horse to where Jodie was brushing the animal's withers, stretching up as high as she could reach.

"What do you think, Jodie? Should I sell Cactus Jack to the sentimental gentleman here?"

"No."

Billie looked at Reese. "There you go."

Reese was quiet, staring at the gray colt. Billie was surprised at how desperate the man was. He had flush bank accounts and prime real estate and dozens of horses and a trophy wife on his arm, and yet for some reason his world was so empty that the only thing he seemed to care about was a two-year-old horse that had just gotten trounced. What was that about?

"The last time I talked to you," he said now, "you told me that this little thing here was a stray that nobody wanted around. And now you're taking business advice from her? Isn't that interesting?"

Billie saw Jodie's eyes and she turned on Ryker. "Really—you're that much of an asshole? I'm having a bad day and every minute I share it with you makes it worse." She leaned forward and dropped her voice. "So why don't you fuck off?"

Reese held up his palms in mock surrender. "You'd better get used to bad days, you keep running that horse."

Jodie didn't speak a word on the drive back to the farm. Billie tried but she wouldn't respond. She sat staring out the side window at the passing countryside, her body language suggesting that she wanted to be as far away from Billie as possible. Even that would be a problem as they pulled up to the barn and saw that the little girl's bike had a flat tire.

"I'll run you home," Billie said.

"I can walk."

"I'm driving you."

The house was a double-wide trailer, sitting on cinder blocks. There were a number of vehicles in the yard, cars and trucks, some up on blocks, most missing engines. An older GMC pickup was parked beneath a limb of a large willow tree. A V8 engine was hanging from the tree by a chain. It had just come out of the truck or was about to go in. Two guys were standing alongside, drinking beer. A woman was with them—thin, wearing a faded blue sundress with straps. She had tattoos on her shoulder and her calves. When Billie pulled into the driveway with the woman's daughter she glanced over and went back to drinking her beer and joking with the backyard mechanics.

"I'm sorry about Cactus Jack," Billie said. "I know you wanted him to win."

The girl's eyes were on her mother and her friends. "I have a question for you."

"What?"

"Did you say that?"

Billie looked out the windshield at the little work party in the yard. She realized now that one of the men was Troy Everson. He wore a lumberjack beard and had put on thirty pounds or more; she hadn't recognized him.

"I said you were a stray," she replied.

"And that nobody wanted me around."

"No. I never said that."

"Then why did he say you did?"

Billie looked at the kid. "Because he's a jerk. He's a jerk who likes to make people feel smaller than him."

Billie had never seen the little girl so sad. It was bad enough that the colt had failed her, but now it seemed as if Billie had, too. The scene in the yard probably wasn't helping. A nine-year-old shouldn't have this much to be sad about.

"I got a question for you," Billie said.

"What?"

"Who are you going to believe—him or me?"

Jodie looked at her mother, laughing with the men, then turned to Billie.

"You."

"Good," Billie said. "See you tomorrow?"

"See you tomorrow."

Twenty-Two

B Y DUSK BILLIE WAS SITTING ON the back deck, watching the broodmares in the pasture. She was trying not to think about the race and all she could think about was the race. She could shift her thoughts to Luke and his sudden transformation into a surly asshole, but that subject was as upsetting as the race itself. Why had he changed his attitude about the horse—and everybody connected with it—overnight? Something had happened to him and whatever it was, it had been significant. Luke could roll with the punches better than anybody Billie knew. She considered that maybe he'd had his heart broken by a woman, but then Luke was always getting his heart broken. It usually took him only a day or two to get over it. Besides, Billie had seen him virtually every day since he'd returned to Kentucky. When did he have time for heartbreak?

She finally told herself to let it go. Whatever had happened didn't matter now. He was gone.

What she should be thinking about was listing the farm on the real estate market and moving on. She should have done it a month ago, when she knew it was the wise move. Instead she had taken advice from David Clay and Skeeter Musgrave and her father's girlfriend and the little girl who lived down the lane. Who could have known that Reese Ryker was the one she should have listened to? Not that she would sell to him even now, but he'd been right all along. There was a reason that her father had been broke his whole life.

She heard the vehicle as it arrived out front, rolling to a stop on the gravel, the engine shutting down. Billie found she couldn't make herself curious as to who it was. A moment later Marian walked out of the house and onto the deck. Billie glanced at her and then back to the mares at their graze.

"What're you drinking?" Marian asked.

"Nothing."

"You're not in the temperance league, are you?"

Without waiting for an answer, Marian reached into her purse and brought out a bottle of Woodford Reserve. She set it on the table and went inside for glasses. When she returned, she poured for them both and then sat down.

"Licking your wounds?" she asked.

"I suppose I am."

"What are you going to do when you finish?"

"Cut and run, I'm thinking," Billie said. "What I should have done."

"So you're back to plan A."

Billie nodded. "Even my trainer agrees, on his way out the door. He says if I keep running the horse and he keeps getting trounced the price will drop to nothing. Best to sell him now. As my father used to say—it would seem the better part of valor."

"He used to say it. I never noticed him practicing it much."

"Well, I'm about to." Billie reached for the glass. "Here's to slow horses."

Marian lifted her glass. "And the men who love them."

Billie drank and then put her glass on the table. She had decided earlier it wouldn't do her any good to get drunk tonight. She needed to think, and usually a thing that seemed like a brilliant idea when she was under the influence lacked significant luster in the morning light.

"Now let's drink to Cactus Jack," Marian said.

"We just did," Billie told her. "Did you miss that part?"

"We drank to slow horses and I don't think Jack qualifies."

"You were at the track today," Billie said. "You watched the race."

"I watched it," Marian said. "What did he get beat by?"

"Christ, I don't know, thirty lengths. Might just as well been a hundred."

"What I know about horses you could hide in a mouse's ear," Marian said. "But I consider myself a bit of an expert when it comes to your father. He might have been wrong about that colt but he wasn't *that* wrong. He wasn't thirty lengths wrong."

"Apparently he was."

"I refuse to believe that."

Billie turned to her. "What are you saying?"

"I really don't know what I'm saying. But I am vain enough to tell you that I've got good legs and good instincts. And I know goddamn well there was something not right about that race today. And now I find you sitting out here with a look on your face that tells me that you know it, too."

Billie decided she would bring Cactus Jack back to the farm while she figured out what to do. She didn't like leaving him in the stall at Chestnut Field, what with Reese Ryker hanging around. At home, at least she could keep an eye on him.

She was on the road ahead of the sun Monday morning. She wanted to leave before Jodie showed up and tried to change her mind. When she got to Chestnut Field there were a dozen or so horses being worked on the track. As she parked along the shed row lane, she saw Tyrone loping a long-legged bay along the rail. He dismounted by the horse's trainer and talked to the man briefly before accepting some cash and walking away. When he saw Billie watching him, he headed over.

"Don't you take a day off?" Billie asked.

"Got bills to pay," he said. "Behind on my rent."

"You're preaching to the choir," Billie told him.

They looked in on Cactus Jack together. The horse didn't seem any worse for wear after running his first race. He was his congenial self, nuzzling Billie with his nose, looking for a treat. Luke had been worried beforehand that the race might take too much out of the animal, but Tyrone didn't think that was the case.

"This is a strong horse," he told Billie.

He didn't ask again about her plans going forward. Instead, he apologized for Saturday's race one more time.

"I wanted to talk to you about that," Billie said. "What were you and Luke arguing about in the ring?"

"I wouldn't say we were arguing."

"You weren't waltzing."

Tyrone looked away, toward the track, where just now a chestnut mare was being pulled up. The rider was off the horse and down on one knee, looking at the animal's foreleg as the trainer hurried over. Tyrone watched as if he couldn't think of anything else.

"Tyrone," Billie said.

He turned back to her, picking his words carefully. "I have to do what the trainer says. That's how it works."

"And when it doesn't work?" Billie asked.

"That's hindsight, Billie. Like I said, he's the trainer."

"And I'm the owner," Billie said. "I need to know what you guys were talking about."

Tyrone shook his head. "It was about the game plan," he said reluctantly. "Sometimes you want to take a horse out quick, set the pace. Maybe make the other horses open up too early. But a good horse most of the time likes to come out of the pack, make his move in the stretch."

"Luke told you to bring him out fast?"

Tyrone nodded. "That was the weird part. We trained that colt to come off the pace. We *knew* he had all kinds of late speed. That was the plan and then suddenly it wasn't. It was almost—" He stopped.

"Almost what?"

Tyrone exhaled heavily. "Almost like he lost that race on purpose."

And so Billie heard in words what she had both wanted to hear and dreaded to hear. Apparently Marian's instincts were as good as her legs.

"Luke told me to sell the colt," she said. "Just before he rode off into the sunset, acting like he'd been the one who got screwed over. I still don't know what the fuck *that* was about."

"I wish you wouldn't do that," Tyrone said. "You need to let him run his race. One time."

"I don't know if I have that option. I don't have a trainer."

"Must be somebody," Tyrone said. "Give the horse his chance, Billie." He hesitated. "There's something else you might want to know."

"What's that?"

"I saw Luke leaving on Saturday."

"Yeah?"

"He stopped by the gate. I was walking to the parking lot and I saw him. And . . . well, he was talking to Reese Ryker."

Billie's stomach dropped. She recalled seeing Luke stop. "About what?"

"Couldn't hear, but they were talking. Not for long, and when Luke left he spun his tires like he was pissed about something."

"He was pissed from the minute he got here Saturday."

Billie thought about it, how just a few minutes after that had happened Reese Ryker had showed up, which probably meant that he knew at that point that Luke had quit. But what had he known before the race? That was the question. Billie didn't want to believe that Luke would sell her out. But something had happened to change his attitude.

"I'd sure like to get another ride on this horse," Tyrone said. "We got untapped potential, me and him both. You too, Billie."

"That's just talk."

"Tell you what—enter him again and I'll ride for nothing."

"No wonder you're having trouble making your rent," Billie said.

After leaving Chestnut Field Saturday Luke had gone back to the farm, fully intent on getting drunk. When he arrived Becky was there, showing her horses to a family of three—a husband and wife and a teenaged girl, maybe thirteen or fourteen. Becky had saddled one of the paints and was trotting the horse in the pasture field, showing the people what the animal could do. Luke had driven up to the house and gone inside, ignoring them.

As he'd been leaving the racetrack, Reese Ryker was waiting for him by the parking lot gate. He had the manila envelope in his hand, the same envelope he'd shown Luke in his office a couple of days earlier.

"See?" he said. "That wasn't so hard, was it?"

Luke made no reply. He took the envelope and tossed it on the seat, knowing that having possession of it meant nothing. Ryker had copies of the pictures and so did the silent goon O'Hara. Luke wouldn't trust either of them as far as he could throw a Clydesdale. The pictures would be hanging over Luke forever; he would always be a phone call away from being arrested.

"You're doing the woman a favor," Reese said. "She'll go broke running that horse. And she's already broke. Face it, she's a second-generation loser. She should be thanking you."

"I gotta go," Luke told him.

"Hold on," Reese said. "I might have something else for you, if you're looking to make a couple of dollars. We both know she's going to end up selling that colt. For some reason, she won't sell to me. If I was to send a surrogate though, and you were to vouch for that surrogate, she'd never know the difference. I could pay you—oh, call it a finder's fee."

While Ryker talked, Luke sat staring out the windshield. Never had he wanted so badly to be on the highway and gone from a place. "I can't even imagine what it's like, being the way you are," he said. "I don't want nothing to do with you again, Ryker. Not now and not ever."

Reese shrugged. "That shouldn't be a problem. You and I don't really travel in the same circles. Do we?"

"We ain't even from the same planet," Luke said and drove away.

At the farm he opened a beer and called Steve on his cell. The quarter horses were in Minnesota now and would be there through the next weekend. Steve was traveling with his mare and Luke's gelding, too. He was riding Luke's horse while the mare's tendon settled down. Luke said he needed to talk to the neighbor kid about looking after the farm before he could head out.

"I'll see you Monday," he told Steve.

"What happened with the thoroughbred?" Steve asked. "He didn't make the grade?"

"Wasn't the horse," Luke said and hung up.

He was pounding the beers and was on his third when he heard voices from the yard and then a vehicle driving off. A minute later Becky was knocking on the door.

"What's up?" he asked when she came in.

"I think I sold my paints." She stayed just inside the door, leaning her hip against the jamb. Luke could smell the horse on her.

"Congratulations."

"There's one problem," she said. "I need to get them to Owensboro and I don't have a trailer. Or a truck neither for that matter."

Luke grimaced. That's what she considered a problem? She didn't know what problems were. "Get your hubby to do it."

"I'm not with him anymore."

"There's a shock."

"Who shit in your cornflakes today?" she asked. "Or are you always like this?"

"You want a beer?"

"No," she said. "Nick's got that tandem trailer out there and you have a truck. These people will pay you to trailer the horses to Owensboro."

"How much?"

"How much do you want?"

Luke had been thinking he'd have to borrow money for gas to get to Minnesota. He did a calculation. It was roughly a hundred and twenty miles to Owensboro. "Two hundred dollars," he decided.

"That sounds okay." She was pretty damn quick to agree.

"A horse," he added.

"What?"

"Two hundred a horse. That's four hundred dollars total."

"I know what two and two is. That seems like a lot."

Luke shrugged. "You know how much gas that Ford takes?"

"What about three hundred?"

Luke drained his bottle and went to the fridge. "I'll do it for three. Now you want a beer?"

"No." Opening the door to go, she stopped. "What is wrong with you anyway?"

"I'm a poor excuse for a human being."

"And you're just figuring that out now?"

"Actually, I am," Luke told her.

Twenty-Three

WHEN BILLIE ARRIVED BACK AT THE farm after her conversation with Tyrone, she expected to find Jodie there. She wasn't, and it was obvious that she hadn't been. The water trough for her animals was nearly empty and they hadn't been fed. Billie took care of them, wondering why the girl hadn't come around. She went to the house and made coffee and the phone rang. It was Kellyanne, her old schoolgirl buddy turned snarky loans manager.

"What's up?" Billie asked.

"I think you know," Kellyanne said. "You need to come and see me."

They sat again in the office that overlooked the street. Today Kellyanne wore a skirt so tight she appeared to have trouble walking in it, and clunky high heels with black stockings. Her eyes flicked over Billie's jeans and T-shirt and she actually shook her head slightly. Billie didn't know she was required to dress the part to talk to the bank.

Kellyanne got right to the point. "I hear your horse is a dog," she said.

"What?"

"I hear he got his lunch handed to him over at Chestnut Field on the weekend."

Billie looked around. "Do your bosses know the way you talk to people?"

"I don't talk to everybody like this," Kellyanne said. "But you told me you'd pay your mortgages once your horse won the Kentucky Derby or something like that. How's that plan coming along, Billie?"

"You tell me. You seem to know all about it."

"I know enough," Kellyanne said. "I have to answer to people. Like I said before, we can't carry you indefinitely. Now you had a plan and it wasn't much of a plan, but we went along temporarily. But now what—do you have another money-making scheme? Did your father have another slow horse stashed away someplace?"

"Do I have a plan?" Billie repeated. "Other than I'm seriously considering knocking you out of that fucking chair—no."

"Did you just threaten me?"

"I might have," Billie said. "Why not call your manager in here and we'll let him decide."

Kellyanne sat back in her chair. "You haven't changed, you know that? You were always just a little bit better than everybody else."

"Not everybody. You maybe."

"Even now, when I'm this close to taking your farm away from you, you're sitting there with that smug look on your face, talking shit. You still think you can lord it over me. Well, look where I'm sitting and look where you are."

"You've got me all wrong, Kellyanne," Billie said. "All these years, I never thought about you once. You're mad at me because you think I fucked Ernie Moscovitz fifteen years ago? Do you know how pathetic that is?"

"That's a ridiculous thing to say. I'm doing my job."

"Then do it," Billie said. "You called me and told me to come in. So far you've insulted my father and my horse and me. How is *that* your job?"

Billie could see the old Kellyanne now, beneath the spiky bleached hair and the Spanx. She was never going to run away from who she was. Neither was anybody else in this world, but the difference was that most everybody else knew it.

"My job," Kellyanne said slowly, "is to tell you that you have until the end of the month to pay your mortgages. If you default, this bank can seize your property and sell it to whomever we please. That includes the house and barns and livestock. Do you understand that or should I go over it again a little slower?"

Billie stood up. "I think I got it. Next time why not just tell me over the phone? That way, I won't have to sit here and listen to you rattle off all the things you wanted to say to me back in high school."

"Go to hell," Kellyanne said.

Billie laughed and left. Her truck was parked along the street a half block away, and when she walked out the front door of the stone building, she couldn't help but notice the very large lawyer leaning against the front fender, eating an ice cream cone.

"That truck is dirty," she said approaching. "You'll ruin your seersucker."

"You want an ice cream, Billie?" Clay asked. "My treat."

"That's the best offer I've had all day," Billie said. "Although there really wasn't much competition."

They walked to a kiosk in the town square that sold ice cream and pretzels and sodas. Clay bought Billie a Neapolitan with two scoops and they sat on a bench beneath the shade of black locust trees to eat.

"So why were you lurking outside the bank?" Billie asked.

"Because I could see you inside," Clay said. "Talking to that poor Kellyanne."

"Poor Kellyanne?"

"The girl has problems. Did you know she's a dipsomaniac?"

"No, but I suspected the last part." Billie ran her tongue around the melting ice cream where it met the cone.

"How's that?"

"The maniac."

"Oh yes, very funny." Some of the ice cream from his cone was running down Clay's wrist and he turned his hand over to lick it. "She was in Mom's earlier today and the talk there was of your colt and its inauspicious debut at Chestnut Field."

"Of course," Billie said. "What else would people have to talk about? Kellyanne heard the story and then hustled over to her office to call me in for a meeting. Where she proceeded to tell me that the bank is about to take my farm and my house and my horses."

Clay scoffed. "They can't take your horses. They don't hold a mortgage on your horses."

"That would be reassuring if the animals were worth anything."

"It's unfortunate that the mortgage is with a branch of First Kentucky," Clay said. His ice cream was nearly gone now and he took a bite out of the cone and chewed it noisily.

"Why is that?"

"Because Reese Ryker has influence with them. He has a large portion of his money—well, I should say his mother's money because the boy has never earned any on his own—in First Kentucky. A substantial enough sum that those in the ivory tower might listen to him if he was to complain about an overdue mortgage out here in the backwoods."

"Jesus Christ," Billie said. "What a world."

"Indeed," Clay said. "What happened at Chestnut on Saturday?"

"As if you don't know."

"I heard the colt got trounced," Clay said. "I heard thirty lengths or maybe forty. I also heard that your jockey brought him out of the starting gate like Lucifer himself was chasing the animal. Why would he do that?"

Billie kept forgetting she was in Kentucky, where every living soul was an expert on horse racing. "Because my trainer told him to do that."

"And why would *he* tell him that?"

"That is the million-dollar question, Mr. Clay. I think Ryker got to him."

"He paid him off?"

"Kinda looks that way."

Clay finished the cone with one last crunch and carefully wiped his fingers with his napkin before tucking it into his shirt pocket. "What did your trainer say when you asked him about it?"

"I never got a chance. He slinked away with his tail between his legs."

"Which is what he would do, had he sold you out."

"Yeah."

"And now what?" Clay asked.

"I trailered the colt home this morning," Billie said. "I'm thinking the smart move would be to see what I can get for him. I've already had one wealthy buyer approach me."

Clay took a moment. "That would be the aforementioned Reese Ryker."

Billie nodded.

"And that's not an option."

"That is not an option, Mr. Clay," Billie agreed. "So I'll advertise the horse and see what happens. The more people try to take that property from me, the more I want to keep it. I can't make a living off it but I can live *on* it. I'll find a job around here somewhere. I'm pretty enough to be on TV, I've been told. Maybe I'm pretty enough for other jobs, too."

"What are you talking about?"

Billie shook her head. "Never mind."

Clay adjusted his bulk on the bench. "I can lend you some money, Billie."

"But how does that improve my situation?" Billie said. "The only difference between owing you and owing the bank is that I don't have any qualms about being in default with the bank, even more so now that I know they might be doing Reese Ryker's bidding. With you, cantankerous old fart that you are, I would be remorseful."

"And to think I bought you ice cream."

Billie stood. "Like I said, it was the high point of my day. But I won't take your money, Mr. Clay." Pausing, she smiled again. "Unless—you're not in the market for a two-year-old gray colt by Saguaro, are you? Lightly raced, I might add."

Clay leaned back and crossed his legs. Apparently he was settled in for the afternoon. Billie could imagine him there, offering encouragement or advice or disparagement to passersby, content in his eccentricities, calculated or not.

"I had a colt once," he told her.

"Serendipity," Billie said.

"Right," he said, realizing. "I already mentioned that, didn't I? Mrs. Clay tells me that I have a habit of repeating myself."

"There are worse habits."

"Oh, I know. Mrs. Clay, for instance, tells me I have a habit of repeating myself."

Billie was laughing as she walked across the square, heading for her truck.

Twenty-Four

MONDAY MORNING LUKE GOT UP EARLY. After drinking two cups of black coffee to clear his head, he backed his truck around to the tandem horse trailer behind the barn. He'd gotten drunk Saturday night and had continued on through Sunday. At some point he had remembered to call Steve to tell him that he had a job to do, trailering some horses, and wouldn't be catching up with him until Tuesday or Wednesday.

The trailer obviously hadn't been moved in some months. Luke suspected that Nick had last used it to bring the horses to the farm, back when he and Becky had been basking in the light of first love, as the songwriters might put it. The recent rain had left the trailer tires sunk in the mud. One was completely flat. Luke had to drag the compressor from the machine shed across the yard to inflate the tire.

At first the trailer wouldn't budge. Luke put the truck in four-wheel drive and rocked it back and forth until the tires finally broke free. As they did, Luke hammered the truck into low gear and gunned the engine—and blew the clutch to pieces. He let off the gas at once and pushed in the pedal. He could hear the springs inside the bell housing, clanking around like loose change in a pocket.

Luke shut the engine down and sat there behind the wheel for a time. He was aware that things weren't going his way lately, and as much as he wanted to feel sorry for himself, he couldn't. He didn't believe that God was watching him and tossing a monkey wrench into his plans whenever Luke acted the fool. He didn't know if God even existed but if He did, Luke had to believe that He had better things to do than fuck with Luke's head.

However, he did believe in karma. And so he had to believe that the hand of karma had been involved in the disintegration of his clutch plate just now. That and the fact that the Ford had nearly 300,000 hard miles on it.

Now he had no idea how he was going to get to Minnesota, just as he had no idea how he was going to deliver the horses to Owensboro. The couple had been back at the farm Sunday afternoon and paid Luke for the job. After a time, he pulled his cell from his pocket and dialed Steve.

"So I'm fucked," he said after telling his story.

"All right," Steve said, giving it some thought. "Call Al's Garage on Bryant Street in Lexington. He bought my old Ram off me for parts and never paid me, always said he'd make it up in repairs. He can fix your truck and then you can owe me."

There was a Jubilee Ford tractor in the machine shed. The battery was dead and the gas tank empty. Luke replaced the battery with the one from his truck and siphoned gas from his tank. The tractor fired up after a minute or so. It ran rough for a time and then smoothed out.

Luke went next door. He knew there was a teenager living there; he'd seen him in the yard a few times and the kid always waved. Turned out his name was Travis and for twenty bucks he agreed to tow Luke's truck behind the tractor to the garage in Lexington.

"Are you sure this is legal?" he asked before they started out.

"Everything's legal as long as you don't get caught," Luke told him.

It was past noon when they pulled into the garage lot. Luke paid the kid and sent him home on the tractor. The garage owner, Al, was walking around the truck as the kid chugged away.

"This is the truck?" he asked.

"This is it." Luke was in the mood for just one stupid question. "What about parts?"

"Place in town has a clutch in stock." Al looked doubtfully at the truck a moment longer. "I'm not making anything on this, you know."

"Thought you owed Steve money."

"I do," Al admitted.

"There you go," Luke said. "How long you figure to fix it?"

"Three or four hours."

"I'll give you my cell number. You can call me when it's done."

"Where you going?"

"Gotta be a bar around here somewhere."

In fact there were a couple of bars, at an intersection a half mile away. One had an Italian name and was some sort of pasta place. The parking lot was full, the lunch crowd. The second place was a strip club called Honey Bunnies. Luke went in and found a corner table. He took off his hat and ordered a beer.

He passed most of the afternoon there, nursing draft beer and watching the girls. There were two stages and nonstop entertainment, as the blinking sign outside promised.

For all his checkered history with the opposite sex, Luke had never been a big fan of strip clubs. He knew guys who were practically addicted to the places, who would spend their paychecks sticking ten-dollar bills in G-strings and taking whichever of the dancers did a little business on the side out back to their trailers or upstairs to a room. To Luke, there had always been something unsexy about the whole arrangement. Watching a woman get naked in front of a couple dozen men seemed antiseptic and bloodless to him. Sex was a contact sport to Luke, and one-on-one up close and personal was the only way to play it. It occurred to him that every woman he had ever fucked he had been in love with, at least a little bit and for a little while.

After a couple of beers, he realized he hadn't eaten much for the last couple days and ordered a hamburger and fries. The waitress was friendly, with nice eyes and a great body. She was in her forties, Luke guessed, and he wondered if she might have been a dancer at one time. With her body and smile, she could still be a dancer. The afternoon crowd was light and they got to talking. He ended up telling her about his troubles—how the clutch was out of his truck and he had horses to haul across the state. He told her he was heading out after that to race the flat tracks. He nearly told her about what had happened at Chestnut Field on Saturday but he couldn't do it. They were getting along fine and even though he would likely never see her again after today he couldn't bear to tell her about his despicable behavior. She kept coming over to talk to him when she wasn't busy. He over-tipped her and she bought him a beer and told him about her Honda that was always overheating. She was funny and smart and Luke found her sexy in a way that he did not find the naked girls on the stage to be.

Al from the garage called at a quarter to four to say that the truck was ready. Luke got up to leave, making eye contact with the waitress standing by the bar. She winked at him over the shoulder of the man she was talking to. The next dancer was being introduced over the loudspeaker as the "mesmerizing Jasmine." Luke put his hat on and was almost out the door when he looked back to see the young woman with cropped hair prancing onto the stage. He stopped in his tracks.

He parked the truck in the lot behind Honey Bunnies, a few yards away from the red Mustang convertible. He'd taken the Ford down the road a couple of miles and back on a test drive and the clutch was working fine. He had no idea how long he was going to have to wait in the parking lot, but it didn't matter to him if it was ten minutes or ten hours. He would wait.

Shortly after five o'clock the lot began to fill up, guys getting off work, Luke assumed. Most were rednecks driving pickup trucks or Jeeps, young guys with money in their pockets, looking to see some naked flesh.

She came out the back door about an hour later. Off duty now, she wore jeans and boots and a denim jacket. She slipped on sunglasses as she crossed the lot to the Mustang and she didn't see Luke until he was a few feet away.

"If it ain't my favorite schoolteacher," he said.

She turned and it took her a moment, but even then she was quick on her feet. Maybe her eyes showed some reaction but they were hidden behind the shades.

"You're mixed up, buddy. I'm no fucking schoolteacher."

"I know you're not," Luke said. "And your name's not Rachel. Or Brenna. I actually kinda doubt that it's Jasmine either, but I don't really care. Whatever it is, you and me need to have a conversation."

"I got no idea what you're talking about." She turned and unlocked the car door. "You keep standing there and I will run you over, you fucking hillbilly. Just try me."

As she got behind the wheel, Luke took his buck knife from his pocket and shoved the blade into the front tire of the Mustang. As the air hissed, the woman came out of the car unhinged.

"What the fuck are you doing?" she screamed.

"I expect you have a spare tire in the trunk," Luke said. "We can talk while you change it. You don't want to talk, then I'll give your license plate number to the cops and you can talk to them. I'm guessing a nice girl like you has a record of some sort. Tell me though—will this be your first time up on blackmail charges?"

"You're a fucking asshole."

"I've been hearing that a lot lately."

Twenty-Five

TUESDAY WAS THE THIRD DAY RUNNING that Jodie hadn't shown up at the farm and now Billie was worried. That morning she tended to the animals and then sat on the bench outside the barn, drinking coffee. She was thinking about smoking a cigarette and was glad that she didn't have one to smoke. She thought about the last time she had talked to Jodie, in the truck after the race on Saturday. They'd been sitting in the driveway of the kid's place, looking at her mother in the yard with her chop shop friends, talking about what Reese Ryker had said. Billie had thought at the time that things were okay between them when she left. Maybe that wasn't so. And now she was worried about a kid she had never wanted around in the first place.

She had other irons in the fire today. She'd posted an ad the night before at Chestnut Field and another on the internet, offering the colt for sale, and had already received two calls. A man named Donaldson was coming to the farm that morning at eleven o'clock. The horse in question was at the moment standing fifty feet away in the pasture with his head over the fence, looking at Billie as if he knew she was planning his fate.

"You had your chance," Billie told him.

Tossing the cold coffee remains into the dirt, she got in the truck and drove over to the double-wide where Jodie lived. With all the vehicles parked in the yard, she couldn't tell if anybody was home or not. A dog was barking as she walked up to the door of the trailer and knocked. When nobody answered she had a look around back. A very large mutt that looked part mastiff was in a chain link run there, drool hanging from its mouth as it barked. Seeing Billie, the dog charged at her, leaping up to plant its large front paws on top of the gate. She stepped back but then realized that the animal didn't seem all that malicious. There were pails for food and water in the pen, both empty. Billie dragged a garden hose from the house over to the run and filled one of the pails through the chain link. The dog came over at once and began to noisily lap at the water. There was nothing Billie could do about the empty food dish.

She went around to the front yard and stood there. Spotting an old brick farmhouse a couple hundred yards to the east, she went back to the truck and drove over.

A woman answered the door, or at least opened it a couple inches, enough to look at Billie in a suspicious manner. She was around fifty, with auburn hair that showed a good inch of gray where the roots had grown past the color job.

"Yeah?"

"Do you know if anybody is home next door?"

"Who you looking for?"

Billie gestured vaguely north. "I have a farm. Jodie, the girl, keeps her animals there and she hasn't been around for a couple days."

"I can't say where she got to," the woman said. "They carted the rest of them off to jail."

Billie turned to look at the double-wide, as if there were something she'd missed. "Carted who off to jail?"

"The woman and that boyfriend of hers. Sheriff showed up with four or five of them big trucks they drive. They all had on that SWAT gear you see on TV and they arrested the whole damn bunch."

"Arrested them for what?"

"Drugs, I'm thinking."

"What happened to Jodie—the little girl?"

"Couldn't say. I reckon they'd a taken her somewheres though."

Billie exhaled. "I reckon."

Back home she made more coffee, and while she waited for the buyer she called the sheriff's department in Marshall. The woman who answered the phone asked who she was and then about her relationship to the family. When Billie said she was a friend, the receptionist—or whoever she was—told her they weren't releasing any information about the family.

"All I can tell you is that the mother's being arraigned tomorrow."

"I'm worried about the daughter," Billie persisted. "I don't care about the rest of them."

"Can't help you," the woman said and hung up.

"But you're supposed to help people," Billie said to the dead line.

The man Donaldson showed up early, driving a black Lincoln Navigator that appeared to be new. Billie met him at the house and they walked to the pasture together. The man was tall and thin and wore a brown suit, no tie, and a tan Stetson. He wasn't a talker and barely bothered with hello. As they walked, Billie saw him looking at the three animals in the paddock by the barn. The pony and donkey were on their feet, watching the approaching humans, while the goat lay contentedly in the dirt. Donaldson smirked at the sight of them, as if he'd stumbled upon a side show.

By the pasture fence the colt came directly to them as was his habit. Donaldson looked the horse over like he was scanning a menu. He didn't bother to go into the field.

"You have the paperwork?"

"Up at the house," Billie said.

"And Saguaro's the sire?" He turned to Billie. "That's what your ad says."

"That's right." Billie indicated the chestnut mare, standing hip-shot by the pond, watching them. "There's the dam."

Donaldson shrugged to show he couldn't care less about the dam. "There was no asking price with the ad."

Billie hesitated. She'd been back and forth on the number ever since she'd posted the colt for sale. What was too much and what was too little? Glancing toward the house, her eyes fell on the new Lincoln in the drive. The horse had to be worth more than the car.

"I have to get a hundred thousand for him," she said. "The colt is fast. I can show you his workout sheets."

"He wasn't very fast at Chestnut Field last weekend."

"He had an off day," Billie said. "Even Secretariat got beat."

"Not at Chestnut Field he didn't."

"Well, that's the price," Billie said.

Donaldson looked at the gray a moment longer, then took a cell phone from his pocket. "I have to make a call."

He tapped in a number and walked down the hill toward the barns as he talked, out of earshot. Billie leaned back against the gate and watched him. There was something about the man that didn't sit right. He had barely looked at the colt, hadn't checked the animal's teeth or feet, hadn't asked to see the workout figures. He never asked to see the ID tattoo, either. He didn't act like any thoroughbred buyer Billie had ever known.

After a few minutes he put the phone in his pocket. Removing the hat briefly to push back his lank blond hair, he started back toward Billie.

"I'll have a trailer here this afternoon."

"We have a deal at a hundred thousand?" Billie asked.

Donaldson nodded. "You'll take a certified check?"

Billie allowed that she would, but she was already second-guessing herself. Whether she was doing the right thing or not, it wasn't what her father would have done. But wasn't the alternative to keep the colt and lose the farm? Even David Mountain Clay was of the opinion that the old man hoped that Billie would hang onto the property. Horses come and go. Will Masterson knew that fact better than anybody.

Then she remembered what Tyrone had pleaded. *Let him run his race. One time.* Billie looked at the colt; the animal was looking back at her. *Goddamn it.*

"I'll need a bill of sale," Donaldson said. "And all the paperwork. I'll bring the money when I come back for the horse."

With that Billie was filled with full-blown seller's remorse, even though she hadn't actually made the transaction yet. She could back out now, find a trainer and run the colt once more, to eliminate any second thoughts she might have next week or next year—or in forty years, when she might be sitting around a home somewhere, telling people about the great horse she *almost* raced.

But Luke had said that another bad showing would drop the price drastically. If that happened, she could lose both the animal and the farm. If only the colt had performed better on the weekend. But it wasn't the horse's fault. She silently cursed Luke for his duplicity, and as she was cursing him she swore she could hear the bark of his truck's exhaust.

And then the sound grew louder. She looked toward the side road and saw the beat-up Ford pulling into the drive, bouncing in and out of the potholes before rolling to a stop by the barn. Luke got out and started toward her, looking suitably hangdog. He stopped when he got a look at Donaldson.

"What the fuck is he doing here?"

Even if Billie had been considering introductions, she wouldn't have had time as Luke charged across the yard to land a right hook on Donaldson's jaw. Donaldson went with the punch and came right back at Luke, dropping into a crouch and firing both hands like a boxer. A very good boxer.

It was a mismatch. Donaldson had obviously done some fighting and Luke was a hundred and forty pounds soaking wet, with a reputation as a man who'd had a lot of fights but never won one. Soon he was on the ground and Donaldson was pounding on him. Billie let it go on for a bit, thinking that Luke was getting exactly what he deserved, but then she told Donaldson to stop. When he ignored her, she told him again, loudly this time, and then she went into the machine shed and came out with a shovel, which she slammed across the man's back. He went down in the dirt and when he attempted to rise, she hit him again. This time the steel spade cracked his head and he stayed down, covering up and shouting he'd had enough.

"What in hell is going on here?" Billie demanded of Luke. "How do you know this guy?"

Luke got up. His nose was bleeding and his shirt ripped nearly off. "His name's O'Hara and he's working for Ryker."

Billie turned to look at the man on the ground. He was on one knee now, groggy from the blow to his head, one hand held up defensively against another whack from the shovel. Billie glanced at Luke.

"Well, that makes two of you," she said.

"They blackmailed me, Billie." Luke ran the back of his hand under his nose, spreading the blood across his cheek. His eyes were on hers, pleading. He was like a little boy telling a tall tale that just happened to be true.

"Oh Christ," Billie said. She turned to Donaldson or whatever his name was. "You—get the fuck out of here. *Now*."

The man got up and when he reached for his hat Luke kicked it across the yard. The man retrieved it and pointed at Luke.

"I'll remember this," he said.

"Anytime, asshole," Luke told him.

"Oh, stop it," Billie said.

Donaldson, or O'Hara, walked away. There was a trickle of blood running down into his collar. When he got to the Lincoln he turned and looked at them both for a long moment, as if he were considering walking back down the hill. He thought better of it and got into the car and drove off.

Billie turned to Luke. "Let's hear your story and make it quick because I want you out of here, too."

She changed her mind, albeit reluctantly, after she heard what had happened. She might have doubted it coming from somebody else but she knew that it was precisely the type of situation Luke could find—and find better than anybody she'd ever known. When she had appeared dubious, he offered to show her the pictures of himself and the stripper/schoolteacher. She had quickly declined and then pointed him to the tap outside the barn door.

"Wash the blood off your face and change your shirt," she told him. "I suppose I owe you a beer for coming to my rescue. Although if you weren't such a fucking jackass it wouldn't have been necessary."

She brought two cans of beer and some ice in a washcloth to stop the bleeding from his nose. He sat on the bench outside the barn, with his head back, until the flow finally stopped. Billie drank her beer, leaning against the fender of Luke's truck, watching him, wondering how she was going to manage to forgive him. Blackmail or not, he had still betrayed her. If she wanted to get all superior and morally outraged about it, she could say he betrayed the colt, too.

In the end she decided that worrying over whether or not she should forgive him was a waste of her time. Expecting Luke to ignore the advances of a pretty girl in a bar would be like waiting for the sun to rise in the west. Let him drink his beer and be on his way.

He set the washcloth aside and had a drink before looking over at her, smiling the goofy smile she'd known since she was eighteen and they had first gone on a drive together. It had worked for him back then. A few nights later they'd had sex in the backseat of his buddy's Oldsmobile.

"We need to make a plan," he said.

"*We* need to make a plan?" Billie repeated. "Okay, here's the first part of the plan. Finish your beer and get into your truck and go back to Idaho or Nebraska or wherever it is you're racing your quarter horse this week. As for me, I have another buyer coming here at two o'clock to look at the colt. With any luck I won't have to hit this one with a shovel."

She could see Luke thinking about it, his brow furrowed. "How do you know that O'Hara wasn't the decoy?" he asked. "And this next buyer is Ryker's guy, too. You can't put anything past him."

Shit, Billie thought. The scenario seemed highly unlikely but how would she know? She hadn't known with O'Hara. She didn't like it when Luke turned out to be smarter than her. The good thing was that it was a rare occurrence.

He tilted the beer back and drank. "Besides, you can't sell that horse."

"I have to sell the horse."

"We gotta run him again."

"He had his chance and so did you," Billie said. "I have no time for tilting at windmills. The bank is on my case. I'm going to lose this place at the end of the month."

"End of the month," Luke said. "Shit, that changes things." He sat thinking. "Okay, how much money do you need—just to keep them at arm's length?"

"I don't know," Billie said. "I was hoping to get a hundred thousand for the horse. Donaldson agreed to it, before I found out he wasn't Donaldson."

"Sure he agreed, on Reese Ryker's dime." Luke had another drink, then shook the can, sending a hint to Billie that it was empty. "We got 'til the end of the month. The way I see it, we can only run him twice, then. How we going to do this?"

"Those punches to the head affected either your thinking or your hearing," Billie said. "I've made up my mind that I want to hang on to the property, which means I'm selling the horse. Don't think you can come around here looking for sympathy just because you can't keep your cock in your pants. You're feeling guilty because of what happened Saturday. Well, you should feel fucking guilty. But you're forgetting that you're the one who told me that running the horse again is a bad idea."

"I was being blackmailed at the time, Billie."

"For picking up yet another girl in yet another bar," Billie reminded him. "Oh, the irony."

"I don't understand irony," Luke said.

At that moment the donkey in the paddock began to bray. The animal probably wasn't laughing at Luke—but it sounded as if it were. Billie watched the expression on Luke's face and then broke out herself. Luke fell into a pout.

"To hell with the both of you." He regarded the donkey and the other two animals in the pen, then glanced around. "Where's the kid, anyway? I thought you two were joined at the hip."

Billie told him what she had learned earlier.

"So where would they take the girl?" Luke asked.

"No idea," Billie said. "Foster home maybe? She has an aunt but I don't know her circumstances. I'm going to try to find out where she is but I've got a lot on my plate today. For starters, I need to sell that colt and send you on your way. But not in that order."

"Shit," Luke said, standing up. "I guess that means I ain't getting another Budweiser. Well, I have to trailer a couple of horses over to Owensboro anyway."

But instead of going to his truck, he walked over to the pasture where the gray colt stood. He ran his palm over the horse's forehead. "That little girl ain't going to like you selling this boy."

Billie watched. She knew what the bastard was doing. "Well, she's not up to her earlobes in debt."

"You gotta give me a chance, Billie," Luke said, keeping it up. "Christ, I was doing just fine on the quarter horse circuit and then you had to show up in Missouri and drag me back here, set me up to train this animal, and now you're going to pull the rug out from under me."

"You left out a few parts of that story, Luke," Billie said. "You don't deserve another chance."

"I guess I don't." Luke stood quietly, as if in deep contemplation, for a long time before turning to her. "But the horse does."

You sonofabitch, Billie thought.

Twenty-Six

BILLIE WAS AT THE COURTHOUSE IN Marshall at nine o'clock the next morning. The arraignments were up first. Those in custody were led into the courtroom through a side door and seated in a prisoners' dock along the wall. Billie saw Jodie's mother, Shelly, as she shuffled in, wearing camo pants and a black tank top with red bra straps showing. Troy Everson was in the row behind her, beside a black guy Billie didn't know—a squat little man with a shaved head and stringy goatee.

The first indictment was against a man named Hickox, who'd been arrested for assaulting his wife. He stumbled out of the box to stand before the judge. He was a small man, and his face was marked up pretty good. Either the wife he'd assaulted had gotten the better of him or the cops had smacked him around when they arrested him. Billie was okay with either scenario. The judge advised the man that bail would be five thousand dollars and held him over for trial.

Troy Everson was up next. Billie thought the bailiff would get winded reading the charges. Possession and trafficking in meth, possession of stolen goods, grand theft auto, violation of parole,

forgery, conspiracy to commit fraud, and fraud. When the bailiff
finished, Troy Everson broached the subject of bail.

"Do you consider yourself to be extremely wealthy?" the judge
asked.

"Nope."

"Then forget it."

Jodie's mother was charged with possession of and trafficking
in meth and possession of stolen goods. Billie assumed the goods
were the car parts scattered about the yard. She also considered the
possibility that the woman was guilty of nothing more than allowing Troy Everson and his fellow Mensa members to hang around
her place. But Billie couldn't know that. Maybe she was the brains
behind the whole operation. It really didn't seem to be a very high
bar.

When the arraignments were done, Billie approached the dock
and called over to Shelly. She was immediately blocked by one
of the escort cops, a tall woman with shoulders like a linebacker.
Shelly turned when she heard her name and was glaring at Billie.

"I need to talk to her," Billie told the cop.

"You can't."

"I just need to ask her a question."

"She's going back to holding."

"I can't ask a question?"

"Fuck you," Jodie's mother said from the dock.

"Where's Jodie?" Billie asked.

"Go fuck yourself."

Now the cop took Billie by the forearm and started to steer her
away. "You're about to get yourself in trouble."

"Hold on," somebody said then.

The voice was familiar. Billie turned to see David Clay
approaching, dressed in a three-piece suit and carrying a briefcase.
She glanced around; it was as if the large lawyer had dropped from
the sky.

"Who are you—Batman?"

"I am a lawyer and this is a courtroom," Clay said. "We needn't call Ripley's Believe It or Not." He turned to the cop. "I will take charge of Miss Masterson."

The cop shrugged her indifference; of course she would know David Mountain Clay. Billie watched in silence as she and her partner led the prisoners out through the side entrance. Leaving, Shelly Rickman continued to stare at Billie. Would she even know who Billie was? They had never met—the day that Billie had dropped Jodie off, the mother had barely glanced her way. Maybe she was feeling belligerent in general. Billie might be the same way, under the circumstances.

"What are you up to now?" lawyer Clay asked, taking her by the arm and guiding her off to the side.

Billie told him her story. While she talked, Clay stood watching as a couple dozen people filed in through the double doors at the rear of the courtroom, his eyes widening and narrowing as he surveyed the group.

"Are you listening to me?" Billie asked.

"I am indeed."

"You don't seem to be," Billie said. "What's the big attraction with the bus tour over there?"

"Bus tour," Clay said smiling. "It's a jury pool, my dear. We are selecting twelve good and honest citizens this morning for a case I'm handling." He waited as the group was seated. They were a diverse bunch, as befitting a jury pool, Billie supposed, but they had one thing in common. None of them looked happy to be there.

"Now back to you," Clay said. "I have to say that I find you to be a constant source of entertainment, Billie. Having you around is going to add years to my life."

"Never mind the horseshit."

"That foul tongue again, and this time in a court of law." Clay shook his head in mock despair. "Blasphemy aside, this is what we'll do. You go on home and tend to your business. I hear you have a two-year-old colt you're trying to unload. I'll attempt to select a dozen semi-intelligent jurors out of this unenthusiastic bunch and then I'll do some digging and try to find our missing child. Does that suit your needs or do you feel the urge to swear at me some more?"

Billie stood on her tiptoes and kissed him on the cheek. "You are a fucking sweetheart, Mr. Clay."

"Good Lord," he said as she left.

Heading back to the farm, Billie had a thought and continued on past, driving down the side road as she'd done the day before. The place was still deserted and the mongrel still in its run, food and water dishes both empty. Before unlatching the gate, Billie petted the animal through the fence until she decided her life wouldn't be in danger by releasing the enormous mutt. After all, she had to assume that the dog was hungry.

It followed her to the truck and sat upright in the passenger seat on the drive to the farm, looking out the windshield expectantly. There was no dog food at the house so she gave the animal half a box of Cheerios with milk. Watching it scarf down the cereal, Billie glanced toward the barn, where the rest of the orphan brigade was in formation in the paddock.

"Noah's got nothing on me," she told the dog.

Chuck Caldwell was in his office at Chestnut Field, feeling beat down, beat up, left out. They were having trouble with the trackside cameras used for photo finishes and inquiries and he'd been on the grounds since dawn. There was a card later that day and without the video they would have to cancel. At ten o'clock he went back to his office and left yet another message for Reese Ryker. He'd been calling a couple of times a day, pressing Ryker on the communications job. Caldwell had decided that there would never be a better time to make a move. His time was up at Chestnut. The place was never going to be anything more than a B track and Caldwell nothing more than a B track manager. He was making sixty-two thousand and hadn't had a raise in five years. He assumed the job with Ryker would pay twice that. *If* he got it. And he'd better get it, after the services he'd rendered. But Ryker was no longer returning his calls.

Hanging up the phone, he leaned back in his chair and put his feet up. After a moment he closed his eyes, thinking he would rest a few minutes. He hadn't been sleeping well of late. He had no intention of going to sleep and so of course he did.

He woke up when he heard his name. Luke Walker was sitting across from him, wearing his stained Resistol, his dirty boots propped on the desk. It wasn't the boots that bothered Caldwell as much as the expression on Luke's face. He looked like a man who'd just drawn to an inside straight.

"What the fuck do you want?" Caldwell demanded.

"You always wake up this cranky?"

"I asked you a question," Caldwell said.

Luke had an open Chestnut Field racing schedule in his lap and now he leaned forward to place it on the desk. He tapped the page with his forefinger. "I'm here to enter a horse in the fifth race next Tuesday."

Caldwell didn't glance at the schedule. "You're not entering sweet fuck-all at this track. I want nothing to do with you."

"Well, I don't want nothing to do with you neither," Luke said. "But I need to enter Billie Masterson's two-year-old in that race next Tuesday. Looks like eight entries so far. You're about to make it nine."

"Get the fuck out of here. Are you stupid?"

"Sometimes I am," Luke admitted. "The difference between you and me is that I know it when I'm stupid. I figure you're one of those guys who thinks he's smarter than everybody else, right up until somebody shows you that you're not."

Caldwell reached for his cell and punched in a number. "I need you in my office," he barked into the phone.

"You're calling security?" Luke asked.

"Gee, you're not so stupid after all," Caldwell said.

Luke got to his feet. "Okay then, I won't make a fuss. I'm in the mood for a beer anyway. I might drive over to this place I know in Lexington—place called Honey Bunnies." He paused. "You know something—I think you and me might have a mutual acquaintance over there. Calls herself Jasmine. She's not the most honest woman I ever met but she's a bobcat in the sack."

Before Caldwell could reply the door opened and a large man dressed in navy blue entered the room. He must have been nearby. He looked Luke up and down briefly. "What's up?"

Caldwell kept his eyes on Luke for a moment, then shifted to the security officer. "Just wondering how things are going with the cameras."

"I can check," the man said, his tone suggesting it was not something he would ordinarily do.

"Do that."

When the man was gone, Luke sat down again. This time he removed his hat and leaned forward to place it on Caldwell's desk.

"What do you want?" Caldwell said.

"You got manure in your ears?" Luke asked. "I want to enter a horse in that race."

"What else?"

"What else?" Luke repeated. "Oh—I get it. You're wondering if I intend to do anything about the fact that you paid a stripper five thousand dollars to pretend she was a schoolteacher and jump my bones and then pretend she was a teenager so that I would get scared I was going to prison and throw the race last Saturday. Is that what you were wondering?"

Caldwell looked back at Luke, his bottom lip bouncing.

Luke smiled. "You see—this here is one of those times when you're about to realize that you're not near as smart as you think. If you were, you would have told Reese Ryker to deal with that little girl Jasmine himself. You know, instead of giving you the five grand in fifties to give to her. Then you wouldn't be having this uncomfortable conversation right now, where you look like you're about to spout a few tears."

Caldwell glanced at his phone again.

"Oh, you want to phone old Reese right now, don't you?" Luke said. "Go ahead. Ask him how he's gonna feel when you implicate him in your little blackmail scam. I'm pretty sure it would make all the papers if his name was involved. Actually, I'm the only one who might come out of this smelling all right. All I did was fuck a pretty girl I met in a bar. By the way, she's twenty-five, pal. Least that's what she told me while she was changing a flat tire and calling me names that by God made even me blush."

Caldwell pressed the heels of his hands against his eyes, as if hoping the act would make Luke disappear.

"Do you think the cops are going to believe a stripper?" he asked when he lowered his hands to find Luke still there.

"Do you think your wife is going to believe *you?*" Luke reached forward and picked up the schedule. "Next Tuesday, fifth race. This horse is named Cactus Jack, owned by Masterson Thoroughbreds. You got the particulars in your files from last time. I expect to see the change made in the schedule by tomorrow morning—else I might have to come visit you again."

"I'll enter the horse," Caldwell said. "Then that's it between you and me."

"I wouldn't say that's it," Luke told him. "Up until now, you've been a real prick to Billie Masterson and we both know why. In the future, you're gonna treat her like she's the Queen of the Furrow. Everything I know about this situation, she knows. You got yourself in a pickle here, Caldwell. If I was you, I'd be on my best behavior from here on in. That how you got it figured?"

Caldwell looked at him, his eyes flat, and said nothing. Luke reached for his hat and got to his feet. At the door, he looked back at the unhappy man behind the desk.

"Ain't life funny? You figured you had this thing you could hold over me and now here I am holding it over you." Luke put his hat on. "I believe they call that irony."

Twenty-Seven

IT WAS AN EVENING CARD AT Chestnut Field that Tuesday. They had trailered Cactus Jack back to the shed row a few days earlier, and since then Luke and Tyrone had been working him every morning. After what had happened the last time, Tyrone had been understandably suspicious of Luke's involvement and Billie had told Luke that he needed to both apologize to the jockey and explain the circumstances. Luke had agreed to do it.

"But he's the last damn person I'm saying sorry to," he told her.

"What about Jodie?"

"Shit," Luke said. "Okay, second last."

"It's good for your soul," Billie told him.

"You never figured I had one."

"Just in case," Billie said.

Billie had collected Jodie from her aunt's place in Marshall over the weekend. True to his word, David Clay had found the woman, living in a third-floor apartment in the old part of town. The aunt's name was Micky Saunders. David Clay had called Billie with the information the day after the scene at the courthouse. She didn't ask where he got it. After all, he was Batman.

She hadn't known what to expect the first time she went to the apartment. Shelly Rickman's reaction to Billie in the courtroom hadn't been particularly warm, but then the woman had been arrested on multiple charges and spent the night in the lockup so it was possible that she wasn't feeling all that congenial. Still, Billie was nervous that the aunt might be of a similar disposition.

Aunt Micky looked nothing like her half-sister. She had a kindness in her manner that her sister did not. She answered the door wearing green sweat pants and a pink hoodie. Her hair was wet, as if she'd just stepped out of the shower.

"Yeah, I know who you are," she said. "I've been hearing all about you and that farm. I sent her to the store for bread, she'll be back soon. You want coffee?"

They sat in the kitchen of the apartment. The house was red brick and had wide oak trim and baseboards. It had probably been built by one of Marshall's leading citizens a hundred years ago. David Clay would know who, or at least he'd come up with some history on the place if Billie were to ask. Now the three floors had been partitioned off and converted into one-bedroom apartments. This one was clean and tidy, tidier than any apartment Billie had ever had.

"I don't know what I'm going to do," Aunt Micky told her. "I waitress in Lexington three nights a week. Those nights I've been paying Alice downstairs to watch Jodie. But Alice is a little off, carries a pistol in her purse, and spends all her money on lottery tickets. My other job is cleaning houses and I take Jodie with me then. She's a good little worker."

"I know she is," Billie said.

"Be different in the fall when school starts. At least then she'll have a place to go during the day. But I'll still be working nights."

"What about your sister—is she going to make bail?"

"I hope not," Aunt Micky said. "Best place for her right now is in jail. She needs to get straight. Hopefully they'll send that Everson off to Eddyville for twenty years and she can be rid of him."

Billie drank the instant coffee. She was inclined to agree with Aunt Micky about jail being the best place for the mother, for the time being anyway. But where did that leave the kid? Billie couldn't imagine she was all that happy, living in the small apartment. And the pistol-packing babysitter sounded half a bubble off plumb.

"I could use some help at the farm," Billie found herself saying. "Would it be okay if she came out there, at least until school starts?"

Aunt Micky sipped her coffee. "I think that would be all right," she said after a long moment's consideration. "She surely thinks the world of you."

"She does?" Billie wondered how she came to deserve that.

Aunt Micky smiled. "Well, she thought that the sun rose and fell on your father, so maybe it's a residual effect."

And so Jodie had moved to the farm. The situation was temporary, Billie had advised her. She brought her clothes and books and other items in a knapsack. She said she would sleep on the couch in the living room but Billie told her she could take the big bedroom upstairs. She was pretty sure that Will Masterson would be okay with that.

Jodie was surprised to find the mongrel mastiff at the farm. Billie had been feeding the dog and giving it the run of the place, although he never traveled far. At night he slept on the back deck, as a watchdog might, but Billie doubted the animal would be of much use in that capacity. A prowler with a handful of Cheerios could buy him off. The dog appeared happy to see Jodie. It seemed she was the only one who paid it any mind at the double-wide.

"What's his name, anyway?" Billie had asked.

"Troy called him Cujo," Jodie said. "But Troy didn't like him much because he wasn't mean."

"He doesn't seem like a Cujo to me," Billie said.

"I always called him George."

"Why George?"

"Because he looks like a George."

And so George it was.

The scene at the track Tuesday night was naturally a repeat of the previous race ten days earlier, with one exception. This time Luke was present in every sense. The race was for two-year-olds with five starts or fewer. The purse was thirty-five thousand, which meant the winner's share would be twenty-one grand. There were a couple of highly regarded colts in the field; both had two wins to their credit already. The favorite was on the board at three to two. The handicapper at Chestnut Field, understandably unimpressed with Cactus Jack's last start, listed him at sixty to one.

Tyrone was again bridegroom nervous and so was Billie. Luke had a calm about him, but then Luke was always calm, even when royally fucking up, so she didn't read too much into it. When the colt was saddled and in the walking ring, Billie took Jodie with her to see him off. Luke was standing at the horse's head, having just given Tyrone a leg up. Neither man said a word. Billie gave the jockey what she hoped was a reassuring smile before turning to Luke.

"Isn't this where you tell him how to ride the horse?"

"He knows how to ride the horse," Luke replied.

And this time Luke was right. Tyrone brought Cactus Jack sharply out of the gate and moved him at once to the rail, where he settled in, middle of the pack. He kept him there through the first two turns and into the back stretch, keeping the colt easily in hand. The field stretched out going into the three-quarter turn and Cactus Jack moved into third place, still close to the rail.

Billie and Jodie stood near the finish line with Luke as the horses came around the clubhouse turn and moved into the stretch. The two leaders were side by side, with Cactus Jack five full lengths behind.

"Now you move him," Luke said, so softly Billie wasn't sure she heard it.

But she could have sworn that Tyrone did. He switched the colt's lead and moved him outside, going to the whip just once. Cactus

Jack leapt forward as if rocket-powered, overtaking the leaders in a couple dozen strides and thundering down the stretch, running flat out, ears back, nostrils wide open. Tyrone tucked himself behind the colt's head and went along for the ride; Billie could see him talking to the animal as they flew across the finish line, beating the favorite by eight lengths. Jodie screamed and Billie turned to look at Luke. Always playing the cool cat, he just nodded. But she kept her eyes on him until he grinned.

They went out onto the track to meet the horse as Tyrone loped him back. Looking at Luke, the jockey gave him a quick fist pump and then jumped down. He beamed over at Billie, like a kid showing off a good report card.

"How's that?"

"That will do just fine," Billie said.

In the clubhouse lounge Reese Ryker stood at the windows overlooking the track. Behind him at a table, Sofia was enjoying a crème brûlée while Caldwell sat miserably across from her. Reese watched until the hot walker led the gray colt away and Billie Masterson disappeared with her reprobate trainer and the orphan kid, presumably to pick up her money.

"Well, that's just fucking peachy," he said when he came back to the table.

Sofia rolled her eyes. "Why do you care? So this horse wins the race. Did you have a horse in this race? No, you did not. So why do you care?"

"Because it's fraud," Reese snapped. "Humphrey Brown bred Saguaro to that ten-cent mare under false pretenses. You watch— if that colt wins a few more races, the woman will stand that horse to stud next year, claiming it's by Saguaro."

"But he *is* by Saguaro," Sofia reminded him. She used her finger to gather up the rest of her dessert.

"The line is tainted." Reese turned on Caldwell. "You should never have let them enter that horse."

Caldwell looked at Sofia a moment and then spoke pointedly to Reese. "I can explain that to you again if you like."

Reese eyed Caldwell with menace but quickly waved away the suggestion. "What happens next? I happen to know that the woman has significant money problems, which means she's going to keep running the horse. Not that I expect it to win again. Tonight was a fluke."

Sofia laughed. "Do you see the time on the board? Is that a fluke in America? It is not a fluke in Spain."

Reese ignored her, keeping at Caldwell. "I know the woman's up against it at the bank time-wise. I'm thinking—what if you were to convince her to run the colt in a claimer? Something with a decent payday? She might risk it."

"She knows you're watching the horse," Caldwell said. "She's not going to let you claim it."

"She might slip up. That mortgage is due and she fucking well knows it."

Once again Caldwell glanced at Sofia. "That's not all she knows, Reese."

Sofia had been watching the horses on the track, coming out for the next race, and now she turned to them. "What is all of this mystery? I feel as if there is something at this table that I should know."

"No," Reese said. "Chuck and I are just talking here. Trying to figure a way to keep the white trash out of the racing game. I guess we'll have to wait for her next move. You will keep me in the loop, Chuck."

Caldwell nodded. He didn't have any choice. With Luke Walker on one side and Reese Ryker on the other, he didn't have much choice in anything these days.

Out of a superstition inherited from her father, Billie hadn't bet anything on the colt. She was afraid of jinxing the animal. She found out after the race that Luke had put his last twenty dollars on it and Jodie had bet two bucks. The colt paid a hundred and twelve dollars for the win. Luke, of course, wanted to spend his money—God forbid he would ever put a nickel aside—and suggested they go for dinner at the Bellwood Hotel in Marshall. Tyrone had a mount later in the card and said he'd catch up with them afterward.

Walking across the parking lot with Jodie, Billie spotted Marian on her way to her car. Billie had looked for her in the stands earlier. Now she called to her.

"Maybe you were right after all," she said.

"You mean maybe your father was right," Marian said.

"Where were you?" Billie asked. "Why didn't you watch with us at the rail?"

"I watched from the grandstand. I have a feeling that you and I do better at arm's length, Billie. But I enjoyed that very much. Cactus Jack looked like a different horse tonight. Can you tell me why?"

Billie shrugged. "We streamlined the operation. Got rid of the strippers and blackmailers and duplicitous billionaires. Your typical story."

Marian's eyebrows lifted.

"We're heading to the Bellwood for dinner," Billie said. "Come with us."

"Not tonight. I have plans."

"You don't have a new boyfriend?"

"Still getting over the last one."

Luke brought the racing schedule into the bar at the Bellwood. They sat in a corner booth and asked for menus, then ordered a pitcher of beer to start, and lemonade for Jodie. The waitress who brought the drinks was a young woman, college age. When Luke began to flirt with her, Billie kicked him under the table. The waitress walked away.

"Just once in your life," Billie suggested.

Luke glanced at Jodie as he reached for the pitcher.

"So what next?" Billie asked, indicating the schedule.

Luke opened the paper. "First we need to see how he comes out of tonight's race. If he's sound, we can think about racing him again in two weeks. So what do we have here?" He flipped through the pages, going forward. "There's a big card at the end of the month, same day they run the Jamboree Mile. Biggest day of the year at Chestnut. Look it here—there's a juvenile sprint that day, second race, with a purse of forty thousand. Open to two-year-olds that have won at least one race, which means we now qualify. Winner would get twenty-four grand. How would that get you with the bank?"

"Closer," Billie said. "Not close enough."

"One step at a time," Luke said and went back to calculating. "Let's say you run him again in mid-September, and twice in October. Hell, you could be out of debt in time for Thanksgiving turkey."

"If he keeps winning."

"This conversation don't work otherwise," Luke said. "Right, Jodie?"

She looked up from the menu. "Jack's going to win."

"Because he's got the best trainer, right?" Luke said.

"Because he's the fastest horse," Jodie said. "I'm going to buy fish and chips with my winnings."

"I'm buying," Luke said.

"You're like a sailor on leave," Billie told him. "You just have to spend every dime you make, don't you?"

Jodie looked at Billie. "Any day you break even is a good day in the racing game."

Billie smiled. "Now I wonder where you heard that."

Twenty-Eight

ON THE DRIVE HOME THAT NIGHT Sofia told Reese that he needed to forget about the gray colt owned by Billie Masterson. She'd had brandy after her dessert and wine beforehand and was a little tipsy, a condition that emphasized her accent.

"It has nothing to do with you," she said. "It is consuming you up."

"I wouldn't say that," he told her.

"I am saying that," she countered. "It is consuming you up and it makes you boring, as well."

Reese had a lifelong suspicion that he was in fact boring. Two of his wives had mentioned it in leaving. And so when Sofia told him that he needed to stop obsessing over Cactus Jack, he spent the next few days pretending to do just that.

Friday morning, he put Sofia on a plane for Los Angeles, where she was due in the studio to record some songs. Reese had intended to accompany her but decided against it at the last minute. To say that he himself put her on a plane was a figure of speech. He had one of his limos take her. When she was gone he had breakfast in the sunroom, waffles and maple syrup, and watched his own TV station's newscast.

With Sofia off to the coast for a week, he had to remind himself to heed her words. But then he'd awakened in the night thinking about the goddamn horse. Lying there in the large bed in the mansion his mother had left to him, he told himself he needed to let it go. Why did he care? Let the woman run the B tracks with her B horse. Reese owned Ghost Rider, perhaps the best two-year-old prospect in North America. That was the horse the racing world would be talking about at the Breeders Cup this fall. And, if the stars aligned, in Louisville the first Saturday in May next spring.

By the time Reese had finished his waffles, lifting the plate to lick up the last of the good Quebec syrup, he was once again ready to put the matter in his rearview mirror. He walked out onto the terrace and looked down to the training track, where just now Joe Drinkwater was standing with Ghost Rider. There was an exercise rider on the horse and he'd obviously just taken the animal for a turn around the track. He and Drinkwater were talking and the trainer was nodding his head. Watching, Reese couldn't help but think how much the colt looked like the gray that had won the race the night before at Chestnut Field. The goddamn imposter that had won the race the night before at Chestnut Field. And with that, it started again.

He took his phone from his pocket and scrolled down to find the number for Herbert Jakes at First National. A secretary answered and Reese asked to speak to the man.

"Mr. Jakes is not here. Can I take a message?"

"Have him call Reese Ryker."

"Oh, Mr. Ryker. How are you?"

"Have him call me as soon as he gets in."

"Mr. Jakes is gone for the rest of the week," the woman on the phone said. "It's the annual convention."

"Where is he?"

"This year they're at Pebble Beach. Bankers and golf, you know how—"

"I'm sure he has a phone with him," Reese snapped.

"Of course. I'll forward the message."

Hanging up, Reese walked into the sunroom again and poured another cup of coffee, which he carried onto the terrace. Ghost Rider was gone now and Joe Drinkwater was fitting a bridle over the nose of a bay filly. Reese had a thought and took out his phone to punch redial.

"Who's at this conference?" he asked.

"I beg your pardon?"

"Who's at this Pebble Beach thing—all the branch managers?"

"Why, yes. As well as various board members and vice presidents. Was there someone else you wished to speak with?"

Reese hung up.

When he got to the Marshall branch of First National, he asked to speak with the manager, Brock, knowing full well that manager Brock was in a golf cart or a sand trap along the Pacific Rim, or sitting in a boardroom nearby, listening to somebody drone on about mutual futures while looking forward to being in a golf cart or a sand trap at some point. Reese next asked to speak with the loans manager.

Her name was Kellyanne something. She was impatient with Reese until he told her who he was, whereupon she practically dropped to her knees in reverence.

"Can I help you with something?"

"Probably not," Reese said. They were sitting in her office. Outside the sun was shining on the denizens of Marshall as they went about their day. Reese half hoped that Billie Masterson would walk by and see him sitting there. It might remove the smug look from her face. That is, if she were smart enough to realize what she was seeing.

"I was passing through town," Reese said then, "and I saw this place and thought I'd stop and inquire about the practices of a small-town bank. You see, I have considerable deposits in the charter branch in Lexington—"

"I'm sure that's an understatement," Kellyanne interjected, smiling brightly.

"Uh, yes," Reese said. "Herbert Jakes runs the show there and I have every confidence that he plays hardball when it comes to deadbeat debtors. But I've been hearing lately that these back-woods branches don't like to play that game."

"That's not true," Kellyanne assured him.

"It's not? Well, maybe I don't understand this thing called a mortgage. I was led to believe that if the mortgagee didn't make his payments, then the bank would be obligated to foreclose. Am I wrong in assuming this?"

Kellyanne took a moment to consider the sarcastic tone in his voice. "You are not wrong."

"No, I'm not," Reese agreed. "Unless, of course, the mortgagee's name happens to be Will Masterson."

Kellyanne had no reply to that.

"Will Masterson died nearly two months ago," Reese said. "He was in default for some time before he died. And yet you continue to carry his loan. Do you anticipate the man rising from the dead? More to the point, do you anticipate the man rising from the dead flush with cash?"

Kellyanne glanced out into the bank, weighing her words. "I'm not happy with that situation. But I don't know that I can discuss it with you."

Reese lifted his hands. "I'd rather you didn't breach any proto-col on my account. I can always bring it up with Herbert Jakes." He leaned forward to take one of Kellyanne's business cards from the holder on her desk. "I'll mention that we were chatting."

"It's the manager's call," Kellyanne said quickly. "But he's got people nattering at him. There's a lawyer here named Clay who thinks he runs the town and I know he's been yapping in Brock's ear. And so all I keep hearing is 'give Billie Masterson some time.' It's bullshit, as far as I'm concerned. The note was due and now it's overdue."

"So why don't you do *your* job and call it in?"

Kellyanne hesitated again. "Like I said, it's the manager's call."

Reese stood up and made a show of putting Kellyanne's card in his shirt pocket. "I won't bother you further." He was nearly out the door when she called him back.

"There is something I can tell you," she said reluctantly.

Reese waited, watching as she struggled with some inner crisis of confidence.

"All right," she said finally. "This information does not concern the bank and as a rule I wouldn't even know about it. It involves a third party, who let it slip to me at a social event recently. We were talking about Billie Masterson and her situation."

"I'm listening," Reese said.

"This person's father holds a demand note on the Masterson farm. Are you familiar with the term?"

"Vaguely."

"It's basically a private mortgage," Kellyanne said. "The debtor is required only to keep up on the interest. However, if the lender decides he wants the note paid in full, all he has to do is say so."

"Who is the lender?"

"An older man, owns a boutique vineyard over near Monticello."

Reese stood looking out the window to the street for a time before turning back to Kellyanne. "This thing called a demand note. Would the lender be free to sell it to another individual?"

"Yes," Kellyanne said. "He would."

Billie wasn't sure how she had managed it, but Jodie somehow convinced the dog now known as George to pull the pony cart she had sanded and painted. As big as the dog was it was still not quite pony-sized, but it did a reasonable job of hauling the little girl out to the road and back. The operation was much more successful with the mutt than it was ever going to be with the obstinate pony. It was midmorning and Billie watched from the back deck, drinking coffee and thinking that it was just the natural way of things. Dogs were dogs and ponies were ponies and just because the conveyance in question was called a pony cart didn't mean that your

average pony would want anything to do with it. Ponies were con-
trary animals that as a rule didn't give a hoot in hell about a little
girl's wishes. The donkey was little inclined to the task, either. A
dog, on the other hand, wanted nothing more than to please its
human counterparts. Sitting in the morning sun and considering
the vagaries of the animal world, it dawned on Billie that she was
now running a dog and pony show.

"Chrissakes," she said out loud.

In truth though, she was surprised to find a feeling of content-
ment creeping into her subconscious of late. There was nothing
to account for it; she was still in dire straits financially, with all of
her hopes in that direction pinned on a horse race coming up on
the weekend. And then on another race after that. And so on. To
think that the colt would win every time out was impractical and
probably downright delusional, but Luke had reminded her that
second and third place paid decent money as well, enough to keep
moving forward.

Her financial future, doomed or charmed as it might turn out
to be, had nothing to do with the change in Billie's emotional
being. For some reason she was no longer restless on the farm,
or at least not as restless as she had been when she'd first come
back. She wasn't convinced that the feeling would last and in fact
doubted it would, but she felt at home for the first time since she
was about fourteen years old. Ironically, she felt at home in the
very same place as when she was that age. She wished she could
tell her father that.

Watching Jodie coming down the laneway once again in the
cart, she thought that it might be time to suggest giving the dog a
breather. The animal seemed to be slowing down, its tongue loll-
ing. In the course of a week it had gone from being penned up in
a chain-link prison to a brand-new life as a draft animal. Billie
reasoned that a career change like that needed to be gradual.

Before Billie could speak, she saw a white Buick SUV turn into
the lane, heading for the barn. The car was moving slowly, dodging

the holes in the gravel drive. Billie got to her feet, wondering who it was behind the wheel.

The Buick made a wide circle around the dog cart and parked. A youngish man in a blue suit got out. He glanced at Jodie and the big mutt before looking up to see Billie at the house, then reached back into the SUV to retrieve a briefcase. There was something about the man's arrival that didn't sit well with Billie. Men with briefcases rarely delivered good news, at least in her experience. She started down the hill.

The man said his name was something Albertson and that he was a lawyer. He appeared just nervous enough to make Billie nervous, too. He was obviously hesitant to say why he was there, which didn't help. Billie regarded him a moment before turning to Jodie, who had pulled the cart to a stop by the barn door.

"Maybe we should give George a breather," she said.

"Okay," Jodie said. "He did pretty good, didn't he?"

"He did very good."

Then Billie turned back to the fidgety lawyer and asked what she could do for him.

They found Luke at the farm outside of Junction City. He was drinking beer on the front porch and reading a paperback novel. His hat was on the newel post at the top of the steps and his worn boots propped on the railing.

"Demand note," Luke said. "Never heard of that before."

"I wish I never heard of it now," Billie said.

"What's the story on it?"

"Some guy over in Monticello lent my father forty-five thousand dollars a few years back. The agreement was that the old man just had to keep up on the interest. Which apparently he somehow did, along with a small bit of the principal."

"But now the guy's calling in the note?"

"Not exactly," Billie said. "The guy sold the note."

"Sold it to who?"

"How many guesses do you need, Luke?"

"Well shit."

"Yeah," Billie said.

"Why didn't you know about this?" Luke asked.

"I knew it was there," Billie said. "Lawyer Clay said not to worry about it. There were more pressing debts."

"Not anymore, there ain't," Luke said. "How much is owed on this thing?"

"Nearly the full boat. Forty-two thousand."

Luke's eyes narrowed and he looked out to the field where the Hereford steers grazed, as if the little herd might offer a solution to the money problem. After a few seconds he stood up, draining his beer.

"You want a pop, kid?"

"Sure," Jodie said.

As Luke went into the house Billie reached over for the novel he'd been reading. It was a Mickey Spillane mystery, a tattered and dog-eared copy that looked to be sixty years old. When Luke returned he was carrying two cans of Bud and a cola for Jodie and he had the racing schedule tucked beneath his arm. He handed over the drinks and then sat on the railing where he took a long drink of beer before opening the paper.

Jodie had a drink of the soda. "Can I go look at the cows?"

"They're steers," Luke said. "Go ahead. They ain't all that entertaining."

"I like their white faces." Jodie went down the steps and walked over to the fence line, where she tried to draw the attention of the disinterested Herefords.

"Forty-two thousand," Luke muttered. "And we got how long?"

"Note's due in ten days," Billie said.

Luke frowned, scanning the schedule.

"Since when did you start reading novels?" Billie asked.

"I always did," Luke said. "Hell, I've spent near my whole life living in motels. What do you think I do in my spare time?"

"Drink and chase women."

"Shit," he said, still looking at the schedule. Suddenly his face lit up. "Hey—we enter him in the Jamboree Mile. We take him out of the sprint and run him in the Jamboree."

"The stakes race?" Billie asked, her voice incredulous. "How many beers you had today? We can't run Cactus Jack in that race. That's way out of his class."

"Says who?" Luke replied. "We win this race on Saturday and you can have the money for Monday morning. Well—provided he wins."

"There is that provision," Billie said sarcastically. "We can't step him up like that. He's raced twice, for Chrissakes."

"But you're out of time," Luke said. "Sometimes you just do something because it's the only thing left to do."

"And that makes sense to you?"

"Well, it don't always work out."

"Cactus Jack can't compete against that field."

Luke shrugged. "I'm listening if you've got a better idea."

"It doesn't matter anyway," Billie said. "The race is five days away and the field will be full. Caldwell wouldn't let us enter him if we wanted to."

"Chuck Caldwell will show up at that race wearing an evening gown and pearls if I tell him to," Luke said.

Twenty-Nine

W HEN CALDWELL CALLED, REESE WAS IN his car, heading for the TV station in Louisville. He hadn't been spending much time there of late and even though he knew that it mattered little whether he was there or not, he felt that his presence should be noted occasionally, in case somebody decided that they—and not he—were running the place.

But then he got the phone call and he turned around, heading for Chestnut Field. He was getting tired of news from Chestnut Field and even more tired of it being bad news.

"The Jamboree?" he said. "Why the hell would they do that?"

"I assume for the money," Caldwell replied. "Why else would they do it?"

They were standing trackside by the finish line, where a few trainers were working horses. When Reese had arrived, Caldwell had been there, talking to a video technician about the cameras.

"What's the purse on that race?" Reese asked.

"A hundred thousand."

That was it, Reese knew then. The winner's take would be sixty thousand, more than what Billie Masterson owed on the demand note Reese had purchased from the old vintner in Monticello a few days earlier.

"So they pulled the horse from the sprint and booked him in the stakes."

"That's what they did," Caldwell said.

"And you didn't tell them no."

"I did not."

"Seems to me that Luke Walker is pretty much running this place these days," Reese said. "Sounds as if he says jump and you say how high."

"I guess I could tell him to fuck off and then we could all talk to a judge about certain things and certain people. You among them, Reese."

"You can't link me to any of it."

"You're the one who showed Walker the pictures of him and the stripper," Caldwell said. "You think he forgot that part?" He paused, watching Ryker. "What are you worried about anyway? That horse is way out of his class in the Jamboree. The favorite is that big bay Jim's Dandy. Horse has won all five of its starts. Every horse in the field can beat that horse of Masterson's hands down. They're doing you a favor, pulling that colt out of the sprint. They're going to end up with zilch, which is what you want. Isn't it, Reese?"

Reese thought about that as he drove back to Lexington, having forgotten all about going to "work" at the TV station. It sounded as if Billie Masterson was desperate, entering her horse in the stakes. Nothing short of a win would save her. And Chuck Caldwell had just guaranteed Reese that a win was out of the question, which meant that come Saturday night, Billie Masterson was out of options.

That is, as long as her horse got beat. But why was Reese willing to trust Chuck Caldwell's guarantee on this or anything else? After all, it was Caldwell who had come up with the idea of getting the stripper to pose as the schoolteacher. It had cost Reese five grand and backfired in the end. Why should Reese trust him now?

When he got to the house, he drove over to the barns to look for Joe Drinkwater. The trainer was in his office on the upper floor on the stable, sipping green tea and going over some paperwork. Reese really didn't know what the man did when he wasn't actually on the track, working horses. He assumed that Drinkwater knew what he was doing and so he left him to do it. His horses kept winning.

"What's up, Reese?" Joe asked when Reese walked in.

"We're running Ghost Rider in the Jamboree Mile at Chestnut Field on Saturday," Reese said.

"What?" Joe snapped. "Since when?"

"Since I just decided."

"That's two days away," Joe said. "We're not doing that."

"Yes, we are," Reese said and left. As he walked to the house, he called Chuck Caldwell to tell him the news. For the second time in two days Caldwell was going to have to expand the field for the race and he immediately began to whine about it. Reese hung up on him.

"That sonofabitch," Luke said when he heard.

Skeeter Musgrave told him the news Friday morning. Skeeter hadn't been coming around the track much of late. He had finally decided to let the doctors replace his left hip and he was waiting for a date for the surgery. He didn't like being at the track when he couldn't do anything constructive, so he'd been steering clear of the place. But he ate breakfast every morning at the Creekside Diner down the road a couple of miles. A lot of track workers frequented the place and it was there he'd heard about Ghost Rider.

"Only the best goddamn two-year-old on the planet," Skeeter said. "According to Reese Ryker, that is."

"According to a lot of people," Luke said.

"Everybody knows Ryker has a bee in his bonnet over that colt of yours," Skeeter said. "But dropping that horse into that race—well, that's beyond the pale. Lot of people pissed off about it."

Luke nodded. He was one of them, although his reasons were different than those of the people Skeeter was talking about. Those folks didn't like Ryker bringing his horse in just to win the race. It wasn't illegal, it was just wrong, and it would make the race a mismatch. All it meant to Luke was that Cactus Jack couldn't win. It had been a stretch in the first place, entering the colt with just two races under his belt.

The horse in question was at that moment standing in his stall a few yards away, picking at some alfalfa. Luke had had Tyrone lope the colt for a couple of furlongs earlier but that was all he would do today, with less than twenty-four hours to race time.

"What are you gonna do?" Skeeter asked then.

"I don't know," Luke replied. "This was a hell of a long shot to begin with and I sure wasn't expecting this." He stood looking at Cactus Jack chewing the sweet hay, oblivious to his fate. "What would you do, Skeeter?"

"The Lord hates a coward."

Billie was in the barn with Jodie when Luke pulled up in his truck. She had decided to replace the rotting boards along the back wall of the building and first they had to move the hay out of the way. They were lugging bales across the floor to the opposite wall when Luke came in with the news.

Billie didn't say anything for a time. She sat down heavily on the bale she'd been carrying, her eyes on the scarred wooden barn floor. "I guess we should have seen that coming."

"Nobody else did," Luke said. "It's a bush-league move, dropping that horse into the race, and everybody knows it. Ryker's name is mud around Chestnut."

"He couldn't care less about that," Billie said. "How did he enter him so late?"

"Same way we did is my guess," Luke said. "He's got his foot on Caldwell's neck, too, I expect."

"So what do we do?"

"We can scratch the horse," Luke said. "Look for another race next week. Maybe even run him at Keeneland or Ellis."

"Nothing that will pay enough, though," Billie said. "You sure this is true? Where did Skeeter hear it anyway?"

"I checked the entries and it's true," Luke said. "The news was all around the track. Skeeter first heard about it at the diner."

Billie stood and lifted the bale onto the stack against the wall. "And what does Skeeter say?"

"Skeeter says the Lord hates a coward."

"I've heard that one before, too," Billie said.

"Is Ghost Rider a brother to Cactus Jack?" Jodie asked.

"Half-brother, yeah," Luke said.

"I bet they'll be glad to see each other."

Billie smiled in spite of herself. "Maybe they will."

Thirty

COME SATURDAY MORNING JOE DRINKWATER WAS in a foul mood for the third day running. At one point Reese thought the trainer was going to quit over the matter. He'd come to the house Thursday night to plead his case.

"We had a plan," he said. "We run the colt in three weeks in the Mercedes Mile and then we take him to the Breeders. There's strategy here, Reese. I'm not throwing darts at a racing schedule on the wall."

"That's still the plan," Reese said. "We're just going to make a little side trip to Chestnut Field first."

"That's another thing," Joe said. "This isn't fair to the owners who run that track all year long, dropping Ghost Rider into that race. This stinks like a dead skunk. It makes us all look bad."

Reese shrugged.

"And it's all because of that Masterson colt," Joe went on. He realized something. "Is that why Luke Walker was here that day? Were you trying to influence that boy somehow?"

"Not at all."

Joe watched him a moment. "You don't want to do this, Reese. Pull the horse now, say it was a publicity stunt, or a clerical error, something. But you don't want to do this."

"We're doing it."

The conversation had done nothing to ease the tension between the two men. They trailered the gray colt to Chestnut Field the next morning. Ordinarily a horse like Ghost Rider would be received like royalty, but not in this instance. Nearly everybody at Chestnut had a connection to one or another of the horses entered in the Jamboree, which meant they were all now resigned to the fact that their horse would be running for second. Anyone who admired Ghost Rider did it while simultaneously resenting the horse's very existence. It didn't help that Reese Ryker showed up on Saturday looking like he'd just stepped off the set of a 1930s movie, dressed in a white linen suit and wearing a wide-brimmed white hat. Sofia was still in Los Angeles, making music, so Reese arrived alone. He hung around the shed row for a bit but soon grew tired of Joe Drinkwater's pout and went up to the lounge to sit with Chuck Caldwell, whose disposition wasn't any improvement over Joe's. He'd been taking heat for days over his allowing Ghost Rider to run in the mile. Reese ignored his petulance and ordered bourbon and water.

Billie and Jodie were at the track a couple of hours before race time. Luke had been there since early morning, even though there'd been nothing to do. He and Billie had talked the night before of pulling Cactus Jack, but in the end Billie had said no. They'd been on the back deck at the farm. Jodie had gone to bed and the moon was just showing in the eastern sky.

"I don't care if he finishes last," she said. "Either we show up or Ryker will think he scared us off."

"Christ, you're just like your old man," Luke told her.

"There was a time I would have taken umbrage at that," Billie said.

The Jamboree Mile was the seventh race on the card. Billie and Jodie went to the shed row to see Cactus Jack a little beforehand. Luke was there, sitting on the tailgate of his truck, looking cool as a cucumber, although Billie didn't believe it. He turned to Jodie as she approached the horse in the stall.

"Did you bring him a carrot?"

"You said I couldn't before a race," she reminded him.

"That was the old Luke."

A few minutes later Joe Drinkwater walked by, leading the big gray Ghost Rider. Joe glanced over at Luke and Billie and shook his head, as if in apology, and kept walking. Billie watched the colt as it walked, the muscles in the haunch and shoulders rippling beneath the silver-flecked coat.

"Jesus, that's a good-looking horse," Billie said.

Luke looked at the horse and then back to Billie. "I ever tell you about the time I went to the prom over at Danton?"

"You went to a prom?" Billie asked.

"Yup. There was this girl over there that asked me. She thought I was a young Brad Pitt."

"You went to a prom with a blind girl?"

"You ain't near as funny as you think, Billie," Luke said. "Her name was Sherri and it was a night. I rented a tuxedo at that place in Marshall. Before the big dance, we were standing in the lineup thing with all the other couples and I'm staring at these girls and I'm thinking—man, there's some good-looking women here. They were all done up in their fancy dresses, and the hair and the flow-ers—what do you call them—corsairs?"

"Corsages," Billie said. "A corsair is a pirate."

Luke shrugged. "So anyway, a week or so later, Sherri comes around with a bunch of pictures from that night."

"Why would a blind girl have pictures?"

"You can stop that anytime," Luke said. "I'm looking at these pictures of all these pretty girls and goddamn, don't I realize that I was with the prettiest one of the bunch." Luke looked pointedly past Billie to Cactus Jack.

Billie turned toward the horse and goddamn if Luke wasn't right. "Whatever happened to Sherri?"

"I borrowed her old man's Lincoln one night without asking and rolled it over six times on Westfield Road. Sherri married an insurance salesman and moved out of state."

Billie shook her head. "I'm sure that's what you consider a happy ending."

She and Jodie headed for the walking ring while Luke led Cactus Jack to the saddling barn. Billie had been watching for Marian but didn't see her. She had even thought she might stop at the farm sometime in the past few days but she hadn't. Billie wondered if she was sticking to the same routine as when Cactus Jack had won twelve days earlier. Billie was aware of how superstitious people were about such things. She'd been thinking about it that morning, as she'd gotten dressed in precisely the same clothes as last time the colt had raced, right down to her underwear.

She spotted Reese Ryker, turned out like a fried chicken huckster, in the saddling barn with Joe Drinkwater. Luke had Cactus Jack thirty feet away. The colt was relaxed and loose as always. The big gray Ghost Rider appeared antsy, sidestepping away from the saddle and tossing his head.

In the walking ring minutes later, Luke stood with Tyrone as the horses paraded in the circle. Billie and Jodie were at the rail a few yards away. Luke's eyes never left Ghost Rider as the horse moved around the circle. The big gray was restive, fighting the bit and shaking his head.

"Well?" Tyrone asked as the walker stopped Cactus Jack beside them.

"Stay with him," Luke said and he didn't say anything else.

The race was announced as the horses were led out onto the track. Luke walked with Billie and Jodie to the rail, as before. Reese Ryker climbed up to the grandstand, where he stood with Caldwell as the entries were being loaded into the gate. The field had been increased from ten to twelve horses to accommodate the two late additions. There was a feeling on the air that the race was now nothing more than a joke. Billie heard one man say that Ghost Rider would win by fifty lengths.

Billie promised herself that she wouldn't look at the tote board and she promptly broke that promise. Ghost Rider was listed at one to five while the handicapper appeared to agree that Cactus Jack had no business even being there and had him at ninety-nine to one, as high as the tote board could list. The real number could have been twice that.

The bell rang and a dozen horses burst from the gate. As they rounded the first turn all twelve were bunched up, striving for position. Coming into the stretch a minute and a half later, ten of them had been left in the dust. There were two gray horses all alone out front and both had been sired by Saguaro.

Tyrone had listened to Luke and parked Cactus Jack a length behind Ghost Rider all around the track, staying just off his hip, stalking him. Both horses had accelerated at the three-quarter pole to leave the field behind. Two hundred yards from the finish line, Tyrone moved his horse outside and once again the colt had erupted. Ghost Rider spotted Cactus Jack on his flank and he too responded with a burst of speed. He held off the challenger until ten yards from the finish and then Cactus Jack caught him with a huge lunging stride at the wire. It looked like Cactus Jack by a nose. The crowd was roaring with excitement, the noise deafening. Nobody there had expected anything like the finish they'd just seen, and if the hordes weren't specifically cheering for Cactus Jack, they were definitely cheering against the interloper Ghost Rider. Billie looked expectantly at Luke.

"Did he catch him?"

Luke wasn't sure. "I think he got him on the stride."

In the grandstand, Reese Ryker turned on Caldwell. "Photo finish!" he barked. "Get your ass down there."

The steward had already called for a photo. Caldwell hurried to the booth, with Reese on his heels. As soon as they entered, they knew there was a problem.

"That camera again," the steward said.

"What do you have?" Caldwell asked.

"I have them a few yards from the wire and then nothing."

Down on the track the photo finish sign was blinking, advising all bettors to hold their tickets. Luke had walked out onto the track as Tyrone brought the colt back. Joe Drinkwater, waiting for his own horse, came over to shake Luke's hand.

"Good job, Luke," he said. "That's a hell of a horse." Then he looked over to where the jockey was bringing Ghost Rider back to the wire. Whatever Joe saw, he didn't like.

Billie and Jodie were by the rail, watching. Billie still didn't want to allow herself to believe they'd won, not yet. Superstitions.

In the booth the steward was running the tape back and forth but the image wasn't there. After a moment Reese took Caldwell by the elbow and pulled him outside.

"My horse won that race," he said.

"It really didn't look that way, Reese."

"I'm telling you."

Caldwell exhaled. "What if we call it a dead heat? That covers our asses."

"Fuck you and your dead heat," Reese snapped. "That horse did *not* beat Ghost Rider."

Caldwell shook his head and started to move away, thinking he might just walk out the front door and out of there forever.

"You want that PR job or not?" Reese demanded suddenly.

And Caldwell turned back to him.

A minute later Ghost Rider was announced as the winner, although the track didn't produce a photo, something nobody present had ever seen before. There was sustained booing from the crowd, shouts that the fix was in. Billie leaned against the rail, her pulse pounding. Jodie reached out to her and held her hand. The prices came up on the board. Ghost Rider returned two dollars and ten cents on a two-dollar bet to win, while Cactus Jack, the longest shot in the field by far, paid eighty-seven dollars to place.

Reese Ryker strolled down to the finish line to get his picture taken with his horse. As he got there, Joe Drinkwater was straightening up from the dirt, where he'd been looking at Ghost Rider's right front leg. His face was ashen.

"We have a problem," he said.

"Later," Reese said, waving him off.

After the picture was taken, Reese headed straight for the rail, where Billie stood with Luke and the girl. None of them were saying anything.

"That little colt of yours ran a good race," Reese told Billie.

"He won the race," Luke said. "You cheating sonofabitch."

Reese ignored him. "Listen, this is just business now, Billie. You and I can come to an agreement and I'll set fire to that demand note today. I can make you a very good offer on the colt right now. Which means you can keep your farm."

"Do you have any idea what you are?" Billie asked.

"What will you take for him right now?"

"You're out of your mind," Billie said. "I mean that. You are out of your mind—aren't you?"

"Not at all. You need to be rational here. I'm trying to save your farm. Isn't this what your father wanted, Billie? I'm offering you something here."

"So am I."

The voice came from off to the side. Billie turned to see Marian striding toward them, a strange look on her face—an expression that was somehow fierce and yet oddly content at the same time. Reese looked at her in annoyance.

"Do you mind?"

"I do mind," Marian said calmly. "I mind everything about you. If I was a man I'd knock you on your ass." She turned to Billie. "How'd you like to sell me ten percent of Masterson Thoroughbreds?"

Billie took a minute. "What's going on?"

"Do you remember that twenty-dollar bill that Elvis didn't sign?" Marian asked. "Well, after Cactus Jack lost the first time out, I told myself I needed to put up or shut up. So I bet that twenty dollars on the horse to win a week ago. That ticket paid over eleven hundred dollars. I took that eleven hundred and bet it on Cactus Jack today."

Reese was getting impatient. "That's wonderful, grandma. You *almost* had a great story there. Too bad the horse didn't win."

Marian took a measured beat. "I bet it to place."

Reese started to speak, then his eyes went to the tote board to look at the prices.

"Don't strain your brain, dipshit," Marian told him. "It comes to just over fifty thousand dollars. And if you call me grandma again, I *will* knock you down." She turned and offered the ticket to Billie. "Like I said, I want to buy a piece of your stable, Billie. What do you say?"

Billie looked from Reese to Marian. "I say welcome aboard, partner."

"Good," Marian said. "I'll let you get back to your conversation with Mr. Ryker."

Billie tucked the ticket in her shirt pocket. "Oh, I think he and I are done."

Reese seemed to feel that way, too. He walked away as if dazed.

"Goddamn, that felt good," Marian said. "I must be getting mean in my old age."

That night Billie and Marian sat on the deck of the farmhouse, drinking Woodford Reserve. Luke had gone into town for steaks and more beer, and he was picking Tyrone up on his way. They had trailered Cactus Jack back to the farm after the race, as Luke didn't want to race him again for a month. Before they left the track, they'd heard a rumor that Ghost Rider had pulled up lame after the race.

"I think we should enter Cactus Jack in the Mercedes Mile," Luke had said. "And then—who knows? Maybe the Breeders."

"Easy now," Billie had told him. But she'd been thinking the same thing.

Now she and Marian sipped the whiskey and watched as Jodie led the gray colt across the pasture to the pond to drink, the horse following the little girl much the same way the mongrel mastiff did.

"What's going to happen there?" Marian asked.

"With the girl?"

"Yeah."

"I don't know," Billie admitted.

"Doesn't sound as if her mother is up to the task, in jail or out," Marian said. "I know some people in the foster child field. That is, if you're interested."

Billie looked out over the farm as dusk crept through the pines and across the fields. Marian watched her for a long while, seeing her father in the woman as she hadn't before.

"Sometimes you don't know what you want until you have it," Marian said. "And sometimes you don't know what you want until you don't have it."

Billie sipped the smooth whiskey. "You talking about the farm, the horse, or the kid?"

"Looks to me like it's a package deal," Marian said. "How does that suit you?"

Billie smiled. "Right down to my boots."

Acknowledgments

A S IS ALWAYS THE CASE, a number of talented people contributed a helping hand in getting this book in print.

First off, many thanks to Skyhorse Publishing and particularly to talented editor/horsewoman Lilly Golden for her unwavering belief in this book.

My appreciation to Diane Turbide, Shelley MacBeth, and Lupe Velez for sage advice, unvarnished opinions, and loyal support.

And a special shout out to Rick Smith—a middling amateur barber but a whiz when it comes to reverse mortgages and demand loans and all that stuff the writer knows absolutely nothing about.

About the Author

INTERNATIONALLY ACCLAIMED NOVELIST AND SCREENWRITER BRAD Smith is the author of twelve novels, including *The Return of Kid Cooper*, winner of the 2019 Spur Award from the Western Writers of America; *One-Eyed Jacks*, short listed for the Dashiell Hammett Award, and *All Hat*, adapted to a feature film starring Keith Carradine, Luke Kirby and Rachael Leigh Cooke. Smith's writing draws on his wellspring of experiences working across Canada, the U.S.A., and Africa at a variety of jobs—including railway signalman, carpenter, bartender, truck driver, ditch digger, school teacher, farmer, maintenance electrician and roofer. He now lives in a ninety-year-old farmhouse in southern Ontario.

Also by Brad Smith

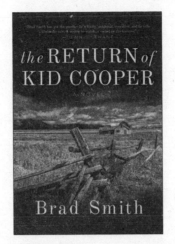

The Return of Kid Cooper
A Novel
Paperback / $16.99 US/ $22.99 CAN (available now)
ISBN 978-1-948924-53-5

WESTERN WRITERS OF AMERICA 2019 SPUR AWARDS WINNER!

"Smith has written tight, fast-paced novels his entire career…and reading one is like riding a thoroughbred."   —*The Chronicle Herald*

The year is 1910. Nate Cooper is an old-school cowboy who spent thirty years in a Montana prison for a wrongful murder conviction. Upon his release, he hardly recognizes his world—horses are giving way to motorcars, his girlfriend has married his best friend, and his nemesis is running for governor. Some things haven't changed. The Blackfoot are still being forced from their land. Nate's moral compass is true and unwavering: he does all the wrong things for all the right reasons. With grit, determination, a quick trigger finger, and the help of the woman he used to love, Nate sets out to settle the score.